MISJUDGED

A LEGAL THRILLER

JAMES CHANDLER

Severn River
PUBLISHING

MISJUDGED

Severn River Publishing
www.SevernRiverBooks.com

This is a work of fiction. Names, characters, businesses, places, events and incidents are either the products of the author's imagination or used in a fictitious manner. Any resemblance to actual persons, living or dead, or actual events is purely coincidental.

ISBN: 978-1-64875-034-2 (Paperback)
ISBN: 978-1-64875-035-9 (Hardback)
ISBN: 978-1-64875-138-7 (Hardback)

ALSO BY JAMES CHANDLER

Sam Johnstone Legal Thrillers

Misjudged

One and Done

False Evidence

Capital Justice

The Truthful Witness

Never miss a new release!

Sign up to receive exclusive updates from author James Chandler.

severnriverbooks.com/authors/james-chandler

For Ann,
my dream girl, then and now.

PROLOGUE

USS *Mercy*, March 2007

Bright lights and surgical masks were all he'd remember.

"Can you tell me your name?"

A woman's voice. He was lying on a bed of some sort, surrounded by people looking down. He couldn't tell which one was talking because all their mouths were covered. The same woman asked him how he was feeling. Sam said he was okay, and she asked if he could feel his legs. He was telling her he could when he felt tingling on his arms and the hair rising on the back of his neck. He attempted to sit.

"We're under attack! My men!"

Several sets of hands pushed him gently back on the gurney. "Lie back, lie back, Captain." The same voice, but quieter and more soothing this time. "Can you tell me your name?"

"Sam. Sam Johnstone. Captain Sam Johnstone."

"Captain, it's over. You're safe," she said. He still didn't know who was talking. Sam looked from face to face, and finally determined the voice was coming from a short woman with blue eyes. "I'm Dr. Margaret Stevens, a trauma surgeon here on the USS *Mercy*," she said. Between the protective goggles, the mask, and the scrub cap, she looked like an insect. He might have laughed, but the pain was too much.

"Do you know why you're here?" she asked.

"Blown up."

"Do you remember what happened?"

"Some."

"Tell me as much as you can remember. It will help us determine what might be going on with you."

The light behind the doctor was blinding. Everything was white. His head and left leg hurt. "I got blown up," Sam offered.

"Can you tell me a little more?" Her eyes were kind, at least.

"Some insurgents—maybe forty or fifty of them—attacked a convoy heading for an FOB—that's a forward operating base—in the Helmand Province. That's Afghanistan, ma'am. Convoy got surrounded. They dropped me and a couple of platoons from my company to see if we could help. We called in an airstrike, then the gunships showed, which seemed to do the trick. Then we started to escort the convoy back to the forward operating base."

"And then what happened?" the doctor asked. "Nurse, hurry up with that IV."

While the nurse administered the IV, Sam closed his eyes. "Stay with me for a minute," the doctor instructed.

"What's your name again?" Sam asked.

"Stevens. Dr. Margaret Stevens. I'm an Army major and doctor. This is a hospital ship."

"Okay, ma'am. So, I was in the lead vehicle. We heard some AK-47 fire from the north, and an RPG round went right over the top of us. I was trying to get an idea of the enemy's direction, but—" Sam tried to sit up again. "My men!"

"Captain Johnstone, please lie back down." Multiple pairs of hands carefully pushed him back down. "Finish your story, Captain," she instructed.

"We must have hit an improvised explosive device. Killed Jones—my driver. The poor bastard just got in theater last week."

The doctor nodded sympathetically, and Sam saw concern in the eyes of the others. "The concussion took off all the doors and blew me out of the vehicle, I think. I don't know. I just know I was out on the road and slid about thirty yards on my side and ass."

"Were you conscious?"

"Yeah, the whole time. I remember skidding along until I came to a stop. I couldn't believe I was still alive. I couldn't feel anything."

"Adrenaline."

"Huh?"

"That was the adrenaline going through your body."

"Okay. Anyway, I patted myself down and was trying to get my shit together and get up when I got shot in my leg, I think. Hurt like hell, but I knew I had to move, or I was gonna die."

"You walked with that leg?" the doctor asked.

"No. I couldn't use my leg, so I was trying to crawl for cover when Jenkins came and dragged me behind another vehicle. I reported contact to task force headquarters and had Jenkins help me to a covered position where I could see. I made it to the driver's door. Jones was halfway out of the truck, hanging on by his seat belt. An arm and half his chest were missing."

The doctor looked to the nurse, who said, "IV is ready, ma'am. Say the word."

She nodded acknowledgement. "What else do you remember?"

"The gunner—Fish—was dead, too. He was bleeding from his eyes and ears. No pulse. Jenkins told me Lieutenant Patterson was coordinating actions on contact. Then I was in some aid station somewhere. They told me I lost five men total. They cleaned me up and gave me a shot. Then Frankfurt. Next thing I know, here I am."

"Okay, Captain. I'm going to administer a little something that's going to make you fall asleep while we look at your leg."

"What's wrong with me, Doc? Where are my men?"

The doctor ignored Sam and nodded to the nurse. "Okay, go ahead."

Once more, Sam struggled to sit up. "I should have seen it coming! The men!"

"Try to relax, Captain. Please count backward from ten for me."

1

─────────

Sam sat quietly, fly rod across his lap, staring at nothing, hearing only the roar of water against rock and feeling the morning sun on his shoulders and the high-mountain, early-summer breeze on his face. He twisted the lid off a pewter flask and took a long pull from it, then wiped his mouth and returned the flask to his vest pocket. Upstream, the small lake formed by snow runoff was beginning to reflect the rays of the sun just peeking over the jagged crests of the highest peaks in this part of Oregon. Somewhere, an eagle shrieked.

He gave a desultory look at the selection of flies in his box. At last, he selected a tiny attractor—a Royal Wulff. Having made up his mind, he leaned forward and began the process of tying the tiny fly to the tippet. The fly would work; at this elevation, the small trout had only a few months to gorge themselves before their world was once again covered with several feet of snow and ice. If he could muster the energy and interest to get going, he would catch fish.

When at last he was rigged and ready to go, he stood and stretched. Sitting for ten minutes on the cold granite had stiffened him; he'd need to be careful, lest he fall. He looked up the face of the mountain and saw a goat looking down at him. They stared at each other until, apparently deciding that its need to get over the ridge was more important than figuring out what that two-legged animal with the stick in its hand was, the goat turned on its heel, leaving Sam alone. He edged closer to the bank of the tiny creek, false-casted a few times, and flipped the fly upstream near a large boulder, behind which were several inches of still water and—if Sam was right—a fish.

He played the brook trout as quickly as possible, removed it from the hook, then carefully released it in the shallows at his feet. "I'm in the books," he whispered. Sitting back down, he took another long pull from the flask.

With his left hand, he reached across his body and drew the pistol from the shoulder holster. He'd purchased the lightweight, compact, double action .38 caliber revolver a couple of weeks earlier. The guy at the gun counter had tried to talk him out of it, explaining that the little revolver held only five rounds. When Sam remarked, "I only need *one*," the poor man had put his head down and finished the required paperwork without another word.

Sam looked at the revolver in the morning sun and took a deep breath. One round and it would all be over. No more pain; no more regret. Over the sound of the rushing creek he heard once more the *thump* of rocket-propelled grenades and the staccato of automatic weapons from more than a decade ago. The soft touch of the high-mountain breeze yielded to the force from the concussion of mortar rounds, and the light from the morning sun gave way to intermittent flashes caused by the bursts. He closed his eyes and heard the screams of his men, wounded and dying and fighting to the end.

―――――――

A thousand miles east, Paul Norquist sat in an uncomfortable chair across the desk from Judge Preston C. Daniels, the Wyoming Twelfth Judicial District's senior district court judge. Paul didn't like being in any judge's chambers—no attorney in his right mind did. A sole practitioner, he had been one of Custer, Wyoming's, preeminent attorneys for almost twenty years.

"You want a drink?" Daniels asked, searching in a cabinet drawer. "I left that goddamned glass somewhere."

"No, thank you," Paul said. "It's not even four o'clock."

"Sure?" Daniels proffered a dingy-looking tumbler. "This is a very nice single malt. I got it from a client."

"I didn't think judges had clients," Paul noted dryly.

"Well, 'ex-client,' if you're forcing me to be accurate," Daniels clarified, pouring himself a healthy dose. Paul was glad he didn't have a client's future riding on the old judge's ability to see and think clearly this afternoon. "Same guy who needs the road."

Daniels had been on the bench for more than two decades now. He was short-tempered, acerbic, and took what some viewed as a sadistic joy in troubling attorneys from the bench. In Paul's opinion, Daniels had long ago given up ruling based entirely on the law, choosing instead to impose "justice" as he saw it. On occasion, Daniels's view of justice and the law coincided. When it did not, Paul appealed. The old judge wasn't supposed to take it personally, of course—but he did. As a result, the two men had experienced more than their share of run-ins over the years.

"This new man—Sam, I think you called him. Tell me about him, Paul."

"An old friend of mine from college. We played baseball together. After graduation, I went to law school and he went into the Army. We stayed in touch over the years—you know, alumni games, reunions, and the like—and at some point, an acquaintance of ours told me Sam had gotten himself into some trouble. Apparently, he got wounded in Afghanistan in 2007. Medically retired, then went to law school, of all things. I offered him a job a while back, but he wanted to do government contracts. Was working in some firm in D.C. but got fired."

"What happened?"

"Not sure. Booze, maybe."

"He okay now?" Daniels asked. "The last thing we need is another drunk in this town—enough of those homegrown." He took a sip from his tumbler.

"Yeah, a lot of that going around," Paul observed. "He got ahold of me a couple of weeks ago and asked if I still had a job for him."

"I've got a lot riding on this deal, so your guy better be up to it."

"He'll do what we need him to do. He's out of options."

"Good." Daniels took a large envelope from his center desk drawer and handed it to Paul. "Here is a retainer."

Paul looked at the envelope and met Daniels's gaze. Finally, he looked away. "I don't like this."

"I don't either. But it is what it is. Take the money. I want that road put in."

———

While Daniels was talking with Paul, Circuit Court Judge Jonathon R. Howard was a floor below, presiding over the initial appearance of a suspected drunk driver. Circuit court was the lower trial court—the "people's court," some called it. Howard had called the case and was reviewing the charges when the young man said, "I want all charges dropped. I'll accept fifty-three dollars in compensation; I'd like it in cash, and I'd like to be paid today."

Howard looked up from the file in his hands. "Mr. Yoder, if you'll hang on for a second, I'll look through this and maybe figure out just what's going on here." Then he turned his attention back to the file. The police report indicated that after driving his truck across a city park's grass, the defendant had purposely rammed a vehicle multiple times before exiting his truck and commencing a drunken rant of some sort. When finally accosted, he began spouting what the arresting officer referred to in his report as "religious gibberish." Ultimately, Yoder had been charged with driving under the influence, felony property destruction, and a host of minor traffic violations.

"Mr. Yoder, did you understand the rights I advised you of?"

"Yes, Judge. My Lord my father explained them to me as well."

"Well, good," Howard replied before asking Yoder several questions to try and discern whether he was oriented to time and place, and understood why he was there and the nature of his charges. Having obtained satisfactory responses, Howard moved on. "Mr. Yoder, are you employed?"

Yoder stared at Howard for several seconds. "My Lord my father and higher power has instructed me not to answer any more questions."

Howard sat back, removed his reading glasses, and took a close look at the defendant. "Well, Mr. Yoder, we might be at loggerheads. My higher power is the Constitution of the State of Wyoming, as well as Wyoming's rules of criminal procedure—particularly Rule 46, which governs pretrial release. Under those rules, if your higher power won't let you answer questions, then my higher power will likely have me keeping you in jail until your trial just to be on the safe side, because I'll be unable to determine the level of danger you pose to the community."

Yoder stared at Howard for another long moment and then replied, "I'm a carpenter."

Howard and Yoder went back and forth for an extended period while Howard tried to discern whether the defendant was troubled or whether his religious beliefs were sincere. Yoder was somewhat difficult throughout the exchange, but Howard let it go due to his concerns for the defendant's mental state. Ultimately, he deemed Yoder able to proceed, appointed him an attorney, and set bond. Finally, he asked, "Mr. Yoder, do you have any questions?"

"Yes, Judge," Yoder replied. "Are you going to pay me that fifty-three dollars?"

"No, Mr. Yoder, I am not."

Yoder looked steadily at the judge, then gave a disgusted sigh and shook his head sadly. "My heavenly father told me you would answer differently."

"Well, Mr. Yoder," Howard said, "when you check back in with the big guy and give him my answer, I'm sure he'll tell you it's not the first time he's been disappointed in me."

Daniels had little patience for, as he put it, "preening, showboating, or wasting time"—meaning he was hard on attorneys, many of whom made a moderately good living by preening, showboating, and wasting time. Today had been especially grueling, and it was about to get worse. He took a sip of his coffee and looked around his chambers, then focused his attention on the woman sitting across from him. "What I ought to do, young lady, is throw your sweet ass out of my chambers. This is blackmail."

"All I want is for my client to get the same sort of consideration that, well, *others* have received—is that so wrong?" Attorney C. Emily Smith replied.

"Your client has been busted for driving under the influence five times in the past three years! He's a goddamned hazard!"

"Judge, I think maybe the cops have been selectively enforcing the law —don't you?"

"They have that right. It's called 'prosecutorial discretion.'"

"Certainly, but when the police and prosecutors enforce the law against people like my client and let—well, let's just say *prominent citizens*—walk for the same offense, I think the public might see that as unfair. If they were to find out about it, I mean."

"You have absolutely no evidence—"

"I have what I need to bring this to the public's attention, Judge, and I think with a little discovery I could get more. The people of this county would be dismayed to find out that certain officials have been accorded considerations not available to my client or themselves. And what with your retention election coming up next fall, well, it would be a bad time for this sort of thing to make its way into the paper, don't you think?" She looked at him, sipping from a paper cup of coffee while she waited.

"Get out of my office," Daniels said.

"Do we have an understanding?"

"This is the last time."

"Oh, Judge," she said sweetly. "That would be such a mistake."

"Just get out."

After she had gone, Daniels called Mary Perry, his judicial assistant. "Call the County Attorney's Office; tell them to send Ann Fulks up to see me."

2

The job in Washington, D.C. had ended badly. What few cases Sam had left at the end were mostly the firm's ash and trash—futile appeals of contracts awarded to his clients' competitors, defense of low-level corporate officers on the wrong end of obscure federal regulations, and holding the hands of big-wigs' children who had been busted for possession. It was an inauspicious end to an inauspicious legal career. When he'd graduated from law school, he wasn't exactly overwhelmed with offers, but an old acquaintance stationed at the Pentagon arranged an interview and he got hired, so he moved to D.C. He was obviously not the typical fresh-faced recent law school graduate that most K Street law firms and their staffs envisioned. Some of his peers openly lauded the diversity he brought to the firm; some looked at the scar on his cheek and the artificial left leg and were put off; some viewed the military background he had tried so hard to conceal on his resume with if not outright antagonism then at least barely concealed distaste.

The beginning of the end had arrived on a beautiful morning in March. With the weather warm, the cherry blossoms around the Tidal Basin were abloom and the source of thousands of extra riders on the Metro. Riding into the city that morning, Sam began to feel uncomfortable tightness in his chest, which increased as each stop resulted in more and more riders boarding the train. He knew he needed to get off, but he was frozen in fear. By the time he got to the Capitol Hill station he was soaked in sweat, seeing explosions and hearing screams of wounded men. He burst out of the train and ran to a wall near the exit, put his back to it, and dropped his briefcase. "Get down!" he shouted. "Get the hell down!"

Hours later, after he'd been seen at the Metro Police Station and cleared of any wrongdoing, a doctor sat down with him and told him he was suffering from post-traumatic stress disorder. "You've got to get some help, son."

"I'll be fine," Sam said. "I gotta get to work, though. I missed a hearing."

Video of the incident went viral, and two senior partners were waiting for him when he got to the office. They gave him a couple of weeks off to get some help, and for a while he tried. He'd gone to a few meetings at the VA Medical Center, and he'd tried AA, but quickly grew disenchanted. His experiences were different than those of the others, and rather than try to find similarities, he focused on differences. After meetings, he'd hit the bar on his way home. Soon after, he'd begun to abuse his pain medications. Things were also different at the office. All but the most senior partners had shied away from him, and he'd found his billable hours in sharp decline. At some point, he was given an all-expenses-paid vacation to a Florida hospital specializing in the treatment of addiction and trauma. That helped, until one Sunday when he was driving back to the city after a perfect day on stream in rural Pennsylvania. He'd started to feel anxious as the traffic built, and had seen a little package liquor store attached to the gas station where he was filling up and thought to himself, "What could it hurt?"

He came to three days later in a Tacoma Park hospital, where he was being treated after having been found wandering in and out of traffic alongside a major two-lane. The managing partner had called him in and cut him loose—albeit with a small severance package. "I'm sorry, Sam," he'd said. "We're gonna have to let you go. I know you've been dealing with a bad situation, and I appreciate what you've done for your country, but our attorneys and staff . . . Well, you scare them."

The inevitable bender had followed, after which Sam had awakened in Walter Reed Medical Center suffering from dehydration, malnutrition, and a host of alcohol- and opioid-related issues. After his discharge he wandered the country in his truck drinking, popping pain pills, and spending the severance check. Then one morning, coming off a booze- and pill-fueled blackout, he'd remembered that several months before he had taken a call from an old college teammate. Paul Norquist had hinted that if Sam would move to Wyoming he'd find work for him, see to it Sam got a part-time contract from the public defender's office, and introduce him to some of the local attorneys. Two weeks ago, in a moderately sober moment, he'd called Paul; the offer was still open.

Now, looking into the gin-clear water, Sam could see dozens of little trout darting about, competing vigorously for insects in all their forms: nymphs, emergers, adults, and spinners. He took a long pull from the flask and swallowed a little white pill, looking at the titanium contraption where his lower left leg used to be and thinking about the five men who'd died under his command. He turned the little revolver over in his hand. For more than ten years now, he'd been drinking to remember and drinking to forget. Now, seventy-two hours and a thousand miles west of a potential fresh start in Wyoming, he had a decision to make.

After a few minutes he holstered the pistol, wiped his eyes with the back of his hand, and strained to look through a veil of tears to find feeding fish in the clear water. "One more," he said aloud.

3

"All rise. Circuit Court for 12th Judicial District, Custer County, State of Wyoming, is now in session," the bailiff announced. "The Honorable Jonathon R. Howard, presiding."

"Please be seated," Howard intoned. "Good afternoon, ladies and gentlemen. Court is in session, and we're on the record. We are here for in-custody arraignments."

Quickly scanning the shackled and orange-jumpsuit-clad defendants, Howard noted a couple of regulars, as well as a few new faces. Each constituted what he often thought of as an entry in what he called the "march of the misfits": alcoholics, addicts, dumbasses, hotheads, and the mentally ill and deficient, each facing charges alleging crimes ranging from the petty—assault and battery, drug use and/or possession, criminal trespass, misuse of a credit card, and the all-too-common drunken driving—to the horrific, including rape and murder. Roughnecks, cowboys, oil riggers, welders, electricians, service workers, and the unemployed, they were to a man or woman heavily tattooed and attitudinally remiss.

"The way this hearing will work," Howard continued, "is as follows: the court will first read your rights to you as a group and take any questions from you as a group. The court will then call you forward individually, verify your identification, read the charge or charges against you as well as the maximum possible penalty attendant to that crime or crimes should you plead guilty or be found guilty of the charge or charges, and then discuss attorney representation and bond. Are there any questions?"

As usual, there were none. As usual, maybe one in five was even paying attention. But Howard had to give the required advisal, for the law presumed he cared, even if most defendants did not.

Howard looked down from his bench at the defendant, who was charged with domestic assault. She couldn't have weighed 125 pounds, despite her obvious pregnancy. "You've indicated you understand your rights as well as the elements of the charge against you and the maximum possible penalty that could be imposed were you to plead guilty or to be found guilty after a trial. Are you prepared to plead?"

"I am, Judge."

"To the allegation that on or about May 12, in Custer County, Wyoming, you violated Wyoming Statute 6-2-511, commonly known as 'domestic battery,' how do you plead?"

"I'm guilty, Your Honor."

"Are you under the influence of drugs or alcohol?"

"No, I'm not."

"Do you understand that by pleading guilty here today that you are giving up most of the rights I advised you of earlier, to include the right to an attorney?"

"Yes," she replied, wiping a tear from her cheek with her chained hands.

"Do you understand that if you plead guilty and if I accept your plea there won't be any trial in this matter, that you won't have the opportunity to confront any witnesses against you, and you won't be able to complain about law enforcement's investigation?"

"Yes, Your Honor."

"Do you understand the only matter remaining would be sentencing?"

"Yes, Judge."

"Has anyone threatened you with anything, or promised you anything in return for your plea here today?"

"No."

"Okay, what happened?"

"Well, I went to my OB/GYN appointment last week, Your Honor. My husband was supposed to meet me there."

"Have the two of you been having problems?"

"I didn't think so."

"Okay, did he meet you?"

"Well, kinda."

"Kinda?"

"Well, yeah."

"What happened?"

"Well, I was in the waiting room, and he came out of the back with another woman—she was pregnant, too."

"So—"

"He knocked this bitch up—excuse my language, Judge—and set the OB/GYN appointments within an hour of each other so he didn't have to miss much work," she said. "But the doctor got behind, so his appointment ran late with the other woman and I caught them."

"Okay, so what about the battery?" Judge Howard asked.

"Well, he came up to me and tried to explain, but I kicked him in the balls," she said. "I'm sorry, Judge. For my language, I mean."

Howard suppressed a smile and looked at the audience with a stern expression until the laughter died down. "Who called law enforcement?"

"I'm not sure. The nurses took me in the back until they got there. All I remember is the women in the waiting room gave me a standing ovation, and the doctor said the visit was at no cost," she said, and then put both hands on her stomach. "Oh! Oh, my God!"

"What? What is it?" Howard asked.

"I think my water just broke, sir!"

Sitting at the prosecutor's table, Assistant County and Prosecuting Attorney Ann Fulks asked herself for the thousandth time why in the world she had suffered through four years of college and three years of law school if all she was going to do with her valedictorian's sheepskin was ring up drunks and tweakers on piss-ant charges in this piss-ant courthouse in this piss-ant town.

In just the past month she'd been spit at by a toothless, meth-tweaking wretch, nearly vomited upon by an old drunk, and attacked by an enraged parent whose son was dealing drugs in the local junior high. Some of her friends had asked why she'd taken a position in what she openly referred to as "this godforsaken wasteland." The answer, of course, was that to get to the top she knew she'd have to put in her time, try some bad cases, and suck it up for a while. She'd been doing just that for five long years, dreaming of the day when the county attorney would allow her to start prosecuting major felonies. Prosecuting some real bad guys and kicking some serious defense attorney ass would get her name in the paper. She was going to be somebody. She could feel it.

Ann frequently daydreamed her way through arraignments and initial appearances. There simply wasn't very much to do. Howard would try to explain to the defendants what was going on, but most were too fried or too ignorant to really get it. In the end, they'd usually plead guilty in an effort to get it over with, whereupon she would recommend a standard sentence for that particular charge. Ninety-five percent of the time Howard would impose the recommended sentence, usually consisting of a fine and a brief stint in jail.

While legislators kept increasing jail time for offenses, they appropriated funds insufficient to build additional jails or prisons, or hire staff, or pay probation officers. As a result, judges were hesitant to throw anyone but the most dangerous into jail—it was simply too expensive to give offenders three-hots-and-a-cot for every little offense, and the overcrowding was serious. The jurisprudential philosophy behind making the guilty pay fines was to offset the cost of doing business. The system didn't always work as designed, because the guilty rarely paid their fines, preferring instead to spend their hard-earned or stolen cash on things like booze, weed, methamphetamine, hookers, and cigarettes—preferably, all at the same time. And since most of the defendants were repeat offenders, each new offense would be met with a new sentence, consisting of jail and a fine added to the existing fine. Ann had plans to change all that.

Because she was dreaming of the day when she'd be in charge, Ann was startled when Howard barked at her. "Ms. Fulks, I'll ask you again: does the State have an objection to a brief continuance?"

Seeing the young woman spread out in the defendant's chair, Ann unconsciously shifted in her chair in an attempt to keep her four-hundred-dollar, handmade Italian pumps dry and calmly responded, "Your Honor, I've no objection to the defendant being excused, although it might be a bit late."

The next morning, Howard was back on the bench reviewing a file while the prosecutor, defense counsel, and defendant waited expectantly. Howard knew the file well, but for tactical reasons he wanted to make the defendant sweat a little.

"Mr. Bryant, you are here on charges that you violated the terms of your bond by failing to appear for twice-weekly urinalysis tests. As I recall, you are awaiting a preliminary hearing on a charge of felony possession of methamphetamine. Is that correct?"

"Yes, Your Honor."

"When the prosecutor alerted me to the fact that you'd not been testing, I signed a bench warrant and had the sheriff do the 'habeas grab-ass' on you. When did you get picked up?"

"Last night, Judge."

"You've had three prior convictions for possession of methamphetamine, young man. You are violating the law so fast I cannot dispose of the matters I've got or put you in treatment before you reoffend. You're leaving me no choice. You are either going to piss in the cup every Tuesday and Friday or sit in jail. Do you understand?"

The defendant folded his arms over his chest. "You think you can make me piss?"

"No. I'm fifty-seven years old. I have enough trouble on my own. But if you don't, I can and will hold you in jail until you're either bound over to district court or you tell me you are willing to pee in the bottle and enough time has passed where I'm no longer irritated with you."

"That sucks." Bryant pouted.

"Indeed. But understand this: I'm gonna put you back out on the street, but if you miss a test, fail a test, show late for a test, or show for a test without sufficient funds, make sure you have kissed your children good-bye, made arrangements for someone to care for your pets, and have your toothbrush with you, because I intend to set a cash bond that would require you or someone who cares about you to mortgage a house. Do you understand?"

"Yeah. So, that's it, huh?"

"That's it. Bailiff, please escort Mr. Bryant back to the detention center and release him."

Howard had no expectation that Bryant would or could stay clean. He had neither the tools to stay sober nor the desire to do it cold turkey. It was a shame he couldn't simply hold Bryant in jail until trial, but a little thing called the Constitution precluded Howard from saving Bryant from himself.

"So, when is Sam getting to town?" Jeannie Norquist asked.

"I'm not entirely certain," Paul said. "I told him he had the job, and he told me he needed a couple of weeks to get things together. I think he is doing some fishing in Oregon. His boss in D.C. told me he is struggling. Memories of the war."

"He needs to move on. Good Lord, it's been more than ten years!"

"Jeannie, don't judge," Paul cautioned.

"Paul, it's time for him to move on," she said. "You said he thinks and drinks and fishes around the country. No good is going to come of that."

"I understand. And maybe I agree with you a little bit, but let's both try not to be so judgmental. We can't understand; let's let him live his life his way."

"That's just the problem, honey: he's not living his life. From what you've told me, he is simply existing. He used to be so full of life."

Paul looked at her closely. "You are over him, right?"

"Of course. That was years ago. Besides, I married you, didn't I?"

"You did. And it was the best thing that ever has, or ever will, happen to me."

"And I've never regretted it either, Paul. Not for an instant. Now, don't be getting all jealous on me because an old boyfriend is moving to town— especially since you invited him."

"I'm not worried, dear."

"Good. Now go holler at the boys to wash up. I think this chicken is just about done."

"Veronica, what's on tap this morning?" Howard asked his judicial assistant while pouring himself a cup of coffee.

"You're going to laugh," Veronica Simmons replied coyly. She was a local who had graduated from the county's only high school a decade or so earlier. She had been Howard's judicial assistant for a little over a year, having come to the court after finding herself a poor fit at the new box store in town, where she stood at a cash register for hours at a time listening to the banal musings of coal miners' daughters and wives and ringing up their purchases of all things made in China. Despite her relatively short time on the job, she had quickly developed a fierce loyalty toward her boss. The way she saw it, her job was to be the gatekeeper, keeping everyone out of her boss's chambers except when absolutely, positively necessary.

"I am?" he asked.

"You are."

"Okay, whose ass is in a wringer?"

"Mark Bryant."

"The same guy I released yesterday?"

"Yup."

"Did he fail a piss test?"

"No. New DUI. Spice. He was passed out in his car in the middle of an intersection downtown, lighter in his hand and a burning pipe of spice between his legs. Then he jumped out of the car, attacking people, yelling about 'jagulinas'—whatever they are—in his pants."

"Good God almighty! He didn't make it twelve hours, did he?"

"Nope. Missed his urinalysis at eight p.m. and was found just before midnight. P.D. took him to the hospital. Said he's okay but walking kind of funny. I guess he's a little tender down there."

Howard smiled. "Nice. Well, let's hold him over for a day or so and let his head clear. He was angry yesterday; let's see how he's doing tomorrow. Maybe he'll be a little more receptive to following the rules when he realizes just how deep the crap he stepped in really is."

It was just getting dark as Sam drove into Custer, Wyoming. Every town in Wyoming seemed to have a junk collector living on its outskirts, and Custer was no different. Sixteen acres of bus and truck hulks, small boats, trailer house shells, abandoned cars, and assorted metal refuse dotted the landscape on the north side of the highway. Sam gazed at the goats and sheep browsing between rusted frames and perused the entire property to see if he could discern which of the trailer houses were occupied.

The airport was next, north of the highway and not looking terribly busy. Then the trailer parks, frantically and haphazardly emplaced during one of the many boom times for coal, oil, or gas—back when time and housing were short. Now, the dirt streets and abandoned bicycles served as a reminder of both better times and innocence lost.

Next came the motels. Full during boom times, the owners now looked out the dirty windows at the weeds encroaching through the cracks in the blacktop. Then came the older homes, and finally, "downtown," such as it existed in a town of eighteen thousand people. He wanted to find Paul's office and have a quick look around town in the September gloaming. The downtown business district had been laid out just after namesake General George Armstrong Custer's debacle across the border in what was now Montana. Two- and three-story buildings lined both sides of the Yellowstone Highway, called Main Street as it passed through the middle of Custer. Seeing the courthouse, Sam slowed and began looking at the stenciled windows on nearby buildings until he found it: Norquist Law Offices, P.C. Located next to First Wyoming Bank, the office was neat, tidy, and bereft of windows, no doubt to preserve a degree of client confidentiality. Having memorized the look of the place, Sam set off to find his lodgings.

The aging one-story log motel was streamside at the north end of town. Access was by means of a key, and parking was restricted to the spot immediately outside the room door. Breakfast, the clerk told him, was "continental," meaning coffee, cereal, oatmeal, and stale donuts. The room itself was clean and tidy, although the ten years since the "No Smoking" designation had been given had done nothing to alleviate the smell. The television was small, and the toilet ran a bit; beyond that, nothing much to complain about.

Sam turned on the miniature refrigerator and heard the electric motor start the compressor. He sat on the bed, adjusted the prosthetic leg—it was rubbing him raw—and opened his suitcase. Finding the bottle he'd packed that morning, he cracked the seal and took a sip, washing down a pill before going to look for some ice.

The next morning, the old friends greeted one another warmly. "Sam, so good to see you. How long has it been?" Paul said, shaking Sam's hand heartily.

"Fifteen years." Sam matched Paul's smile with one of his own. "I appreciate this, Paul. Thank you for the opportunity."

"It's my pleasure. I needed a guy, and when I found out you were available, well, it was a no-brainer. How was your trip?" Paul could smell the booze on Sam.

"Great. Caught some fish, saw some country."

"When did you get in?"

"Late last night."

"Where are you staying?"

"Out on the Yellowstone Highway, log place—stopped at the first place I saw with a 'Vacancy' sign."

"Kind of a dump, ain't it?"

"It's okay. I think my fridge is out. Asked them to fix or replace it. We'll see."

"Well, good," Paul said. He turned and sat behind an ornate oak desk, gesturing for Sam to join him. "You come highly recommended, you know."

"Paul, you and I both know that's bullshit," Sam said, taking the chair. "I got fired."

"Well, given what happened," Paul began, and then, trying not to stare at Sam's leg, added only, "I'm sorry."

"Thanks," Sam said, and noting Paul's glance, tapped his leg. "I'm not going to be shagging any flies, but I'm over it."

"I haven't thrown a pitch in years myself. No company softball team, either." Paul smiled. "But we're glad you're here; we've been a little short-handed. Ever worked collections?"

"No."

"Well, not a lot to it. Everyone hates it, and since you're the new guy I think we'll start you out with some of those, and then gradually work you into the more complicated stuff as you get familiar with Wyoming law. Later on, I've got a private road situation I'm gonna need you to handle. How's that sound?"

"Good with me."

"Good thing about Wyoming law is that there ain't a whole hell of a lot of it. This is a small state, and a newer state, so in some areas of the law we're making law, rather than adhering to precedent."

"That will be different."

"And I'll need you to handle the majority of the criminal defense stuff as well. Nothing too serious—DUI, domestic violence, pissing in the street, possession, stuff like that."

"Sure."

"We got a methamphetamine problem here in town, just so you know. I haven't done a lot of serious criminal defense stuff because I don't want some tweaker sitting in my waiting room next to the little old lady waiting to get her will done," Paul said, and then abruptly changed the subject. "How's your drinking?"

"I've got a grip on it."

"D.C. guys said it was an issue sometimes."

"It was." Sam was looking at his shoes.

"What about now?"

"I've got a grip on it today, Paul," he said. "It's a one-day-at-a-time deal."

"Good. I can't have any trouble, Sam. I know this place ain't much." He gestured around his office. "But it's all I've got."

"You got it. Hey, how are the boys?" Sam ventured. "They must be in high school by now."

"They're doing great. I think Ronnie has a shot at starting this year, and he's only a junior. First game is in a couple weeks. Friday night lights in early September—nothing better! Why don't you come with us? It's a home game. Weather is usually perfect."

"I just might do that."

"Paul—we call him P.J. for Paul, Jr., get it? He's too small right now. He's just a freshman, playing junior varsity. Gotta game on Saturday in Casper."

"Sounds like you've got your hands full. How is Jeannie?"

"She's a handful, too," Paul said, smiling. "In all sincerity, she is well. We look forward to having you over for dinner. How's tomorrow night sound?"

"Sounds good."

4

No one, to Jack Fricke's knowledge, ever grew up wanting to be a janitor. Notwithstanding, here he was, thirty-five years old and armed with mop and bucket, swabbing the courthouse floors for the umpteenth time on this snowy day in Bumfuck, Wyoming, and praying like hell some old bag didn't fall on her butt on a slick floor, which would result not only in his getting his ass chewed by the building manager, but probably one of the courthouse commissioners would demand he be docked a day's pay.

In between jobs Fricke and his assistant—a kid named Michael who was apparently related to one of the county commissioners, and whom courthouse wags had christened "Frac"—would ogle women and await a call from elsewhere in the courthouse whenever some drunken defendant vomited or urinated on the courthouse floor. All in all, it wasn't a bad job, and since it was a county job it came with benefits, like two weeks' vacation and a couple of sick days per month. Fricke had been through rehab four times, but he still drank a bit, and once every couple of weeks or so he'd call in sick while he slept it off. No one seemed to mind too much, except for the building manager, who was a Type-A asshole and hated being stuck alone with Frac.

"I don't understand how you can work with that kid, Fricke," he'd say. "He's got a brain the size of a pea."

The benefit, from Fricke's perspective, was the sheer entertainment available. It wasn't just anyone who could laugh at the drunks and addicts and ogle their women and get paid for it. In addition, Fricke looked forward to snooping through attorneys' and judges' files and garbage cans, as well as pocketing change left on desks and in chair cushions. On a good night Fricke and Frac could pick up two, maybe three bucks. They split it fifty-fifty, or so Frac thought.

Plus, there was the opportunity to watch arraignments, or as Fricke had long-ago named them, "Night Court," in honor of the old television show. In truth, in-custody arraignments in the circuit court occurred every afternoon. But like the television show, they were unpredictable and generally funny as hell—if you weren't the one in a jumpsuit and chains, of course.

Fricke and Frac had gotten into the habit of watching arraignments just after Frac came on board. Fricke wasn't sure that Frac ever really understood what was happening, but he laughed obligingly when Fricke did, and on those rare occasions when he didn't, Fricke elbowed him in the ribs. Today was a Monday, and there had been a full moon over the weekend, so Fricke suspected the "local color" had been out in force.

―――――――――――

"State of Wyoming versus Mark Bryant," Judge Howard announced. He was looking into a television monitor. Defendants appearing before the judge often appeared remotely from the jail, saving the county the time and cost of transport. A dozen or so young men and women were sitting on plastic chairs in a jail room equipped with a similar monitor. The judge had earlier advised the defendants as a group of their constitutional rights. It was now time to speak to them individually.

"Uh, here, Your Honor," Bryant said.

"Mr. Bryant, why don't you have a seat in that chair up front?"

"Yes, sir."

After Bryant was seated, the judge continued. "Mr. Bryant, you are here pursuant to a warrant that alleges you violated the terms of your bond by consuming spice, a controlled substance and/or altering substance. More particularly, you were placed on bond a couple days ago pending trial in a possession matter—do you remember?"

"Yes, Your Honor."

"The allegation is that at approximately ten p.m. the night before last, you were reported to police by passersby after you were observed doing seventy-five miles an hour on 2nd Street, crashed the car, got out, stripped naked, and began berating folks who tried to assist. Says here you accused them of 'bathing in the blood of the jagular'—whatever that is—and 'trying to steal your, er, penis.' You then, according to witnesses, dropped your trousers and defecated."

"Well, I had to go—"

"Just a minute, Mr. Bryant." Judge Howard held up a hand. "According to the officers on scene, you could not remain still, had pinpoint pupils that did not react to light, could not maintain a train of thought, and kept clenching and unclenching your jaw—all signs of methamphetamine use, according to the drug recognition experts. You were cited for use of a controlled substance and taken to jail. Now, do you have an independent recollection of the events of that night?"

"Kind of."

"Good. Now, do you remember me saying that a bond was a sort of agreement between you and the court?"

"Yes, Judge."

"And I explained that, were you to appear in front of me as the result of an allegation that you were using or drinking, I was probably going to deal rather harshly with you, didn't I?"

"Yeah."

"So, you understand your rights in this matter?"

"Yes."

"And you understand the allegation?"

"Yes."

"Okay, you've indicated you understand your rights and the allegations against you. To the charge that on or about the 21st day of September you violated the terms of your probation, do you admit, or do you deny?"

"Well, I admit, Judge."

"Okay, Mr. Bryant, what happened?"

"Well, my girlfriend picked me up after you released me. But she has been bathing in the blood of the devil, so I got out of the car . . . no, I took her home, and because she was morphing into a jagular, I took her car to get away."

The judge raised his eyebrows and stared at Bryant. "She was attempting to harm you?"

"Well, of course. Jagulars live on human flesh."

"Okay. So, you took off in her car?"

"Yes."

"And later you were stopped on 2nd Street after you crashed the car?"

"Yes. I did that on purpose."

"You crashed the car on purpose? Why?"

"Because I had a jagular in the car with me, and it was in my pants."

Howard stared hard at the courtroom audience, then those in jail, quieting their laughter. "Okay . . ."

"So, that's why I crashed that car."

"Okay. Let me ask you this: at any point that night—and I'm talking about before you had the jagular in your pants—did you use meth-amphetamine?"

"No . . . spice. Spice is the only way to keep the basilisks away."

"I guess I'm not sure what a basilisk is, Mr. Bryant."

"A basilisk is a reptile that can kill you with a single glance. But they won't look at someone who has taken spice, so as soon as I heard there was a basilisk loose in Custer, I went and got me some."

"And you used that spice?"

"Yes, sir. You would too, rather than have a jagular in your pants."

Again, Howard stared hard at the other inmates and the audience in the courtroom. Having decided that Mr. Bryant was truly troubled and not just putting him on, he made his decision. "Okay, Mr. Bryant. I'm going to suspend proceedings here and order you held without bond until you can be examined by a mental health professional. Ms. Fulks, please prepare the appropriate order."

5

By early October, Sam was starting to get the rhythm of his new firm. Norquist Law did some collections and—true to Paul's word—as the new guy, Sam had been assigned to the unenviable task of collecting debts for some of the physicians in town. The job was not a difficult one, but it was unpleasant.

Not infrequently, the debtors were angry at the world, suffering from an addiction disorder or marital/relationship issues, and were being pursued by multiple creditors who employed various tactics to get their money. It was a volatile business, and in just a few weeks, Sam had observed various blow-ups.

Today's defendant owed money to Sam's client, one of the town's OB/GYNs. She showed up late, snipped at the receptionist, and was shown to a conference room. Sam entered a couple of minutes later and found the defendant on the phone. She kept talking while Sam noted the time. At some point, she said, rather disdainfully, "I'll be with you in a minute."

Sam replied casually, "Okay with me. It's your money."

"What?"

"The judgment against you includes attorney's fees, which—much like the interest on your debt—accumulates. In my case, in six-minute increments."

The phone was snapped shut. He had her attention. Decent-looking gal, Sam thought, but a very hard edge to her. She was wearing the tightest jeans he had ever seen. Her T-shirt showed it all, and there was plenty to see, courtesy of a very talented plastic surgeon somewhere. Sam began the questioning.

"So, you say you've been unemployed for several months."

"Right. I was pregnant."

"And how old is your child now?"

"Ten months."

"Well, let me ask you this . . . when you are working, what is your usual occupation?"

"I'm a dancer."

Sam couldn't resist acting like the dork she assumed he was, so he adjusted his reading glasses and asked her with a straight face, "Ballet or tap?"

"I'm a stripper," she said. "Exotic dancer. I do parties, private homes, and sometimes establishments throughout the Midwest and Rockies. . ."

Sam was tempted to ask if she'd ever sat on his lap in Denver, but he bit his tongue. "Really, how very interesting. . . Are you employed by a particular outfit, or—"

"I'm an independent contractor; I work on a cash-basis only. Sometimes I do escort work."

The next few minutes consisted of a back-and-forth, Sam trying to figure out what assets she had while she tried to convince him that she didn't own squat. She was street smart, wary as hell, had no bank accounts, and was paid in cash under the table. He concluded there was nothing he could grab or garnish to get his client's money back.

Tiring of the game, she finally asked straight out, "How can we take care of this bill?"

"Do you have a cowboy hat?" Sam asked.

"What?"

"Are you allergic to feathers?"

"Are you serious?"

"Look, you owe $1,500. How 'bout you pay $750 and do a lap dance for each of us at the next office Christmas party and we'll call it good-to-go?"

"I'm out of here, sicko," she said, and stalked out, slamming the door behind her.

"What was that all about?" Paul's secretary asked.

"Professional differences," Sam said.

"So." Howard shifted on his barstool. "I sentenced a couple to a lifetime of connubial bliss this weekend."

"Yeah? Anyone I know?" asked Sean O'Hanlon, current president of the Custer Chamber of Commerce and Howard's long-time drinking buddy.

"I doubt it. This wasn't exactly your Chamber of Commerce type."

"So what happened?"

"Well, I got called in at the last minute because the groom was and is a probationer of the judge who was scheduled to preside," Howard said. "The bride was maybe thirty-eight or forty, and the groom was ten years older or so."

"Younger woman, huh? So what happened?"

"Well, I had noted on their paperwork that both were from Indiana. Anyway, we get done with the ceremony and they exchanged a lengthy, rather stomach-turning smooch, and I couldn't help but overhear as the groom gazed deeply into the bride's eyes and said, 'I'm so happy your name is Cooper'—which was the guy's last name—'again.'"

"Yeah?" said O'Hanlon. "Hey, gimme a second, here's the waitress." After ordering them another round, he said, "Continue, yerhonor."

"Well, I figured maybe they were on their second go-round together, but they didn't say anything, and I didn't ask."

"Hey, none of your business if a guy wants to get back on a horse that has already bucked him off!" exclaimed O'Hanlon.

"True enough. Anyway, the groom says to me, 'She's my niece!'"

"His niece? Holy shit, what'd you do?"

"Well, I was thinking it through, and I must've looked rather odd, because the guy says to me, 'No, no—she's my step-brother's daughter, so it's legal, see?'"

"Which is true—right, Judge?"

"Right. The gal says, 'Bob and I have been in love forever!'"

"What'd you say?"

"Well, I bit the shit outta my tongue, because what I was thinking was along the lines of, 'No shit. That's exactly what I'm afraid of.' Instead, I just smiled, and watched as they left, wondering how his being his stepbrother's new son-in-law will change things during gift exchange next Christmas."

"I wonder how long it'll take for the gal to quit calling her new husband 'Uncle Bob?'" O'Hanlon cackled, raising his glass. "Here's to you, Judge!"

"You know everyone already thinks we're having an affair," Veronica said.

"Who? I haven't been here six months yet." Sam looked up from his salad. "Hardly anyone even knows me."

"Everyone," she said, indicating with her fork the rest of the restaurant. "This is a small town, Sam."

"You're not married, and neither am I," Sam said.

"I know." She picked at her salad. "But still."

"Well, let's give 'em something to talk about. Wanna play a little footsie?"

"What are we, fourteen?"

"Yeah, you're probably right. Besides, with this leg that'd be difficult for me. And from what I've seen so far, we'd have to be doing the deed right here on this table to draw any serious interest."

She laughed aloud. "It is a problem."

"Besides," he said, "I don't like to eat alone. It's lame."

"Get a dog, maybe?"

"And I can only eat so many bologna sandwiches in my room per week."

"I'm one step above bologna?"

"No, you're one step above the dog; this BLT is one step above bologna." Sam took another bite of his sandwich. "And don't knock it; I'm buying."

"I appreciate it. Can I ask you something?"

"Sure."

"It's personal."

"Okay."

"How did you lose your leg?" Veronica asked. "I know it's maybe kinda rude to ask, but there's lotsa rumors. People talk."

"I got blown up in Afghanistan."

"Oh my God! I mean, I kinda knew—"

"Yeah. Not one of my better days."

"I just don't know how you deal with it."

"I'm okay."

"The rumor is you've had some problems."

Sam swabbed a potato in ketchup, then put it in his mouth and started chewing, looking steadily at Veronica. "I guess I'm trying to figure out what business of yours it is."

"I like to know who I'm having lunch with. It's a dangerous world."

"I'm okay," he said at last. "I got blown up and then shot. I lost five of my men. But I'm dealing with it."

"How is the drinking?" In response to his raised eyebrow, she offered, "I heard you might have a problem."

"People talk?"

She nodded.

"I'm holding on. It's a day-to-day deal. I don't want to get too comfortable, but right now I'm doing okay."

"Good. We've had a lot of problems over the years with attorneys coming to court drunk, dealing with their clients drunk, or generally just being drunk. That's the whole reason they stopped holding the annual County Bar Association Christmas party. I was told it turned into a real shit-show, with the judges leading the way."

"Really? That surprises me. Judges are usually stuffed shirts."

"Not in this town."

"How do you know?"

"I work for one of them," she said. "I know everything about him."

"Everything?"

"Almost. Everything I want to know, and a lot I don't want to know."

"You'll have to tell me sometime."

6

Tommy Olsen let himself in the back door using a key Emily Smith had palmed him earlier that evening and dropped it on the kitchen counter. Without turning on the lights, he made his way slowly through the kitchen and into the living area, where Emily sat cross-legged on the couch sipping a cup of something that looked to be iced tea in the light of a Tiffany lamp. Tommy knew Tiffany lamps. He'd stolen a couple of them when he was a kid and sold them to buy beer.

Everyone in town knew Emily Smith was a local attorney—her ads and billboards were everywhere. But what they didn't know was that, since yesterday, she'd been his lover. As far as he knew, only he and Emily were in on that one.

He'd come back from Afghanistan a hero five years prior, but with a little more iron and lead in his body than was biologically necessary, and the physical and mental scars to go with it. As time passed, his physical wounds had healed, but he had some other "issues," as his wife Becky called them, that he'd yet to deal with. When he flat refused to do so, Becky had packed up the car, piled the kids in, and left for her mother's. He'd kept calling her until finally she answered, and they'd talked about working things out, but it soon became clear that the bitch had no intention of ever coming back—or even of letting him see the kids—so he had decided to file for divorce.

After he'd gotten out on bail following his second drunk driving bust, he'd met and hired Emily, a local divorce attorney, to swordfight on his behalf with Becky's bulldog of a lawyer. They'd been working together for a couple of months now; she'd draft a pleading and run it by him for his approval, and then file it. They were an odd pairing—anyone could see that. But at some point—yesterday on the desk in her office, to be specific—the tentative flirtation that had gone on for weeks had somehow turned into something more. He'd gotten back from the shop, cleaned up, and had just barely made it to his appointment—her last of the day, as it turned out. The staff had left soon after he arrived, and the deed was done.

Today was Halloween, and they'd run into each other at a party downtown earlier in the evening. She'd invited him over, so he'd left the party and arrived at the appointed time. She was still wearing her lady of the evening costume. He was dressed as an assassin.

"What are you drinking?" he asked.

"Long Island iced tea." He loved her voice. Feminine, but somewhat deep for a little gal her size.

"Never heard of it."

"Vodka, tequila, rum, gin, triple sec, maybe a little coke and sweet and sour—"

"Whoa. I'm not supposed to drink—Doc says it'll interfere with my meds. But I've been known to shoot tequila."

"I'm in," she said, moving toward the kitchen—and Tommy. "How about you slice us a lime?"

He watched as she retrieved a knife from the drawer under the cabinet and a lime from the refrigerator, anticipating the heat of the tequila and the contrasting tastes of the salt and lime, and—if he was lucky—maybe a little of Emily, too. He hadn't shot tequila since a bad night in Juarez some years back. But then, until last night, he hadn't had sex with anyone other than Becky in a while, either. If he was gonna be single again, he might as well start acting like it.

"Bring it on," he said, and was slicing the lime when she approached him from behind and goosed him. "Shit!" He turned to show her a deep gash on his forefinger that was already bleeding.

"Jesus, I'm sorry! I didn't mean to scare you. I just wanted to, uh, touch you. I didn't mean—"

"Not your fault. I'm a little jumpy," he said, and turned on the tap and put pressure on the finger.

"Keep your hand under the running water while I go and get you something," she said. "Will a small bandage work?"

"Maybe." He watched the blood leak from the wound into the sink. Seeing the knife on the counter, he placed it in the sink. "Get that out of the way."

"You've got blood all over your shirt," she said. "You need to soak that, or it will be ruined." She helped him remove the shirt.

"I might need some stitches."

"You're fine, tough guy," she said. "Now, just hold that in the air for a couple of minutes. Between the pressure and the elevation, it ought to stop pretty quickly."

"I think I'm ready for a shot of tequila—for medicinal purposes, of course."

"Of course," she said.

Much later, when the sun had just begun to illuminate the rim rock and pinnacles that marked Custer's eastern horizon, Tommy kissed her one last time and left by the back door. What a night. His bleeding had slowed, and aside from a slight headache, he felt better than he had for months.

"Wait until I tell the boys about this one," he thought, smiling as he started his truck and punched buttons on the satellite radio until he picked up an artist he favored. Blood began to soak through the bandage again, and he decided to run by the emergency room and get the finger looked at before work. Stopping at the intersection a block from Emily's house, Tommy waited for a fancy foreign job, a cop car, and then a car that looked like Becky's to proceed. Couldn't be, he thought. Her lazy ass wouldn't be out of bed yet. He hit the gas, looked at his watch, and put things in perspective.

"It's gonna be a good day," he said aloud, "when you get laid and hear Cody Jinks—all by five-thirty."

7

"Ms. Knight, why don't you step up to the podium, if you please?" Howard said. The defendant, a woman of about fifty, slowly made her way to the podium and elaborately placed her chained wrists atop it. "Did you hear and understand your rights?"

"Yes."

"Any questions?"

"No."

"Ms. Knight, you've been charged with a violation of the terms of your bond. You'll recall that you appeared in front of me a while back and entered a plea of not guilty to a charge of driving under the influence—fourth or subsequent offense in five years. Do you remember?"

"Yes."

"The allegation is that you blew a .42. That means you are alleged to have been driving at an alcohol concentration five times the legal limit, a level that would kill most people," Howard said. "So, you sat in jail for about thirty days because you couldn't make the bond I set—$1,500 cash or commercial surety. Do you remember?"

"Yes."

"Your lawyer asked me to reconsider bond, and I did. I released you after a hearing that started at 4:30 p.m. yesterday with the admonition not to use, consume, or possess alcohol and your agreeing to participate in a daily testing regimen. Remember that?"

"Yes."

"So, I've got a police report here that says you were arrested by the Custer Police at nine p.m. last night on a charge of public intoxication. Says here you wouldn't leave the library, then you passed out and vomited in the entranceway. Do you understand that?"

"Oh, yeah, that was me."

"So, do you admit or deny that you used alcohol yesterday evening after getting out of jail?"

"I admit."

"Ms. Knight, what were you thinking? You weren't out of jail more than three hours!"

"I was thinking after thirty days in jail I needed to get good and drunk, Your Honor."

"Well, I appreciate your honesty, Ms. Knight. Unfortunately, you've shown me you're not a good candidate for pre-trial release, so I'm going to reinstate the original terms of your bond and add a little bit to it. You'll be held in lieu of $2,500 cash or commercial surety. If you do get out. . ." Howard then advised her of the terms of her bond. After the advisal, she had a question.

"Judge, is there any way I can get out again tonight?"

"If you or a bail-bond outfit posts $2,500, yes."

"And I can't drink if I get out?"

"No."

"Then I don't want out."

"Well, Ms. Knight. I'm sorry, but I guess I can't say I'm surprised."

"The world is an ugly place for a sober woman, Judge."

Mary Perry was irritated. Judge Daniels had only one more hearing today —a custody matter that could be handled in a few minutes—and everyone was present and ready to go, except for the petitioner's attorney, Emily Smith. As the judge's judicial assistant, her job was to keep the docket running smoothly. Plus, it was in her best interests, as delays would not infrequently send him into a fit. Especially of late.

With a District Court judge and a Circuit Court judge holding hearings almost all day long—and with everyone running late some days—it was not uncommon for attorneys to find themselves scheduled for two hearings simultaneously. Generally, when an attorney was a no-show, Mary would simply call their office and get an explanation.

Dorothy Johnson, Ms. Smith's receptionist, had only said that "Emily was not in," before—with some prodding—she had explained in confidence that she had no idea where she was.

Daniels was generally unwilling to grant a continuance without being given a valid reason and would usually order someone else from an attorney's office to appear. But since Ms. Smith was a sole practitioner, there was not a lot anyone could do. Mary would simply have to find another setting to insert for the judge's four o'clock, lest they waste an hour and get even more backed up than they were already.

Just down the street from the courthouse, Dorothy Johnson, or Dot, as her friends called her, had just about had it with Mary Perry—and her boss, Emily Smith. Before the latest phone call, when Dot finally had to admit she had no idea where Emily was, Mary had called three times to set hearings, check on pleadings, etc. Because Emily kept her own calendar, it wasn't like Dot could just agree to the setting and be done with it.

This had happened before, Dot recalled. A year or so ago, Emily had disappeared for a couple of days. No warning before she had gone; no explanation afterward. She'd gone to the annual bar convention and simply not returned. No explanation; just didn't return when all the other lawyers did.

Later, Emily had appeared to listen closely as Dot explained that as her receptionist, she had a right to know where the boss was, et cetera. In response, she got only a muttered apology—and no commitment to ensure it didn't happen again. Emily was very private and never once discussed her private life. In fact, Dot didn't even know where Emily was from, whether she had siblings, or anything. What kind of woman was so secretive? Emily was sweet, but she was stubborn, too, and clearly not interested in revealing her past, which only made Dot more determined to find out what Emily was hiding.

When by mid-morning yesterday Emily had not arrived for work and missed her first appointment, Dot had gone into her office to check the calendar on Emily's desk. That revealed nothing, because Emily had taken to keeping her calendar on her computer, which she could access with her new cell phone. Dot did not have Emily's computer password so she had left several increasingly plaintive phone messages. In response, she'd heard nothing.

She hadn't seen Emily for almost two days, and too many people were looking for her now to ignore it. Even that Tommy Olsen—the man who had the last appointment with Emily two days ago—had called. She remembered him because he looked so dirty, sad, and tired the first time he'd come in, but he was as clean as a whistle the other day—so much so she'd hardly recognized him.

She would have to do something if Emily didn't show by tomorrow.

"Dude, you must be one horny sonuvabitch," said Tommy's new "friend" Elk, so called as the result of his having only two toes on one foot. Elk had only recently arrived in town and was a resident of the local halfway house, so Tommy had felt safe in confiding to him that he was drilling a really nice-looking lawyer.

"I can't understand why she isn't returning my calls or texts." Tommy squinted as he tried to read the little numbers on his phone.

"Mebbe you didn't rock her world like she rocked yours," Elk opined.

"Dude—" Tommy began.

"Mebbe she's checkin' some associate's briefs!" Elk guffawed.

"C'mon, man, this is serious. It's been, like, forty-eight hours."

"Dude, you got it bad, but remember: that kinda chick don't owe you nothin'. To her, you're just a blue-collared, one-night stand. She probably considered it a charity deal. You need to move on, like to that fat redhead down the end of the bar," he said, pointing.

"Screw it, I'm gonna go see what her problem is."

"I ain't so sure that's a good idea, boy," said Elk. "You gotcha a belly full, so even if you don't get busted for DUI, you're just gonna show up pissed off and blow whatever shot you got."

"Yeah, well. I'm pissed off now. So what?"

"So tomorrow you might find your dumb ass in the can, is what. Or maybe you'll be back here, bitchin' and moanin' with nothing to look forward to."

"Judge, how you doin'?" O'Hanlon asked, pulling a chair out for Howard.

"What a day." Howard took a long pull from the frosty mug O'Hanlon had waiting for him. "Had a gal in front of me who was up for an initial appearance on felony possession of methamphetamine. I advised her of her rights and read the charges against her, advised her of maximum possible penalties and all that shit," he continued as he sat down. "Then I started asking questions so I could set an appropriate amount of bond in order to protect the community and ensure she'd make her court dates. So I asked her about employment (none), phone number (none), residence (none), contacts with the community (few). Then I asked her if she'd ever been convicted of a felony. 'No, Your Honor,' she said. So, just to make sure, I asked the prosecutor, 'Does the State show anything different?' The prosecutor said she was convicted of felony possession in 2012." Howard grabbed a handful of mixed nuts and tossed them into his mouth.

"She was lyin', huh?"

"Right. So, I looked at the defendant and asked her, 'Ring any bells?' and she said, 'I forgot.'"

"They always do, I bet," O'Hanlon said.

"Indeed. I was getting ready to set her bond when she said, 'Judge, I can explain!'"

"So, I said, 'Please do. It might make a difference in how many zeroes are in your bond amount.'" Howard took another sip of his beer. "So she said, 'I was convicted because my boyfriend put Viagra in my pants.'"

"I'll bet that made for a stiff sentence!"

Howard smiled. "Yeah, I choked down comments about 'hardened criminals,' too. I think she meant Vyvanse, which is a stimulant."

"Whatever. Judge, I don't know how you deal with those folks every day." O'Hanlon shook his head.

"Well, I find people interesting. Can't say I love people, but I find them fascinating. At a lower level trial court like mine, most of the defendants are there due to drug and alcohol problems—they're generally good people who're making bad decisions."

"Speaking of which, you want another drink?"

"No, thanks. I gotta get home before Margaret has dinner on the table."

"Well, I don't even mean the criminals. The lawyers, Jesus, they are hard to work with!"

"I hear you, but honestly, these local attorneys are pretty damned good overall. These are small-town, bread-and-butter lawyers. They go to work, represent their clients, and go watch the kids' ballgames or recitals or whatever. You get an honest day's work for your money. No one around here is billing $1,000 an hour to review transcripts or harass the other side with electronic discovery requests or any of that crap you see in the cities. They keep the nonsense to a minimum. I like working with most of them."

"Yeah, well, my divorce attorney charged me a pretty penny and that bitch didn't do shit."

"Who'd you have?"

"Emily Smith. You know her, of course."

Howard finished his beer and wiped his mouth with the back of his hand. "Yeah, I've had some dealings with her."

"Tell you what. She's easy on the eyes, but weird as cat shit."

It didn't appear anyone was home, but then, with a two-story apartment you could never tell. After ringing the doorbell and pounding on the door and getting no response, Tommy checked the handle—locked. He tried the first-floor windows. Same thing.

He was turning to leave when an old guy in a dirty white tank top stepped out of the apartment next door.

"She ain't here," he said.

"Who are you, and how do you know?" asked Tommy.

"I'm Gus, and I look after this place," the old man replied. "Who the hell are you?"

"My name's Tommy. I'm looking for Emily."

"You ain't the only one, boy."

"Seen her around?"

"Can't say for sure, but there ain't been no one answer when the others come callin'," he said.

"When's the last time you saw Emily?"

"Who's Emily?"

"The gal that lives here."

"Sorry, didn't know her name. Never met her. She's kinda stuck up, you ask me."

"When's the last time you saw her?" Tommy asked.

"Well, I think it was right before you went into the house the night before last—'bout ten-thirty, weren't it?" the old guy responded, and then, seeing Tommy's look of surprise, he continued, "You is that guy, ain'tcha?"

"Uhhh... yeah, I guess it was about ten, maybe eleven."

"Lotsa guys here trying to see her."

"Swell," Tommy said, knocking one last time before turning to face the old man. "Look, man, how about letting me in?"

"I can't do that—you know that."

"But I'm worried about her!"

"Sure you are, son." Gus leered at him. "But you ain't got nothin' to worry about. I been keepin' an eye on this place and ain't seen no one go in or out since you left two nights ago."

"Then she's in there."

"Might be. Maybe I missed her. But you'll have to wait until she comes on out, just like everyone else. Now git, boy, afore I call the cops."

Tommy stared at the old man for a moment, considering his options, then slowly turned and departed.

———

Howard was signing a stack of paperwork when Veronica entered his chambers. "What's on the docket today?" he asked.

"Arraignments, followed by a change of plea. Light day," she said.

"Who is the defendant?"

"Albert Smith, the wife-beater."

Howard hated family violence matters. Smith had been busted twice already; if not for his wife's prior recantations he'd be looking at a third conviction, which, under Wyoming law, would make it a felony. Unfortunately, like so many other victims, Mrs. Smith had a shortage of self-esteem and a surfeit of fear, and had twice gotten cold feet, forcing the county attorney's office to accept a plea to a reduced charge of breach of peace. It was the best they could make of a bad situation. Everyone knew that within a week or so of Smith's release law enforcement would be called to the residence again.

"Who is counsel for the defendant?" Howard asked. It made a difference. Some defense attorneys could turn even a change of plea into a grind.

"Emily Smith." Howard noted the not-quite-concealed distaste in Veronica's response. Never in his life had he come across anyone who engendered such emotion without saying a word—or even being in the room, for that matter.

"Any relation?"

"Not that I know of."

"Well, get ahold of her office, would you? I hear she missed a couple of appointments yesterday in Judge Daniels's court. I'd like to slip out early, if possible, and in any event, I don't want to have to reschedule the setting."

———

Dot had made up her mind: enough was enough. Mary and Veronica had now called her four times. She was going to find Emily, and when she did, she was going to read her the riot act—boss or no boss. It just wasn't right, Emily leaving her to answer the phones, make excuses, and worry without telling her in advance that she was going on a little dalliance.

Certainly, what Emily did was her own business, but not when it affected her. Dot knew full well there were legal assistants in town who did a lot more for their bosses than cover up the occasional absence or forgotten appointment. My goodness, Lucy, the secretary over at the Lemke Law Office, was said to have practiced more law than a lot of third-year associates because of her boss's more-than-occasional imbibing. But Dot wasn't Lucy, and enough was enough.

She picked up the phone and made the call.

8

Officer Ron Baker had not been a cop very long, so it was with some degree of trepidation that he knocked on the door. He had the feeling this was not going to end well. "Police! Please open the door, Ms. Smith."

He waited a few seconds and, hearing no answer, knocked again. "Ms. Smith, please open the door! This is the Custer Police Department; we are doing a welfare check."

Consistent with his training, Baker proceeded to move in a clockwise direction around the small house, cupping his hands over his eyes as he peered through each window. At the back door, he repeated his demand for Emily Smith, whom he knew to be a local attorney, to answer. Still hearing nothing, he turned to Smith's secretary. "What do you want me to do?"

"Well, no one has seen her in a couple of days," Dot said. "She's missed several appointments and court appearances. I am worried. That's kind of unlike her."

"What do you mean, 'kind of?'"

"Well, there've been a couple of times where she disappeared without telling me, but she didn't miss any court."

"Okay, hang tight. I am gonna make a call back to dispatch. I will be right back." Several minutes later, Baker returned, this time with a piece of curved metal in his hand. "Ma'am, I'm gonna ask you to go sit in your car and wait until I come get you. It's for your own safety."

Dot complied, lighting a cigarette as she walked back to the car. Baker disappeared around the rear of the house and was gone for what seemed like forever. When he returned, he was ashen.

"Did you find her?" Dot asked.

"I did."

"Is she okay?"

"No."

"What does that mean?"

"That means it's time for you to go back to your office. I have some calls to make." Baker turned around and vomited. "We'll call you when we need a statement." Wiping his mouth with the back of his hand, he walked unsteadily to his squad car and got in the front seat, then took a long swig from a plastic water bottle and plucked the microphone from his vest. "Dispatch, this is Baker. We have a situation."

Deputy County Attorney Ann Fulks was detailing recommended bond conditions when Veronica entered the courtroom from Howard's private chambers passageway and passed him a note reading, "I need to speak with you. Now. Very urgent." Howard hated to take recesses—especially with only one more defendant to arraign—and Veronica knew that. For that reason alone, Howard knew it had to be something important.

"I am very sorry, ladies and gentlemen, but the court needs to take a five-minute recess," he said.

"All rise!" the bailiff bellowed as Howard departed.

"What's going on?" the defendant asked the bailiff.

"I dunno," the bailiff replied, moving his toothpick from left to right with a twitch of his lips. "But I know this: this ain't gonna do you any favors."

"But it's just weed and meth!" wailed the defendant. "Ain't like I killed somebody or nuthin'."

Howard followed Veronica back to his chambers. "What is it?"

"Your Honor, she's dead," Veronica said.

"Who's dead?" Howard asked.

"Emily Smith."

"What? My God—how?"

"Well, the police department is saying someone attacked her—cut her throat." She unconsciously massaged her own neck.

"Good Lord!" exclaimed Howard. "Who would do such a thing? She's an attorney, for Christ's sake!"

Daniels was growing increasingly impatient. Prior to his entering the courtroom, the parties had represented to his staff they had reached a plea agreement. In Daniels's court, the normal procedure was that, following the announcement of a plea agreement, the prosecutor and defense attorney would put the terms of the agreement on the record. The judge would then take the plea, ask some questions to ensure the defendant was in fact guilty as charged, and then sentence. Today, however, the defendant was refusing to admit certain salient elements of the charge. Daniels was beginning to think the defendant was wasting his time.

"Your Honor, may I have a moment?" Sam asked.

"Yes, but please make it brief, Mr. Johnstone," replied Daniels. "I have a full docket today."

"I will be very brief, Judge." Sam covered the microphone at the defendant's table with his hand and turned to his client. "Listen to me," he began. "I told you, before we agreed to this plea, that if you came in here and pleaded guilty you'd have to give a factual basis, and that you'd have to answer the judge's questions. All of them. You keep dorking around, telling them you 'don't know,' and you 'forgot,' and you're gonna piss that judge off and he's gonna queer the deal—got me?"

"Dude," began the defendant, who was looking at three counts of conspiracy to deliver methamphetamine as well as two counts of delivery, "I start coughing up names and places and I'm gonna get killed."

"If you don't, you're gonna get eight-to-twelve in the pen, man," Sam replied. "With your priors, there ain't gonna be any work farm or any of that shit, get me?"

"Better twelve years than eternity. These bastards scare me," admitted the defendant. "Sam, I still owe the Mexican mafia about $30k for the shit I got busted with."

"Just try and lay out as much as you can, then, okay? You gotta get enough on the record so the judge will accept your plea," Sam counseled.

"Yeah, yeah—I hear you, man. But I ain't no stool pigeon."

Like every other meth user, the defendant was a "dealer." He'd buy a quantity of meth with the idea of selling enough of it to cover his expenses, and then keep the balance of it for his own use. Of course, as his use and tolerance increased, he'd found himself keeping an ever-increasing portion of what he got. As a result, he needed to sell more to get his needed share, and as he gradually outpaced the circle of users he sold to, he'd started doing dumb stuff—like selling to strangers in the alleys behind bars. Inevitably, he'd sold to a so-called "confidential informant," cop-speak for "another user/dealer who'd already been busted and who had agreed to do controlled buys for law enforcement" in return for consideration when it came time for sentencing.

Sam was speaking in earnest to his client and Daniels was doodling on his yellow legal pad when Mary entered the courtroom through the anteroom off the judge's chambers and handed him a note. Daniels abruptly stood and announced, "We will take a brief recess at this time. Please be seated at 10:30 sharp."

The bailiff had everyone rise until the judge left the courtroom. "Know anything about that?" Sam asked the bailiff, who might have some insight since he'd worked in the courthouse for decades.

"You didn't hear it from me, but the word in the halls is that the P.D. did a welfare check and found a body this morning. It's Ms. Smith."

"Who?" Sam asked.

"Emily Smith," the bailiff said. "The lawyer."

"What happened?"

"From what I heard, someone gutted her like a fish," the bailiff said. "But that's just what I heard."

9

"Who found her?" Detective Ken "Punch" Polson asked while toeing a portion of the newspaper scattered on the bedroom floor with a handmade alligator boot. It was the editorial page, he noted. Ironically, it featured a three-column rant demanding something be done about the crime rate.

"Ron Baker, about an hour ago," replied Corporal Mike Jensen, tipping his head toward the back of the house. "Apparently, her secretary called the station."

"Welfare check?"

"Yeah."

"Where's Baker?"

"Back of the house. Puking."

"How long has he been on the force? Thought he'd seen some of this," mused Punch. "Did he get the scene secured before he started yakking?"

"Yeah, he got calls into forensics and the EMTs right away and did a sweep of the place to make sure the perp wasn't still here. I think he was okay until the EMTs got here and started workin' on her."

"Working on her? Wasn't it obvious?"

"I guess one of the techs went to check for a pulse and his hand almost went right through her. That's when Baker lost it the second time."

"Well, when he gets done un-swallowing, have him see me."

"Roger."

Punch looked around at almost a dozen folks, most of whom were in their "bunny suits"—white clothing resembling hospital scrubs, designed to protect the wearer from biological hazards associated with death, especially violent death. "Get a list of everyone in here. Find out who absolutely, positively needs to be here, and who is just here to gawk or have something to talk about tomorrow. Run anyone who doesn't have a purpose."

"Right, boss," Jensen said.

"Then get some tape up here and start limiting people's ability to move around in here. I want everyone coming in and leaving to use the same routes. We can't let this scene get any more screwed up than it already is —got me?"

"Got it."

Punch turned his attention to the coroner, who was on his knees looking closely at the body. "How long?"

"Won't know for sure, but I'd say two days or so," replied "Doc" Fish, who wasn't a physician but had been the county's elected coroner for more than thirty years.

"So, what—maybe Halloween night?"

"I'd say that's maybe about right, but I don't want to get pinned down yet, Punch," Doc replied. "Help me up, would you, son?" Punch helped Doc to his feet.

Punch had come in through the front door and noted no signs of a break-in. Turning to Officer Jensen, he asked, "You check the doors and windows?"

"You bet. Nothing there, Punch. I'm waiting for the print guys now."

"Find the knife?" Punch lifted the sheet to get a look at her injuries.

"Not yet. Got the boys out back looking as we speak." Then Jensen added helpfully, "I checked her knife set—it looks complete. 'Course, it coulda just been something he got out of her kitchen. Hard to tell. I don't know what the hell it was, but it was a damned big blade."

Punch didn't say anything, but pushed back his cowboy hat, rubbed his forehead, and sighed. He knelt next to her and took a deep breath, then let it out and pulled back the sheet. She was on her stomach, with her head turned to one side. The killer had apparently been behind her when he cut her throat. "Yep. It was that." Punch had seen knives like that before—in the Army as a young man. Of course, around here there were a lot of veterans and almost as many hunting, hardware, and Army/Navy surplus stores as there were people. Complicating matters, you had the internet—where anything was for sale—so finding the guy who bought a knife that could inflict these wounds would be a matter of sheer luck. Praying silently for a really dumb suspect, he replaced the sheet.

"Anyone see anything?" he asked Jensen, noting the blood spatter high on the wall three feet from her head. Apparently, she'd been standing when he'd cut her. There were no real signs of a struggle, but there had to have been noise.

"We're still canvassing the neighborhood, Punch," replied Jensen, who was looking a little peaked himself.

"Call dispatch and get a coupla cars here to pound on some doors. Someone had to hear or see something. You okay, Jensen? You look like you just saw your own mother nude."

"I'm okay." Then, as if to explain, "I seen a lotta bodies in my time, but nothin' like that. He damned near took her head clean off."

"I noticed. Look, when Doc finishes, run everyone but the lab boys and the photographers out of here. I want a first-class effort, here—got it?" Punch looked closely at Jensen, who nodded.

In the kitchen, Punch noted several open bottles of booze, a cut lime, three shot glasses, and blood in the sink. The tequila was high-end stuff. A vase full of dead flowers sat on the counter. There was no card. "Jensen, make sure we get a sample of this blood, and check that vase for prints."

"Right, boss."

"I'm going to run downtown for a bit," Punch said, heading toward the door before stopping. "And Jensen?"

"Yeah?"

"Let me know when Baker's got it together."

"Will do, boss."

Punch was headed to the office to do some coordinating. Nothing for him here until the forensics team got their jobs done. He'd learned a long time ago that sometimes the best thing a leader can do is get out of the way and let people do their jobs. As he got into the unmarked county sedan, he swept the crowd with a practiced glance, memorizing faces and looking for anyone acting suspiciously. Murders just didn't happen in Custer, so the scene had drawn a crowd. It was not uncommon for killers to come and watch what was going on. In any event, other than the courthouse janitor and a couple of small-town punks, he didn't see anyone he knew.

10

"Unbelievable," Howard said to the ice in the bottom of his fourth—or was it fifth?—highball. Emily didn't do much criminal work back then, so she didn't generally appear in his court. At least, that's how he had justified it to himself afterward. The bar convention had been in Cody that year. He'd gone, as always, and had sat through all manner of continuing education classes, as well as the mandatory judicial meetings.

One night early in the week, he'd been cornered by some of Custer's attorneys, who were bound and determined to drag him and the rest of the Custer judges out for drinks. It was the first pub crawl he'd participated in for a while, and he'd overdone it.

He was awakened by movement next to him. At some point he realized he was dead drunk, alone at the hotel bar, and looking at his watch in a vain attempt to tell what time it was. He was weeping, like one of the goddamned street drunks who routinely appeared in front of him.

"Your Honor, can I help you?" was how it all started. The touch of her fingertips at his elbow thrilled him, even as drunk as he was. He wiped at his eyes and mumbled, "Just having a little trouble reading my damned watch—getting old, I guess."

"It happens to all of us, Judge," was all that Emily said.

Astonished, he could only stammer, "My name is Jon. Call me Jon."

"Are you sure?" she asked. "I don't want you to regret that—or anything else—in the morning."

"Where are the others?"

"They've all gone to their rooms. I think we drank them under the table." She was on the barstool next to him, looking at him in the mirror. He looked around with an unsteady gaze, and saw the tin roof above him, the bottles lining the wall, and Emily next to him. Uncomfortably close to him, in fact.

"Would you care for another?" she asked, placing her lips on the straw and slowly sipping a drink that had miraculously appeared, never breaking eye contact. He couldn't deal with it and looked down.

"I don't think so, Ms. Smith. I think that I've had more than enough, thank you very much." He focused on the stains on his slacks until they began to whirl. It was bourbon, if he recalled correctly. Or maybe scotch. Single malt. Who the hell could remember? That was a couple of stops ago. He rose unsteadily, determined to get back to the room before he made a complete and utter fool of himself. The last thing he needed was to do something dumb here; he'd never live it down.

"Let me help you, Jon," she said, taking a hand and an elbow. "And call me Emily, please."

Things had quickly gotten out of hand when they got to his room. Predictably, he'd performed poorly, if at all (he really couldn't remember). Back home, she had resisted any contact with him for several weeks. They had exchanged some office emails that alluded to what went on, and he had made some phone calls, sent some text messages, and—to his everlasting shame—had gotten loaded one night and sent flowers and a hand-written love note to her (in his own name, for Christ's sake!), all to no avail.

As time passed, he was able to be around her and transact business as if nothing had ever happened. Until a few months ago, when the demands came.

"Judge, I wonder if I might bother you for a moment," she'd said. It was a statement, not a question. She'd known damned well that he would let her bother him anytime, anywhere.

"Come in, Ms. Smith." He had motioned for Veronica to close the door on her way out, which she did after shooting the judge a scathing look. "How might I be of assistance?" he had said, loud enough to ensure Veronica could hear.

"Well, as you know, I missed the deadline to get my response to Mr. Marquez's motion filed; I'd like an extension," she had said as she glided toward his desk and sat down. She had a terrific voice.

"Ms. Smith, this is an improper, *ex parte* communication—you know that. Besides, even if the other side didn't object, I'm not sure I can do that. Mr. Marquez's motion is dispositive, and the relevant deadlines are clearly stated on the case management order. I—"

"Oh, I'm sure you can, Judge," Emily had cooed. "You're the judge, Jon. You have 'discretion,' I think it's called."

"Emily, Mr. Marquez is a conscientious attorney with a reputation for getting things done. If I allow you to get away with a late filing, well, I'll have to let everyone get away with it," he had protested.

She had stared at him levelly. "How is your wife, Jon? It's Margaret, isn't it?"

He'd felt his bowels loosen ever so slightly. "You know damned well what her name is."

"Well, I've always thought that while infidelity probably shouldn't be a crime, it is still somehow wrong—do you know what I mean? Do you happen to know how Margaret feels about the subject? I mean, does she think someone ought to be prosecuted, or is she content with a simple civil proceeding for dissolution or, in your case, maybe divorce?"

Howard sat very still for a long time, and then said, "Well, Ms. Smith, I suppose if you got me a response to the motion real soon I could overlook the late filing date."

Emily stood, reached out, and smoothed a couple of stray hairs on his head. "I knew you could, Judge. Thank you."

He had watched her sashay out of his chambers and close the door. Hating himself, he pressed the intercom. "Veronica? Get me the Thompson file, please."

After that, she'd made an occasional demand for a favorable setting, a motion to be decided in her favor, or the dismissal of a charge. To his shame, he'd acceded to every demand she had made. They had never gotten as frequent as he had initially feared, but somehow that made it worse. He'd lived with a sense of foreboding for a while now—one that clouded his entire outlook.

11

Veronica and Catherine Schmidt were in Judge Howard's outer office, awaiting a defense attorney's arrival. "The word is," said Veronica, "that she had a lot—and I mean a lot—of boyfriends, if you know what I mean."

"I don't know." Catherine, one of the assistant prosecutors, fiddled with the stapler on Veronica's desk. "I never socialized with her much, and I never, ever saw her out with anyone—except in Cody a couple of years ago."

"Who was she out with then?"

"Oh, a bunch of us went out one night during the bar convention and bar-hopped for a while. We even got your boss to join us, although it took some talking to get him out of his room."

"Really?" Veronica asked, surprised.

"He was pretty funny that night," Catherine recalled. "And I will tell you this: he can hold his liquor."

"I'd never have suspected," Veronica replied, careful not to look toward his office, where the bottle was kept. Time to change the subject. "Who is going to prosecute, assuming the cops catch the guy?"

"Well, I'm assuming it will be Mike Shepherd," Catherine said. "He's the chief deputy."

"Do you think he can handle it?" inquired Veronica. "He just seems so . . . fragile, I guess."

"I haven't thought about it, but Mike will have to take the case. The county attorney hasn't been in a courtroom in years."

In truth, Catherine had given quite a bit of thought to the matter. Even a dolt like Veronica could see that Mike wasn't up to the job. By all rights, then, as the next most senior deputy, Catherine would be in line for the jump. But she hadn't gotten to where she was by jumping willy-nilly into things; she would step forward if—and only if—the bust was righteous, and the outcome was a foregone conclusion. She damned sure wasn't gonna stick her neck out on something like this.

"God, this is all so terrible. I can't believe it happened," said Veronica.

"I know," agreed Catherine. "I just hope it's over."

"What do you mean?"

"Well, we don't really know what we're dealing with yet, now do we? I mean, this person or persons—he or she or they or whatever—could be some sort of nutcase."

"Oh my God. I—I just assumed we were dealing with someone who had it in for Emily," Veronica said. She hadn't even considered anything else.

"That's probably what we've got. But until we know it for sure, you need to be extra careful," she said, adding as she left Veronica's office, "We could have a Ted Bundy running around."

"Dude, they almost cut her head clean off," Fricke was telling Frac as the latter mopped the floor. Fricke had just hung up the phone, and now he took his feet off Veronica's desk and hollered to Frac in the hallway, "And they gutted her like a fish!"

"Cool," said Frac, not quite knowing what a gutted fish looked like. Fricke was mad at him—again. Frac didn't like people being mad at him. It made him sad. Maybe if he did an extra special job on this floor, Fricke would be nice to him.

"'Cool?'" Fricke exclaimed. "Gal gets her head cut off and dissected like a science class frog, and all you got to say is, 'Cool?' Boy, you are one dumb sonuvabitch. Finish that floor, dummy. I got another call to make."

Ann felt guilty, but she was so excited she was about to jump out of her skin. "This is it!" was all she could think. Her chance to shine. Certainly, the case would go initially to Mike Shepherd, but sure as hell he would kick this football to whoever else wanted it. Shepherd was a good guy; in fact, he had been an excellent mentor and source of knowledge for her over the past couple of years. But no way could his health withstand a capital murder trial, which was exactly what this would be if what Ann had heard —that Emily had been decapitated—was right.

She picked up the phone and called Shepherd's office. Bonnie answered on the first ring.

"The boss in?" Ann asked.

"No, Ms. Fulks, he is not. He's at the pharmacy, having a prescription refilled. Shall I tell him you called?"

"No. Just put me on his calendar for whenever he is supposed to be back," Ann replied, feeling her heart pounding. "I need to speak with him personally."

"I'm afraid his calendar is quite full," Bonnie replied. "Him being gone was unscheduled, and I had to scramble to rearrange his calendar."

"He'll see me," Ann replied testily. "It's very important, and I have news that he will want to hear."

By all rights, the case should belong to Shepherd. But if he couldn't or wouldn't do it, then Cathy Schmidt would be next in line. Cathy was no risk taker, however, and all murder trials were high-wire acts for the prosecution. If things went as planned, Ann thought, she would soon be sitting first chair in a murder prosecution.

Tommy was standing in mud up to his knees in a field south of town when his phone rang. He wiped the muck from his hand and answered. "Hello?" He didn't recognize the number.

"This is Gino from the Longbranch."

"Yeah?"

"Where you at?"

"In the field—maybe twenty miles south of town. Why?"

"You listening to the radio?"

"When I'm in the rig. Right now I'm changing a drill bit. The muck out here is like gumbo and I can't get the damned thing to bite, so I'm gonna try another one. Why?"

"Listen, I'm sorry to be the one to tell you, but you know that lawyer you been layin'?"

"Yeah?"

"Cops just found her. Someone cut her head clean off, from what I been told."

"Jesus!"

"Yeah, no shit. I only seen her once, but she was sweet lookin'. Sorry, man."

"Yeah. . . Sure. . . I gotta go."

Tommy jumped out of the rig and found his crew chief. "Boss, I gotta get to town."

"You'll be there in another three hours or a hundred feet, whichever comes first."

"Someone killed her."

"Who?"

"That lawyer I been seein'. Emily."

"That gal with the phone-sex voice you been tellin' us about?"

"Yeah."

"Jesus! Sorry. Look, let me call another rig. I think Number 7's on the way to town. Maybe they can swing by and pick you up."

"I'm not sure I ever met her," Sam said. "Maybe at a meeting of the bar association or something?"

"She was something else." Paul turned to check his e-mail. "Divorce attorney. Recently started doing some criminal defense, I'm told. Mostly small-time stuff. I didn't do a lot of stuff with her; I found her difficult to work with. I will say she was easy on the eyes."

"So I heard," Sam said.

"In any event, the courts will shut down for the funeral."

"She a local?"

"Oh, yeah. Parents are ranchers from east of town. Judges will want to attend. We do that here. Hell, we're lawyers—if we didn't attend each other's funerals, who would go?"

Sam laughed aloud. True anywhere.

"Sam, I want to change the subject for a minute."

"Sure, what's on your mind?"

"How are things going?"

"Pretty well, I think. I'm kind of enjoying the way business is done around here. The courts are a lot more flexible in terms of pleadings and timelines, and the prosecutors are damned sure easier to work with. On the civil side, counsel are much, much easier to work with than they are in D.C."

"Got a theory?"

"Sure. I think it's because as an attorney around here, you're going to have to interact more with your peers. So while in a particular case I might have the facts and the law on my side, I'd best keep in mind that the next time counsel and I meet she might have the hammer. Attorneys have to cooperate. On the other hand, in a place like D.C., lawyers can try and bury each other, because the opportunities for retribution are few and far between."

"Interesting take. Well, it looks to us like you've gotten the hang of things quickly."

"Thanks, Paul. I can't thank you enough for the opportunity. Not a lot of folks would have given me this shot."

"Well, I figured you'd be up to the job," Norquist said, doodling on his desk pad. "Sam, I'm kind of uncomfortable asking this, so I'm just going to say it: word is you been drinking a lot."

"Anyone say I'm drinking on the job?"

"Of course not. If I'd heard that, you'd be gone. But word is—"

"Word is irrelevant," Sam interrupted. "It's no one's business what I do when I'm not on the job."

"Sam, this is a small town. People talk. I can't have people thinking that we're anything other than God-fearing, toe-the-line types. I've spent my professional life building something here. This practice is my life's work. It's all I have."

"I respect that, Paul. I really do. And I respect everything you've done for me. You gave me a shot. But I don't like being watched."

"Fair enough. All I'm asking you to do is keep it on the down-low."

"Done."

"And one more thing," Norquist said.

"Yes?"

"You're not giving any thought to taking on the defense in Emily's case, are you?"

"I hadn't given it any thought, no," Sam said. "Have they caught the guy?"

"No, but it's just. . . It's just that this is a small town, and folks won't take kindly to someone defending her killer."

"The law says—"

"Oh, screw that. I know the law, Sam, and I'm just as convinced of the need for a righteous, vigorous defense as you are. But everyone in this town knew Emily. It ain't right, but folks won't approve of whoever helps the guy. That's the kinda thing could ruin me."

"I understand."

"Again, I don't give a damn what anyone says, I built this and I don't want to see it go to hell over one guy."

"I hear you, Paul." Sam looked at his watch. "I've got a hearing in front of Daniels here in a few minutes."

"Do it," Norquist replied. "When you get back, I want to talk to you a little more about that private road matter I mentioned some time back."

12

Punch was getting moderately irritated. He'd parried the boss's questions now for about an hour. And while it was true that—unlike a fair number of police chiefs—this one had law enforcement experience, it was just as true that he hadn't worked in the field since Christ was a corporal.

Chief of Police William "Buck" Lucas had been appointed by the city council when Clinton was president and had served at their pleasure since. Punch had all the respect in the world for the chief's ability to manage an office, but because he had little recent field experience with serious crimes, Punch didn't see the value in having him grading his paper on a murder investigation.

"Chief, you've got to understand. We've only had this case a couple of days. You've got to give me some time to get folks in there to fully develop the evidence. Once I do that, then we can start to get you some answers," Punch said, as calmly as he could.

"Was there a struggle?"

"No, I don't think so."

"Really, I'm surprised. I'da thought she'da fought like a cat."

"I don't think she saw it coming, but just in case she did and maybe got her licks in I've already got people watching the emergency rooms and the walk-in clinics all over town."

"Any footprints?"

"Yeah, but I don't know whose they are yet. We had a lot of people tromping around before we got the crime scene guys on scene."

"Ah, shit. The prosecutor is not gonna like that."

"The prosecutor's not the one who is trying to deal with this real-time."

"I know that, Punch, but goddammit, we have to give them the best evidence that we can! That's our job. That's what we get paid for."

"I know what my job is, boss. And I'm trying to do the best I can. These situations develop quickly, and it's not like my people are seeing murders every day. I think we've done a pretty damned good job so far, and I think if you give me some time we'll have the evidence we need for you and the county attorney to get a conviction and keep the taxpayers happy."

"When?"

"As soon as possible, boss. What's it been—forty-eight hours?"

"What are you thinking right now?"

"Well, there was a knife. I always figure that anyone using a knife is either really, really pissed off or a nutcase. In this case, it was one clean cut."

"Did he beat her?"

"No apparent evidence of that. It looks to me like he came up behind her and did the deed quickly and cleanly."

"Where'd you find her?"

"In the upstairs hallway."

"Was there blood anywhere else?" Lucas asked.

Punch shook his head no, and then remembered. "Yeah, there was, and I don't think it was hers. It was downstairs in the sink. No way she could have bled both places from a neck wound like that. Maybe he cut himself during the attack. Too soon to know."

"She was killed right there in that hallway, right?"

"As far as I can tell. Looking at all the blood spatter on the walls, there was a lot of spray, and looks like he walked up right behind her and grabbed her by the forehead, tilted her head back, and slit her throat in one quick motion."

"So, she turned her back on him. That means she knew him, right?"

"Maybe. Or maybe she didn't know he was in the house at all," Punch countered. "Could be they did not know each other. Could be that he is some kind of a freak who's been watching her. Could be that she was just really, really unlucky and he picked her house for no reason at all. I just don't know yet."

"Your working theory is going to influence how you go about solving this case."

Punch looked at him dolefully. "I know that, which is why I want to wait until I've got something from the crime scene boys."

"I want you to keep me posted on this, Punch," Lucas said. "I don't need people panicking. For right now, our working theory is going to be that we think it is someone that she knew."

"But I am not that far," Punch protested. "I just can't say that yet."

"You don't have to—I will. I'm going to say that to try and quell any rumors of a goddamned nutjob running around this town," Lucas said. "I'm gonna do a press conference at five o'clock day after tomorrow, and the city council wants a full report at tomorrow night's meeting."

"I wish you wouldn't do that, boss."

"Got to be done, Punch. My job is public safety, and part of that job is to keep people from panicking."

"Ann, come right in." Chief Deputy County and Prosecuting Attorney Mike Shepherd closed the door behind her as she took a chair in his cluttered office. Shepherd had been County Attorney Rebecca Nice's right-hand man and loyal confidant for the entirety of her four-year tenure. He was smart, wary, and extremely political, Ann knew. "What can I do for you?"

"You can assign me to assist you with the prosecution of whoever killed Emily Smith," said Ann.

"What in the world are you talking about?"

"Emily Smith's murder."

"Has there been an arrest?" He pulled an egg from a paper bag on his desk and tapped it on his desktop.

"Not yet, but from what I hear they are moving pretty quickly," Ann lied. "They expect to make an arrest any time now."

"Goodness," said Shepherd, peeling the egg. "I guess we better start thinking about how we are going to deal with this."

"Well, Mike, you are the chief deputy prosecutor, so unless the prosecutor takes the case from you, this is your case."

"I know that. But I haven't tried a murder case since that drug deal went bad in 2010. That was before you got here. I don't have a burning desire to do that again," he said, and popped the egg into his mouth.

"I want it, Mike," Ann said. She felt a little queasy watching him.

He held up a finger while he chewed, then took a drink from a bottle of soda on his desk. "I admire your ambition, but you don't have a lot of experience yet. Murder investigations and prosecutions are not for the novice."

"Mike, I've been a prosecutor here for five years! I am tired of dinking around with misdemeanors and minor felonies. I can promise you a conviction. How else am I gonna learn if I'm stuck dealing with penny-ante bullshit? Let me sit second chair, at least."

"I'm gonna have to talk to Rebecca," he said. He reached into the bag and retrieved another egg. "It's her call. She answers to the voters."

"Obviously. But when you talk with her, tell her that I want the case."

"I'll do that. But you know that if I don't take it, by all rights it should go to Cathy. She's the next most senior prosecutor."

"Mike, I understand. But I don't think she's gonna want it, either."

"I will check with Rebecca and let you know," he said, tapping the egg lightly on his desktop.

"Thanks, Mike. That's all I can ask."

"Ann?"

"Yeah?"

"Are you familiar with the old adage, 'Be careful what you ask for?'"

"I am." Ann laughed. "Don't worry about me, Mike. This is exactly what I want, and I can handle it."

13

It was just before the sun came up—what the Army termed "early morning nautical twilight"—and still hot. The choppers had left half an hour ago to take advantage of the cover of darkness. Sam and his men had exchanged gunfire with an unseen enemy, but after a few passes by the AC-130 gunships, whatever enemy was out there had likely been killed or skulked away. Sam's troops had spread out among the convoy's vehicles, intent on getting everyone back to the forward operating base safely. As if in slow motion, Sam saw trouble coming. He heard the gunfire, tried to determine the direction of attack, and then felt the concussion. He flew from the vehicle and was skidding down the middle of the road. He tried to get up, then felt the round impact his leg, looked up, and saw a wall of blood headed for him. It was a red tide, and it caught him and overtook him. He was trying to swim to safety, but his leg wouldn't work. His men were on the bank telling him to swim to them, but he couldn't make it. He was floating down a river of blood, screaming for help.

"Sam! Sam, you're safe! You're here with me!" Veronica was shaking him.

"O-Okay," Sam said. "I'm fine."

"Oh my God! No, you're not!" she said. "I've never seen anything like that."

"I'm cold. Just give me that blanket." He managed a weak smile. "Just a nightmare. I'll be fine."

"Are you sure? You're covered in sweat," she said, pulling a blanket over him. She was nude from the waist up. He remembered the red panties. "The sheets are soaking wet. I've been trying to wake you up." She put her hand on his wet chest. "Your heart is pounding."

"I'm fine."

"You are not! What is wrong?"

"Just had a nightmare. It happens." He was out of breath but attempted a smile. He looked at the digital red numbers on his clock showing two a.m., then pushed himself up on the mattress and gestured toward his leg, which was leaning against the nightstand. "Can you hand me my leg?"

"Of course," she said. He watched as she went to the nightstand, grabbed his artificial leg, and handed it to him. Unlike others, she seemed unfazed. "Can I help?"

"No, I've got this," he said, while positioning the leg and beginning the process of affixing it to his body. "I'm pretty good at it by now."

She sat on the bed, watching him intently. The perspiration had literally soaked him, and his hair was plastered to his forehead. "Sam, I don't know what to say. Obviously, I'll never be able to understand how terrible it was. But you've got to get some help."

He said nothing, still focused on getting the leg on properly. "Do you hear me?" she asked.

"I hear you. Look, lots of bad things happen to people every day. I'm no different. I just need to work through this. I'll be fine." He slid off the bed, the artificial leg now firmly attached. Then, flexing the leg, he stood and walked to the bathroom. "I gotta take a leak, and I need a shower."

Veronica lay on her back, staring at the ceiling and listening to the shower for a long time. When he didn't come out after fifteen minutes, she dressed and left.

14

Since murders in Wyoming were still rare enough to make the front page of every paper in the state, Lucas knew a lot of attention would be paid to this one. Still, he wasn't prepared for the crowd of reporters assembled on the steps of the law enforcement complex. The local newspaper guy and radio reporter were there, of course, as was a young woman he recognized as being from the Casper paper of record. He was surprised to see television cameras—one from the Denver metropolitan area, and one from Rapid City. This didn't bode well, because as far as he knew, the more salacious details of the crime had yet to emerge. Once those were out, he might well have a real shit-show on his hands.

He gave a statement while one of his deputies handed out copies of his resume. A little publicity couldn't hurt.

"Chief, do you have any suspects?" It was Sarah Penrose, a writer with the local newspaper, the Custer *Bugle*.

"Not yet; we're in the early stages of our investigation."

"But isn't it true that the first forty-eight hours are arguably the most critical to an investigation?"

"Generally, yes."

"And yet you have no suspects?"

"None that I'm prepared to name at this time." This was not going as well as he had hoped.

"So you do have one or more suspects?"

"We have some people we're interested in, is all I'll say," he responded tersely, recognizing his mistake.

"Could this be the work of a serial killer?" asked the Denver television reporter.

"Doubtful."

"Why do you say that?"

"Because we've got no evidence of any other crime."

"But if another murder was committed, that would be evidence, right?"

"How the hell can I answer that right now?" he snapped.

"Have you discerned a motive?"

"No. As I mentioned, we are still in the early stages of our investigation."

"Is terrorism a possibility?"

"Excuse me?"

"I'm asking if this could be a terrorism incident."

"I think we can safely rule that out," Lucas said, shaking his head.

"On what basis?"

"On the basis that a) there is no evidence of terrorism, and b) that it's stupid."

"But if you don't yet have a motive, how can you know that it isn't terrorism?"

"In the same manner that I know that Sasquatch didn't cut her throat."

"Her throat was cut?" interjected the Rapid City reporter, keying in on the newly-released evidence.

Punch, watching the spectacle live on his office television, crushed his paper coffee cup and threw it against the wall. "You've got to be freaking kidding me," he said as he hit the mute button. "Are you recording this, Jensen?"

"Yes, boss."

"Okay. You watch this farce and make me a list of all of the facts that he discloses to the press."

"What are you gonna do with it?"

"Nothing," Punch said as he put on his hat and headed out the door.

"But I'll know what information the average idiot has, so when I interview someone who wants to confess, I'll know what he could have found out compliments of the chief."

"Where are you going?"

"I'm going out to look for clues."

"Where?"

"Wherever I can find one. But I'm gonna start at Emily's house."

Jensen un-muted the television and focused on the press conference.

"Is the public in danger?" a reporter asked.

"We don't believe there is any significant danger to the public," Lucas said, trying to choose his words carefully.

"So, you are unable to rule out a threat to public safety at this time?"

"What I'm saying is we have no indications of a threat to public safety at present."

"Well, you have a dead girl and an unsolved crime, don't you?"

While Lucas tried to formulate an answer, Jensen rummaged through a desk drawer, trying to find pen and paper.

"So, just out of curiosity, when they find out who did this, would you consider defending the guy?" Veronica asked. She was pushing peas around the plate with her fork, apparently not very hungry. This was the second time they'd been out to dinner together. It had been a couple of days since Emily's body was found, and her murder was topic number one around town.

"I don't think so." Sam gestured toward the bartender for another scotch. "Paul has already warned me off."

"Word on the street is that Paul's in trouble. Could be tempting."

"How do you know that?" he asked.

"I know a lot of things about the law firms in this town," Veronica said.

"Well, I don't think you have to worry about me on this one. This is the end of the line for me. I've got nowhere left to go."

"I would hope you wouldn't take it. Whoever takes it on is going to be the most unpopular man or woman in the county. Whoever did that to

Emily needs to fry. Let them bring in one of those shoulder-pad-wearing shrews from down in Cheyenne. That's the difference between practicing in a city and in a small town. Here, we all have to get along."

"Speaking of which, word I got is that you hated Emily's guts, and she felt the same about you."

"That's just small-town gossip. It's true that we had our differences, but that was because she wasn't particularly good at managing her schedule, which screwed with my boss's docket—and I don't like anyone dicking with my boss's docket," she said, giggling.

"Come on, Veronica, she slept with your ex-husband while you were married. You can't tell me that you don't hold a grudge over that."

"How do you know that?"

"I've got my own sources."

"Touché."

"You wouldn't be normal if you could just let that go. That's not how love works. No one gets over that kind of stuff."

"Kind of like you not getting over getting hurt?" she said, sipping her wine. "That was weird the other night. Tell me what happened, Sam."

"Yeah, like that," he said, too quickly. Then, "I don't want to talk about it. I haven't talked about it for ten-plus years, and I'm goddamned not going to start now."

"So, let me get this straight: you can talk about my personal life, but yours is off limits—is that how this works?"

Sam took a couple of deep breaths. "Veronica, I don't want to argue. I am just not ready to talk about it yet. I want you to know I tried to set up an appointment with the VA, but at this clinic it'll be six weeks before they can see me."

"Good. You need to talk to someone. Maybe then you wouldn't drink so much. Maybe you wouldn't take so many pills."

Sam looked at her steadily until he shifted his eyes and met the waiter's, mouthing, "Again, please."

15

"The body is that of an un-embalmed, well-developed, healthy, white female of slender build. Body length is sixty-seven inches. Estimated weight is one hundred twenty-five pounds." Dr. Ronald B. Laws had a voice-activated microphone attached to his lab coat so he could record his findings as he made them. Laws had done a residency in pathology some years ago before turning to internal medicine, and now contracted with "Doc" Fish—the elected coroner—to do the actual work of pathology for the county.

"The body was found no more than thirty-six hours following death; post-mortem decomposition, therefore, is underway," Laws continued. "The head is normal, the pupils round and equal; the irises are brown. The nose, ears, jaw, chest, abdomen, and extremities are normal. The neck and throat sport an incision approximately four centimeters in width and running from jawline to jawline."

Punch stood nearby, watching. "Detective Polson, would you assist here?" Laws asked. Together, the doctor and detective moved Emily Smith's body into a semi-reclining position. Laws then placed a plastic object shaped like a block underneath the body, near her upper spine. "Okay, let her down."

This resulted in the chest protruding upward and her arms falling to the sides, like a whole chicken ready for deboning. As Punch watched, the doctor made a Y-shaped incision, with the branches of the Y just under each breast and the base of the letter near her pelvis. Since the blood in her body had long since coagulated and settled, there was no bleeding. "The organs are in normal location and have normal relationships," Laws dictated after a quick inspection.

Wielding the scalpel, the doctor warned Punch, "You're not gonna like this; you might want to have a seat."

Punch nodded, determined to hang in there. "I've seen 'em before, Doc."

"Whatever," was the response, and the dissection, or "internal examination," began, whereupon the doctor proceeded to remove, weigh, measure, examine, and comment on the internal organs of what had once been a vibrant young woman—somebody's little girl.

Punch hung in there for an hour or so, but the tedious nature of it all got to him, and he pulled up a chair and sat down. He half-listened as the doctor dictated the findings as he went along, choosing instead to review his notes on the case so far. At last, Laws stood up, straightened his back, and retrieved a saw from the small table behind him. It was, he informed Punch, time to examine her brain.

"Doc," Punch said, standing and looking at Emily. "I'd love to stay, but I've got things to do."

"What?"

"I dunno," Punch said. "I'll think of something. Call me."

16

"Mr. Hadley? I'm Officer Jensen from the Custer Police Department," Jensen said through the crack in the door.

"Lemme see your badge, boy," was the response. Looking from the daylight into the darkness in the house, all Jensen could see was a white sleeveless T-shirt and silver hair. He could smell the bourbon, though. Excellent. Another drunk who saw and heard things no one else did. Jensen was busy, with the boss and half the department all over him. He really didn't have time for this. Nonetheless, he showed the guy the badge, just as he might someone who would actually know what he was looking at.

"Mr. Hadley, you called and said you had information that might help us?"

"I did." Hadley opened the door to reveal a remarkable mess of an apartment. "I think I seen him, but I wanta be put into that there witness pro-tection program 'fore I says anythin'."

"Mr. Hadley, why don't you tell me what you know, and then I'll make a determination whether or not your information is helpful, and whether you might need protection as a result."

"I ain't sayin' shit lessen I git protection," said Hadley, scratching at his armpit like an old, gray ape. "And I want a re-ward."

Jensen's eyes had adjusted. "Mr. Hadley," he said, looking over the old man's shoulder. "Is that marijuana in that frisbee under that chair behind you? Because if it is, I'm gonna have to arrest you and take you downtown and ask you a whole bunch of questions about where you got it, et cetera."

Hadley turned and considered his living room, then faced Jensen again. "Well now, Officer, I don't see any reason why we can't work something out. . ." Hadley trailed off, realizing things hadn't gone quite the way he had planned.

Jensen had pushed past Hadley and was now in the living room. He bent over, cleared a place on the couch by moving a pile of empty beer cans and a pizza box, and somewhat reluctantly sat down. "Now, tell me what you know, Mr. Hadley," Jensen said. "Beginning with why you waited several days to call."

Lucas and Punch were in Lucas's office several days after the discovery of Emily's body. Press queries were incoming, and the mayor was getting impatient, so Lucas had called Punch in for an update. "So, what do we have?" he asked, sipping coffee from a mug with a handle shaped like a pistol grip.

"It looks to be pretty straightforward," Punch opined. "No sign of a break-in; nothing is missing as far as we can tell; killer cut her with a purpose."

"So, someone she knew," Lucas said.

"Starting to look that way," Punch said. "Way I see it, she let the guy in, something was said, and at some point he lost it."

"He?"

"I think so. Never known a woman to do something like that. Besides, she was slender, but the word is that she was a fitness fanatic. She wouldn't have been a pushover."

"Speakin' of which, anything back from the lab? Prints?"

"Lots of prints—maybe a half dozen distinct sets so far. One's hers, of course—even I can see that, but the rest are unidentified right now. Cale is running them through the FBI's Integrated Automated Fingerprint Identification System to see if we can get a match, but so far we don't have squat."

"AFIS? That's just bad guys, right?"

"Not anymore. Nowadays, you buy a gun, work in a bank, or do any number of other jobs you get fingerprinted. All the records end up in the database."

"So our guy could be a first-time offender and we might have a shot?"

"Or even a never-offender, if he ever bought a gun or did any security work," Punch said, and then, with a devious grin, added, "Or was a cop."

"Jesus Christ Almighty! Don't even think that—gives me the runs just thinking about it!" Lucas took a deep pull from a can of soda on his desk. "Blood?"

"What I said before: most of it was hers. Some—what was in the sink—maybe wasn't."

"So maybe he cut himself?"

"I figure either his hand slipped when the blade got wet and he washed up later, or maybe she got to him first—like I said, she was no wilting lily, by reputation."

"Weapon?"

"All of her kitchen knives are accounted for, and her mom said she didn't have anything else around the house."

"So, premeditated?"

"I'm thinking so, yeah. Looks like he brought it with him and left with it."

"Boyfriends?"

"Mom and secretary don't know. We're asking around."

"Pictures of the gawkers?"

"Yeah. Jensen had the photogs go outside and shoot crowd shots every half-hour or so in case our boy is a ghoul."

"Anything?"

"Not yet."

"Phone records?"

"We're working on it. Can't find her cell."

"What about the neighbors?"

"Jensen got a call about an hour ago; guy lives in the next stairwell. He's on it; I haven't heard anything yet."

"So, tell me what your gut says, Punch. This a pissed-off boyfriend, or do we have a weirdo running around?"

"I can't tell yet, Chief. I don't have enough yet to even hazard a guess. I only hope—"

"Hope ain't a method, Punch," Lucas interrupted. "We need to know, and we need to know ASAP."

"I know that. I'm on it. There's nothing more I can do right now."

"I don't need to tell you, Punch, that this is a big deal. The city council is in an uproar. There's an election pending. I want this mess wrapped up and put before the public wrapped in a big red bow long before that—got me?"

"Gotcha, Chief."

"Just remember something. Come election day, if this case is still open, detective or not, you could very well find your ass checking parking meters on Yellowstone Avenue in a new administration."

Cale Pleasance had been a fingerprint examiner for almost twenty years, and he was, as he liked to say, "in all modesty—a damned good one." He'd been the on-duty examiner, so he'd gone to the scene and pulled a number of the fingerprints himself. There were fingerprints everywhere, which, contrary to what one sees on television, was to be expected. He'd lifted as many of those as he could and dusted for latent prints just in case whoever had done this had been dumb enough, or panicked enough, to leave behind his or her prints. He'd then glue-fumed the hallway where the body was found to pick up additional latent prints. Finally, he'd treated some of what he saw as the clearer prints with gold nanoparticles and attached cotinine antibodies; this could tell him if the individual who left the prints was a smoker.

The team had taken the victim's prints at the scene, and Pleasance had a copy of those on hand for the sake of comparison. Accordingly, he'd been able to quickly eliminate about ninety-five percent of the visible and latent prints as belonging to the suspect, simply because they were those of the victim.

The unidentified prints he was left with were located on common items, to include lamps, wineglasses, the open bottles of wine in the kitchen and bedroom, the bedposts up by the headboard, the handles to the entry door, the window sash in her bedroom, three shot glasses, the bathroom taps, and the towel rack. There were also a couple of unknowns on the refrigerator handle and a vase full of dead flowers on the kitchen countertop.

Now he had to submit the prints to AFIS to see if any of the donors had a criminal record, had been in a sensitive position, required a special license for work, or had ever worked with children, the infirm, or had been or currently was a member of the military. Based on his experience, it would take AFIS a little time to give him an answer, so Cale decided to get a cup of coffee while he waited. He was pouring it when the phone rang.

"Custer Police, Technician Pleasance. May I help you?"

"Yo, Cale. Jensen here. You got anything? Punch and the chief are on my ass."

"Just kicked things off to AFIS. All I know right now is you got six or seven sets of prints in the house, and one set belongs to a smoker." Cale took a careful sip from the steaming cup. "You in touch with her folks or relatives?"

"We're tryin'," Jensen said. "Why?"

"I'm thinking if you can talk with them, find out the last time—if ever—they were here. If we can get a set of prints from them, maybe we can start eliminating a lot of these unknowns."

"Okay, I'll talk with Punch. Call me as soon as you know something, okay?"

"I'll do it."

"Have you ever seen a doctor?" Veronica asked. She and Sam were having lunch at a small café near the courthouse.

"I've seen a lot of doctors," Sam said. He knocked on what should have been his leg with his knuckles.

"I'm sorry. I meant—"

"I know what you mean. Look, they took my leg on a hospital ship somewhere on the Red Sea. I got shipped out of theater to Frankfurt, Germany. There's a big hospital there. They got me stabilized and worked up, and I got sent from there to Walter Reed, near D.C. Spent almost a year there recovering physically, learning how to use this." He pointed at the leg. "And they sent me through counseling, and the like. Saw lots of docs."

"That must have been terrible. You are a hero, Sam."

"I'm no hero. A guy like Corporal Jenkins, who ran through gunfire to drag my ass to safety—that's a hero. I was a guy doing a job who got blown up and shot. A guy who got his men killed—"

"Stop it!" Veronica whispered. "You can't blame yourself."

Sam looked at her for a long moment. "I fought against a medical discharge, but at the time and given my specialty, well, the Army said I had to go or change my specialty. I didn't accept that very well, so I went on a bit of a bender when I got the news."

"That's understandable."

"I didn't have any idea what I was going to do next. I'd never really thought beyond the Army. Fortunately, a guy I knew was friends with the admissions officer at a law school nearby. They pulled some strings and I got in."

"That was good of them."

"It was. Without my disabled vet status, I doubt I'd have gotten in."

"Did you enjoy law school?"

He laughed. "Show me someone who enjoys law school and I'll show you someone who's as crazy as a shithouse rat. I finished in the middle of my class, which wasn't bad since I was generally three or four beers to the good during class." Seeing her look of horror, he added, "It was night school."

"So that makes it better?" she asked.

"It does." Sam finished his sandwich, wadded up his napkin, and dropped it on his plate. "Anyway, while I was in school I tried the mental health counseling thing, but I wasn't getting much out of it and there were a lot of guys who needed it more than me, and since there was limited space I just kind of decided to let someone else see if they could get anything out of it."

"Who could need it more than you?"

"Lots of guys." He looked at the floor. "You don't know the extent of damage to some of these guys and gals. I mean, I'm screwed up, but I've got so many advantages over so many of them . . . It's hard to explain, but I'm okay."

"Are you?"

"I am, really. Just had a bad night. I have some of those."

"Hey, Judge, what do you know about that murder?" O'Hanlon asked Howard. They were tipping a few, and O'Hanlon was feeling a little loose.

"You know I can't talk about pending cases," Howard said.

"Well, I suppose not," O'Hanlon said. "Think you'll get it?"

"If they find the guy, I could do his initial appearance and then preside over his preliminary hearing." Howard took a long pull from his glass. "If I didn't recuse myself."

"Why would you?"

"Oh, I don't know. You never know. Could be someone I know."

"Well, I hope they find the guy. It's creepy, some guy killin' a lawyer and all—especially a good lookin' one like her."

"Yeah." Howard raised his glass to the bartender. "Another round for my friend and me, Pete."

17

"Get a description?" Punch asked, hoping beyond hope it was a black guy or a Hispanic, not because he was racist but because there were relatively few of each in town, and it would make finding the suspect much easier. What Punch decidedly did not want to hear was that the suspect was a white, blue-collar-type male with facial hair and driving a white 4x4 pickup, because that description would fit most everyone in town.

"You bet," replied Jensen.

"Whatcha got?" Punch readied his pen.

"Witness says the guy is a white male, late twenties to early thirties, average height, goatee, wearin' a baseball cap and driving a white Ford F-150."

"Aw, shit!"

"But we got a lead—the dude has a tat," Jensen said eagerly.

"I hate to break it to you there, stud, but aside from my wife—and I ain't so sure there—everyone in this town seems to have a tattoo."

"This one's different."

"How so?"

"It's a bulldog with writing that says 'semper-something' on it."

"He's a Marine," Punch said.

"Huh?"

"He's a Marine. One of their symbols is a bulldog, and 'semper fidelis' means 'always faithful.'"

"How do you know?"

"I was a soldier. I knew some Marines."

"Got it. The neighbor gave us a description of his truck, too."

"Plates?"

"No luck. But he did mention that the suspect's truck was lifted and has real expensive tires—twenty inches or so."

"Great," Punch said sourly. "This is getting better and better. I could stand on Main Street and swing a dead cat by the tail and hit three guys matching the description of my suspect or his truck."

Jensen smiled. "What's next?"

"I've been to her house; I want to get in her office—you know where it is?"

"Yeah. Little place a block or so from the tracks."

"Let's go. You drive."

On the way, Punch made a couple of calls. Turning to Jensen, he asked, "Did you know this gal?"

"No, never met her. I don't think she did much criminal defense work. Did divorces, mostly."

"Hear anything about her?"

"Yeah. My sister says she's a cunning bitch."

"Was."

"Huh? Oh, yeah."

"Your sister?"

"Yeah. Her and her old man—name is Tommy—are splitting the sheets, and this gal Emily was representing him."

After speaking with Dot, they were allowed in Emily's office. It was a disaster; papers were strewn everywhere, and houseplants were placed haphazardly about the room. "Ain't much here," Jensen commented while poking around the tiny space. "I don't even see any lawbooks."

"I think they got them all on computer nowadays," opined Punch. "But this place does look more like a grow room than a law office. She see clients in here?"

"Not sure. I'll ask her secretary. This isn't like on TV. On TV lawyers spend all night looking through stacks of books, any one of which is that thick." Jensen held his thumb and index finger several inches apart.

"Yeah, well, on television, they're all good-looking too."

"This one was," Jensen mused while looking at a small framed photo of Emily and a little girl.

A loud knock came from the outer door.

"You expecting someone, boss?" asked Jensen.

"Yeah. One of those computer forensic guys. He's going to image her hard drive so we can look at it later. Show him where everything is and get him started. And tell him not to touch anything if he can avoid it. Have him glove up just to be sure."

"Right."

"And get his prints, just in case."

"Right."

"And when the hell is the rest of the team going to get here? We called them an hour ago." Punch rubbed his eyes with one hand.

"They got diverted."

"Diverted?"

"Yeah. Evidently some dude got popped for diddling the ten-year-old twins of some doctor. He was mowing the doc's lawn, met the kids, and somehow got 'em alone."

"Jesus!"

"No shit. There ought to be a special place in hell for guys like that."

Punch had been going through Emily's desk and found what he was looking for—a small pocketbook-sized planner. "Here we go."

"Whatcha got, boss?"

"Just a minute. Let's start by looking at the day she was killed. . . After-noon court appearance . . . She missed that, which is why her secretary called us in."

"Missed that morning one, too."

"Yep."

"What about the day before?"

Punch turned the page. "Looks like a couple of meetings with clients and then one after five with 'T.'"

"Who is that?"

"Now how the hell would I know?" Punch asked.

"I don't know, boss. I just thought—"

"Look. Everyone else, she's got first and last names. This person is just 'T.'"

"Why?"

"Well, that's what we need to figure out. You write down the names of all these folks and arrange for us to visit them. I'm going to talk with that secretary of hers and see if she knows who 'T' is."

"Punch?" Jensen was looking at the picture of Emily and the child, thinking.

"Yeah?"

"Maybe 'T' stands for 'Tommy.'"

"Tommy?"

"Yeah. My soon-to-be ex-brother-in-law."

"You said she was his attorney—right?"

"That's what my sister said."

"What's he look like?"

"Maybe six-foot, 180, shaved head, wears a hat a lot, drives—"

"—an F-150?"

"How'd you know?"

"I'm psychic. Has Tommy ever been in the service?"

"Hey, I ain't sayin'—"

"Has he ever served?"

"Well, he was a . . . uh . . . a Marine. Served in Afghanistan."

"Know where he lives?"

"Of course. Same house he and Becky lived in before she left."

"Where does he work?"

"I don't know. He's a roustabout in the oilfield. Different company all the time."

"Would your sister know?"

"Not sure. I'll call her and ask."

"Do it. I want to talk with this guy. If he's our guy that would be some small-world shit there, huh?" Punch said. "I'm gonna stay here and look around."

While Punch and Jensen were searching Emily's office, Officer Greg Goodrich, one of Custer's newest patrol officers, took a call from dispatch.

"This is Unit 32."

"See the lady at 101 Bighorn Street. Name is Roberta Saathoff. Report of a purse-snatching."

"Roger, en route. 32 out."

Goodrich arrived at the address two minutes later. Approaching the mobile home, he surreptitiously unsnapped his holster as he rang the doorbell.

"Police. Dispatch asked me to check out a report of a theft. Are you Ms. Saathoff?"

"Yes, Officer. I was in the yard—just coming back from the casino where I won $77 on the video machine –when this gal jumped outta the bushes over there, grabbed my purse, and ran that way," she said, indicating the direction of travel.

"Ever seen her before?"

"I don't see so good." She lit a cigarette.

"Can you describe her?"

"Well, she was a young'un. Maybe twenty-five years old. Washed-out lookin', you know?"

"How tall?"

"Dunno. Maybe five-foot-four," she said, squinting through a plume of smoke.

"How much did she weigh, do you think?"

"A lot."

"Like—?"

"Oh, jeez, I dunno. She was a big ol' gal."

"But she ran off?"

"Well, kinda. I guess it was more of a waddle. A fast waddle."

"Hair?"

"Purple."

"Her hair was purple?"

"Last I seen, yup."

"What was she wearing?"

"She had a Harley-Davidson halter top and camouflage cutoffs. Flip-flops."

"You're certain?"

"'Course I'm certain."

"Okay, Mrs. Saathoff—"

"It's *Ms.*"

"Okay, Ms. Saathoff. Let me make a call to dispatch and we'll start looking around." Goodrich dutifully reported the description, and thinking it unlikely anything would come of it, returned to talk with the victim.

"Well, Ms. Saathoff, I've called it in—"

"There she is!"

"What? Where?"

"There! At the end of the block!"

Goodrich turned and saw a heavyset woman walking down the street approximately three houses away. He began to walk toward the woman, who—seeing him—turned and walked away.

"Stop! Police!" Goodrich yelled, and gave chase. Hearing him, the woman increased her waddling to a near-run and made her way around a corner.

Goodrich called in his location and activity as he ran, surprised at the obese woman's speed. As he rounded the corner, he saw her throw something into the bushes in front of a small, white, craftsman-style home. Deciding to continue the pursuit, he made a mental note of the location of the evidence and continued after the suspect. After rounding another corner, he determined that he'd lost her and called in his location, the situation, and requested a dog.

Returning to the bushes, Goodrich found and bagged what turned out to be a discarded wallet. Moments later, he showed Ms. Saathoff the bag and its contents.

"Ms. Saathoff, I'm not sure where your purse is, but I believe I've got your wallet."

Ms. Saathoff looked at the wallet, then at Goodrich. "That ain't mine," she said, drawing on her cigarette.

"What?"

"That ain't my wallet, Officer."

"Well, I saw her throw it in the bushes while I was chasing her."

"Don't know what you saw, but that ain't my wallet."

Opening the wallet, he found a driver's license and other identification belonging to one Chastity Clausen. He thanked Ms. Saathoff and told her he'd be right back. Jumping in his vehicle, Goodrich quickly drove the three blocks to the address on the driver's license.

He called for backup and, after help arrived, approached the door of a dilapidated ranch-style home, gun at his side. Knocking on the door, he yelled, "Police! Open up!"

Seeing no response, he pounded again, whereupon the door was opened by a heavyset, purple-haired woman wearing a Harley-Davidson halter top and camouflage-patterned cutoffs.

"Can I help you?"

"Are you Chastity Clausen?"

"Yes, what is this about?" she asked, dabbing accumulated sweat from her forehead.

"I was chasing you—why didn't you stop?"

"I guess I don't know what you are talking about, Officer. I been here all day—"

"Let me see some identification."

"I'll have to get my purse."

"Please do. Don't try to run, and don't make any sudden movements or do anything weird. My partner is out the back door, and he's kind of skittish."

Clausen returned to the door with her purse and began searching, presumably for her wallet. It soon became clear that it wasn't in her purse.

"I don't understand," she said. "I been here all day, and it was right here."

"No," Goodrich said. "You stole Ms. Saathoff's wallet, ran, and when I was chasing you, threw it into the bushes. Or so you thought."

"Whaddaya mean, 'or so I thought?' I don't know what you're talking about."

"Ms. Clausen," Goodrich said, showing her the wallet in his possession and allowing her to see it through the protective baggie. "I know it was you

I was chasing. I saw you throw a wallet into the bushes. I retrieved that wallet. This is it. Look at it."

Clausen looked at the wallet. "That's my wallet!"

"Yup. And I'll bet that's Ms. Saathoff's wallet right there on the coffee table." He nodded in the general direction of her living room.

"You mean—?"

"Yeah. You threw away the wrong wallet when you were running away from me."

"Aww, shit!"

"Would you please turn around? I need to cuff you and read you your rights."

18

Punch walked around Emily Smith's office with his hands clasped behind his back, looking at everything in turn. Pictures and mementos of a life cut short: shots from the beach with what appeared to be friends, a selfie taken atop the Eiffel Tower, and a group shot from a bar somewhere, featuring the decedent as well as several local attorneys and one obviously drunk Judge Howard. "So, Mrs. Johnson, did Ms. Smith have any enemies?"

"She's a divorce lawyer, for crying out loud," Dot said. "Of course she made enemies!"

Punch's face reddened slightly, but he bit his tongue, wishing Jensen were still here so he could let him deal with this. "Got any names, or should I just insert 'human race' into my report?"

"Well, there've been a few of these guys who didn't get the deal they thought they should have who blamed Emily. It's not like they are going to take responsibility for anything they've done."

"Do you have any names?"

"Well, not that I can think of right off the top of my head. . . She's also done a couple of child support cases lately—those are always ugly."

"How has she been acting lately?"

"What do you mean?"

"Well, has she been nervous, concerned, or afraid? Has she mentioned anyone following her, threatening her, or anything like that?"

"No. I'd have told you if she had."

"Was she seeing anybody?"

"I don't rightly know, Detective. Is there anything wrong if she was?"

"Mrs. Johnson, I'm just trying to figure out who might've had a reason to harm her."

"You ask me, it was some nutcase what just moved here from out of state. We seem to be getting the worst of that lot out here."

"Well, that's possible." Then it hit him. For whatever reason, it hadn't occurred to him that he hadn't seen a cell phone anywhere. "Did she have a cell phone?"

"You bet. She had one of those fancy ones," Dot said.

"Thanks. I need to make a call. I'm gonna step outside." Once outside, Punch called Jensen.

"Jensen here."

"Where are you?" Punch asked.

"I'm doing backup for Goodrich. He's arresting this great big gal for theft. She's being a bitch."

"I was just thinking—I never saw a cell phone. Is there one on the inventory?"

"I don't know. I'll have to check."

"Well, did you see one?" Punch asked.

"Not that I recall."

"What about Baker? He say anything about a phone?"

"I'll ask him, but I don't think he'll remember anything but all the blood."

"Try him," Punch instructed. "And Jensen?"

"Yeah?"

"Didn't we already have one of the county attorneys draw a warrant for all of her phone records?"

"Yeah, but I ain't seen it. Why?"

"Because I want to see who all she was talking to before she died."

"What kind of time frame you got in mind?"

"I don't know. Let's start with a month prior to her getting killed and see what turns up. We can always go back for another bite at the apple later."

"I hear the cops are all over town trying to solve that murder," O'Hanlon said to Howard. Howard had been buying the drinks for an hour now, and O'Hanlon was interested in getting the inside scoop on Custer's biggest story in years.

"Yeah?" Howard asked.

"What I hear," O'Hanlon said. "Hey, you signing any warrants? Is what they're saying true?"

"Who?"

"What?"

"Who's 'they?'"

"Well, you know, Judge, just 'they.' People. People are talking."

"You know I can't talk about a pending matter," Howard said. "By the way, I saw this twenty-two-year-old gal last week on a meth possession rap —her second time being charged. So I took her not guilty plea and set her up with an attorney."

"Yeah. She employed?"

"Of course not. I think she is exchanging sex for a spot on a couch and meth. She drags her kids around with her from guy to guy."

"Tragic."

"Right. She's a mess. Without exception, every area of her life is a mess. So, in court I listened to her cry and spill her guts, and as always, I fought back two emotions: anger, over what she's done to her life through her poor decision-making, and sadness, because no matter what she does, I can't get it out of my head that she was and is somebody's little girl."

"So, what did you do?"

"I had to let her out of jail, so I did."

"And?"

"And she was back in front of me this morning."

"No shit." O'Hanlon shook his head. "What happened?"

"Well, she apparently took a couple of hits off a meth pipe en route to her appointment at Department of Family Services."

"Nice."

"Addiction is a bitch," Howard said, taking a swig from his beer. "So, anyway, seems the folks at the Department of Family Services got concerned about her behavior, so they gave her a urinalysis. Then they asked her how she got there, and she said, 'My boyfriend gave me a ride.' So they looked out the window and watched the guy she'd said was giving her a ride apply a tourniquet and then inject meth into his arm—right there in the parking lot."

"Holy shit!"

"Yeah. We're fighting an uphill battle."

"Doc, anything new?" Punch was in the medical examiner's office, looking at the diplomas on the wall.

"Yes, a couple of things," Dr. Laws said, looking at his report.

"Yeah?"

"Yeah. First, she had sex shortly before she died."

"Was she raped?"

"No signs of that."

"So, maybe a boyfriend. What else?"

"Well, we got enough of a specimen to get a DNA analysis done."

"Good stuff, assuming he's ever been asked to give a sample. Maybe we'll get lucky. Anything else?"

"I found a very small shard of metal in her throat where she'd been cut."

"Part of the murder weapon?"

"I can't be sure until I see the rest of the weapon—and I'm not a weapons expert, you understand—but I would think so."

"This is good stuff, Doc." Punch nodded. "I'll tell the sheriff we're working on it."

"Detective, there is something else."

"What?"

"The blade that was used on her. It was enormous."

"Like a hunting knife?"

"Bigger."

"Bigger?" Punch looked at the doctor thoughtfully. "How about a bayonet?"

"Why would you think that?"

"Just a hunch."

"Well, I'd have to see the weapon, but that might well do it."

"Okay. How long before you get the DNA results back?"

"Well, since we're not matching them with a known sample, it'll probably be a couple of weeks. And you understand that if this individual is not in the Combined DNA Index System, we might not get anything useful back?" It wasn't really a question.

"Got it, Doc. Any way you can hurry them up? I'd kinda like to know one way or the other."

"No."

"Thanks, Doc. Do what you can. We need to get this guy." He reached for his phone. "Sorry, gotta take this . . . Polson."

"Punch, this is Cale. I got good news."

"Hit me."

"We identified six distinctive sets of prints in the house. The victim's, of course. Her mom. Her housekeeper."

"She had a housekeeper?"

"Apparently, and some from one Thomas Olsen. That set was registered years back by the military."

"Bingo! We've been looking at him, anyway. He was one of her clients." Punch felt his heart begin to pound. "Where were his prints?"

"Everywhere."

"Gimme a little more, Cale."

"All over the house. On the bottle, on the shot glasses. At the sink. All over her bedroom," Cale said, obviously reading from a list.

"Great. Look, let me get going, and thanks a lot."

"No problem. Just let me know if you come across someone else you want to try and match to these other two sets."

"Will do."

19

"Seriously, could you defend someone you knew was guilty?" Veronica asked Sam as they sat in a restaurant, waiting on their drinks. No one had been arrested yet, and the murder was still a topic of conversation.

"How would I know they were guilty?" Sam asked.

"Well, the evidence."

"I guess I'm kind of surprised to hear you say that—how long have you worked for Judge Howard?"

"About a year."

"So you know that no one is guilty until a jury says they are. Until then, they are presumed innocent."

"Well, I know that's what the law says, but the reality is a lot of the time everyone knows they are guilty. It's just a matter of going through the motions, isn't it?" Veronica took a long pull from a margarita. Sam liked the way her mouth pursed around the straw. He was sipping scotch tonight.

"What everyone *knows* is maybe there is evidence tending to indicate guilt, but a person is not guilty until he or she is adjudicated as such by a judge either following a plea of guilty or after a finding by a judge or jury. Until then, the person is not guilty."

"You are such an idealist! Who knew? But really, a lot of times people know—"

"People don't really know. Even if a person admits to, say, shooting someone, it does not mean they are guilty under the law. The law recognizes any number of defenses and allows the presentation of mitigating or extenuating circumstances which can result in someone being found not guilty of murder, for example, even where they have admitted killing the person."

"Well, thank you, Professor Johnstone," Veronica teased. "So, seriously, you'd take the case?"

"Oh, I doubt it. There would have to be a reason for me to get involved. But the thing is, for our system of justice to work properly, the question is not, 'How do I defend this guilty man?'"

"What is the question, then?"

"The question is, 'What is this man entitled to under the law?'"

"I understand, but I find it repulsive to even think about defending a murderer or child molester or someone like that," Veronica said.

"I'll grant you, there is a high 'ick' factor in a lot of cases," Sam allowed. "And I think most people agree with you, because most people look at what lawyers do, and unless they or a family member have a problem, they want to denigrate the entire profession and the people in it. But that comes from a misunderstanding of what the profession is about."

"What do you mean?"

"Well, as an attorney I'm neither a judge nor a member of the jury. My job is not to decide or even to be seriously concerned with whether the defendant is guilty. My job is only to advocate on behalf of my client and insist that she is afforded all of the rights she is entitled to under the law." Sam signaled the waitress for another scotch. "What that means is that I have to ensure that she is not punished until and unless the State demonstrates beyond a reasonable doubt that she committed the crime as charged. When I sign on to defend someone, I have to understand that gal is placing her property, liberty, or—in a case like this—even life in my care. For an attorney, 'the truth' is what the law and the evidence show."

"That's a little idealistic, isn't it?"

"Absolutely," Sam agreed. "But our system doesn't demand 'absolute truth'—we don't speak of 'God's truth' or 'scientific certainty' or anything along those lines. The system demands only that a defendant's guilt be determined beyond a reasonable doubt by a jury of his peers."

"Good enough for government work?"

Sam smiled. "How about, 'close enough to the truth to allow the public to continue to allow our somewhat disorderly system of justice to operate?' It is the lawyer's job to ensure that the system works as well as possible."

"Of course, but I guess I still don't know how you can stomach it," Veronica said.

"It's not always easy. Some defendants are incredibly difficult people," Sam allowed. "The clear majority have substance abuse issues; along with that come the usual co-occurring disorders. Most have a visceral dislike of authority and anyone they perceive as being part of a system they believe is arrayed against them. But even if defendants are a total pain in the ass—and a lot of them are—and even if I think a client is technically guilty of the crime charged, I have to set aside my personal ethics and prejudices and replace them with what I like to call 'the lawyer's conscience.'"

"I didn't know lawyers had a conscience," she teased.

"And until I became a lawyer, I didn't, either," Sam said. "But understand a 'lawyer's conscience' is not everyone's conscience. A lawyer's conscience is a unique way of viewing a legal situation. In forcing the State to play by the rules and prove a defendant's guilt, we not only serve the client we've got but the innocent ones to follow, and hopefully we continue to distinguish our society from those that eschew an open, transparent system of justice."

"All that said, would you—could you—represent whoever eventually gets arrested for this?"

Sam sat back in his chair and twirled the ice in his glass. "I doubt it."

"After all that? Why not?"

"I'm probably not the right guy. I'm newer to town, so I don't know all of the players who would be important in a case like this," Sam said. "Assuming I was on my own, I'd have limited resources. Murder trials are incredibly expensive and time-consuming. So, that's the *could* side."

"You'd get a high fee, right?"

"Potentially. But despite what you see on television, most people accused of murder are not particularly well-off. Most defendants are appointed public defenders. Those who aren't are generally represented by firms that are well-off—you've got to have the resources to be able to independently investigate and test evidence. It's the rare firm that can do so," Sam said. "The other issue is time. Big trials are huge time-sucks, so once you take the case on and get paid your fee—if you get paid—that's it. You're stuck with the deal you struck. In the meanwhile, new clients and new problems arise. It's a huge commitment, and I don't know that I'm professionally or personally ready to commit myself to something like that."

"I'm glad to hear that," she said. "Personally *and* professionally, I mean."

"But as far as the *would* side goes, well, I'm not saying I wouldn't at least give it a look," Sam said. "I've always kind of wanted to try a murder case."

"Bucket list?"

"Personal challenge."

20

Punch had been on the phone all morning and hadn't put it down when it rang again. "Polson."

"Punch, this is Jensen."

"Tell me something good," Punch said.

"Roger. State lab just called. They've got an ID on the DNA they got from the victim—the stuff that wasn't hers, I mean."

Punch's heart skipped a beat. Just as predicted, it had been weeks. "Whose is it?"

"I don't know, they said they can only tell you."

"For Christ's sake." Punch hung up and dialed furiously. "This is Detective Punch Polson from the Custer Police Department. I need to talk with whoever is doing the DNA for the Emily Smith murder here in town." Predictably, he was switched several times until he was finally connected with someone who knew something.

"I'm told you have a match for that DNA sample we asked for?" Punch asked.

"We do," the technician said. "Your man's name is Thomas Olsen."

"You sure?"

"I can say with a reasonable degree of scientific certainty that the DNA in our possession would match fewer than one man in a billion. So, in language even a cop would understand: 'Fuckin' A.'"

Punch laughed. "All right, I deserved that. Thanks a lot." Then he had a thought. "Does that DNA from Olsen match all of the DNA on the scene?"

"No."

"No?" Punch said, taken aback. "Let me ask that question this way: you got a match for Tommy Olsen, right?"

"Right."

"And you've obviously matched the decedent's, right?"

"Right."

"So, are you saying there's another set of DNA on scene that you haven't matched?"

"I am."

"Where?"

"There was some semen on her sheets that doesn't match Tommy Olsen."

"Christ. So, that means what?" Punch asked. "That she had sex with two guys before she died?"

"It appears that way."

"Let's assume that. At the same time?"

"That's not something we'd be able to tell you," the technician said. "But assuming she did laundry on occasion, I'd guess within a tight time-line. Sorry, we can't do better than that."

"Any idea who the other guy was?"

"No."

"Can you get me a match?"

"Doubt it. If he was in the system, we would have matched this one. So, not unless you bring me a second, known sample you want to see matched to the first."

"Can you check?"

"It would take a miracle without a suspect's DNA to compare to. It would be expensive as hell, and I'd need a directive or order or something with your name on it. It costs money to run a blind check, and my boss won't authorize it without something in writing from you or your boss."

"Well, hold off for now," Punch said. He hung up and sat at his desk for several minutes, thinking through the various possibilities and the meaning of what he'd been told. It was a complication, but the evidence against Olsen was good. He dialed Jensen.

"Jensen."

"Find Olsen."

"You want me to arrest him?"

"Not yet. But I'm going to try to get a warrant, so just watch him until I get one and then we'll bang him."

"You think he did it?"

"Yeah. I'm pretty sure he did. But I'd feel better if the dude would confess. Me and him are gonna have us a little 'Come to Jesus' here soon."

Punch had been kept waiting for ten minutes before he got in to see County Attorney Rebecca Nice, and was irritable as a result. She was oblivious to his anger, however. "So, what do you have?" she asked.

"I've got Olsen's prints all over the murder scene, his DNA in her, and an eyewitness who can place him or at least a guy who looked like him at the scene the night she was killed," Punch replied tersely.

"Is that it?"

"She had her throat cut by a big-ass knife. Olsen was a Marine."

"What does that tell you?"

"Knives are particular weapons, for particular people."

"You got the weapon?"

"Not yet. That's why I want a warrant."

"Motive?"

"I haven't spoken with him yet. I'll need to talk with him to fully develop a motive, of course."

"Did she know him?"

"Yeah. He was her client. She was doing his divorce."

"Why would he kill his own divorce attorney?"

"I don't know. Maybe her fee was excessive?"

"Hilarious. Okay, let's take it from the top, but let me tell you something: you damned sure better have the right guy."

"Thanks for the vote of confidence."

"Get me your affidavit, and I'll draft the warrant. In the meanwhile, this needs to be our little secret."

"Okay."

Tommy was hungover. The light hurt his eyes, his tongue tasted like a scout troop had spent the night on it, and the pounding in his head sounded like someone banging on the wall. The pounding continued as he came out of his fog, until he finally realized someone was at the door and opened it.

"Thomas Olsen?"

It was a cop. Or at least he looked like a cop. "Yes?" Tommy said.

"My name is Ken Polson. I'm a detective with the Custer Police Department. I'd like you to come downtown and talk with me."

"This is about Emily, right?"

"Right."

"Are you thinking I did it? Because I didn't. She was kinda my girlfriend."

"I just want to ask you some questions," Punch said. "Also, Mr. Olsen, I've got a search warrant here."

"For what?"

"For a knife."

"Why? You think I killed her, don't you?"

"Tell me you didn't."

"I didn't."

"Then you won't have a problem with my men looking around, will you?"

"Not really."

"Not really?"

"Well, what if you were to find something else?"

"Like what?"

"Something, uh, illegal."

"How illegal?" Punch asked.

"Like maybe a little weed."

"I'm not here for weed, Mr. Olsen. I'm here for murder."

"I already told you—"

"Yeah, well, you'll excuse me if I don't take your word for it," Punch replied. "I'm gonna leave some guys here to execute this warrant. How about you come with me in the meantime?"

"What if I don't want to come?" Tommy asked.

"Well, that'd cause me some difficulty. I'd either have to arrest you here and now or apply for a warrant from the judge. Either way, it would be a lot easier for both of us if you'd just accompany me down to the station."

"But I don't know nothin'."

"Sometimes people know more than they think they do. You want this guy caught, right? I mean, she was your girlfriend."

Tommy stood quietly, thinking. "Right."

"Well, if you didn't do it, then I'd hope you'd tell me everything you know, so I can figure out who did do it."

"I don't like this," Tommy said. "But if it will help figure out who killed Emily, then I'll do it."

Half an hour later, Punch and Tommy were in the interview room, getting ready to begin, when Punch's phone rang. "Just a minute," Punch said. "I need to take this." He stepped out of the interview room and said, "Polson."

Jensen was excited. "Boss, we found it!"

"What'd you find?" Punch asked.

"One of those big army knives that attaches to a gun."

"A bayonet?" That would do the trick.

"Yeah!"

"Excellent," Punch said. He'd moved to a position behind a two-way mirror, and was watching Tommy cool his heels, awaiting more questions. It was an old trick, but like most old tricks, it was an effective one. "Tell me more."

"It gets better: it's got what looks like a little chink in it, and blood and hair on it."

"No shit," Punch said. "Please tell me you handled it properly."

"I did, boss. I didn't want to blow this one."

"Good. Get it to the lab boys as soon as possible."

"We're already on our way to Cale's office."

"Mr. Olsen," Punch said as he opened the door to the small room. "We've had a development."

21

"So, tell me about this guy," Sam asked Veronica as they had dinner in one of the town's locally-owned restaurants. She'd told him that the police had a suspect, someone she knew.

"Well, I actually went to high school with him," she said.

"And?"

"Nice enough. Didn't know him well. Shop guy, you know? Partied, drank a lot, raced cars he built, that kind of thing."

"Didn't hang out with the cool kids like you, eh?" Sam smiled, cutting a piece off his steak.

"Why no, he did not." She returned the smile. "Why are you interested? As I recall, you recently told me you probably weren't 'the right guy.' Has something changed?"

"My sources tell me he is a veteran. That could change the calculus."

"A veteran who maybe killed a lawyer."

"He hasn't been arrested. And even if he ever is, the correct phraseology will be that he *allegedly* killed a lawyer—remember?" She smiled, so he continued. "And I've already told you I'm not going to represent the guy. I'd just like to talk with him, kind of on the down-low. My motto regarding vets is, 'Give all you can, and then give some more.'"

"He was fun, you know?" she said. "I remember him going off to the

Marines and everything. Then I remember hearing he got hurt. Then he got back to town and, well, you know. . ."

"No, I don't. I'm not a local, remember?"

"Well, he got back from the war and it's just been one thing after another. Drinking, drugs, fighting—they say he's just different. Poor Becky. It's that way with a lot of these guys. We've been sending men and women over there for almost a generation."

"I know."

"I'm sorry." The silence grew uncomfortable. Sam was trying to figure out how to get access to the accused.

"Janitors are invisible," he mused.

"What's that?" Veronica asked.

"Nothing," Sam said. He wiped his mouth. "Just talking to myself. Interested in dessert?"

22

"Jensen, where the hell are you?" Punch asked. He'd finished his initial questioning of Olsen, and had him on ice.

"I'm a coupla blocks off Main Street," Jensen responded. "I'm waiting on a search warrant."

"What happened?"

"Well, near as I can tell, the landlord and tenant got into a dispute over the tenant not paying his rent or utilities."

"Sounds normal."

"Yeah, but here's where it goes off the tracks: the landlord got tired of this guy not paying his utilities, so he cut the power to his apartment."

"Okay," Punch said. Local landlords called the technique "self-help."

"So, the tenant, he snakes a power cable through his bedroom window, fires up his 2kw camping generator, and—voilà!—he's got power."

Punch couldn't help but smile. "So?"

"Well, that was fine as far as it went, but because the apartment was in a four-plex, it wasn't very long before the neighbors got tired of hearing the generator running."

"I can see that," Punch said.

"Yeah, so they tried to get the tenant to cease and desist, but he told them to get screwed."

"Nice."

"Yup. So, apparently, our guy was in his house smoking a little of the evil green weed, which I'm not sure really bothers the neighbors, but given his un-neighborly ways, they called us. We got here and the guy wouldn't let us in."

"So, what'd you do?"

"Well, we started talking with the guy's mom, who answered the door. She took a swing at me, so we arrested her."

"Good."

"Then the guy's brother and girlfriend drove up, so I went to speak with them, and they were drunk, so I busted her for DUI and him for possession, because he had a warrant out for his arrest. When I did the search incident to arrest, he had a little baggie of weed with him."

"Okay."

"Yeah, except that when I was taking the brother into custody, he got to scuffling with me, and the dog he had on a leash bit me!"

"For Christ's sake!"

"Yeah. So, we've arrested the guy's mom, brother, wife, and dog."

"It's like a George Jones song!"

"I know, right? I think I'm okay, but the dog ruined my boot. Got teeth marks in it."

"Okay, well, hang tight and await that warrant. I'll take care of things at this end."

"Wilco, boss. We spoke with the landlord, turned off the tenant's unapproved power source, and are just waiting to search the house and arrest the dude."

"Okay. Keep me posted and be safe!"

"Roger."

"Paul, what's the matter?" Jeannie asked. "You've been short with the boys and short with me. I feel like you're never home, and even when you are, you sit and look at your damned phone and ignore us."

"I'm sorry. I'm just a little concerned."

"Talk to me, Paul. What is it?"

"Well, with the oil and gas industry tanking, business is down. I've got secretaries looking at taking jobs with the state and county, because God knows they don't have to worry about their overhead. Sonsabitches pay outrageous salaries and don't give a thought what it does to guys like me. I just . . . I just don't know how much longer I can continue to do this."

"Paul, we've been through this before. We'll make it through this. We always have."

"Well, maybe," Paul allowed. "But when is it going to get easy? I see people every day who have so much more than we do, who have worked so much less. It isn't fair, damn it!"

"Well, of course not. But just like you tell the boys, 'Life isn't fair.' Right?"

"I know, but goddammit, I'm getting tired of busting my ass just to put a roof over our head. At some point, don't I have a right to enjoy my life?"

"I thought you did. Enjoy your life, I mean." She picked up a magazine and thumbed through it.

"You know what I mean, Jeannie. I'm just saying that it'd be awful nice to be able to run my office without having to worry about making ends meet. And now, on top of everything, word is Sam is sniffing around, thinking about taking on that murder case."

"Oh, I'm sure he wouldn't," Jeannie said. "He's got to know that would damage your practice."

"I'm not so sure he gives a shit," Norquist said.

"Oh, Paul, I'm sure he does. After all you've done for him . . ."

"He's not like he was twenty years ago. He's a different man nowadays. In fact, I'm not sure what he cares about."

23

Tommy slumped in a tiny plastic chair, which, along with an identical chair and a gray metal desk, were the only pieces of furniture in the room. The walls were masonry, with a gray metal door at one end and a one-way window along the side. He looked around and shifted uncomfortably in the chair, awaiting Punch's return. On the other side of the glass, Punch watched Tommy while he spoke on the phone with Jensen, who had called and demanded to speak with him.

"Polson."

"Boss, we got more!" said Jensen.

"More than the bayonet? What?"

"This guy visited the emergency room on the Sunday morning after our victim got it."

"What was wrong with him?" Punch asked, feeling his stomach tighten.

"Had a cut on his finger. Told the doctors that he had cut himself slicing limes," said Jensen. "Docs say it took seven stitches to close a cut on his finger."

"Good job, Jensen. I'm about to talk to our boy right now. Let's see what he has to say."

Tommy looked up from the chair when Punch entered the room. Punch walked over to the little plastic chair, and as he sat down, he extracted a small voice-activated tape recorder from his pocket.

"Am I under arrest?" Tommy asked.

"Not yet. You're still free to leave at any time," Punch responded. "I just want to ask you a few more questions. You still okay with me recording what we say here?"

"No problem," Tommy said.

"Okay, we're back on the record. Today is November 27. It is 1235 hours, and my name is Kenneth Polson. I am a detective sergeant with the Custer Police Department. I am in room number five with Thomas Olsen, whom I am questioning about the circumstances surrounding the death of Emily Smith. Mr. Olsen has agreed to answer questions and understands that he is not under arrest and is free to leave at any time." Looking at Tommy, Punch asked, "Mr. Olsen, did I accurately state all that?"

"Yeah."

"So I'd like to ask you a few more questions, if you are okay with that."

"Sure. Like I said, anything I gotta do to get out of here."

"Okay, so, you knew her professionally?"

"Yeah. I already told you that."

"Did you know her personally?"

"No."

"Ever been in her house?"

"No."

Tommy was not a good liar. "You sure?"

"Well, maybe once or twice."

"Ever sleep with her?"

"No."

"Mr. Olsen, I'm going to advise you to be honest with me. Are you sure that you've never slept with her?"

"Yes."

"Well, maybe you can explain why your DNA is in her."

"Say what?"

"We found semen in her. Ran a check and it's yours."

"You're full of shit."

"No, I'm not. Remember when you were at Parris Island and they ran that cotton swab around the inside of your mouth? Well, they were collecting your DNA in case they ever needed to identify a piece of you on a battlefield somewhere. But it turns out it's also handy to match your DNA to crime scenes. So, let me ask you again, did you ever sleep with her?"

Tommy looked at his shoes for a long time. "Yes," he said at last.

"Why did you lie to me?"

"Well, I didn't want you to think bad about her. I didn't want you to think she was a whore or something."

"So, in your mind women who sleep with guys are whores?"

"Not in my mind, but I didn't know what you thought."

"So, how many times have you been over to her place?"

"Just the once."

"And when was that?"

"Well, it was Halloween night, I guess. That's why you're asking me these questions, right?"

"Well, that and your prints and your semen and the fact that you were seen there. So, the two of you had a thing going?"

Tommy was still for a moment, thinking. Punch watched him closely. Tommy sat back in the chair, then shifted position, leaned forward, and put his elbows on the table between them. "Yeah, I was doin' her. Does that make me a suspect?"

"I'll ask the questions, if you don't mind. You just need to answer them. When's the last time you had sex with her?"

"I suppose it was Saturday night. You want to know how we did it?"

"Not particularly—unless you're gonna tell me that she liked it rough and with knives."

"What are you talking about? I ain't no pervert, if that's what you're sayin'!" Tommy insisted. "You think I did it?"

Punch stared at Tommy for a long while to make him uncomfortable. It was a standard ploy. "How well did you and Emily get along?"

"We got along great."

"Then how come she's dead?"

"I have no idea. Look, we had a few drinks, we did our thing, and I left. The last time I saw her she was asleep with a smile on her face. And that's the truth."

"About an hour ago, we found a bayonet in your garage."

"Of course you did. I brought mine back from the sandbox. A lot of guys did."

"Yeah, but the blade on yours has a chink in it and is covered with blood."

"What?" Punch watched as the color literally drained from Tommy's face.

"There's blood on the blade," Punch said, thinking Tommy looked genuinely surprised. "But then, you know that."

"I don't know what the hell you're talking about!"

"You know if that blood matches hers, well. . ." Punch looked at Olsen, who was now pale. He decided to change tactics. "Where'd you get that cut on your finger?"

"Me and Emily were making some drinks and I was cutting some limes and cut myself."

"Let me see that." Punch held out his hand.

"Sure." Tommy extended his, palm up.

"Looks like a professional job," said Punch. "Where'd you get that done?"

"At the emergency room," said Olsen. "You can check."

"Already did. Just wanted to see if you'd tell me the truth. What time did you go to the emergency room?"

"If you already checked, then you already know the answer to that question. Am I a suspect?"

"Everyone is a suspect until I rule them out. But in all fairness, Tommy, you're the only guy whose semen is in her, fingerprints are all over the house, and whose bayonet is covered with what I think we'll find is her blood. And I'm asking you what time you went to the ER."

"I don't know, maybe 5:30 in the morning? I couldn't get the thing to stop bleeding and I was going to the field that day, so I thought I'd walk into the ER before I went to work."

"When did you cut yourself?"

"Are you listening? Because I already told you that I cut myself when I was cutting limes the night before."

"You took seven stitches—is that right?"

"That's what the doc said, yeah."

"You cut yourself sometime during the evening, and then waited until 5:30 the next morning to get the stitches put in?"

"Yeah."

"I don't believe you. That had to be a serious cut."

"You ever seen that gal? Because if you did, I can tell you that if she was willing there's no way that you would leave before you tapped that. Ain't no way I was gonna leave unless I was bleeding to death. I put a Band-Aid and a piece of hundred-mile-an-hour tape from a roll she had in her garage on it real tight to stop the bleeding. No way was I walking away."

"Did she agree to have sex with you?"

"Absolutely. It was her idea. She had her own mind; she knew what she wanted."

"Did you two have an argument?"

"Absolutely not. Everything was good with us."

"Ever sleep with her before that Saturday night?"

Tommy looked at the floor for some minutes before answering. "I don't want to answer that question."

"Why not?"

"Because I'm getting divorced. Answering that question might get me in trouble."

"Tommy, we are investigating a murder. It's possible that if you were arrested for this crime and convicted, the State of Wyoming could seek the death penalty. I guess I'm not sure what could be more troublesome than that."

"Yeah, well. I didn't kill Emily. But I did screw her, and if my old lady finds out she'll probably hose me in my divorce."

"Let me ask you a couple more questions. Then we can get you out of here." Punch softened his tone. "I know you've got things to do."

"I don't think this is a good idea."

"What's that?"

"Talking with you. I think that I'm gonna need a lawyer before I answer any more questions."

"Tommy, you've already told me that you were in her house, that you had sex with her, and that you are probably the last person to see her alive.

I have your blood on the scene, your fingerprints in her house, your DNA in her and on her, and what I think is her blood on the murder weapon, found in your garage. What else can you tell me that I don't already know?"

"I want a lawyer."

"Look, because you are technically not under arrest, you really don't have a right to a lawyer. Just answer a few more—"

"If I ain't under arrest, then I can leave, right?"

"Does that mean that you do not want to answer any more questions at this time?"

"Yeah, that's what that means. I want a lawyer." Tommy stood. "I'm getting the fuck out of here."

"Fine. It is 1255 hours, and at the request of Mr. Olsen I am terminating this interview." Punch picked up his tape recorder and turned it off, then put it in the pocket of his suit jacket and stood up. He looked at Tommy. "This would go a lot easier if you would cooperate."

"I've said enough. I told you I didn't do it. I'm not saying anything else until I get a lawyer."

"Okay, give me a minute. Gotta out-process you. You know how the government is." Punch turned and exited, closing the door behind him.

Tommy was alone in the room. He looked around, sighed heavily, and put his head in his hands. "What in the hell have I gotten myself into?"

Punch had walked directly into the adjoining room and was looking through the one-way mirror. "A helluva mess, is what he's gotten himself into," he said to Jensen, who was back at the jail.

"You gonna hold him?"

"No, let him go. I'm gonna talk with Ann. I've got enough for an arrest warrant, I think. But just to be sure, I'll run it by her. Don't want to screw this up. Meantime, you keep an eye on him."

———————

Time had dragged on and on while Ann waited for Rebecca to decide. It seemed simple enough: Rebecca wouldn't touch it—a case like this would draw far too much press attention. Lose this case and the voters would show you the door. This one would be delegated.

Mike wanted no part of it; his health was bad, and even if it wasn't, this case was way out of his league at this point in his career. She'd watched him over the years; he was fine driving deals and maybe prosecuting the occasional possession with intent to distribute, but a death penalty case would be more than he could handle. Besides, his appearance was terrible—Rebecca wouldn't want an obese, obviously unhealthy man serving as the "face" of her office for the weeks the trial would take. The real question was how to get Cathy out of the picture, and soon. With her gone, Ann would be next in line, leaving Rebecca with a stark choice: go out of town for "assistance," and thereby tacitly admit the office wasn't up to the job, or appoint her to try the case. She needed to move quickly; the rumor on the street was that Polson was close to making an arrest.

She thought it over for a moment, then made her decision, picked up the phone, and dialed. "I've got some information for you. When can we meet?"

Punch was in Rebecca Nice's office. "Rebecca, we need to talk," he said.

"What's up?" asked the prosecutor. "Anything new?"

"Spent an hour or so with Olsen."

"And?"

"He's our guy, but he's denying everything."

"Get anything at all?"

"He now admits it's his blood in the sink downstairs, and he has a cut on his hand. Says he got it that night, and the hospital records back that up."

"That isn't much."

"It's one more thing someone is going to have to explain. Would you want to explain what your blood was doing in a murdered woman's house?"

"No."

"He admits being in her house, and he admits having sex with her."

"That's good. Only a couple of dozen guys could say that."

"Wow."

"Sorry. Never did care for her."

"Most women didn't."

"What are you saying?"

"I'm saying most women I've spoken with didn't like her. Look, I think the evidence is there. I let him go, but I'm not gonna lie—I'm worried he'll run. Let's do this. A guy like that might be hard to find if he doesn't want to be found."

"What else?"

"Well, the prints, the DNA, and we've got what I think is the murder weapon. A bayonet. Found in his house with blood on it."

"Is it hers?"

"I don't know yet, but Jesus Christ, Rebecca—who else's could it be? Can I grab him?"

"Not yet. Put a tail on him for now. Ann's putting together an affidavit of probable cause for you to sign, and then we'll see if we can get Howard or Daniels to sign an arrest warrant."

Tommy had an old duffel bag and was stuffing it with everything he could think of as he walked through his house. He dialed the phone. Elk answered on the second ring.

"Yo."

"Elk, I need your help."

"Tommy boy, what's up? Haven't heard from you for a few days. Let's get a coupla cool ones."

"Sounds good. Maybe one of these days. Right now, I need something."

"Sure, bro. Whatcha need?"

"I need a bus ticket."

"A bus ticket? Ain't no one take the bus, man."

"Just get me a ticket."

"Where?"

"Shit, I don't know. Maybe east. Minneapolis?"

"Okay. Uh, you wanna front me some cash?"

"Sure. I'll meet you at the bus stop in an hour. I'll give you the money, and you buy the ticket."

"But then what? How you gonna get on the bus? You ain't me, and them bus drivers check."

"We're about the same size. You buy the ticket and bring it back to my truck. Give me the ticket and your ID. We'll switch shirts, I'll put on a hat, and it will work. Those drivers are just going through the motions."

"What if they got some of that facial recognition stuff, man?"

"What if Napoleon had rocket artillery?"

"Huh?"

"Never mind. They don't. Just meet me and we'll do the deal. Then, when I get somewhere where I can, I'll mail your ID to you."

"I dunno. This sounds a little risky."

"How much?"

"Huh?"

"Quit jerking me off. How much do you want?"

"Uhhh, how about $50?"

"Done."

"Done? Maybe—"

"Fifty bucks, man. We got a deal."

"Okay, man, okay. I'll be there. Just bring the money."

Half a block from Tommy's house, Jensen was taking a bite from a sandwich when he got a call.

"Yeah?"

"Jensen, this is Punch."

"Yeah, boss. What's up?"

"You got eyes on?"

"Well, I can see the front of his house. His truck's there. Front window's open, and every once in a while I see someone walk by in the living room, but I can't tell if it's Tommy. Want me to knock on the door?"

"Hell, no! I want you to sit and watch and report!"

"Okay, okay! No reason to get loud on me, Punch."

"Jensen, it is very important we not lose him—you get me? Finish your sandwich and get focused."

"How'd you know I was eating?"

"I'm clairvoyant."

"Huh?"

"Just keep an eye on him."

―――――――

Howard was reading the affidavit of probable cause provided by an officer seeking a warrant to search a home for drugs. According to the warrant, a guy who'd been arrested for dealing drugs had consented to a search of his phone. Reading the affidavit, Howard laughed aloud, concluding that cell phones were the best thing that ever happened to law enforcement.

"What's so funny?" Veronica asked.

"You know, so much of what we see is so very sad, but the drug trade. . . Well, these people are hysterically funny sometimes."

"What do you mean?"

"Well, so many dealers, they just cannot resist taking pictures of their supply and then sending them to other people. I've signed dozens of warrants over the years as the result of pictures of guys holding pounds of weed, gallon bags full of opiates, or blocks of methamphetamine or cocaine."

"I know that, but why is that so funny?"

"Listen to this one: you know how guys usually adopt a euphemism for their supply—something like 'pizza?'"

"Sure."

"So, the conversation would usually go like this: 'Hey, you got any pizza?' 'Yeah, fresh. Just made it.' 'How much?' '$100 for the whole pie; $50 for half a pizza.' Or something along those lines, right?"

"Right."

"Well, this friggin' genius," Howard explained, pointing to the affidavit, "this guy decided to refer to his drugs as 'kittens.' So, when the cops got their hands on his phone, they came across this gem: 'Got any kittens?' 'Yeah, just got a new litter.' 'How much?' '$100 per kitten.'

"So the buyer says, 'I don't have that much,' and the seller replies, 'That's retail, dude.'"

"Oh, no," Veronica said, knowing what came next.

"Yup. The guys asks, 'Can I get half a kitten?'"

They shared a laugh as Howard signed the warrant. "People," he said aloud, and handed the signed document to Veronica.

"Judge Howard?" Ann Fulks called from his outer office.

"It's open."

"I've got a warrant I'd like you to look at," Ann said, handing it to him. She waited uncomfortably while Howard read the affidavit for probable cause supporting the arrest warrant for Tommy Olsen. Eventually, he sat back and took the readers off his nose.

"Lot of evidence," he said.

"Punch does good work," she said.

"He does. He's got a lot of common sense." Howard leaned forward, squinting as he scribbled his signature. "Good luck, Ms. Fulks. This is a big one."

She grabbed the warrant and was digging her cell phone out of her pocket before she'd left his chambers. Howard took a deep breath, held it, and let it out. Decades before, one of his bosses had turned him on to that relaxation technique. At the time, he'd belittled the practice, but had reinstituted it when he took the bench, and had found it invaluable since.

24

"Polson."

"Punch, this is Ann Fulks." Her heart was pounding. "Howard signed the warrant; I'm emailing it to you here momentarily, and a hard copy is en route with one of my clerks. Need this done cleanly, Punch," she continued. "Put your best men on this one. We can't have any mistakes."

"Thanks for the vote of confidence."

"Nothing personal, but this needs to be done right. We cannot have this one fucked up."

"Well, I'll try, but honestly, it's mid-afternoon and I haven't stepped on my own dick yet, Counselor, so I can't in good conscience promise anything."

Ann was silent for a moment. "I'm sorry. Who's on it?"

"Well, Jensen, Baker, and me. It's not like I've got a SWAT team to call on. Jensen's been following Tommy since he walked out earlier this afternoon."

"Good."

"I think he's ready to move on my command," Punch said, envisioning Jensen finishing his sandwich. "I'll be there in three minutes. If you want to have one of your folks meet me out front, I'll grab the warrant, then radio Jensen and we'll get this show started."

"Done."

"On my way."

The three-minute drive was uneventful, and—just as promised—as Punch approached the courthouse, one of the county attorney's clerks flagged him down. Punch rolled down the window, grabbed the document without fully stopping, and radioed Jensen. "We're a go. Hang tight for further instructions."

"Roger."

A few minutes later, Punch watched as Tommy made his way down the street in an aging Ford F-150 with the window down and Jerry Jeff Walker blaring from the speakers.

"Well, he's got that going for him," he mused. He had followed Tommy from his home to a nearby gas station on the north end of town, watching as he met and exchanged cash for papers with a man Punch couldn't identify. Then, Tommy and the man exchanged shirts. As the realization of what was going on began to dawn, a commercial bus pulled into the parking lot. "He's gonna try and take the bus!" Punch said into the radio. "Get him as soon as he starts to cross the parking lot!"

Punch watched as Tommy grabbed a duffle bag and hoisted it over his shoulder. As he began to cross the parking lot toward the bus, Punch yelled, "Now!"

Tommy was immediately surrounded by the Custer Police Department's finest, with guns drawn. "Put your hands behind your head!" one of the officers yelled. Tommy complied.

"Now on your stomach with your hands outstretched to the side!"

Tommy did so, despite some trouble with his hands on his head. Jensen put a knee in his back and cuffed him roughly. "What is the problem?" Tommy asked.

"I have a warrant for your arrest."

"On what charge?"

"Suspicion of murder. Emily Smith."

"I knew it. Goddammit. I knew it would end shitty."

"Keep your head down," Jensen instructed as he assisted Tommy into the back seat of the sedan. "We'll be with you in a minute."

Punch got into the sedan's passenger seat, moved the laptop and other items out of the way, and turned to face Olsen. "Mr. Olsen, at this time I am going to review your constitutional rights. Please pay attention so that I don't have to do this again. I want you to know that this vehicle is equipped with a voice recorder, and anything you and I say is being recorded."

"Anything?" asked Tommy.

"Well, yes," said Punch. "As long as the microphone can pick it up, it will be recorded."

"Okay, well, let's get this on the record. Kiss my ass. I didn't do it. That's my statement."

"Swell. Now how about shuttin' the hell up so I can read you your rights?"

"Sam, there's a call for you on line two. It's Sarah from the *Bugle*," Norquist's secretary said. "Do you want to take it?"

"Did she say what it was about?"

"No. Should I ask?"

"No, that's fine," Sam said, and switched lines. "Sam Johnstone."

"Mr. Johnstone, this is Sarah Penrose from the *Bugle*. I wonder if you have a few minutes to do a quick interview with me?"

"About what?"

"About the murder of Emily Smith."

"I don't know anything about it," Sam said. "I don't think I ever even met her."

"That is what I'm made to understand," Sarah said. "I've heard you will be defending the accused."

"Who told you that?"

"Well, I cannot reveal my sources; I'm sure you understand."

"Well, I don't know where you're getting your information, but I don't know the guy, have never spoken to him, and as far as I know I've never laid eyes on him. Your *source* is flat wrong."

"Mr. Johnstone, my sources are rarely wrong. Now, do you know the accused, Tommy Olsen?"

"I already told you I don't."

"So, do you agree with me that, because you know neither the deceased nor the accused, that you'd be a good choice?"

"Not really, and I think there's a little more to defending a murder case than who you know."

"Well, you'll agree with me that generally, it's better if the attorney has little or no personal involvement in the matter?"

"Well, yes, but—"

"And since you're one of the few lawyers in town who didn't know either party, you may well be the right choice?"

"I don't agree."

"If you were to be asked, would you accept the case?"

"Well, no one has asked. It's far too early to say whether—"

"Fair to say you'd give it some consideration?"

"Well, of course. But—"

"Thank you, Mr. Johnstone. I'm on deadline, so I've got to get to a keyboard," she said, and hung up.

25

The jail was unusually loud for this time of evening, Sam thought. He was sitting in a small room reserved for lawyers to meet with prisoners when the jailers brought in Tommy Olsen. "Mr. Olsen." Sam stood and indicated where Tommy should sit. "Thank you for seeing me. Did Jack Fricke talk to you?"

"The janitor?" Tommy asked. He looked smaller than Sam had imagined.

"Yes."

"He did. Said some mouthpiece wanted to speak with me." Tommy looked at Sam closely.

"That's me. I'm Sam Johnstone and I'm an attorney. I'd like to talk to you for a couple minutes."

"Why is that?" Tommy asked. "Are you a public defender?"

"No, I'm not. I'm just a guy who does a little criminal defense work, heard about your situation, and thinks that maybe you and I should talk."

"Then you're screwed, Mr. Lawyer. Because I don't have any money. Been paying temporary child support to that crazy old lady of mine, and I'm gonna lose my job. I don't have anything to say. I think I'm screwed. I didn't do it. This is a bunch of shit."

"Well, whether it is or isn't, you're gonna need an attorney," Sam said. "And the sooner you get one, the better off you'll be."

"Seems to me that cop has his mind made up," Tommy said. "Seems to me I'm screwed. They're gonna bend me over the stump."

"Not necessarily. That cop's job is to collect evidence and make his best determination whether a crime was committed and, if so, who did it. The prosecutor's job is to put that evidence before the jury, which makes the final determination."

"Frigging lawyer-speak."

"Like it or not, that's how justice plays out."

"Justice? I don't give a rat's ass about *justice*, man. I just want out of jail. I don't know who did it, and I don't care. All I know is that I didn't do it. Why me? And who the hell are you? I've been around town for a while, and I've never heard of you."

"I'm kind of new to town. There's no reason for you to know who I am."

"Where you from?"

"Washington, D.C."

Tommy laughed aloud. "You must be one lousy-ass lawyer to move from D.C. to this hellhole."

He had a good laugh, Sam thought. "I'm okay. I've worked with veterans over the years who found themselves in trouble."

"What's your angle?" Tommy looked Sam over. "Did you serve, or you just a fan boy?"

"I did my time."

"Branch?"

"Army."

"JAG?" The Judge Advocate General's corps was comprised of the Army's lawyers.

"No. Infantry."

"You look like an officer. You a ring knocker?" A "ring knocker" was a derisive term for a graduate of the United States Military Academy at West Point.

"No. Officer Candidate School."

"Well, I guess that's good."

"What'd you do?"

"I was a Marine; therefore, I was a grunt. Did a tour in Afghanistan. That's my claim to fame."

"How come you got out?"

"I guess I just got sick of the shit after I redeployed. Felt like I fought my war, time for me to come back home." Tommy looked at his feet. "But after coming back here, I wish I'd never got out. I think I was a good fit in the Corps. I'm not sure I'm a very good fit anywhere as a civilian."

"Lotta that going around. How long were you in?"

"Four years."

"What was your rank at discharge?"

"Private. You?"

"Captain."

"Why'd you leave?" Tommy asked.

"Medically retired," Sam said, and knocked on his leg. "They got me."

"Bastards."

"Yup."

"Miss it?"

"Every day." Sam looked at Tommy for a long time, weighing how far to go, then decided to see how he would react to what had to be some painful questions. "So, you were in the Corps for four years and you left as a private? Who did you piss off?"

"I had a little disagreement with an officer and lost rank."

"But you got an honorable discharge?"

"Barely. I had a good war record."

"What happened?"

"I got in a dispute with a female lieutenant when I was out-processing before I went on terminal leave."

"What you mean by 'dispute?'"

"I mean the bitch was being disrespectful to me and a couple of my buddies when we were out-processing. That woman had never deployed, and she had a real attitude. I said something to her, and she pulled rank on me. I said something back, and she got in my face, screaming at me. Next thing I knew she was lying on the ground."

"You are damned lucky you didn't end up in Leavenworth."

"She's damned lucky she's not dead."

"Do yourself a favor," Sam said.

"What's that, sir?"

"Whoever your lawyer ends up being, don't say shit like that to them."

Tommy laughed. "Sure, sir."

"Tommy, do you draw a disability check from the Veterans Administration?"

"Yeah."

"Can I ask you for what?"

"They tell me I suffer from post-traumatic stress disorder and traumatic brain injury. Sometimes I get really pissed off and I guess it scares people. But I've always been that way. I think it's bullshit, but I'll take the money."

"IED?"

"No. Mortar landed in the compound—right outside my hooch. Knocked my ass out!" Tommy grinned. "They told me later I staggered around like a drunk for two days before I could get medevac'd."

"Not good. Been seeing your counselor?"

"You seeing yours?" Tommy bristled.

Sam met his stare. "I'm not charged with murder."

Tommy looked away, then back at Sam. "When I can."

"What does that mean? You are supposed to make those counseling appointments—it's important."

"Gotta pay the bills, man. My boss don't care if I'm nuts. He only cares whether my ass shows up on time. Besides . . . C'mon, sir, sitting in a small room with a bunch of rear echelon motherfuckers, talking about what's bugging us? I ain't got time for that."

Sam nodded in understanding. "You been drinkin'?"

"I like to have a few beers, sure. Like anyone else."

"Taking your meds?"

"Yeah. Pretty regular. Sometimes I forget, and some days I don't like the way I feel when I do."

"You need to take them no matter what," Sam advised. "How much trouble you been in with the law since you been out?"

"No more'n anyone else."

"Been convicted of any crimes of violence?"

"Well, yeah."

"Like?"

"Assault. Had an aggravated assault that got dropped to a simple, and a DV."

"These all separate incidents, or what?"

"Well, the assault was a bar fight. The aggravated assault and DV happened when I came home and found Becky—that's my soon-to-be ex-wife—alone with our neighbor. I beat his ass with a three wood I kept in my closet for just such an occasion, and apparently I slapped the shit out of her."

"Ugh."

"I'd do it again tomorrow. Bitch deserved it. Can't say I blame him too much, as Becky is really hot, and his old lady is a hag. But it happened and I admitted to it. We got the aggravated pled down to simple assault and I did thirty days right here for that. She left with my kids, got a no-contact order, and filed for divorce. That's how I came to know Emily, er, Ms. Smith."

"Any other convictions?"

"Just minor stuff."

"How minor?"

"DUI. Possession. Drunk and disorderly."

"Awards?"

"All the usual shit: Bronze Star, Purple Heart, stuff like that," Tommy said. "We don't give awards like the Army."

Sam smiled. "Does anyone around here know about your awards?"

"Hell no, sir," Tommy said. "As far as I can tell, the only guys talking about combat and fruit salad are those drunks down at the American Legion, most of whom never left the States. Mr. Johnstone, I want you to know—"

Sam interjected, "First, call me Sam." He held up his hand. "Second, don't tell me anything important right now. I am not your attorney, so anything you tell me could be asked about by the prosecution. I just wanted to get some background from you today."

"Are you gonna represent me?" Tommy asked.

"I doubt it. I want to see if we can line up an experienced criminal defense guy for you—someone who understands Wyoming juries and has maybe done a murder case or two. It's one thing for me to represent veterans who have gotten themselves into minor scrapes, but this is another thing entirely. Besides, my boss would fire me, and defending a murder charge costs hundreds of thousands of dollars, which I don't have, and which I doubt you have."

"Sir, I need you," Tommy said. He was standing now, gesturing with his arms.

"Not so sure. There are plenty of capable attorneys in the public defender's office," Sam said. Then, seeing Tommy's reaction, he continued. "I know that a lot of people disparage the public defender's office—call them 'pubic defenders,' 'public pretenders,' and all that shit. But the truth is, no one spends more time in courtrooms, and no one tries more cases than those guys and gals. If you can find a guy who has spent his career as a public defender, you find a guy who is not only a believer but very likely a damned good trial attorney."

"But they're not gonna believe me."

"It doesn't matter, Tommy—that's not their job. Their job is to defend your rights, and they will do that whether or not they believe you."

"It matters to me."

"I hear you, and I appreciate that. But I have a landlord, a car payment, and several bartenders and liquor store clerks who depend on me to bring in a little bit of money every month. I can't take on something like this and still pay the bills."

"I did not kill Emily . . . Do you believe me, sir?"

"Tommy, I don't . . . It doesn't . . . Tommy, like I said, it isn't important."

"Sir, I need help," Tommy said. "If you don't help me, they said they're gonna stick a needle in my arm and put me to sleep like an old beagle."

"Let me see what I can do."

The newspaper on Paul's desk featured the headline: "Sam Johnstone to Defend Marine Accused of Killing Lawyer." Paul tossed the paper on the desk in front of Sam. "I told you I did not want you to take this case," he said. "What part of that didn't you understand?"

"Paul, this is bullshit. I'll admit I went and spoke with the guy, but he's a fellow vet, and I haven't agreed to do anything," Sam said. "All I've done is look at the situation and try to determine if I can help a fellow G.I."

"I want you to stay away from this case, Sam. I told you that. The phone has been ringing off the hook all morning, and Monique says the calls are running about five-to-one ripping us for defending a killer. This could ruin me."

"I understand," Sam said.

"Then how the hell could you do this to me? Let somebody else do this one, somebody who knows what they're doing. Someone who can defend a murderer."

"I'm not so sure this guy did it," Sam ventured.

"Right. Because the police arrest the wrong guy all the time. Have you seen the evidence against him?"

"It happens, Paul. And no, I haven't."

"Sure it does. And who knows whether the cops got it right this time. But guess what? It doesn't matter, because you're not taking the case."

"Paul, I can never thank you enough for the opportunity you've given me. But I'm going to have to look at this matter, and if I think this guy needs representation, and if I think I'm the right guy to do the job, then I'm going to take it."

"Why? Why in the world would you stick your toe into that swimming pool full of shit? You're off to a good start here, have a future and an opportunity to do good things for people. Why throw it all away?"

"Throw what away?"

"Well, to begin with, your affiliation with this office. Your clients here. If I find out that you're talking with Olsen, you're done. Do you understand?"

"I understand," Sam said, his decision made.

"Good. So I have your word that you will not pursue this any further?"

"No, I can't give you that." Sam shook his head. "I can't tell you that I will not represent Tommy Olsen."

"Sam, I can't have this. I've explained to you why."

"I understand. And I can respect that. But I'm not sure I can respect myself if I turn my back on a disabled veteran who needs help."

"Leave it to the public defenders, Sam," Paul said. "They're the experts."

"I know," Sam admitted. "Paul, you will have my letter of resignation by tomorrow. And Paul?"

"Yes?"

"Thanks again, for everything." Sam extended his hand. "I'm sorry. This is just something I think I might have to do."

Paul took Sam's hand and shook it firmly. "I know. But Sam, I'm not gonna lie. I'm thinking very soon you're going to look back and regret your decision."

"Tommy, sign here," Sam said. They were back in the small jail room. Sam had used one of Paul's forms to craft a representation agreement.

"What's this?"

"It's a representation agreement. I need you to sign this before I will agree to represent you. It lays out all the terms of my representation, to include my fee, who pays costs, under what circumstances I can back out, and stuff like that."

"I've been thinking, Sam. I can't ask you to do this for me. I can't afford to pay you. I already filled out an application for the public defender like you said. I think I'm supposed to see the guy tomorrow."

"This county has well-qualified public defenders who know their stuff. Nothing wrong with them representing you at all," Sam said.

"Then why do you want the job?"

"I don't know, Tommy. Maybe because I served my country and you did the same. Maybe I'm a little worried about you." Sam indicated the spot for Tommy to sign. "And maybe I'm a dumbass."

Tommy took the pen. "Do you know what you're doing?"

"Well, I've never tried a murder case," Sam allowed. "But I've been in and around courtrooms for a while now. Besides, I've got something going for me that few others will or would."

"What's that?"

"I actually believe in you."

Tommy looked steadily at Sam. "Yeah, okay. But how in the hell am I ever gonna pay your fee?"

"Well, I've got a little income, some VA disability, and some money from other things I've done. Let's agree that, like it says here, you give me some money upfront, and then you sign a promissory note for the balance—a big one."

"This how they teach it in law school? What if I don't get out?"

"Well, I guess I will have made a bad investment. But let's cross that bridge when we come to it."

"If."

"Yes. *If* we come to it," Sam said, pushing the documents in front of Tommy, who signed as best he could, given his hands were chained together.

"Now, let's get to work," Sam said.

26

Days later, Sam was in the courthouse, dropping off business cards with his phone number on them.

"Hey, Sam, I heard Paul let you go," said Fricke. Sam did not like anything about the janitor. Nothing he could put his finger on—just an immediate, visceral dislike. He was already regretting using him to get to Tommy.

"Yeah? Where'd you hear that?"

"I hear stuff. People tell me stuff."

"I'm sure."

"So, since you took on Tommy Olsen—"

"Where'd you hear that?"

"I told you. People tell me stuff. Anyway, you gotta be looking for some office space, right?"

"So, you're like a realtor, or what?"

"I know a guy."

"Oh, you know a guy. So, this 'guy' you know—what's he got?"

"Well, he's got a little office—about 650 square foot is all. But the price is right, especially for a guy like you who might not even get paid."

"How did you—? Never mind. Where is it?"

"Just across the street from the courthouse."

"That's the high rent district. I thought you said the price was gonna be right?"

"Not across *that* street. *This* street." Fricke jabbed his thumb over his shoulder.

Sam knew the area. Tattoo parlors, bars, and thrift stores. "Is there a storefront?"

"No, it's upstairs. Above the thrift shop. It ain't much, but—"

"I'll take a look at it. Who has the key?"

"I just happen to have one with me."

"I'm shocked."

Sam looked around the place. It wasn't much. A realtor would describe it as "modest." Three tiny rooms: an entryway that could serve as a reception area, a small room that could serve as an office, and a slightly larger room that could become a conference room. The restroom was downstairs, and there was no kitchen.

But the price was right.

"I'll take it," he said to Fricke. "Get me the lease and let me look at it."

"Lease? We don't do business that way around here, Counselor. Around here, a man's word is his bond," Fricke said, showing his yellow teeth.

"Here's thirty dollars." Sam flashed three tens in Fricke's face. "Go to the stationary store and buy a lease form, have the landlord fill it out, and get it to me. Keep the change and buy yourself a drink, and we've got a deal. No lease, no deal."

Fricke thought for a couple of seconds, then snatched the tens from Sam's hand. "Deal, Counselor," he said.

Sam's investigation had been fast and furious. To date, the evidence against Tommy seemed solid, but Sam was determined to speak with every potential witness he could identify. Last night, he'd gotten ahold of one Gus Hadley, Emily's neighbor, and had wrangled an interview.

"So, Gus," Sam said, looking around for a place to sit, but afraid to do so lest something crawl up his pants leg, "what can you tell me about Emily?"

"Well, lawyer-man," Gus said, eyeing Sam closely, "let me ask you something: what's in this for me?"

"Well, you can talk to me here and now, or I will go file a subpoena and you can meet me at a time and place of my choosing, at which point I'll put everything you say on the record."

"I get it. Ain't gotta go getting all huffy on me." Gus was sitting on a pile of clothing covering what looked like an old recliner. Looking up at Sam, he reached down, grabbed a can of beer, and spat tobacco into it. "Now, I ain't a snoop, so I don't spend my time watching what goes on, know what I mean? But I get paid to upkeep this here place, so I keep my eyes open as necessary. That Emily, she was a good looker. She had lotsa guys callin' on her. Some young, some older; some lookin' rich, some not so much. One great big guy. The day 'fore she died, I seen a young fellow call on her. Wearing a costume, but I could see he was thirty or so, mebbe six-foot, one-eighty— good shape, you know what I mean?"

"Sure."

"Yeah, so he come up in a big truck, jumped right out, walked on up to the door, and went right in."

"Then what?"

"Then nothin'. I tol' you, I ain't nosy."

"So, when was the next time you saw Emily?"

"Never did."

"Did you see my client leave?"

"Nope."

"So, you don't know what time my client left—is that right?"

"Well, I know it was before six o'clock in the mornin', 'cause that's when I get up to pee. Truck was gone then."

"So, fair to say you saw a costumed man you think was my client go into the apartment at around 10:30 p.m., and he was gone at 6:00 a.m. the next day?"

"Yep."

"But you didn't see him leave?"

"No, but his truck was gone. Why would he leave without his truck?"

"I hear you," Sam said. "But you'll agree you don't know when he left, right?"

"'Course I will."

"And what time did you go to sleep that night?"

"What night?"

"The night you think you saw my client go into Emily's house."

"I know what I seen, Mister."

"Okay. So, you saw a guy who looked like my client go into her house, and at some point, you went to sleep, right?"

"Yup. Right after *Bonanza*. I watch *Bonanza* every night."

"So, that comes on at—what?—about 10:00 p.m.?"

"Yup. Ends at eleven. That's when I go to bed."

"So, on that night you went to bed at eleven?"

"Yup. Right to sleep, too."

"You a light sleeper?"

"Not really."

"So, you don't know anything about what happened at Emily's place after eleven for sure, and really after the guy you think was my client arrived—because you're not nosy, right?"

"Well, yeah. But I know what I seen."

"And you're convinced it was my guy?"

"Oh, yeah."

"How so?"

"'Cause that picture them cops gave me, I recognized him."

"You recognized him from a line-up?"

"No. They just showed me the one picture of the guy, but I recognized him right away 'cause he came around here the day after she was kilt lookin' for her."

"Are you sure?"

"Oh, yeah. It was the guy. Same truck, same fella. All upset, though."

"About what—if you know?"

"I don't. I just figured he was alley-cattin' around," Gus mused. "Maybe she'd blown him off, you know? She had lots of boyfriends."

"You've said that twice, now."

"What?"

"That she had a lot of boyfriends."

"Well, she was a looker, that girl."

"Did you ever go out with her?"

"Well, no."

"Did you let him in the house?"

"Who?"

"My guy."

"Nope."

"You sure?"

"Sure, I'm sure. Why would I? He coulda been some nut or broken-hearted Romeo or somethin'."

"Did you ever ask her out?"

"Naaaw, not me, now."

"Ever been in her place?"

"Sure."

"When was the last time?"

"Mebbe a coupla days before she died."

"So, between the time my guy showed up and you seein' his truck was gone, you didn't hear or see anything?"

"I didn't say that, now."

"Excuse me?"

"Well, sometime during the night I heard something—I imagine it was your boy leaving."

"Did you look?"

"No."

"What time was it?"

"Dunno. Didn't look."

"So, sometime during the night you heard something, but you don't know what it was or what time it was—true?"

"Well, yeah, but I just figured it was your client. Didn't have no cause then to think he'd kilt her."

27

Tommy's initial appearance had drawn a full house, Howard noted as he approached the bench. It was to be expected in a rural American town like this, where murders had historically occurred about once every other year or so. Most of the murders Howard had seen over the years involved drunken husbands killing wives or wives shooting battering husbands, so one like this would naturally draw a lot of interest. And since Emily had known practically everyone in the courthouse, it was no surprise that a lot of the courthouse staff had given up their lunch hour or otherwise taken time off to watch.

"The first matter before the court is State of Wyoming versus Thomas Olsen," Howard said. As a circuit court judge, Howard didn't have the jurisdiction to take a plea. Instead, the purpose of the hearing was to ensure the defendant understood his rights, the charges, and the possible penalty should he plead or be found guilty; to arrange for attorney representation if necessary; and to set the terms of his pre-trial release. "Mr. Olsen, would you please step to the podium?"

Tommy dutifully arose and shuffled to the podium, his feet constrained by steel shackles, where he was met by Sam.

"Your Honor, Sam Johnstone, appearing for the defendant."

"Welcome, Mr. Johnstone. Have you been retained by Mr. Olsen?"

"I have, Your Honor." An audible murmur went through the courtroom as those who didn't know Sam asked those beside them who he was, and those who knew him expressed surprise that an attorney in Paul Norquist's office would take the case.

"Mr. Johnstone, because this is an initial appearance on a felony, we'll go through this rather quickly, and then we'll talk about bail."

"Yes, sir."

Howard asked Tommy his name, social security number, address, and phone number.

"Mr. Johnstone, will your client waive an advisal of rights?"

"He will, Your Honor."

"Thank you, counsel," Howard said. "Mr. Olsen, you are here pursuant to an Information and Warrant alleging you are guilty of one count of first-degree murder, a violation of Wyoming Statute—"

Howard stopped talking when a tremendous clapping sound reverberated through the courtroom. He was looking around, startled, when Sam began yelling, "Get down! Incoming! Everyone get down!"

The bailiffs immediately drew their weapons and began scanning the audience, yelling at Howard to get under his bench. Sam was behind the table, scanning for enemies and calling for his platoon leaders. He could hear the *thump* of mortars being launched at his men. "Get everyone down! Now! Incoming!"

The bailiff was looking at Tommy, who was under the table, staring at Sam. The courtroom was very quiet. "Sam." Tommy cautiously put a cuffed hand on Sam's arm. "Sir, it's me, Lance Corporal Olsen."

Sam peered cautiously up over the table, then got back down and looked at Tommy. "Sir," Tommy repeated. "It's me."

"What's going on?" Sam said. He was sweating heavily.

"That easel thing there in the corner fell down," Tommy said, gesturing behind them. "Made a helluva noise. You, uh . . . You freaked out. But it's okay." He again placed a cuffed hand on Sam's forearm. "We're all okay."

Courtroom security cautiously approached Sam and Tommy and determined all was clear. One of the officers moved to Howard's bench and was whispering in his ear. Howard nodded and looked at Sam, then stood and declared, "We'll take a fifteen-minute recess. Counsel, in my chambers, please."

"Damn, son, you scared the shit out of me." Howard wiped his forehead with a paper towel he'd gotten from the restroom in his chambers. Handing one to Sam, he asked, "You all right?"

Sam asserted he was fine but accepted the towel. "My apologies, Your Honor."

"How about you, Ms. Fulks?" Ann was looking at one of her shoes— apparently a buckle had been broken in all the excitement.

"I'll take care of that," Sam assured her. "My fault. I'm, I'm sorry. I thought—"

"We know what you thought, counsel," Ann said. "It was clear to every-one. Your Honor, I'd like to put something on the record. I cannot abide by Mr. Johnstone's antics—"

"Antics?" Howard asked. "Surely, Ms. Fulks, you cannot think that Mr. Johnstone would create such a disturbance on purpose?"

"I don't know," Ann said. "What I do know is that we are in the middle of an initial appearance on a charge of murder. If Mr. Johnstone cannot, or will not, represent his client without . . . theatrics, then I would ask the court to see to it that he is replaced."

"Your concern is noted, counsel." Howard turned to Sam. "Mr. John-stone, are you all right?"

"I'm . . . fine, Judge. I just got startled, that's all. I'll. . . I'll be okay."

"Are you fit to continue?" Howard asked. He was up and handing out bottles of water from the refrigerator in his office. "We can continue until tomorrow, if you prefer."

"Your Honor, the State will object to any continuance."

"Ann, we're not on the record here, so shut up for a moment, would you?" Howard stared her down. "Now, Sam, how would you like to proceed?"

Five minutes later, the parties were reassembled. The judge had put the matter back on the record and was in the process of reading the charge to Tommy. Still shaky on his feet, Sam rose, holding onto the table for support. "Your Honor, my client waives his right to a reading of the charges against him, and—" Sam was hoping to avoid a reading of the charges and penalties.

"Not that quickly, Mr. Johnstone. This is a serious matter. I'm going to read the elements of the crime and the possible penalties to the defendant, then I'm going to ensure he understands what he's been charged with."

"Your Honor, I'll represent to the court that before appearing here today Mr. Olsen and I discussed the warrant and the charges against him—to include possible sentences."

"I'm sure you did, counsel. Now, may I continue?"

"Yes, Your Honor," Sam said, sitting down and listening impatiently while Howard read the statute and the warrant verbatim. "Mr. Olsen, do you understand all that?"

"Yes, sir," Tommy said quietly.

"The statute goes on to say," Howard read, "that 'a person convicted of murder in the first degree shall be punished by death, life imprisonment without parole, or life imprisonment according to law.' Mr. Olsen, do you understand that?"

Whispers and groans had run through the crowd at the mention of a possible death penalty. Tommy sat quietly, looking at the chains on his wrists, and said nothing. Sam leaned over and whispered in his ear, "Tom, did you hear that?"

"Yeah," Tommy said. "So I could die?"

"Well, technically, but that isn't going to happen. Answer the judge."

"What do I say?"

"Tell him you understand."

"I understand, Your Honor," Tommy said in a near-whisper.

"Thank you, Mr. Olsen," Howard said, shuffling through papers on his desk. "Does the State have a recommendation for bond?"

Ann rose and stepped to the podium. Her moment had arrived, and she was well-rehearsed, aware that newspaper writers from all over the state were present. "Your Honor, as the court knows, Mr. Olsen has been charged with first-degree murder. While the State is still trying to determine whether to seek the death penalty, this is the most serious crime on the books. A young woman has lost her life. Mr. Olsen does have a prior record, one which includes prior assaults on women. For that reason, we would ask that the court allow no bond, and order him held until trial."

Howard, who had been taking notes, looked toward Sam. "Mr. Johnstone, does the defendant care to respond?"

"Yes, Your Honor," Sam replied, gathering his notes and walking to the podium. "As the court well knows, my client is presumed innocent until proven otherwise. Mr. Olsen vehemently denies these charges and looks forward to the opportunity to defend himself. He is married, has a wife and kids here in town, and is employed as a rig hand. He is not a flight risk. Further, Mr. Olsen is a decorated veteran who spent several years of his life defending the rest of us in Afghanistan and elsewhere. While he acknowledges his criminal record, I am made to understand that it consists primarily of driving under the influence and domestic difficulties. Further, I understand that these incidents stem from an underlying, untreated post-traumatic stress disorder. Basically, he's been self-medicating with alcohol, Your Honor. Because my client presents no threat to the community when sober, I'd ask that you set a reasonable bond in order to ensure that he appears for trial. We feel a bond in the amount of $25,000—"

"Twenty-five thousand bucks? Where the hell am I going to get that kind of money?" Tommy interjected.

"Mr. Johnstone, please restrain your client," Howard said sharply.

Sam leaned over to Tommy and whispered earnestly, "Tom, are you interested in spending the rest of your life in jail, or worse?"

"Of course not. But I ain't got no money," Tommy replied.

"I need you to trust me. I need you to be quiet for just a minute and trust me. Can you do that?" Sam looked Tommy in the eyes.

Tommy met his stare, then looked down. "I didn't do this."

"I understand that. But will you trust me?"

"Yes, sir."

Turning his attention to the judge, Sam concluded, "Your Honor, I apologize for the interruption. We believe that Mr. Olsen does not present a danger to the public, and a bond in that amount is sufficient to ensure his appearance at all further hearings in this matter. I'd ask that you set bond in that amount, order my client to comply with a house arrest order, and abstain from the possession or use of controlled substances, alcohol, and weapons. Thank you."

Sam sat down and watched Howard. Tommy leaned over and asked in a low voice, "Does that mean I can't hunt?"

"Yes," Sam said, jaw tight.

"Sam—"

"Tommy, I need you to sit tight. We'll talk about this later."

"But Sam—"

"Tommy, we'll talk later. Rock steady, now."

Howard looked to Fulks. "Ms. Fulks, does the State have a response?"

"We do, Your Honor," she said, rising. "I recognize that Mr. Johnstone is new to this jurisdiction and to this state. And I don't know how they do business back in Washington, D.C., but in Custer County, Wyoming, twenty-five thousand dollars is insufficient for a crime of this magnitude—"

"An *alleged* crime of this magnitude," Sam interjected, half out of his chair.

"Mr. Johnstone, please let her finish," Howard scolded. "In this jurisdiction, counsel do not address each other—all comments must be addressed to the court."

"I apologize to the court," Sam said.

"Continue, Ms. Fulks," Judge Howard said.

"As I was saying, twenty-five thousand dollars is insufficient, Your Honor, and the State renews its request that the court deny bond. Thank you."

"Well, having heard and considered the arguments of counsel, this court is going to deny bond. The reasons therefore are the severity of the allegations and the defendant's prior criminal record." The judge looked at Olsen. "Mr. Olsen, you are remanded to the custody of the detention center pending trial."

"Tom, I'll be over to see you tonight. Need you to stay out of trouble," Sam whispered.

"Okay," Tommy said. "Sam, I didn't do this."

After Tommy was led from the courtroom, the public arose and left as well, eager to discuss the events they had just witnessed. Sam remained behind. He wasn't surprised or even disappointed—no judge in his or her right mind would allow a man with Tommy's background, who was suspected of murder, out of jail pending trial.

Outside the courtroom, the press was ready with cameras and microphones. "Ms. Fulks, how are you feeling about the denial of bond by the judge?"

"The charge is first-degree murder. The court's job is to ensure that the defendant will appear for trial, and that the public's safety is assured. Given that the death penalty has not been taken off the table, the State feels the denial of bond was appropriate," Ann said, just as she'd rehearsed.

"Are you nervous? This is your first murder trial, is it not?"

"It is my first murder trial, and no, I'm not nervous," Ann replied, and then mustered what she hoped was a look of grim determination. "I'm not on trial." And with that, she turned on her heel and walked swiftly away from the reporters, feeling pleased with herself.

A few days after the initial appearance, Punch was on his way to the county attorney's office to give her an update. He was still trying to tie up some loose ends. He was running late and looking at his watch when his phone rang. "Polson."

"Hey, boss. Baker here."

"Baker, what's up? Make it quick; gotta meet the county attorney momentarily, and I'm running late."

"Lucky you. Hey, we got some good shit on Olsen."

"Tell me."

"You remember we did a request for his military records?"

"I do."

"Well, we got the results."

"I'm listening."

"Turns out he almost got a dishonorable discharge. Apparently, he punched an officer!"

Punch thought back to his brief career and the countless times he'd come close to nailing some pin-headed officer—especially majors. There was something about majors. "So what?"

"So . . . it was a broad!"

Ignoring for a moment his subordinate's politically incorrect language —he'd worry about that later—Punch directed Baker to get on with it. "Gimme the skinny."

"Well, it was right before he got out. He was out-processing, this gal said something, he said something, and she slapped his ass. According to the Corps, he went crazy and knocked her out. Took three of his buddies to get him off her. But because she had slapped him, they just busted him a couple ranks on the way out the door."

Punch considered his next action. "Whattaya got—hard copies or is this all electronic?"

"All I got is one hard copy. The Marines don't give out the electronic version, apparently."

"All right. Make one copy and throw it in my inbox. I'll get to it tonight," Punch said, feeling a little better. It was one more nail in Tommy Olsen's coffin. Maybe he and Rhonda could take the kids out to eat tonight.

28

"So, how are you doing?" Sam asked, eyeing Tommy carefully. It was mid-December, and Tommy had been in jail for more than a month. His preliminary hearing would be next week. He had gotten a haircut, revealing several unusual scars on his head. The orange jumpsuit was hanging on him, indicating a loss of weight. Jail food was obviously not agreeing with him.

"I'm locked in a cage for a crime I didn't commit. How the fuck you think I'm doing?" Tommy asked. "Where the hell have you been?"

"Got that out of your system?" Sam asked. Tommy looked at the floor. "Tommy, I told you I was not going to be able to get in to see you every day. I'm here as often as I can be. But I've got other cases, bills to pay, and a lot of work to do in preparation for this case. I'm doing the best I can, and I need you to believe in me—just like I believe in you."

"I'm sorry, Sam," Tommy said. He stood up and walked the small cell's perimeter. "Time goes slowly in here, and it's hard not to get pissed off. I'm thankful for what you're doing for me, but I'm going ape-shit in here."

"No problem," Sam said. "Serious question: how are you feeling?"

"I'm okay. I've been doing some push-ups to try to keep my strength up. They only let me exercise out of the cell for one hour a day, and only inside, so I'm not getting much cardio."

"You look like you've lost weight."

"Well, the chow here sucks."

"You gotta eat. Have you been reading those books I got you?"

"Yeah, I'm okay with the Alcoholics Anonymous book, but some of those others just seem like a bunch of hocus-pocus."

"Fine, just give them all a try if you can, Tommy. They'll help. I'm taking a look at them myself."

"You need to, after that shit-show in court. Jesus, you scared the hell out of everybody!"

"I know, and I'm working on it," Sam said. "Listen, I need to talk to you about something. The way criminal defense works is this: you either did it, you didn't do it, you were justified in doing it, or you did it but weren't responsible for doing it. Those are the four defense possibilities."

"I didn't do it."

"I understand—"

"I didn't do it!"

"Tommy, quiet down! I understand what you're saying. But it is my responsibility as a lawyer to provide you with the best defense possible, and it may be that your best defense is to admit killing her but assert that you were not responsible for your actions at the time that you—"

"What? Killed her?"

"Well, yeah. It might be that given the evidence that we face, your best bet to avoid the death penalty or a long jail sentence is to say, 'Yeah, I did it, but at the time I did it I was not in control.'"

"What part of 'I didn't do it' don't you understand?"

"Tommy, I hear you. But if you hang your hat on being found not guilty by a jury, and if they don't like you or don't believe what you are saying, you could find yourself in a trick."

"I don't care. I didn't do it. They won't be able to find me guilty."

"Tommy, ever have a situation where you find out you did something, and you don't remember doing it?"

"Well, yeah—but only when I was drinkin'."

"Well, you were drinking with Emily the night she got killed, right?"

"Yeah, so?"

"So, how do you know you didn't do her, and then black out?"

"Because I remember everything. Trust me. She ain't a gal you forget about."

Sam smiled despite himself and motioned for Tommy to sit beside him. "Tommy, a jury is comprised of twelve human beings. None is perfect individually, and they are not perfect as a group. I can't sit here today and tell you or promise you—let alone guarantee you—that the jury in your case will not make a mistake. So, we need to look at all possible defenses. To that end, given your military service, I want you to agree to be evaluated by a psychiatrist to see if you are fit to stand trial now, and if you were legally sane at the time of the killing. We can get a doctor from the VA—"

"I won't do it. I am not a nutjob!"

"Tommy, I can't make you, but as your lawyer, I can ask the judge to order you to undergo an examination. I don't want to do that. What I want is for you to sign a consent form so that I can order up an examination."

"I am not crazy. I was not there when she was killed. For Christ's sake, I didn't do it, Sam! Why won't you believe me?"

"Just humor me. Just go along with this for me, and let's see what the results are." He looked steadily at Tommy, who met his stare for a moment, then looked to the floor.

"I'm not going to consent. There's nothing wrong with me. I maybe have a temper, and sometimes maybe I drink too much, but I'm fine."

Sam grasped Olsen's forearm and looked him in the eye. "Tommy, I can't have you die on my watch. I've been there and done that. I can't deal with it again. I can't live with it. I need you to do this, for you and for me. And if you won't do it, then maybe you're going to have to retain another attorney."

"Damn, Sam. You'd walk away? I misjudged you, man. I thought you were straight up." Tommy watched Sam, who had turned to stare at the cinderblock wall. "Sam, I'm fine. Just like you, I'm driving on."

"That's where you are wrong, Tommy." Sam's eyes were wet with tears. "We're not fine. We're all screwed up. It's just a matter of degree."

29

The sun's warmth on the back of his neck contrasted with the temperature of the water swirling around his lower legs. Having caught a few decent fish, Sam waded to the water's edge and sat heavily in the bent grass lining the bank of the spring creek. The breeze was slight and the sky was azure, with no clouds visible above the canyon walls looming over him.

Sam had little enthusiasm today. Normally, an early winter day spent on stream served to clear his head of all but fishing-related thoughts. He'd simply focus on the fishing and let everything else go. But today was different, because this case was different. The stakes were high—hell, they couldn't be any higher.

The fish were cooperative, and Sam had matched the hatch, but he'd missed several solid strikes. Maybe it was all that whiskey last night; maybe the fish weren't quite taking the fly like he thought. That didn't make sense. He'd been fishing since he was a kid; he knew a solid strike when he saw one. Maybe his focus wasn't what it should be—or maybe it was. Maybe this was a bad idea; maybe he should be back in the office getting ready for a preliminary hearing on behalf of a man whose life literally depended on his having it together.

Slowly and deliberately, Sam retrieved his line, clipped off the fly, and attached it to the drying patch on his vest. Even now, with the advancements in equipment, Sam still wore a decades-old vest containing a bladder that could be inflated with the pull of a cord or by blowing into a tube. It had been a gift from a girlfriend, the result of one too many tales of a fall into a creek, a misstep that resulted in his tripping into the river, or a bank giving way that ended up with him swimming downstream until he could regain his footing. She always hated those stories, and when a drunken buddy had ignored her look of shock and horror and regaled everyone at a party with the tale of how Sam's waders had filled with water on Arkansas's White River and only a fortuitously overhanging branch had saved him from drowning, she had spent more money than she could afford on what was, at the time, a state-of-the-art vest.

He wondered idly whatever happened to her, then rooted in the pockets until he found the flask, took a long pull from it, and lay back in the grass. Somewhere among the prairie oaks lining the valley floor, tom turkeys called mournfully for mates.

"Dude, what is your problem?" Tommy asked. He was at the door of the adjoining inmate's cell. The inmate, a young guy by the name of Vargas, had been running his sink and flushing his toilet all night long. "I'm trying to get some sleep."

"What does it look like I'm doing, man?" Vargas replied. "I'm doing laundry. My girl is coming tomorrow, and I need to be looking good."

"Do it during daylight hours, please."

"Fuck you, man. I'll do it when I want. You can go—"

Tommy had crossed Vargas's cell much quicker than the young convict had anticipated and was on top of him in an instant. Vargas tried to fight back, landing one punch under Tommy's right eye. But it had little effect, and Tommy beat Vargas until the little man was unable to fight back.

Stepping away, Tommy heard the prisoners shouting in the adjoining cells. He backed himself into a corner in case anyone came to assist Vargas, heard the alarms, and waited. Moments later, the jail's quick response team arrived, geared up and ready to go.

"It was me," Tommy admitted, turning and putting his hands behind his back as he nodded toward Vargas on the floor. "This little fucker was being disrespectful, and I got sick of it."

––––––––––––––––

"Tommy, let me make sure I have this straight," Sam said. "Some asshole is being an asshole, so you—charged with first-degree murder and potentially facing the death penalty—get pissed off and assault the guy? Are you kidding me?"

"Sam, I'm sorry," Tommy pleaded. "I was tired, it was late, and I've been feeling a little stressed out."

"Well, no shit." Sam shook his head. "I'm sure I've heard of something someone did that was stupider; I just can't remember what it was right now. Another little trick like this and you're gonna have to find yourself another boy. You understand?"

"I understand, Sam," Tommy said. "And I want you to know something."

"What's that?"

"I don't usually let people talk to me like you are right now. Just so you know."

"For Christ's sake, Tommy! Really? You're going to threaten your lawyer now?" Sam signaled for the guard through the window. "You know what? Get yourself cleaned up, and let's go do this."

30

"Good morning, Circuit Court for the County of Custer, State of Wyoming is in session," Howard began. "This is the matter of State of Wyoming v. Thomas John Olsen. Today is the 12th day of December. I note the presence of Deputy County and Prosecuting Attorney Ann Fulks. Mr. Olsen is here and is represented by Sam Johnstone. We are here for a preliminary hearing."

Seeing the mouse over Tommy's eye, Howard asked, "Mr. Johnstone, is your client able to proceed here today?"

"Yes, Your Honor," Sam said.

"Ms. Fulks, is the State prepared to proceed?"

"We are, Your Honor."

Sam had explained what was going to happen at this hearing to Tommy earlier in the day. "Under Wyoming law, Tommy, when a defendant is charged with a felony, he has the right to a preliminary hearing," he had begun.

"What's that?" Tommy had asked sullenly.

"It's a hearing to determine if there is probable cause to bind you over to district court—the higher court having jurisdiction over felonies—for further proceedings," Sam responded. When Tommy looked at him blankly, he continued. "Probable cause means that an ordinary person could reasonably believe that the offense was committed and that you did it."

"But I didn't do it," Tommy interjected. "And I've been in jail for weeks already."

"I understand," Sam said. "But this hearing is not to determine whether you did it; it's only to determine if you might or could have done it. In other words, for the State to prevail today and bind you over, they don't have to prove your guilt beyond a reasonable doubt, but only that a crime was committed, and it is reasonable to believe that you did it. Do you understand that?"

"Hell, no. I didn't do it, Sam!" Tommy said.

"Tommy, I hear you. But that's not what this is about. In this hearing the State will present evidence, then I will cross-examine the State's witnesses —okay?"

"You need to rip them a new one, Sam."

"Tommy, I'm not your big brother. I'm your lawyer. There are rules."

"Screw the rules, Sam! I'm innocent!"

"Tommy, pipe down!" Sam exclaimed. Then, softening, "Tommy, I hear you, okay? I know what you want. You want out, but I cannot do that right now. And you aren't helping things by sounding off and acting like a hothead. I need you to keep your poise. Do you understand that?"

"Put me on the stand. Let me talk to the judge. He'll see—"

"No."

"Damn it, Sam!" Tommy banged his fist on the metal table between them, rattling the chains on his wrists.

Sam didn't respond, so Tommy sat sullenly staring at the table between them. After a moment, Sam looked at his client. "Tommy, look at me."

Tommy looked up at Sam. His eyes were red, his face was blotchy, and he looked tired.

"I need you to suck it up right now, Tommy," Sam said. "A lot of this is theater. I need you to go into the courtroom today looking confident and ready to show your innocence."

"But you just told me we're not going to do that," Tommy said.

"Not yet. It's not the time. I need you to trust me, and act like we've got this in the bag. And when Howard binds you over, which he will, I need you to act like it's no big deal."

Now, two hours later, Tommy was holding up his end. He was sitting up straight and appeared to be listening closely as Howard called the case.

"Counsel, before we begin, are there matters preliminary?"

"No, Judge," Ann said.

Sam had spent the last few weeks attempting to convince Tommy to change his plea to one of not guilty by reason of mental illness, but Tommy had steadfastly refused. Under the rules, Sam could go ahead and ask for an evaluation of his client. Now, taking a last long look at Tommy, Sam decided against it.

"Mr. Johnstone?"

"No, Your Honor," Sam said.

"Thank you, Mr. Johnstone." Howard turned to Ann, ordering her to call her first witness.

"Your Honor, the State of Wyoming calls Detective Kenneth Polson."

After swearing an oath, Punch took the stand.

"Mr. Polson, please state your full legal name for the record," Ann said.

"Kenneth Polson—but everyone calls me Punch, ma'am."

"Why is that, Mr. Polson?"

"Well, I got in a lot of fights as a kid," Punch said. "Wasn't much good at it, neither."

The capacity audience briefly tittered but quieted under Howard's glare.

"Mr. Polson, are you employed?"

"Yes, ma'am."

"What do you do?"

"I am a detective with the Custer Police Department, assigned to the major crimes unit."

"And how long have you been assigned to the major crimes unit?"

"Five years."

"What did you do before that?"

"I was a patrol officer."

"And how long did you do that?"

"Oh, I suppose it was three or four years. I can't remember exactly. I started after I got out of the Army. I did a year or so as a detention officer, and then went to the law enforcement academy, then out on patrol."

"So, you started as a detention officer at the jail, spent a year or so doing that, then went to the law enforcement academy, and then came back to Custer County?"

"That's right. Then I was a patrol officer, and then I made detective."

"Your Honor," Sam said as he stood. "The prosecution is repeating itself. The defendant will stipulate Detective Polson is who he said he is, and that he lost a few fights."

Again, the audience laughed nervously. "Mr. Johnstone, please be seated," Howard said. "Your objection is overruled. Ms. Fulks, please continue."

"Thank you, Your Honor," Ann said. "Detective Polson, were you ever in the service?"

"Yeah, I was an MP." She was nervous, Sam knew, and working from an outline without listening to the answers.

"Where did you do that?"

"Primarily at Fort Drum, New York. Spent a little time in the Middle East, as well."

"And before that?"

"High school."

"Where?"

"Here."

"Did you graduate?"

"Barely," Polson replied, glancing at Howard, who was not amused.

"Were you on duty as a member of the major crimes unit on or about October 31?"

"No, I was on call."

"And on that date, were you called to a residence on Custer Avenue?"

"Yes."

"Please tell the court what happened."

"I was on call and had gone home a couple of hours earlier. Was home and got a call. It was Officer Ron Baker. He told me we had a stiff, er, dead person at that address."

"And what did you do then?"

"I got up, showered, and went to that address."

"And what did you find?"

"Well, first I met with the first officer on the scene and asked him what he had found."

"What did he tell you?"

"He told me that he had been asked to do a welfare check on a female named Smith, because she had missed a couple of court appearances. So he went to her residence and looked around. There was no answer, so he decided to get in the house and see what was going on."

"What happened next?"

"The officer broke a pane of glass on the back door, reached through, unlocked the door, and effected entry into the home. Said he knew something was wrong. Went upstairs and found her."

"Found who?"

"Found a woman we later identified as C. Emily Smith, lawyer."

"What condition was she in?"

"She was dead."

"How did the officer know?" Ann asked.

Tommy leaned over to Sam. "Shouldn't you be objecting or something?"

"Just hang tight and let me listen to what's being said," Sam said. "I promise I'm on this."

"Okay."

"You just know," Punch said.

"How?"

"Well, she was lying on the floor with a cut across her throat like this"—he gestured with a slashing motion across his own neck—"and more blood than . . . well, there was a lot. It was on the walls, ceiling, everywhere."

"What happened then?"

"The officer called the desk sergeant, who called me. The officer secured the scene and I showed up."

"The scene you mentioned—is that in Custer County, Wyoming?"

"Yes."

"Okay, so what happened next?"

"We processed the scene forensically and began our investigation."

"How did you do that?"

"Well, first we secured the scene—literally blocked it off so only people known to us, like crime scene photographers, forensics people, etc., could get in. Then, we let those experts do their thing. After they had done their job, I went through the scene to see if there was anything I could find out."

"And what did you find out?"

"Well, as I mentioned, there was a lot of blood. She'd almost been decapitated—I'm sorry," he said, when he heard the crowd gasp.

"Go on."

"And at some point, I saw blood in the kitchen, which I thought was significant."

"Why?"

"Well, because the way the victim had been attacked, there's no way her blood would have gotten into the kitchen unless someone else put it there. I mean, she never moved—she couldn't have. So, the blood in the kitchen, I figured, was likely someone else's."

"What else?"

"Well, the forensics folks later told me she'd had sex prior to being killed."

"Was she raped?"

"Inconclusive on that, but they found, uh, semen."

"Were you able to determine whose semen it was?"

"Some of it."

"Some?"

"Some belonged to Tommy Olsen, the defendant."

"And the rest?"

"Unknown donor at this time."

Ann allowed the murmuring to die under Howard's scowl before she continued. "What else?"

"Well, the fingerprint folks went over the whole house, gathering prints. They found quite a few. And we had Emily's—Ms. Smith's—prints, so we were able to tell which prints were hers and which were not."

"And did you find prints in the house that did not belong to Ms. Smith?"

"Our print guys did. Yeah. You bet."

"And were you later able to obtain identification of those prints?"

"Most of them, yeah. The ones we found belonging to the defendant were all over."

She interrupted him. "I'm sorry, what do you mean by 'all over?' All over her?"

"No. All over the house. On the bedposts, in the bathroom, on a bottle of wine and glasses in the living room."

"When did you identify the fingerprints?"

"I can't recall, exactly."

"Would it help refresh your memory if I showed you your report?"

"It would."

Ann looked to Howard for guidance. He turned to Sam. "Any objection, Mr. Johnstone?"

"No objection, Judge."

"Your Honor, may I approach the witness?" Ann inquired, holding a sheaf of papers in her hand.

"You may."

Ann approached Punch and handed him a copy of his report. While she returned to the podium, he perused it quickly and then looked up at her. "It looks like we got Emily's, er, Ms. Smith's fingerprints identified the next day," he said. "We got the others identified around the middle of November. There's still at least two sets we haven't identified."

"So," Ann asked, looking at Sam, who was scribbling on a legal pad. "After the defendant's fingerprints were identified, what did you do?"

"Well, I spoke with Mr. Olsen and asked him if he knew Ms. Smith, and if he'd come in and talk with me."

"What day was that?"

"That would have been the day after we identified his prints," Punch said. "I remember because I got the call we'd identified his prints while I was watching the Broncos playing the Chiefs."

"And did he?"

"Did he what?"

"Well, both. Did he admit knowing her?"

"Yes. Said she was his lawyer."

"And did he willingly come in to meet with you?"

"You bet. Came right in."

"And what happened then?"

"Well, he denied knowing anything about Ms. Smith's death, but said he'd been in her house and they'd had consensual sex."

"And so what did you do?"

"Well, at the time I let him go. Honestly, his story seemed to be standing up, he had an explanation for being there, and I just didn't think I had enough to hold him."

"But at some point, you changed your mind?"

"Yes."

"Why was that?"

"Well, we already had a match on his fingerprints in the kitchen and elsewhere in the house—that was bad for him. He had already admitted to being with her, his truck was seen in the neighborhood about that time, and then the DNA came back as a match with his from the federal database."

"Anything else make him a suspect?" Ann asked.

"Well, his name was in her scheduling book, and after speaking with him it was clear that he was the last one we could find who'd seen her alive, and, well, he had military training and knew how to use a blade."

"How did you find that out?"

"He told me."

"Okay. Anything else?"

"He lost several ranks in the Corps because he hit a woman."

"Move to strike," Sam said. "Hearsay, irrelevant, unfairly prejudicial—"

"Overruled," Howard said. "For what it's worth."

"Anything else?" Ann asked.

"Well, like I said, we got a warrant to search his house, and we found a bayonet matching what the forensics guys told us to look for."

"When did you get the warrant?"

"It was November 13. I remember because it was Friday the 13th."

"So, you searched Mr. Olsen's house under the auspices of a warrant?"

"Uh, yes. We had a warrant."

"The bayonet, I think you called it. What is a bayonet?"

"Well, it's sort of a knife."

"What do you mean, 'sort of?'"

"Well, you can hold it in your hand and use it as a knife, or you can attach it to the barrel or body of a military rifle and use it that way," Punch answered, gesturing with his hands.

"Was there anything of interest found?"

"Yes."

"What was that?"

"The blade was missing a small piece, which was interesting because the medical examiner had found some metal in the deceased's neck area during the autopsy. And there was blood on the bayonet. It turned out to be Ms. Smith's."

"How did you determine that?"

"We sent it to the lab. Didn't take long to get a match because we already had a lot of her blood on hand." An audible groan emanated from the audience. "Sorry," he added.

"What did you do then?"

"We matched some of the prints on the bayonet to the defendant."

"And then?"

"I went back to my office and put together an affidavit and an arrest warrant."

"And then what?"

"Well, then I got it reviewed by you, and eventually it got signed by Judge Howard. I'd had Mr. Olsen followed, so we arrested him as he was trying to leave town."

"He was trying to leave?"

"Yes."

"Did he say anything?"

"He said he didn't do it."

"Anything else?"

"He told me to kiss his ass."

Ann waited a moment for the laughter to dissipate. "Anything happen since that time to make you think you got the right guy?"

"Yes."

"What, Detective?"

"Well, he got in a fight with another inmate in a holding cell. According to the victim of that attack, Mr. Olsen here told him that, 'He'd get his, just like that bitch got hers.'"

Again, the small crowd gasped.

Tommy leaned over to Sam and whispered fiercely, "That's bullshit. I said—"

"Not now, Tommy," Sam said. He gave some thought to objecting, but because hearsay was admissible, it wouldn't do any good. Besides, you can't "un-ring the bell," as the old trial adage went, and Howard had already heard it. An objection would give Ann the opportunity to restate what was said, so that anyone who might not have heard it—to include the reporters present—would get a second chance.

"Your Honor, may I have a moment?" Ann asked, wanting the last point to sink in for a moment before she yielded the podium.

"Of course," Howard said, staring down the audience members to ensure silence.

Ann appeared to consult briefly with Nice, who always sat second chair during major trials. Second chair allowed her to be present and take partial credit for a good result while shielding herself if everything went south. "Your Honor, the State has no further questions."

"Mr. Johnstone, care to cross-examine?" Judge Howard asked.

"Your Honor, could I consult briefly with my client?"

"Make it quick."

Sam and Tommy consulted for a couple of minutes. Sam didn't have a lot of questions to ask. When it came to preliminary hearings, the defense was at a decided disadvantage. There wasn't a lot he could do beyond locking down some key testimony.

"Any cross-examination, Mr. Johnstone?" Howard asked impatiently.

"Yes, Your Honor."

Howard sighed and stared at Sam levelly. "Then get to it, son."

Sam moved to the podium. "Detective Polson, did you know the deceased?"

"No, sir."

"Where exactly was that bayonet located?" He skipped to another subject, just to keep the witness off balance.

"It was in his garage, in a toolbox."

"Does the garage door lock?"

"Yes."

"How did you get in?"

"I got the combination for the automatic door opener—there's a pad on the garage door frame—from the defendant."

"And you just opened it and went in?"

"I had both a warrant and his consent."

"Anyone with that combination could've done the same?"

"Sure."

"Who else had the combination?"

"Well, I guess I'm not sure. The defendant, I suppose his wife, although she moved out a coupla months ago, he says. Unless he changed it. His kids, maybe."

"And maybe some other people, too—true?"

"I don't know. Couldn't speculate."

"Why were you looking for a bayonet?"

"I was not necessarily looking for a bayonet; I was looking for a large knife that could have made the kind of wound the medical examiner described. But we knew he was a former Marine, so it didn't surprise me. Jensen said he came across the bayonet and it looked like it might fit the bill. Plus, it had what looked like blood on it."

"Did your men find a scabbard anywhere in the house?"

"Yeah. The scabbard was in his gun safe. They found that first."

"How did you get access to the gun safe?"

"The defendant gave me the combination."

"Willingly?"

"Well, I explained to him that if he would not give me the combination, then I would have someone drill the safe. My men found the empty scabbard in there, so they started looking around and then found the bayonet in the toolbox."

"Does the toolbox lock?"

"It does, but it wasn't locked."

"So, anyone could have gotten in there?"

"Yes."

"Do you know why he would keep the bayonet anywhere other than in the scabbard?"

"Objection. Calls for speculation," Ann said. It was a harmless question, but Sam was getting too comfortable.

"Your Honor, I'm not asking the witness to speculate," Sam said. "I'm merely asking if he knows. I can re-phrase, if necessary."

"I'll hear it. Answer the question," Howard instructed.

"No."

"Detective Polson, how many sets of fingerprints did you find in Emily Smith's home?"

"At least six."

"At least?"

"Well, the lab boys said they can identify six separate sets for sure. There are others around that are smeared or incomplete or whatever," Punch said. "They can't tell if some are from one of those six people or not."

"How many have been identified to this point?"

"Four. The deceased, her mother, her housekeeper, and the defendant."

"So, you checked the bayonet for fingerprints?"

"Yes."

"And what did you find?"

"There were two sets of prints on it. The defendant's, and another, unidentified set."

"Does that unidentified set match any of the unidentified sets in the decedent's house?"

"Objection," Ann said.

"Overruled," Howard said. "You may answer."

"I'm told it is not a match."

"So there are three sets of unidentified prints that are relevant to this case?" Sam asked.

"Objection; not a lawyer," Ann said.

"Your Honor, it's a prelim—"

"Sustained. Mr. Johnstone, I see where you are going. But you and I both know that line of questioning is not going to be dispositive given the limited purposes of this hearing."

Sam looked at Howard for a long minute, then turned back to Punch to try another tactic. "Detective, you said you found evidence that she had sexual relations prior to her death?"

"Yes, as I said—"

"And you said my client was not the only man she had sex with immediately prior to her death?"

"Your Honor, I object!" Ann said. "Misstates the evidence, and the deceased is not on trial here."

"Mr. Johnstone, you know well that a preliminary hearing is not a discovery device. I am willing to allow you a 'lap around the lake,' figuratively speaking, but be careful. No fishing," he warned. Then he turned to Punch. "But I will overrule the objection. Answer the question."

"No," said the detective. "As I mentioned before, two samples of semen were located."

"And they belonged to different men?"

"Yes."

"And you identified only one sample?"

"Yes."

A thought came to Sam's mind. He considered his options, then decided he might as well get this out in the open. "And one sample matches my client?"

"So I'm told. I'm not an expert."

"But the other sample is that of another, unknown man?"

"That's my understanding. We collected the DNA from someone other than Defendant Olsen on her bed sheets," Punch said. "But we haven't been able to match it."

"So, you have matched only one sample to a donor?" Sam asked.

"DNA guys tell me one sample is from Tommy Olsen."

"But you've no match for the other?"

"No," Polson said.

"But you're working on it?"

"Yes."

"How long might it take?"

"Well, it could be quick—if we had a potential donor or suspect or whatever and could get a sample of his DNA. Maybe weeks in that situation."

"And if not?"

"Well, that could take a long time. It would be prohibitively expensive, and—"

"And?"

"Well, it'd be like finding a needle in a haystack."

While awaiting Punch's answer, Sam leaned down and whispered in Tommy's ear, and then listened as Tommy whispered back. Sam thought for a moment, then returned to the podium. "Judge, I have no further questions for this witness."

"Detective Polson, you can step down," Howard said. "Ms. Fulks, any other witnesses?"

"No, Your Honor."

"Well, then, I'll hear from each of you before I announce my decision."

Ann stood and addressed the court perfunctorily. "Your Honor, the State has made a sufficient showing that a crime was committed, and that the defendant is the person who committed it. We ask the court to bind Mr. Olsen over to the district court for further proceedings."

Howard nodded, then turned his attention to Sam. "Mr. Johnstone, any response?"

"Briefly, Your Honor."

"That would be appreciated."

"Your Honor, the State has shown by a preponderance of the evidence that a crime was committed, but it has failed to show probable cause that my client committed it. There are simply too many unanswered questions regarding the so-called evidence. My client, during his interview with Detective Polson, admitted he's been in the house, that he had consensual sex with the victim. He explained the presence of his blood. There are unexplained fingerprints, and evidence that she had sex with another man at some point—"

"Mr. Johnstone, don't you agree that goes to the weight of the evidence, and is not particularly relevant to this hearing?"

"Your Honor, again, I would ask the court to heed—"

"Mr. Johnstone, I'm heeding. I simply don't place the kind of weight on your argument that you do. Anything else?" he asked pointedly.

"No, Judge."

"Thank you both," Howard said, then looked at Tommy. "Mr. Olsen, in a hearing like this, the State's burden is set at 'probable cause.' As I said earlier, the State's task today was merely to show that a crime has been committed, and that a reasonable person with the information before him could conclude that you committed that crime. Having heard and considered the evidence here today, this court finds that there is probable cause to believe that on or about October 31, in Custer County, Wyoming, the crime of first-degree murder, a violation of Wyoming Statute Section 6-2-101, was committed, and that you were the person responsible. Mr. Olsen, your case will be transferred to district court for all further proceedings."

He turned to Ann. "Ms. Fulks, are there other matters to be addressed in connection with this defendant?"

"No, Your Honor."

"Mr. Johnstone?"

"Yes, Your Honor, I'd like to revisit the issue of bond. I—"

"Denied."

"Your Honor, we've heard information that brings into question whether my client—"

"Denied, Mr. Johnstone. I am not going to hear it. You can take the motion up at district court."

"But, Your Honor—"

"Is there anything further to come before the court?" Howard asked, looking around the courtroom. "If not, we'll be in recess." He pounded his gavel and left the courtroom.

The crowd filed out, abuzz with discussion regarding the day's events. After his client left with court security, Sam sat alone at the defense table, reviewing in his mind the judge's various rulings. He'd told Tommy he'd see him tonight and explain the events more fully, but right now he needed a drink.

31

"The preliminary hearing went well," Ann began. "Got him bound over—"

"Any idiot could do that," Daniels said, looking through a cabinet. "Shit! Where are those little glasses?"

"We can't have this talk, you know," she said.

"What do you mean?"

"I mean any communication between us about the case is a violation of ethics rules. You know that."

"Seriously? You want to lecture me about ethics?" Daniels opened his desk drawer and rummaged around. "I thought I had a couple of those little airplane bottles in here. You want a drink?"

"Your Honor, I'm uncomfortable with this. The more time I spend in your chambers, the more likely it is that people are going to talk," Ann said, shaking her head to decline the offered bottle in the judge's hand. "I just don't think it is very smart."

"And I don't give a shit what you think. You need to do what you are told. I thought I made that clear the last time we had this little discussion."

"I just—"

"Ann, you don't understand, do you? You think it's an accident that you got this job? That you were assigned to prosecute this case because of the great work you have done?" Daniels paused to take a swig. "Because if you do, let me make something clear: you are trying this case because you are the best of a lousy bunch of prosecutors. That's it. Do you understand?"

"I understand."

"Good. Now, because I don't want to have to try this sonuvabitch twice due to your inexperience, tell me what is going on in this case. I heard Johnstone freaked out during the initial appearance."

"Yeah, he did. It was weird. An easel fell in the back of the courtroom, and I think he had a flashback or something. The guy's not right." She recited the recent events of the case, to include the status of the probable witnesses, the evidence that she intended to present, as well as an outline of her trial strategy. Daniels listened and sipped the whiskey from a plastic cup he had found in his desk, occasionally nodding in agreement or furrowing his brow in apparent disagreement.

"How was he during the prelim?"

"He was fine."

"What questions did he ask?" When she had finished explaining, Daniels asked, "What do you think Sam's strategy will be?"

"Well, if I were him—"

"Ann, that is a different question. I'm asking you what you think Sam will do."

"Well, as I understand it, he has already tried to get his client to cop to an insanity plea. That failed. So he really only has three choices. He can use the 'some other dude did it' defense, or he can try to justify it as self-defense, or he can try to show that what happened was not premeditated. I think he'll see that self-defense is a loser, so I would expect to see him defending with an eye toward demonstrating that his guy killed Emily as the result of an accident. But maybe he'll try some sort of disabled vet thing."

"Will he file a motion to have an examination done?"

"I thought he would ask for one before the prelim, didn't you?"

"I did. But maybe his client won't go for it."

"In his shoes, I would have," Ann said.

"Well his client probably won't agree to it," Daniels said. "What is your plan to attack those defenses?" he asked, changing subjects.

"Well, actually, I am still working on aspects of my own case. I have not yet had the opportunity to look at ways to present my case to preclude his defenses."

"You damn sure better start! You've got about ninety days to get ready. You need to be ready as soon as possible, and then you can refine from there."

"I understand."

32

On a Sunday afternoon late in January, Sam blew on his fingers to warm them and tried to tie a size twenty blue-winged olive pattern onto the tiny tippet he had affixed to his leader for that purpose. After a couple minutes of struggle, he realized that he had dropped his cheaters in one of his many vest pockets. After rummaging through the vest, he finally located them, got the fly tied to the tippet, and was ready at last. After double-checking to ensure that the vest was packed with water, beef jerky, sunflower seeds, a book of matches, his flask, and a cigar, he locked the door of his truck and set off across the snow-covered hillside for the stream.

The day had dawned clear and cold, no clouds in sight. The water was somewhat high, but surprisingly clear given a recent warming spell and the subsequent runoff. The temperature was just about freezing, and Sam anticipated a hatch of some sort if the wind stayed down long enough for the sun's rays to warm the water's surface.

He sat on the bank, lit the cigar, and looked around. Across the stream in a stand of cottonwood were half a dozen turkeys. Seeing him, they had closed ranks and were now peering at him, attempting to discern his motive. On the hillside, a pair of mule deer looked down at him. Apparently satisfied he meant them no harm, they shook their huge ears and browsed off. Sam listened to the soft murmur of the water and scanned the small stream for signs of fish. He didn't see any shadows out of place, any "noses" indicating feeding trout, or swirls in the water that might indicate subsurface feeding going on. In short, he didn't see anything that would indicate fishing was worth his while. But he'd come to fish and was intent on doing just that.

He cast upstream maybe twenty-five feet or so, a medium-length cast designed to probe a small pool formed by a trickle of water pouring over the gap between two large boulders. The cast met with success, and less than thirty seconds later he was removing the fly from a small rainbow trout's mouth. "I'm in the books," he said aloud.

For the next ninety minutes, he fished his way upstream. At this time of year and in this water, the fish were slowed by their core temperatures and did not react particularly quickly to the appearance of Sam's fly. For that reason, he eschewed fishing in the rapids and focused his efforts instead on the small pools in the stream. Walking carefully along the bank, he looked ahead for likely spots and then maneuvered into position where his left-handed casts could place the fly on the water.

The leg was causing him pain, so as the sun started to sink behind the mountain range to his west, he decided to call it a day. He had kept a couple of fish for dinner, stopping to clean them using his pocketknife. When he'd finished, he placed them in a small plastic bag that he kept in his vest and commenced the hike out. It was dark when he reached the truck, and he stumbled around until he was able to start the vehicle and turn on the headlights. He then dressed in the glow of the brake lights, walked around his parking spot to ensure that he hadn't forgotten anything, and departed the area. He'd spent time by himself, caught some fish, gotten a little exercise, seen some country, and avoided all contact with human beings. Success.

"Sam, you've got to get me out of here," Tommy said. He was unwrapping a candy bar Sam had brought him. "This place is driving me nuts."

"Tommy, I can't do that. You know that. Judge Howard denied bond weeks ago when we had the preliminary hearing. I'll ask Judge Daniels to reconsider. But it's a longshot. I know you don't like it, but it's almost certain you're gonna have to ride this out until after the trial."

"Then what?" Tommy asked, taking a huge bite from the candy bar.

"Then, if you're acquitted, you'll be free to go."

"And if I'm not acquitted?"

"We can't think that way. We need to remain positive."

"We?"

"Tommy, I'm in this with you. As much as I can be. As much as anyone could be."

"I know that, Sam," Tommy said. He stood and threw the wrapper in a small trash can in the corner. "I'm just getting a little squirrely, is all."

"How are they treating you?"

"Who?"

"Anyone."

"The other inmates are okay, ever since the incident with what's-his-name. I keep pretty much to myself. The guards . . . well, I think they just try and stay above it all. Basically, they're all authoritarians. Control freaks —you know what I mean?"

"I do."

"I mean, most of 'em, they're just doing the jail thing until they get a slot at the law enforcement academy. They're okay. But the ones who like this shit—overseeing inmates—I mean, who would lock himself in with a bunch of criminals for twelve hours a day, right?"

Sam smiled.

"Sam, what do you think?" Tommy asked.

"Tommy, I can't tell you what's going to happen," Sam began. "I'm doing everything I can. We have about three months to get ready. But there's an alternative. You give any thought to pleading out?"

"Screw that, Sam. Told you last time you asked. I'm not crazy, and I didn't do it!"

"Tommy! Lower your voice. Look, I hear you, okay. But a plea is the only way—the *only* way—you can be absolutely sure you don't end up with a life sentence or worse. Just say the word and I'll talk with Ann. Maybe she'll take second-degree. You'd be looking at maybe twenty years."

"Twenty years! No way! I didn't do it. When the jury hears my story—"

"I've told you before: juries are made up of people. People make mistakes."

Tommy was out of his chair, pacing the small conference room. "That's not going to happen. It can't happen."

"Tommy, let me ask you something."

"What's that?"

"As long as we've been together, I've never heard you talk about your wife. I need to know about you and her. It's Becky, right?"

"Right. What's to know? We got married after I'd been out of high school a couple of years—right before I enlisted. I took her to Quantico. She didn't like the humidity and being away from her mom at all, so when I got orders to deploy, I took a couple weeks of leave and moved her back so she could be near her folks."

"How'd it go after that?"

"You know, Sam." Tommy was staring at the cinderblock wall. "You first get in-country they got all kinds of USO facilities, and you call home and talk about the kids and stuff happening back here. But as time goes by, you get more and more wound up with patrols and recovery and ops planning, and so the calls get fewer and fewer. Meanwhile, she's back here having to run the household by herself. Then one day, you're on the phone and the wife is bitching about something that isn't important and you make the mistake of putting it in perspective for her and she gets pissed off, and then you get pissed off, and then the whole passive-aggressive thing starts. Next thing you know you're calling only on a kid's birthday or a holiday and then it goes downhill from there."

Sam watched Tommy in silence. There was nothing to say.

"Got back and realized I'd spent a couple years doing stuff no one around here understood or wanted to hear about. My first sergeant had recommended I talk with someone at the VA when I got back, but I said, 'Screw that.' I think maybe I kinda held some stuff in. Started drinking too much, and, well, Becky gave me an ultimatum one night and I guess I thought about it and felt like she was hassling me for no reason."

Tommy was pacing again. "I got on her phone and seen she'd been talking with this guy we went to high school with while I was gone. You believe that shit? I'm ten thousand miles away humping a hundred-pound ruck, dodging goddamned bullets and IEDs, and she's back here talking with some pencil-necked banker dude who was on the fucking debate team. And it ain't like she's perfect, neither. She got arrested down in New Orleans years ago for drunk and disorderly."

Sam continued to watch Tommy.

"So," Tommy continued. "One night she took the kids and filed for divorce. I honestly thought things were gonna be okay, that we could do this—what's the word? 'Amicably,' I think—and then she tells me she wants the car, the house, everything, plus full custody of the kids. Said I was 'dangerous.' Bullshit on that. I ain't giving her everything I worked for while she sat back here on her fat ass and collected my check. So I lawyered up with Emily the week after she packed up the kids. I called her bluff, man."

"How did you come up with the money for a retainer?"

"Oh, you'll love this. I get a little disability check from the VA, right? I've been putting that in a separate account every month. I'd been planning on buying a boat when I got enough. Even had one picked out. Then this shit happens, so instead of buying a goddamned boat that I figured she'd get half of, I had to use it to pay an attorney. Took the whole wad."

"I'm gonna need to talk with Becky at some point," Sam said. "Probably soon."

"Why?"

"Well, it might be important. Do you think she'd agree to come to the trial? She didn't come to the prelim, did she?"

"I didn't see her. Why?"

"Because I think it would be good if the jurors saw her there. They'll find out about the pending divorce, sure, but if she was there every day it would give the appearance that she still supports you, still believes in you. Think she would?"

"I dunno," Tommy said. He was sitting in the plastic chair again, staring at the floor.

"When's the last time you spoke with her?"

"Well, I dunno, Sam. Before Emily got killed, for sure. I mean, I was pissed off and she was ragging my ass. She wouldn't let me see my kids!"

"I'm gonna talk with her, Tommy. I'll see what she has to say." Sam stood and extended his hand.

"Okay," Tommy said. "And Sam?"

"Yes?"

"When you talk with her, tell her . . . tell her . . . well, tell Becky I said hi."

"Will do." Sam pushed the button to summon the guard. "Take care of yourself," he said as he left.

"Boss, what's going on?" Jensen asked. "You're not yourself." He pulled a donut from the box on the table between them. They were in the break room at the station. Punch was pouring himself a cup of coffee.

"What do you mean?"

"Well, you've been a little short. Baker said you bit his ass over nothing. That's not like you."

"Baker needs to quit being such a candy-ass," Punch said. He took a sip from his cup. "But I'll tell you what: I am irritable. It's the Olsen case."

"Why? You got the right guy. He got bound over. Trial starts here in a couple of months, assuming his lawyer don't plead him out."

"I don't like loose ends."

"Well, no one does, boss. What loose ends are you talking about?"

Punch stood, walked to the window, and looked outside. It was early spring. In a lot of places, the grass would be turning green, trees would start to put out leaves, and birds would be returning. Not here. Here, it was clear and cold and looked not unlike it did in October. "The three shot glasses—one with a print we can't match. The semen from an unknown male. The unknown set of prints on the vase and an unknown print on the murder weapon. All of that gives Johnstone an opening."

"Olsen's the guy, boss."

"I know he's the guy. But those loose ends give reasonable doubt. If Johnstone's any good—and I think he might be—he could exploit those loose ends and walk his guy."

"So, what do you want to do about it?"

"We need to tie this up," Punch said, rubbing his eyes, "so I can sleep again."

33

Sam was in an examining room at the VA clinic in Custer when his counselor appeared on the desktop's monitor; he didn't even know where the counselor was logging in from.

"Mr. Johnstone, my name is Bob Martinez. I'm a counselor with the VA. How are you today?"

"I'm well."

"Really? Then why are you here?"

Sam sat quietly, thinking about it. "I'm here because I'm all screwed up. I can't sleep, I'm drinking and quaffing pain pills and having nightmares and . . . well . . . I had a little episode a while back and it scared everyone around me."

"Scare you?"

"Yeah."

"Need a change?"

"I do."

"Need some help?"

"I guess."

Martinez smiled. "Of course you do. If you had been capable of fixing yourself, you would have done it by now, right?"

"Right."

Martinez was looking at another screen. "You were a captain, am I right?"

"Yeah."

"Lost a leg?"

"Yes, sir."

"Call me Bob. Now, tell me about losing that leg."

"What do you want to know?"

"Everything."

"I don't like to talk about it."

"No shit." The abruptness of the counselor's reaction made Sam laugh out loud for the first time in days. "Tell me what happened," Martinez said. "All of it."

For the next thirty minutes, Sam recounted in detail that day in 2007. When he finished, he said, "Bob, I know you don't understand—"

"Oh, I get it," Martinez said, waving a prosthetic hand dismissively. Seeing Sam's surprise, he made a show of looking at the device. "This? Oh, I lost my arm in Kuwait in 1991. 2nd Brigade, 1st Infantry Division."

"The Big Red One," Sam said, referring to the division's nickname.

"If you're gonna be one," Martinez began.

"—be a big red one," Sam finished, and they both laughed.

"I'm no hero like you are, "Martinez said. "Got my arm caught between the back of an Abrams tank and a track recovery vehicle right after the war ended."

"Ouch!" Sam said. "You gave it up, Bob."

"I did. See you Thursday."

Sam smiled again. "This just might work," he thought as he walked to his car.

Punch sat back and rubbed his neck, then removed his readers and rubbed his eyes. It was ten p.m. and he'd been working his way through more than a thousand pages of printouts from Emily's computer. For the past couple of days, he'd been spending an hour or so every night working his way through the contents of her desktop—calendar, contacts, email, and the like. He'd had a young officer go through her social media accounts months ago, but it hadn't turned up anything of significance. Following Olsen's arrest, of course, the review of her desktop had gone to the back burner, as new cases arose and took precedence. The contents had only been brought to his attention when Ann had passed on a request for pre-trial discovery from Johnstone seeking copies of all electronic information in the State's possession relevant to the case. It was prudent, of course, to review everything before he kicked it out to Ann to pass along.

He took a bite of his sandwich and continued to scan the left-most column containing the senders' names. Because Emily had both her personal and professional email forwarded to her desktop, the volume was incredible. Some of the retailers sent her more than one email per day. Coupons, advertisements, solicitations, old friends staying in touch. Nothing appearing relevant to the case had caught his eye. Her contacts were apparently mundane, as well. He knew many of the names, which included most of the attorneys and judges in the region. The appointment feature showed about what you might expect, with a couple of exceptions. She had calendared a couple of appointments with Judge Daniels and several with Judge Howard over the months leading up to her death. "Seems odd," he mused, downing the last bite of his sandwich.

"What's that, sir?" Jensen asked from directly behind Punch.

"Jesus, Jensen! I didn't know you were still here! You scared the hell out of me!"

"Sorry. What's odd, boss?"

"Emily Smith. She had a lot of appointments with a couple of the judges prior to her death."

"Which ones?"

"Daniels and Howard."

"Daniels seems like an ass."

"Well, he's a judge."

"Yeah, but even for a judge," Jensen said. He looked at Punch, clearly thinking. "You know, I'm just gonna say . . ."

"What?"

"It's just gossip."

"Spit it out, man!"

"A while back there was a rumor going around."

"I'm listening."

"Rumor was that the lawyer and Judge Howard were a thing."

"You have got to be shitting me."

"Seriously!"

"Jensen, why would a young, attractive woman have an affair with an old . . . well, judge?"

"I ain't sayin' they had an affair. I'm just saying I heard they had a thing."

"I can't see it," Punch said. "On the other hand, why would she have that many meetings with judges? One, who would want to; and two, you can't talk about a case without the other party's lawyer there. What was she doing?"

"I'm just telling you what I heard, boss. Take it for what it's worth," Jensen said. "I gotta go check on Baker. He called in on his way to the park for some sort of disturbance—typical Friday night stuff, but dispatch hasn't heard from him in a while."

After Jensen left, Punch stared at the stack of papers in front of him, recalling the picture of a drunken Howard with several lawyers—including Emily—he'd seen in her home. "No way," he said at last.

34

"Thank you for seeing me on such short notice," Sam said, entering the small living room. Becky Olsen closed the door behind Sam and gestured to an overstuffed chair. She walked over to the couch, moved some toys, and sat down, crossing her ankles and looking steadily at Sam. "Can I get you something to drink?"

"No, thank you, Mrs. Olsen, I'll just be a few minutes."

"Becky."

"Okay, Becky," Sam began. "I'd like to ask you a few questions, if that's okay."

"Sure," she said. "I'm going to get myself a beer, though. You sure you don't want anything?"

"Little early for me," Sam lied.

"Well, me too," Becky said from the kitchen. But my mom's got the kids today, so what the hell." She returned from the kitchen with a bottle of beer, sat, and took a long pull from it. "Ask away."

"How did you meet Tommy?"

"Oh, we went to high school together. He was three years older. Didn't know each other much, but after I graduated, we ran into each other at a party and started going out. He was big and strong and I thought he was everything a girl could want." She finished the beer and rose. "You sure you don't want a beer?"

"I'm sure. Was he?"

"Was he what?" she asked from the kitchen. Sam heard the refrigerator door open and close.

"Everything you wanted?"

"I was popular then," Becky said. "Cheerleader, even runner-up for homecoming queen." She was looking in a mirror over the couch. "Of course, I weighed thirty pounds less."

"And Tommy?" Sam prodded.

"Things were fine to begin with," Becky said. "But then I got pregnant and we didn't have money for medical bills. Tommy ran into a recruiter at a softball game, I think. He came home all excited and told me he was going to be a Marine and that would solve all our problems. And it did help. I mean, we had insurance and a steady check and all that. But I hated being a Marine wife. 'Cause that's what you are when your husband's in the Corps —a wife. A dependent."

Sam waited while she took a few gulps from the beer.

"So, when he got orders to deploy, I told him I wanted to come home, so we came home and he got me set up here." She finished the beer. "He was gone for more than a year, you know?"

"I heard."

"And so it was just me and the kids. I was scared and lonely. No one understands what it's like to be a wife in that situation. And then he came back, and he expected to be in charge of us just like we were in his squad or platoon or whatever. But we're not troops," she said, her voice trailing off.

"He was angry," she continued. "And he was drinking, and he'd get quiet and just sit in his chair and brood. Then all at once he'd yell for me and the kids to shut up and get out of here. The kids were scared, and I didn't know what to do. There was no intimacy. . ."

"Was he ever violent with you or the kids?"

"Not the kids. Oh, he'd yell at them and tell them to be quiet or whatever, but he never laid a hand on them." She lifted the bottle and shook it slightly. Satisfied it was empty, she got up and headed for the kitchen. Sam waited while she retrieved another beer.

When she was seated again, he asked, "And with you?"

"Not really. It was more of a constant tension. A constant fear. He scared me. He'd lose his temper over nothing and get up in my face yelling. He'd ball his fists, his eyes would get red, and he'd just . . . just lose it. That's the only way to describe it."

"And he'd not been that way before?"

"Not like that," she said. "I mean, he was no angel when we were younger—I'd seen him drunk and in fights and stuff. But this was different. This was a loss of control."

"Becky, I need to ask you something," Sam said, leaning forward in his chair. She took another slug from the beer, lit a cigarette, and looked at him expectantly. "Do you think he killed Emily?"

"I—I don't know," she said. She stared at the floor for a moment before looking up at Sam. "I mean, the man I married? I don't think so. But he was different when he got back, Sam. And that Emily . . . well, I'm just going to say she was an evil bitch."

"What do you mean?"

"Sleeping around with other people's husbands, is what I mean."

"Do you know that for a fact, Becky?"

"Of course. People talk."

"Do you know names?"

"Oh, no. I'm not going there. This is a small town. Naming names is how you get yourself run outta here."

"Becky, it could be important," Sam implored her. "It might make a difference in Tommy's case."

"So, you think I oughta be helping him?"

"He's your children's father," Sam said. "Look, Becky, at some point things were good between you. Things happened, and now they're not so good. But he's still your children's father."

"He screwed that lawyer," Becky said.

"What makes you think that?"

"I know."

"How?"

"I just know."

"Well, forgetting that for a minute, I want you to consider something."

"What's that?"

"I want you to attend Tommy's trial."

"Play the supportive wife? After I already packed up the kids and moved out?"

"Well . . . yeah. I mean, it could make a difference."

"Jury sees little wifey sitting there, looking all supportive of her hubby, huh?" She blew a smoke ring to the ceiling.

"Well . . . yeah. Might help."

"Even though he'd been screwing the victim." She pushed a lock of hair out of her eyes.

"Look, Becky, I know you're hurting. I know—"

"You don't know shit."

"You're right. I'm sorry." Sam stood to leave. "Will you at least consider it?"

"She screwed a judge, too," Becky said, then burst into drunken laughter. "Can you imagine? Sweet little Emily Smith banging a fat old judge."

Sam watched as she laid her head back on the couch and laughed, and he headed for the door as her laughter slowly turned shallow. She'd stubbed out the cigarette and begun to cry as he closed the door behind himself.

"You ever hear anything about Emily sleeping around?" Sam asked Veronica. The small coffee shop was empty on this cold February morning. The young woman at the counter was microwaving him a piece of pie, as he'd missed breakfast. Veronica was looking good today, he thought. She'd obviously slept better than he had.

"Of course," Veronica said. "Everyone knew she was loose. Bit of a skank, if you ask me. I told you that."

Sam smiled. "But what do you really know?"

"Well, I know where there's smoke there's fire."

"That it?"

"I know that most of the men in this town were in one of two groups: those who were tryin' to get in her pants, and those who maybe had already been there and were afraid."

"And how do you know that?"

"The first group's easy. You'd see them on the make at any social event, any restaurant, even the recreation center. Guys making fools of themselves left and right."

"And the second?" Sam asked, accepting the pie from the young lady.

"She acted like she had something over some of these guys, and they responded to her every beck and call. She had access to bankers, doctors, businessmen, and lawyers like you wouldn't believe."

"Well, she was attractive. Are you sure there was more to it than that?" Sam wiped crumbs from his mouth and smiled. "I'da got ala mode, but it's a little early."

"Sam, men are tools. You know it; I know it. As women, we know how to get what we want." She sipped her coffee. "But this was different. From what I hear, and from what I saw, she wasn't asking favors; she was demanding them."

"You saw?"

"What?"

"You said, 'you saw.' What did you see?"

"Well, just the way she dealt with people—with men, I mean. Can I have a bite?"

"Of course."

Sam handed her his fork and watched as she carefully cut off a piece of his pie and moved it to her mouth with one hand while cupping her other below the fork. "Crumths," she giggled.

"Do you think she slept with Judge Howard?"

Veronica sputtered, then covered her mouth. After a couple of coughs, she drank coffee and then swept imaginary crumbs from her breasts and lap. "Why would you think that?"

"Just wondering."

Veronica looked at Sam for a long moment. He was a good man. He deserved the truth. But she didn't really know, and she told him that.

"You don't know, or you won't say?"

"I don't know. I mean, he would always see her, and he's not that way with any other lawyer. But I don't know what they would talk about when she was in his chambers. My desk is too far away to hear, and he closes the door."

"You don't suppose they were—"

"No, she was never there long enough for that," she said, smiling.

Sam smiled back. "So, all you know is she had access that maybe others don't."

"Right."

"Maybe he's in the first group?"

"No, it's not like that. There's something . . . there. A history of some kind. I just know it. Call it a woman's intuition."

"Right. Want another bite?" Sam offered.

"No, I've got to get back. Judge's got a sentencing here in a minute."

Howard and O'Hanlon were at the bar, holding down their usual spots at a corner table. O'Hanlon appeared to be telling a joke. Howard listened closely, and then laughed and signaled the waitress for another. Punch sat at the bar, nursing a club soda and lemon, watching the ballgame and occasionally looking at his watch. Rhonda was going to be pissed. Another Friday night, another meal missed with the boys. He'd make it up tomorrow, he decided. Pile them all in the car and take everyone to the movies. There was some remake of a comic book action flick the boys had been wanting to see, anyway. Rhonda would hate it, of course, but that was part of the deal when you were a mom with two boys. He smiled wryly and shook the ice cubes in his glass.

"Another one, Officer?" the bartender asked, clearly irritated with Punch's presence. In the last hour, Punch had seen at least three men enter the bar, lay eyes on him, and then leave. Probably probationers. He found it moderately amusing but understood why the bartender—who owned the place—might not.

"Yeah, why not?" Punch decided, eyeing Howard and O'Hanlon. They looked to be winding it up.

"That'll be ten bucks." The bartender slid the drink in Punch's general direction.

"For club soda?"

"No, asshole. For ruining my Friday night take."

Punch stared at the barkeep for a moment, then peeled a ten-dollar bill off a small money clip. "Keep the change."

"Thanks for nothing, Officer."

"Detective Polson, how are you?" Howard was obviously inebriated.

"I'm well, Judge. How are things down at the courthouse?"

"Crime is a growth industry, I'm afraid," Howard said, shaking his huge head sadly. "But it keeps us in beer and peanuts, I guess."

"Indeed it does, sir."

"Well, Detective, please be safe. I've got to get home. I think Margaret has a chicken in the oven."

"Drive carefully, sir."

Howard made his way out the door while the bartender eyed the recently vacated table. Punch needed to act fast. Acting as if he were going to say something to O'Hanlon, he swung his arm wildly and knocked over his club soda. "Ah, shit!" he exclaimed. "Let me get something for that." He hurried toward the men's room, which was just on the other side of Howard's table. Moments later, he emerged with a wad of paper towels. "Can I help?"

"I already got it, goddammit," the bartender said.

"I'm sorry," Punch said. "Look, I'll just get on out of here, okay?"

"Please do, and I'd appreciate it if you didn't come back."

In his car, Punch carefully transferred the beer glass he'd swiped into an evidence bag, closed it, and fumbled through his pockets for a pen. Protocol required that he label the bag with the date and time of collection, initial it, and get it to Pleasance. Anything short of that would interrupt the chain of custody, meaning it would be inadmissible in court. Finally locating his pen, Punch paused and considered his options while watching snowflakes build up on his windshield. "He's a judge," he said at last, and pocketed the pen.

35

On a rainy February morning, Punch was at his desk, eating a sandwich and reading the box scores from the spring training games, when his phone rang. "Polson."

"Punch, Cale here."

"About time. What the hell? It's been days. I'm dying here!"

"I've been busy. Damned budget cuts are kicking my ass. You want what I got, or what?"

"Spit it out."

"So, there were two sets of unidentified prints in that gal's house, right?"

"Right."

"And this print you gave me? It matches one of those sets."

"No shit."

"Yeah, no shit. So whose print is it? You didn't label the sample."

"I can't tell you that, Cale."

"Can't use it as evidence."

"I know that. Don't insult me." Punch's heart was pounding. "The glass I gave you—the print you matched. Where in the house was its match?"

"According to your crime scene guys, the print matched one they found on a vase full of dead flowers."

"Any others?"

"I don't think so. Like I said, lotta variables, lotta unusable prints."

"Can you tell me how long the prints had been there?"

"No. Find out when the flowers were sent, maybe. But whoever it was might've touched the vase later. I mean, who knows?"

"Yeah, who knows . . . Cale," Punch implored. "You have absolutely, positively, got to keep this under your hat."

Ann was pacing in her office. "Same guy? Are you sure?"

"Yeah," Punch replied, stirring his coffee.

"Holy shit! Where were his prints?"

"On that vase with the dead roses."

"Oh, shit. What does that mean?"

"Red roses? Ever been in love?"

"Wise-ass, I mean what does it *mean*?"

"We've got a set of prints from the victim, her mom, and her house-keeper, as well as our suspect and now Howard, and one other set that is still unidentified," Punch mused.

"Jesus! I think I might need to tell Rebecca. We might need a special prosecutor," Ann said, sitting back down and making a note. "Honestly, he doesn't strike me as the type. On the other hand, he's certainly got the size and strength. I just don't know about motive. What would a judge gain by killing a lawyer?"

"Peace and quiet?"

"Personally, I mean. Smartass."

"Do you know if they knew each other? Personally, I mean? The flowers and all . . ."

"I don't know, but I mean to find out," Ann said, then looked at Punch. "Detective, you don't seriously think the judge might have done it? Christ!"

"I don't think anything yet. I just know I need to talk with him, and I need to ask him why his prints were there. But I'd rather volunteer for a prostate exam by a first-year medical student."

"Just wait. This doesn't change your case against Tommy, does it? We can't even use it. The chain of custody is broken and all."

"Well, not right now. But I reserve the right to call him a suspect when and if something develops."

"I've known him a while; he wouldn't do anything like this."

"And if I were a defense attorney, when I found out his prints were on the scene, I'd be all over that. More importantly, I'd peel the investigator—in this case, me—like a banana. Howard signed the arrest warrant and presided over the preliminary hearing, for Christ's sake. This is fucked up, if you'll excuse my French."

Ann sat for a long while, staring blankly at the papers on her desk. "So who knows about this?"

"Right now, just you and me. I played a hunch. Not even Cale Pleasance, the fingerprint guy, knows who the donor is. Like I said, I sent him a blind sample. Just asked if the print on the beer glass matched any in the house."

"Let's keep it that way for right now."

"Can we get a warrant?" Punch asked.

"For what?"

"I don't know. To get his prints, maybe to search—?"

"Hell, no! What are you looking for? We already have everything we need. We've got a trial in six weeks."

"I'm aware. That's your problem, counselor, and I don't believe we ever have everything we need," Punch said. "By the way, don't we have to turn this information over to the other side?"

"You let me worry about that, Detective," Ann said. "And as for the warrant, even if we wanted to go that way, not sure we've got probable cause for anything. We've got his prints on a vase. Close the door on your way out, please. I have a call to make. And keep this between us."

Punch looked at her for a long moment before he left, closing the door behind him.

As soon as the door closed, Ann picked up the phone and punched the number for Mike Shepherd. "We need to talk," she said.

Several minutes later, Ann was in Shepherd's office. "Thanks for seeing me." She took a seat somewhat gingerly. The office was a pigsty. Papers were strewn about his desk, file boxes full of reports and evidence lined the walls.

"Always good to hear from the lead prosecutor in a death penalty case," he said. "How's it going?"

"I think it's going well."

"What've we got?"

"Well, we've got the suspect's prints all over the house and on the murder weapon, which we found at *his* house. Her blood was on the weapon, and a piece of the weapon was in her neck. We've got a DNA match—his semen. His blood at the scene. His name in her appointment book. His vehicle was placed at the scene. He admits being there the night she died. The neighbor saw him in the area as well."

"Sounds solid. Anything exculpatory?" He reached for a paper bag.

"Potentially," Ann said. Seeing him rummaging through the bag made her feel bilious. "Another semen sample—"

"Excuse me?" Shepherd stopped rummaging and looked at Ann.

"A spot of semen on her sheets."

"Christ. Got an ID?"

"Only the suspect's, so far."

"This isn't good." He reached in the bag and withdrew a foil-wrapped package.

Ann watched as he carefully unwrapped the package. "We've got another complication."

"What's that?" He held up a sausage link. "Want one?"

"No, thank you," she said, trying to hide her disgust. "Six identifiable sets of prints in the house. Most were left by the deceased, of course. Some are those of her mother and her housekeeper. The suspect, Olsen, of course, and two other sets."

"Shit. Two sets of unidentified prints? Johnstone will be all over that." He popped the sausage link into his mouth and chewed. "My doctor says it is better to eat a series of small meals throughout the course of the day," he said at last.

"Good advice," she said, watching as he fingered another sausage with stubby fingers. "It gets worse."

"Really? How so?" He popped the link into his mouth.

"We've got a tentative ID on one set. Someone whose prints are problematic."

"You're making my stomach hurt," Shepherd said. He chewed, swallowed, and took a drink of soda. "Why?"

"Well, he's a prominent citizen." She watched as he shook an antacid from a bottle and put it in his mouth.

"How prominent? Like, bank president prominent? Country club president?"

"A member of the legal community."

"I don't like this, Ann," Shepherd said, chewing the antacid. "What's the problem?"

"He's up to his size-eighteen neck in this matter."

Shepherd swallowed. He had to ask. "Is this individual a suspect?"

"Not at this point," Ann said, selecting her words carefully. "We have no reason at all to believe he had anything to do with Emily's death."

"Is the individual aware of what you've found?"

"No. But based on the evidence, and based on his position, the guy is sophisticated enough to know that we must have figured it out by now. And just so you know, Punch considers the investigation open, at this point."

"Open? He's made an arrest, for Christ's sake! You're going to trial in what—six weeks?"

"I know that, Mike. I'm just reporting to you where we are. Look, Punch is convinced we've got the right guy. We got through the preliminary hearing in one piece."

"So, the individual's role diminished after the prelim?"

"Yeah."

Shepherd took a drink of soda. "Has the individual contacted you, or attempted to contact you?"

"No."

"Has the individual attempted to influence the investigation in any way?"

"No."

"Do you believe the fingerprint evidence is exculpatory?"

"Of course not. I think, based on the evidence that I have seen, that the case against Tommy Olsen is solid, and that Judge Howard's prints would only serve to confuse the jury."

"Howard? Jesus Christ!" At the mention of Howard, Shepherd had leapt to his feet and was now pacing his office.

"My words exactly."

"So, what's your plan? Are you going to reveal the presence of these prints to the other side?"

"I don't know what to do," Ann said. "See, the manner in which they were collected was, uh, unconventional."

"Unconventional? You mean, like, without a warrant?"

"Yeah, but in a public venue."

"Chain of custody?"

"None."

"Oh, hell no!" Shepherd said. He walked to his window and parted the shades to look out. "You wanted this case. This is a tactical decision to be made by the lead counsel."

"But you're the chief deputy prosecutor! Surely you—"

"Who else knows about this?" Shepherd said. He turned to face her.

"Well, me, now you—"

"—I don't know shit."

"—Polson, I'm not sure who else."

"Print guy?"

"Not sure. The judge, of course. He doesn't know that we know, but he kind of has to know." She was looking at her shoes, in part to avoid staring at a spot of grease on his chin.

"Damn it, Ann, why'd you tell me this?"

"Because you're my boss, Mike." She made eye contact with him, trying to avoid looking at the grease.

"Well, who else knows you've been here to see me on this subject?"

"No one."

"Then that's the way it is going to stay. No one is to know that we have discussed the matter of this additional evidence—do you understand?"

"Mike, I need your help. I'm not sure what to do here."

"I'm not going there," he said. He sat down at his desk. "My advice is to decide one way or the other and stick with it."

"But if I make the wrong decision—"

"Then it's gonna get ugly." He was rummaging through the bag again. "But I'm having no part of it."

"Will you speak with Rebecca about this for me?" She watched his hand in the bag.

"Absolutely not. And neither will you. She must not know about this, just in case something goes bad. She needs plausible deniability."

"But Mike, you can't leave me hanging like this!"

"You wanted this case, Ann. You've got it. And now you've got one hell of a problem on your hands, so you better get to thinking about how you're going to deal with it."

"Let me ask you this: what if I disclose the information to the other side?"

"Then you will likely ruin Howard's career, and you will be *persona non grata* with everyone in the state bar." Shepherd was sweating profusely now. He withdrew a small candy bar, ripped the wrapper open with his teeth, and popped the entire thing in his mouth. Chewing furiously, he continued. "It probably doesn't matter, given the evidence you've got on Olsen. But I think you know what most ethics professionals would tell you to do."

Ann said nothing, thankful it was only a candy bar. Shepherd continued, "On the other hand, the good news, at least for now, is that Howard already bound Olsen over, and you didn't know those prints were his, and what you've got can't be used by the State. Maybe not disclosing would be deemed harmless error by an appellate court. I don't know. I do know it sucks to be you."

"So, I'm on my own, huh?"

"Well, yeah. I hate to say, 'I told you so,' but if I remember correctly, a couple of months ago I advised you to be careful what you ask for."

"Ann, I don't like this," said Punch. "It just doesn't feel right."

"Detective, you do your job and I'll do mine, okay? I already explained to you that exculpatory evidence is only exculpatory when it would tend to show that the accused did not commit the crime. Those fingerprints—and anything else you have or will find, for that matter—don't matter given the weight of the evidence that we have accumulated, that *you* have accumulated, against Tommy Olsen. All it's going to do is confuse the jury."

Ann looked at Punch, expecting an affirmation of some sort. Seeing none, she continued. "The last thing we need is twelve of these local mouth-breathers getting their feet tangled and acquitting the sonuvabitch. I am not going to let that happen on my watch."

"I guess I don't understand how in the hell Judge Howard can do the preliminary hearing when his prints are at the scene of the crime. This is bullshit."

"Not your call," Ann said. "If we assume he knows his fingerprints—"

"He does."

"How the hell would he know that?"

"He has to know. He left them."

"But they were on a vase. It could have been delivered. And does he know we know?"

"He has to, unless he thinks my people and I are incompetent. And he knows I'd tell you."

"Right," Ann said. "That means the judge made an informed decision not to recuse himself. He's an experienced jurist. We need to respect that. The investigation is closed."

"Counselor, you do your job, and I'll do mine. This is an open investigation."

"You made an arrest!" She angrily shuffled papers on her desk. "We have to assume the judge has examined the situation and determined he does not need to recuse himself."

"How in the world could he be impartial when his own damned prints are there?"

"Because it was only a preliminary hearing, and all he had to do was conclude that a crime was more likely than not committed, and that Olsen committed it. Besides—and I remind you again—what the judge did is not your concern."

"How about you? Could you ask for a mistrial? This isn't right!"

"Not yet. The trial hasn't even started. I could disclose what we know to Johnstone, but I'm not going to, and I remind you, we are not in the 'right' and 'wrong' business. We are in the 'lawful' and 'unlawful' business. Again, you need to do your job and let me do mine. If you can't do that, then maybe the chief and I need to have a talk."

"I gotta think about this, Ann," Punch said.

"Think all you want, Detective. But when we get to trial, listen to the question, answer the question and only the question, and then shut the hell up. Do not admit or reveal that a set of prints that you found belongs to Howard."

"What if his lawyer asks me?"

"He won't. That crazy bastard is as nervous as a short nun at a penguin shoot. He's in over his head and clearly falling apart. He's got no reason to expect complications with fingerprints, does he?"

"Not right now. But what if he asks?"

"He won't. He's an alcoholic, half-crazy disabled vet trying his first murder case. He's only in town because Paul was doing him a favor. Now he's in way over his head, financially and in every other way. No capital murder experience, no money, no resources. He's falling apart; he just doesn't know it yet."

"You don't seem to think much of the guy."

"I don't think about him at all. He's just in the way."

"I think you might be misjudging him."

"I don't care what you think, Detective. Do your job and everything will work out."

"Right," Punch said, turning to leave.

"Oh, Detective?"

"Yeah?"

"Just remember, a preliminary hearing is just a formality, really. You've been around long enough to know that. Howard bound Olsen over, just like any other judge would have any other defendant. Whatever Howard did or didn't do in his private life really didn't matter. Cut the guy some slack."

"Kenneth, what is the matter? You haven't eaten anything." Rhonda was the only person in the world who called him by his first name. Even his own mother called him Punch.

He lifted his gaze from his plate of uneaten lasagna and saw the concern in her dark brown eyes. "It's just this case, honey. Stuff bothering me."

"You'll do fine, Kenneth. You always get your man, right?" she said playfully. "But you cannot let it get to you like this. You're not eating. You'll get sick."

"I'm fine," Punch protested.

"No, you're not. You're not eating, you're drinking like a frat boy, you're snoring like a freight train, and you're short with me and the kids."

"Well, if I'm such a pain in the ass, maybe I'll just leave!"

"Well, why not?" Rhonda cried. "Why don't you just go on down to the office like you did last night and seventy percent of the nights before that and just leave me and the kids here by ourselves?"

"I will. I don't have to listen to this," Punch said, donning his jacket.

"Daddy?"

Punch stopped in his tracks. He'd thought Joey was asleep. It was long past his bedtime. "Yes, son," Punch said. "What are you doing awake? You should be asleep." With a dark look at Rhonda, he walked over and picked up Joey, took him down the hall, and put him to bed.

"Story," Joey demanded.

Punch complied.

Later, lying next to Rhonda, he explained.

"Surely Jon Howard didn't kill her. And they can't hide evidence, can they?" she asked.

"I don't know, honey. I'm not a lawyer. I do know Judge Howard shouldn't have been involved in the case at all, and I think the presence of his prints should be given to the defense. But some of it is my fault. I played a hunch and I should have gone by the book."

"Well, honey, it's early in the case, right? Maybe Jon will speak up. Maybe Ann will do the right thing. And besides, the guy you arrested—that Tommy Olsen—he's the right guy, isn't he?"

"Oh, I'm positive of that. I'm not questioning whether he did it, but that's not the point."

"Well, what is the point?"

"If the system is to work, it has to be fair. If it isn't fair, no one will believe in it. Things will begin to fall apart."

"My husband the idealist. Who would have thought my tough cop would have a soft heart for defendants?"

"It's not a matter of having a soft heart. It's—"

"Kenneth. Go to sleep. Better yet, roll over here first."

Daniels was in the master bathroom shaving when he heard something in his bedroom. He opened the door to find Marci up and about.

"Did I wake you?" he asked.

"Oh, I don't know. I guess I just can't sleep. Thought I'd make us some breakfast this morning before I go to work. You've got a big day."

"Thank you," he said, and moved to kiss her.

"But I haven't brushed my teeth!"

"I'll live with it." He gave her a peck. "And thanks for breakfast."

Thirty minutes later they were sharing eggs and toast. "So, do you really think the trial will take two weeks?" Marci asked.

"Oh, it'll take every bit of that," he said. "Could be much longer if the jury finds him guilty and we have to go into the death penalty phase."

"I guess the good news is that you're never too late getting home during trials."

"Gotta take care of the jurors," Daniels said, taking a bite of toast. Marci's strawberry-rhubarb jam was legendary.

She was drinking coffee and watching him closely. He noticed. "What?" he said.

"I'm just looking at you," she said. "I'm very proud of you, you know."

"And I'm proud of you, too."

"In three months, I'll be retired and just an aging housewife." She looked at her coffee.

"And I'm just an old judge a couple of years from retirement. Soon I'll call it quits and we can sit and drink coffee to our heart's content every morning. I look forward to it."

"I don't," she said.

"What? Why not?"

"I know you. You'll be making a mess and napping and generally getting in my way. I'll be cleaning up after you all day long!"

He was up, putting on his jacket. "You can't wait, and you know it," he said, reaching for her.

She was in his arms. "You're right. I can't wait. Now get out of here so I can get breakfast cleaned up and get to my office. Go do your trial."

36

Sam took a moment to stop and survey his surroundings before entering the courthouse, a three-and-a-half-story building constructed in 1932. Despite the ongoing depression, the men who held elected office at the time had vision and possessed a degree of optimism that Sam felt was lacking in contemporary officeholders. He could write what he knew of architecture on the head of a pin, but someone who did understand the field explained the structure was "classical modern"—whatever that meant. From the front, the view was of a symmetrical, commanding building of cut limestone dominated by six evenly spaced Ionic columns, three of which framed either side of the double entrance doors, which were at present jammed with potential jurors and onlookers. A rectangular stone carved with "Custer County Courthouse 1932" rested on the pillars.

All in all, Sam thought, it looked a little like the depository at Fort Knox.

On the side of the building was a circular drive where on Veterans Day in 2003, while 9/11 was still fresh in the minds of local elected leaders, an area of lawn was dedicated to all who had served or will serve in the military. Local artists had been contracted to create sculptures at great cost; the result was an eclectic mix of classical, modern, and downright odd testaments to the American fighting man and woman.

Inside, stone wainscoting complemented floors of gray marble. Thirty feet above, ceiling fans circulated air above the gathering throng. At the north and south ends of the building, broad, curving stairways led to the second floor's district court courtroom. At present, the stairways were filled with chattering residents and potential onlookers from outside of town. Bailiffs, augmented by contracted off-duty law enforcement, struggled to maintain order among the crowd. Janitors, at the bailiffs' direction, were attempting to emplace dividers on the stairway with an eye toward allowing traffic to proceed both up and down the stairs. Both Fricke and Frac struggled mightily to meet the expectations of the officers, who were losing patience by the minute.

The courtroom where Tommy's fate would be decided was a large, square room with no windows. At the front of the courtroom were the judge's bench, the witness box, and a box for the judge's law clerk. An area immediately below the law clerk's perch was reserved for the court reporter. The jury box, complete with fourteen chairs, including two for alternate jurors, was to the judge's right. A lectern in the center of the courtroom was flanked by two library-type tables manned by the attorneys and parties from the prosecution and defense. On the walls were portraits of all those who had presided in this judicial district to date; each gazed upon the courtroom's occupants with a stern, unyielding glare. Behind the tables, and serving to separate the trial's active participants from the audience, was a waist-high divider known as "the bar." Since the mid-twentieth century, all courtrooms in Wyoming contained such a barrier.

The clerk of court had called the first extract of the jury panel and seated them numerically in the first six pews located behind the bar. Jurors' reactions would be mixed, Sam knew. Some would be excited, anticipating being part of such an important, maybe even historical, event. Others, especially the gainfully employed, would be fervently hoping they would not be selected.

At the far rear of the courtroom was a large double door through which all but the judge, his staff, the bailiff, and the defendant would enter and leave. The bailiffs standing inside the courtroom on either side of the doors were charged with ensuring that the number of spectators, participants, and media did not exceed the fire chief's maximum, and that those who did make it inside were on their best behavior. The sheriff had duly assigned two of his burliest deputies to the job, and they had adopted a suitably surly disposition. Spectators were seated on a first-come, first-served basis. Woe be it to the spectator with a kidney that required relief, as seating was reserved, and anyone who left for any reason was replaced by the next person in line.

Ann Fulks, Rebecca Nice, Punch Polson, and Buck Lucas sat at the prosecutor's table. Lucas had no real reason to be there, of course, but for the sake of appearances he would occupy the State's table until the first break, at which point he would return to his office and get some work done.

At the defense table, positioned closest to and perpendicular to the jury box, Sam sat closest to the lectern, with an outwardly nervous Tommy next to him. Sam was nervous as well. He'd seen his counselor three times in the past week, and it was helping, but he was feeling anxious. Trials were thought to be the lifeblood of the judicial system, but in fact they were few and far between. The tremendous costs precluded most defendants from mounting a defense, and—in a nod to the mutual avoidance of risking a bad outcome, and faced with a possibility of *this* versus the certainty of *that* —ninety-nine percent of trial attorneys would persuade the client into accepting a deal rather than present a case to twelve strangers whose knowledge, motives, intelligence, and interests were a mystery.

Two weeks before the trial, the clerk of court had provided both Ann and Sam with copies of completed questionnaires that had been provided to potential jurors. The forms provided a baseline of information about each juror: name, age, marital status, employment status, education, and similarly bland background information. In theory, these juror questionnaires existed to provide counsel information by which informed decisions could be made prior to enduring jury selection. In reality, the juror questionnaires did no more than provide counsel with "profiling" information, suitable only to exclude those jurors who would most likely be averse to a party's position. For example, prosecutors would generally exclude teachers and service workers, while defense attorneys would try to exclude law enforcement officers, their families, and friends.

Sam watched Ann, knowing she was silently rehearsing her introduction and her first few questions for the potential jurors, while Punch and

Buck Lucas chatted amiably. Nice was careful to nod a greeting to those voters she knew. From time to time, as the courtroom filled, Sam and Tommy spoke, Sam occasionally placing his arm around his client's shoulders. Ten minutes after the scheduled starting time, Mary entered the courtroom and looked to the prosecutor's table.

"Ms. Fulks, is the State ready to proceed?"

"We are."

Turning to Sam, Mary asked, "Mr. Johnstone, is the defense ready?"

"We are," Sam said, as deeply as possible, despite the butterflies in his stomach.

"The judge will enter momentarily," Mary said, and left the courtroom through an unmarked door leading to Daniels's chambers.

Nervous chatter began anew. Moments later the clerk reappeared, and the bailiff—seeing the judge following in her wake—ordered, "All rise!"

"Thank you," Daniels said. "Please remain standing and join me in reciting the Pledge of Allegiance." Thereafter, Daniels turned from the flag positioned immediately behind his chair and ordered all present to be seated.

"Good morning, ladies and gentlemen," he began.

"Good morning," the audience replied, like a Sunday morning congregation in response to the preacher.

"We are here in the matter of the State of Wyoming versus Thomas Olsen. My name is Preston Daniels, and I will be your judge. The State is present and represented by Deputy Custer County and Prosecuting Attorney Ann Fulks. Mr. Olsen is present and wearing the sports jacket with an open-collared shirt. He is represented by Sam Johnstone of the Norquist Law Firm. We—"

Sam was on his feet. "Your Honor," he said, as politely as possible.

Daniels glared at Sam. "Mr. Johnstone?"

"For the sake of an accurate record, Your Honor, it is incumbent upon me to tell the court that I am no longer affiliated with the Norquist Law Firm," Sam said.

"Can't hold a job?" Daniels asked. The audience tittered with laughter. Sam reddened but held his tongue. "So noted," Daniels said as Sam sat back down.

"We are here for a trial," Daniels continued, looking out on the assembled audience. "I want to start today by speaking a little bit about jury service, and I'd like to begin by extending congratulations to you for being selected."

Hearing the audience laugh, Daniels continued to gaze upon them. "Do congratulations sound strange?" Seeing the nods, he continued. "Many people consider jury service to be at best an inconvenience, and at worst an outright intrusion in their lives. That is unfortunate, in my opinion, for while jury service is one of the responsibilities of being a citizen, it is much more. It is a privilege. Very few governments trust their citizens sufficiently to allow them to perform this function."

Daniels looked about the courtroom, and then commenced a lengthy monologue on the history of the American jury system, ending with a ringing endorsement of its importance to criminal jurisprudence. Those at the library tables had swiveled their chairs to face the potential jury members as the judge began his speech. Sam was attempting to make and hold eye contact with each juror. He took notes on a yellow pad, marking for his later reference which men or women held eye contact, refused it, or avoided looking at him altogether. As the judge continued, Sam was looking at Juror 465, a pinch-faced woman of about fifty-five, and recalling an adage from one of his trial advocacy professors: "Never allow to be selected for the jury a woman with a mouth like a cat's ass." At the time, Sam had no idea what the old lawyer meant. Now, looking at the woman's pursed lips, folded arms, and generally defensive demeanor, he knew exactly what his mentor had so inelegantly tried to communicate many years ago.

Sam watched the jurors while Daniels outlined the procedure that would be followed to select the jury. Occasionally, he would look at his notes, trying to memorize each juror's face and match his notes from their questionnaires. Daniels had moved on and was now providing a general overview of the roles of everyone involved. "Before we begin jury selection," he said, "I need to tell you about the main players in this trial. I'm one of the judges in this judicial district. The judge's role in the trial is sometimes compared to that of an umpire. I will keep order in the court, and I will ensure that the evidence is presented in an orderly manner. I will also ensure that the evidence presented to the jurors is proper and lawful, meaning that I will allow admissible evidence to be presented for the jury's consideration, and I will exclude improper evidence. I will also instruct the jury on the law that you must follow in this case. Thus, in an ideal situation, I will be seen but rarely heard."

The audience laughed, as expected. Juries and audiences always laughed at a judge's jokes. Pointing to counsel, Daniels continued. "As all of you know, the attorneys have an important role in the trial. They lie at the heart of what we call the adversary system. Our system rests on the assumption that if both parties come before an impartial body and argue their positions aggressively, the truth will emerge from a clash of positions. In other words, our system is based on the belief that, from the consideration of competing arguments, the jury will be able to reach a correct result. It is through the attorneys that evidence, the testimony, the documents, and other items will be presented for the jury's consideration. The attorneys will explain and argue the case and try to help the jury understand what's going on."

Daniels gestured toward the potential jurors. "The jury finds the facts and, as part of the fact-finding process, decides which witnesses are believable and what weight should be assigned the testimony and other evidence. The jury applies the law as instructed and decides the case.

"At this time, I will read the charges to you. Before I do, I want to caution you that you are not to consider what I'm going to read as evidence of guilt on the part of Mr. Olsen. It is only an allegation made by the State to give the defendant notice of the crime with which he is charged so he can prepare to meet those charges. Remember, Mr. Olsen is presumed to be innocent of any crime, and the State must prove his guilt beyond a reasonable doubt."

Looking to the document, Daniels read, "In this case, it is alleged that on or about October 31 of last year, in Custer County, Wyoming, the defendant, Tommy Olsen, did violate Wyoming Statute Section 6-2-101 by killing C. Emily Smith purposely and with premeditated malice."

The judge looked up from his reading as an audible rumble went through the courtroom. "Ladies and gentlemen. . . Ladies and gentlemen, I will have order!" he said. "This seems as good a time as any to talk about your decorum in this courtroom. We are here on a very serious matter, and I will not allow spectators, members of the media, or anyone else to disrupt the proceedings. I expect each of you to remain quiet and in control of your emotions. If I must stop this trial because of the reaction of one or more of you, I will have that individual, or those individuals, removed. If it occurs repeatedly, I will simply clear the courtroom of all but the necessary parties. Is that clear?"

The courtroom was now deathly quiet. After gazing about for a few seconds, Daniels turned to his clerk. "Madam clerk, would you please administer the oath for voir dire?"

After the oath was read, Daniels had everyone re-seated. "Now, beginning with juror number one, I will have each of you stand and provide us the information we asked for, which is spelled out on that board in front of you." Formally, the process of jury selection had begun, although Sam had already made some preliminary selections, and he knew that Ann had as well. Each prospective juror would now stand and provide the court and counsel with the information contained on the board. Most of the general information was already included on the juror questionnaires, of course, but having the jurors recite the same information not only served to fact-check but also to allay any nervousness on their part. In addition, it gave counsel a final opportunity to "eyeball" each potential juror.

After the seventy-five potential jurors had introduced themselves, it was the judge's turn to ask some perfunctory questions.

"This trial is expected to last approximately two weeks," he began. "Is there anything about the length or scheduling of the trial that would inter-fere with your ability to serve?" Predictably, some potential jurors raised their hands. Daniels had them come forward individually to the bench, where he, Ann, and Sam spoke with them. Most indicated a lengthy trial would interfere with their ability to earn a living—a very real concern for all except the unemployed or retired. Unfortunately, as Daniels explained, no one can truly "afford" to spend the time to serve on a jury—a fact, Sam knew, that was the basis for the old adage that defendants having a jury trial "put their future in the hands of twelve citizens not smart enough to get off jury duty." Having heard the jurors' objections, and having overruled them, Daniels sent them back to their seats, and Sam—who had been watching their reactions carefully—made a note to exclude a couple of them, if possible.

"Does anyone here have health conditions that would preclude their serving?"

"Is everyone here a United States citizen?"

"Has anyone here been convicted of a felony?"

After weeding out potential jurors for cause, Daniels assembled a pool of men and women who were at least notionally qualified to perform the duties. "At this time, ladies and gentlemen, we are going to call several numbers. If your number is called, please take a seat in the jury box as indicated by the bailiff." The clerk of court read fourteen numbers, and after some movement and a bit of shuffling, those jurors were seated in the jury box, forming the initial jury pool for the trial. As each potential juror's number was called, Sam checked that name off the list that he had compiled from the juror questionnaires. A quick glance at the names indicated that the initial jury contained several that he was glad to see, and an equal number he would want removed.

"Now, ladies and gentlemen, I will turn over the remainder of jury selection to the attorneys. Ms. Fulks, you may begin."

"Thank you, Your Honor. Ladies and gentlemen, as you know, my name is Ann Fulks. Judge Daniels has ensured that those of you remaining meet the basic qualifications for jury duty. My first job is to see to it that those of you who are seated as jurors will serve in good faith and in accordance with the dictates of the law." She then asked questions designed to ensure that any juror selected would attempt to follow the law as prescribed by the judge and have no qualms about imposing the death penalty. Accordingly, her questions quickly headed in that direction.

"Are you in favor of, or opposed to, the death penalty?"

"Whatever your position on the death penalty, will you obey the law?"

"Are you able to set aside your personal preferences to ensure a just verdict and sentence?"

Occasionally, a juror would indicate some hesitation. At that point, a conference with the attorneys, the juror, and Daniels would again be held out of earshot of the other potential jurors. Sometimes, the juror was unsure of exactly what was being asked. Other times, he or she was clearly hoping to get off jury duty by appearing to be more resistant to imposing the death penalty than was actually the case. Each time, Daniels listened carefully before sending the juror back to his or her chair. Experience had shown him that, once you started releasing people from duty for any reason, the number of people seeking to be excused would increase exponentially. Accordingly, Judge Daniels drew a hard line when it came to excusing potential jurors.

Just before noon, Ann was finished with her examination of the fourteen jurors. "Ladies and gentlemen, this looks like a good time to take our lunch break," Daniels announced. "Those of you in the jury box, please go with the bailiff. Everyone please be seated again at 1:30 p.m. I want to remind you that you are not to talk about this case with anyone—period," he concluded, knowing full well that his order would not be followed.

At 1:40 p.m., the bailiff called the courtroom to order and Daniels entered. "It is now the defense's turn to ask questions," he said. "Mr. Johnstone, please proceed."

As Sam stood to address the jurors, Daniels added, "Mr. Johnstone, I want to remind you that it is the court's wish that we complete jury selection today, so be cognizant of the time."

Sam was momentarily knocked off his game. It was improper for the judge to make such a remark, as it tended to have jurors looking at their watches rather than paying attention. But he could do nothing about it, so he took a deep breath and looked at the jurors.

"May it please the court, Ms. Fulks." Sam paused for a moment, deliberately making eye contact with each potential juror. Eye contact was not a strong point for him; in fact, it made his stomach hurt, but it had to be done.

"Good afternoon, ladies and gentlemen. As Judge Daniels told you, my name is Sam Johnstone. I've only been a lawyer here in town for less than a year, but I've been practicing for a while. It will be my honor and privilege to speak to you in this case on behalf of Tommy Olsen." Sam placed his hand on Tommy's shoulder.

"Now, as you may have figured out, Ms. Fulks and I are going to disagree on a lot of things. Most importantly, we disagree whether my client murdered Emily Smith," Sam said. "But one thing we agree on is that under our system the right and fair way to decide a case is to submit it to a jury—a group of people selected from all parts of the community and from all walks of life.

"Now, the rules say that during a trial I cannot speak with you. So the only time I have to get to know you is right now. I'm going to be as brief as possible, but part of my job is to ensure that each of you is willing to give Tommy Olsen the fair shot that he deserves.

"This case is about who killed Emily Smith. The State says Tommy Olsen did it, but Tommy Olsen denies that. We say someone other than Tommy did it," he said, looking at each juror in turn. Indeed, after Tommy had declined a deal and refused to plead guilty "by reason of mental illness or deficiency," Sam's sole alternatives were the "some other dude did it" defense, or self-defense, which was not supported by the evidence, given that she'd been cut from behind.

"Right now, I am responsible for acting on behalf of Tommy Olsen to ensure that he will get his fair day in court. If you are chosen as a juror, you'll share that duty with me for a while. But at the end of the trial, after I have done everything I can on behalf of my client, I will have to step aside and put Tommy Olsen's fate in your hands. Is everyone here comfortable with that responsibility?"

Again, Sam attempted to capture each juror's eye. Two male jurors—one a coal miner, the other a small business owner—held his stare. Most of the others looked away quickly. Sam would focus the remainder of his time on the two men; he had concluded they might well prove persuasive behind closed jury room doors. He needed to know now how they might react.

"Right now, you are not required to know all the law that may apply to this case. At the end of this case, right before the lawyers' final argument, Judge Daniels will give you some specific instructions as to the relevant law of this jurisdiction regarding the crime of murder. But the judge is going to tell you at the end of this case that to find Tommy Olsen guilty of murder, you will have to find that on or about October 31, and with premeditation, Tommy Olsen killed Emily Smith by cutting her throat.

"Now, I can see that upsets some of you, so I need to know before we get started how you feel about that law and whether it is acceptable to you. So, does everyone agree that if, after hearing all the evidence and the law given to you by Judge Daniels and applied to the facts of this case, you would follow that law and be guided by it in arriving at a verdict?"

All the potential jurors noted their assent. The two male jurors he had identified continued to meet his stare.

"What if the judge gave you an instruction about the law of murder and you personally did not agree with that law? Would all of you follow a law that you personally don't believe in and disregard your own feelings? Is there anyone here who would not follow a law that you did not believe in?"

No one raised a hand.

"Can any of you think of any reason why a person who is accused of a crime wouldn't want to testify other than the fact that he might be guilty? Do any of you believe that no innocent person would choose to remain silent?"

No hands. And on it went, well into the afternoon. At last, Sam felt as if he had exhausted the list of questions he had prepared and had a good feel for the jurors. "Ladies and gentlemen, I appreciate your honesty, your candor, and your patience. We look forward to presenting our case to you. Thank you, Your Honor. The defense passes the jury for cause."

"All right, I am glad you are *finally* finished, Mr. Johnstone. Because Mr. Johnstone took so long, we are going to take only a five-minute break before we begin final selection," Daniels said.

Sam looked at Daniels, astonished. Again, this was clearly improper, as the comment could tend to prejudice the jury panel against the defendant. But, again deciding the better part of valor was to hold his tongue, Sam simply seethed.

Five minutes later, all parties were re-seated. Each side had a number of peremptory challenges to exercise against jurors, meaning that juror could be excused for any reason or no reason at all. As Sam had been addressing the jury, he had been watching all jurors closely, silently confirming or denying the initial impressions he had gleaned from their questionnaires. In addition, he had Tommy watching the jurors and attempting to make eye contact with each. The task—the art, really—before them now was to combine all the information and try to select a jury panel that would be as fair to his client as any fourteen people could be.

"Tommy," Sam had said during the brief recess, "in my mind, we've got a pretty good panel. I've got some peremptory challenges to use. The problem is I think there are only seven jurors on the panel who are good for you. Tell me who you think needs to go."

"Sam, I don't like the gal in seat number ten, that fat guy, or that old lady in number two."

This was not good news. The number two and number ten chairs were jurors Sam had wanted to keep. He was most worried about the juror in seat seven, as well as those in seats eleven and twelve. The thing to do now, and quickly, was to prioritize the removal of jurors and hope that the prosecution would remove a couple of those that Sam and Tommy didn't like.

"Well, let's see what happens," Sam said. He was hoping against hope that Ann would remove some of those who really concerned him so he could justify keeping jurors two and ten.

"Ms. Fulks, are you ready to proceed?" Judge Daniels asked.

"We are, Your Honor."

"Mr. Johnstone." It wasn't a question.

"The defense is ready, Your Honor."

"Ms. Fulks, please hand the bailiff your first challenge slip," Daniels instructed. The bailiff retrieved the slip from Ann and handed it to him. "Juror 274, you are free to go. Will the clerk call a replacement?"

It was the juror in seat seven. Sam and Tommy exchanged a look. Tommy was almost smiling. Sam put a hand on his leg and patted it. "Hold your poise," he whispered.

The clerk called a replacement juror, who, after gathering her coat, purse, and other belongings, took chair number two.

"Mr. Johnstone?"

Sam handed the bailiff a piece of paper with the number eleven written on it. The process was repeated, alternating between the prosecution and the defense, until all of the peremptory challenges had been used.

"Ladies and gentlemen," Daniels said. "At this time I will give counsel a brief time in which to inquire of the newly-seated jurors. This brief questioning will take no more than thirty minutes. Each side will then have one additional peremptory challenge, after which the jury panel will be final. Mr. Johnstone, do you understand?"

"Your Honor, I understand. But I must say that—"

"Sit down, Mr. Johnstone," Daniels said sharply. "Ms. Fulks, you may begin."

Sam's ears were burning, and he heard little to nothing as Ann completed her questioning of the new jurors. He was still angry and preoccupied when he felt Tommy pulling on his sleeve. "Sam, you're up!"

He asked a couple of perfunctory questions and passed the new panel for cause. "Anyone you don't like?" he asked his client.

"Well, I still don't like that guy." Tommy pointed at the fat man's name on the chart.

"I understand that, but I have a feeling about him. Besides, if we cut him, we have no say in who will take his place and no way to get rid of them. I'd prefer to go with what we got."

"Okay, Sam. I trust you."

Sam got rid of a middle-aged man with his last peremptory challenge. To Sam's horror, Juror 465 was randomly summoned to fill the empty seat, albeit as an alternate.

Jury selection had taken two days, but they had a jury. Trial would begin tomorrow. Sam looked at his watch. It was going to be a long night.

37

Frac was mopping the marbled hallway in front of the courtroom where the trial had begun that morning while Fricke used an electric floor burnisher to apply wax. The courthouse had been empty for hours, the only sounds coming from the two of them.

"So, Frac, let's make us a bet," Fricke said.

"A bet?"

"Yeah. A bet. I'll bet you four-to-one that Tommy gets convicted."

"What's that mean?"

"What's what mean?"

"What's that four-to-one thing mean?"

"Dude, haven't you ever placed a bet?"

"No."

"Well, if I'm giving four-to-one, that means if you bet a dollar, and Tommy gets off, I'll pay you four dollars. But if he gets convicted, then I'll take your dollar—get me?"

"What's 'convicted' mean?"

"You don't know nothin', do you?"

"How did it go, honey?" Marci Daniels asked, putting a plate of meatloaf in front of the judge.

"Fine," he responded. "I just hope these two are up to the task. I don't want to have to try this case twice."

Bad lawyering led to more reversals and remands than bad judges ever did. Good lawyers tried clean, well-planned cases. Evidentiary questions, questions of procedure, and even objections were meticulously planned. Arguments made by good lawyers were characterized by citation to case law and relevant statute. Poor or novice lawyers were generally "winging it," whether as the result of sloth or inexperience. It didn't really matter; whatever the cause, bad lawyering made a judge's job exponentially harder.

"How did Ann do?"

"Fine. Bigger case than she's used to, so she was a little nervous, but I think she'll be okay," he said, taking a bite of meatloaf. Marci's meatloaf was legendary in Custer. It was one of the few things she knew how to make when they got married forty years ago, and at his request she'd been making it every week since.

"And the other fellow—Johnson, was it?" she asked.

"Johnstone. Sam Johnstone. I suspect he'll be fine. Biggest issue with him will be keeping up with all the State throws at him. He's a one-man show and that's difficult, especially for a guy without a lot of criminal defense experience."

"I heard Paul fired him for taking the case."

"I heard the same thing. Not surprising. Paul can't have one of his guys defending murderers," he said, sampling the mashed potatoes. Lots of butter. "That'd be bad for business."

"Aren't you glad you don't have to worry about clients anymore?"

"Every day, honey. Every single day."

"So, how did it go?" Howard asked.

"It was interesting." O'Hanlon signaled the waitress for another round. "I've never been on a jury before. Been required to show and all that, but never got picked to serve before now."

"Civic duty," Howard toasted.

"Here's to it." O'Hanlon returned the toast.

"What's your initial impression?"

"Well, that Fulks gal was a little nervous—'course, I'd probably be nervous, too, if I were her age and tryin' a case like that. That other guy—Johnson or whatever—he seemed pretty cool about it all, but his client looks guilty as hell."

"Well, I think it's safe to say that the cops get more right than wrong."

"Yeah, I hear that. But you know, I been watching some of them shows on television, and it seems there's a fair number of guys who get convicted and didn't really do it."

"I suppose," Howard said, taking a long pull from his glass. "But I think you'll find there's a lot of differences between what you see on television and in real life."

"Yeah. Hey, Judge, I got a question."

"Shoot."

"After we got selected, and before we got released for the day, Daniels ordered us all not to talk with anyone about this case. That didn't mean you, did it?"

"Well, I am an officer of the court, so technically I think you could. But you know what? Probably better that we just kind of keep this under our hats, okay?"

"Okay. Hey, you know better than I do."

"Probably," Howard said, finishing his drink and putting it on the table. "Another?"

"You betcha, Judge."

———

Ann was afraid she was going to vomit. "What's the matter, dear?" her mother asked, looking at the half-eaten meal on Ann's plate. "Isn't it good?"

"Mom, it's fine. I'm just not hungry."

"But you need to eat! Tomorrow you have your big trial."

"Mom, I'm well aware of what is happening tomorrow."

"You'll do fine, dear. You always do."

"*Fine* is not good enough, Mom. 'Fine' is not going to get me out of this hellhole."

"Now, Ann, don't talk like that. Rebecca and Mike have given you a wonderful opportunity. You're making a name for yourself. You just keep working hard and all your dreams will come true. Speaking of which, are you seeing anyone?"

"No, Mom. I don't have time—I told you that last time you asked me."

"Well, I know. But I worry. Your sister is only two years older and she already has two kids and—"

"And a mortgage, and a husband who drinks too much and can't hold a job, and a fourteen-year-old minivan that breaks down every week."

"Ann! Bobby's got his problems, but he'll find something one of these days. Now, try not to be so judgmental. Your sister loves Bobby."

The silence was lengthy while Ann tried without success to finish her meal. She had invited her mother to Custer for the trial, thinking her presence might be calming. "Look, Mom, I think this was a mistake. I'm just a little uptight, okay? I'm looking at the biggest trial of my career." She took her mother's face in both hands. "I know you want to help, and I love you for it. But I think I'll be better off spending these last few hours alone, preparing for tomorrow. Are you okay with that?"

"Of course, dear. At least take a piece of pie. I made strawberry, your favorite."

Moments later, after her mother had gone upstairs, Ann threw the pie in the garbage. Strawberry was her sister's favorite.

Sam thought he was going to die, but he saw no light, nor did his life flash before his eyes. Instead, he simply skidded and slid along the road for what seemed like forever. Coming to a stop at last, he felt the impact of the round before he heard the report of the rifle. There was intense pain, but the only things that crossed his mind were getting to safety and then killing the bastards who did this. He could barely breathe, and panic was setting in when he saw Jenkins appear in slow motion and drag him back to the vehicle. He feared he'd be shot. "Hurry up! Hurry up!" he yelled. He watched as he found his driver and his gunner dead. He looked at their wounds and smelled the coppery odor of their blood and knew. He tried to look for the others, but he couldn't walk. He was furious and wanted to act but was overcome—tired beyond exhaustion. "My men!" he screamed.

Sitting on his bed, he looked at his alarm clock. The red numbers showed 03:05. Too late to go back to sleep—which wasn't likely, anyway—and too early to go to work. He strapped on his leg and made his way to the bathroom, then brushed his teeth and got a drink of water. Looking in the mirror, he saw the age in his eyes. "How much longer are you going to torture yourself?" he asked aloud.

At 03:15 he was sitting at his dining room table listening to the coffee brew. Atop the previous day's mail was a copy of a book on mindfulness Martinez had mailed him. When the coffee was ready, Sam moved to his recliner, sat down, and began to read.

Punch had gotten in early—he couldn't sleep. In the pre-dawn silence, he'd finished a couple of reports that were due and completed an affidavit of probable cause on a couple of teenagers who'd been "car-hopping"—going through neighborhoods, getting into unlocked vehicles, and stealing whatever they could get their hands on to sell for booze and drug money. Now, he had a couple of things to do on the Olsen matter. Taking care of loose ends. He called the lab in Cheyenne.

"State crime lab, Technician Simmons."

"Just the guy I wanted to talk to," Punch said. "This is Detective Polson in Custer. I'm working a murder case up here. I've got a fingerprint on a beer glass. I want you to go ahead and see if you can get DNA off that print from the beer glass. Then I need to know if it matches a sample of semen we found. I think that's already been sent down your way."

"Okay. We're going to need a service agreement."

"I'll get it."

"Right. And we'll need authorization from the lead prosecutor."

"Really? I'd really rather not involve her."

"Well," Simmons said, "the sole exception is if we already have on file a Form LPPM8A—do we have one of those?"

"Uhh, I'm not sure."

"Well, we've already done some work on this case, haven't we? I seem to recall doing something?"

"Yes," Punch answered, sensing an out. "I think you have."

"I'm assuming you've got clearance, Detective?"

"Go ahead and assume that."

"Detective—"

"Simmons, trust me. I'm the guy. And do me a favor. Keep this under wraps, okay? Send your report directly to me." Punch gave Simmons his contact information and extracted a promise that any and all information would be given directly to him. "I'll buy you a beer next time I'm down in Cheyenne."

"Sure," Simmons said, and hung up.

Punch poured another cup of coffee and looked at his watch. Another hour, and trial would start.

38

"Ladies and gentlemen of the jury," Ann began, "your job begins right now." Her voice held a slight tremor, and Sam was glad to see he wasn't the only one who was nervous. "As lead counsel for the State of Wyoming, my job during this opening statement is to give you a preview of the evidence that you will see. I'm not allowed to argue the evidence, and I'm not going to do that. What I am going to do is give you a brief overview of what the evidence will be, and what it will show. I believe that when you see the evidence you will be convinced beyond a reasonable doubt that the crime of felony murder was committed, and that Tommy Olsen"—she dramatically pointed in Tommy's direction—"was the man who committed it."

Standing behind the podium in a navy-blue pantsuit, she looked polished and professional, Sam thought, although her hair was perhaps a bit severe for his taste. "You will hear from neighbors that Emily Smith and Tommy Olsen had an affair. You will hear from the police officers who found Emily's body. They will tell you of the horrific nature of her injuries. You will hear from the medical examiner, who will tell you when, where, and how Emily died. You will hear from Detective Kenneth Polson, who will outline every step he took in investigating this horrific crime. You will know by the end of the trial why he eliminated others from suspicion. And when all the evidence is in, we will ask you to render a verdict of guilty."

Sam watched the jurors carefully during Ann's statement. He was stunned by its brevity, and as a result was not quite ready to begin his own. Although he had rehearsed it many times, and although he had addressed large audiences as well as juries over the course of a lifetime, his stomach fluttered as he rose to address the jury.

"Ladies and gentlemen, I want to begin by thanking you for your service in this matter. Lord knows jury duty is a difficult and thankless task. This is a matter of no less than life or death. You hold Tommy's future in your hands. I don't believe I am exaggerating when I say it is likely that nothing you will ever do will match the level of responsibility that you will be asked to exercise over the course of the next few days." Sam paused to let the enormity of the task sink in. Juror 465 was watching Sam with a look of disbelief.

"Beginning in a couple of minutes, the attorneys for the State will parade a number of witnesses before you and show you a bunch of exhibits in an effort to convince you that my client killed Ms. Smith. I ask only that you listen to each witness and examine each piece of evidence with this in mind: what does this mean, and how does it prove Tommy Olsen guilty of murder?"

Sam walked from behind the podium and stood behind Tommy. He wanted the jurors to have to look at him, to see he was a living, breathing human being. "I ask this because a lot of what the State will present will *not* tend to indicate that my client, and no one else, committed the crime. A lot of it will be perfunctory and a lot of it will be window dressing to show you that they did their job. Ladies and gentlemen, I contend that the State has not done its job for the very simple reason that the State has arrested and charged the wrong man."

Sam looked at each juror, focusing on the spot between the eyes of each man or woman and holding his stare. Then he placed a hand on each of Tommy's shoulders. "My client did not commit this crime. Now, I seriously doubt I will be able to prove that," he said. "However, as the judge has already instructed you, I do not have to prove that my client did not commit the crime. Rather—"

"Mr. Johnstone, counsel, please approach the bench!" Daniels barked.

Ann and Sam dutifully approached the bench. The reporter was

donning a headset, and when she had it on, the judge turned off his microphone and leaned over his bench so that only Ann and Sam could hear
before angrily addressing Sam. "What in the hell are you doing?"

"Your Honor?"

"You are arguing the law! I will not have it!"

"Your Honor, I'm simply making the point that my client doesn't have to
prove anything—I'm echoing your earlier instruction!"

"Mr. Johnstone, I'm going to tell you one time to stop arguing the law.
Do you understand?"

"Yes, Your Honor." Sam looked at Ann, who was staring at the floor.
Daniels's interference was improper. As an officer of the court, Ann could
technically intervene, and Sam hoped she would do so.

"Return to your places," Daniels instructed when nothing was said.

Sam could feel the jurors' eyes upon him as he returned to the podium.
From a legal standpoint, the jury had no idea what was going on, of course,
but they would know Sam had just been admonished for *something*. And
while it was true that Daniels had earlier instructed the jury to disregard
conferences and his interruptions of counsel, Sam knew that it was not
favorable for his client to have the judge interrupting him during his
opening statement. The only thing to do, of course, was to try and continue
as if nothing had happened. Looking through his notes very briefly, Sam
attempted to pick up where he left off.

"The State of Wyoming has the burden of proving each and every
element of the crimes charged," Sam began, noting that the fat juror was no
longer meeting his glance. "Tommy Olsen asks only that you listen to each
witness, and examine each piece of evidence, with that burden in mind."

Noting that a couple of the jurors were preoccupied with examining
their nails, shuffling the pages of their notebooks, or simply staring off into
space, Sam decided to cut it short. "We believe," he said, "that at the conclusion of this trial, after having examined each piece of evidence and having
heard and observed each witness, you will have no choice but to find my
client not guilty of felony murder. Ladies and gentlemen, thank you for
your time."

With a curt nod to the jurors, Sam sat down next to Tommy and stared
hard at Daniels.

39

"Your Honor, the State calls Officer Ronald Baker," Ann said.

All eyes turned toward Baker as a deputy led him into the courtroom. He'd testified before, so he knew the drill, but never at a trial of this magnitude. His voice was shaky as he swore his oath.

"Officer Baker," Ann began. "Please state your full name for the record."

"Ronald Eugene Baker."

"And Mr. Baker, are you employed?"

"I am."

"What do you do?"

"I am a patrol officer with the Custer Police Department."

"And how long have you held that position?"

"Just over a year."

"And what other employment have you held since graduation from high school?"

"I went to college for a while, then worked as a ranch hand on the Swenson place south of town. Then attended the Law Enforcement Academy."

"So, you are a certified peace officer in the State of Wyoming?"

"Yes, ma'am."

"And in your capacity as a police officer, what are your duties?"

"Run patrol of my sector, file reports, assist other officers as required."

"And were you on duty on the afternoon of November 2nd of last year?"

"I was."

"And did anything unusual happen during your shift that evening?"

"Yes."

"And that was?"

"At approximately 1400 hours—that's two p.m.—dispatch contacted me and asked me to do a welfare check on a woman named Emily Smith. I proceeded to the location given, met with her secretary, I think, and after doing some initial looking around determined to enter the decedent's, er, Ms. Smith's home to see if she was okay."

"Was she?"

"No."

"What was her condition?"

"Dead."

"How did you know?"

"You can tell."

"Was her home in Custer's city limits?"

"Yes."

"And what time did you discover her body?"

"I made a note. It was 1417, er, 2:17 p.m. exactly."

"What did you do next?"

"I told her coworker, who was waiting on the stoop, to leave the scene."

"And what did you do next?"

Baker looked around the courtroom sheepishly. "I puked." Some in the audience tittered, drawing a severe look from Daniels. Ann, feeling bad for the officer, quickly followed up.

"And what did you do then?"

"I called it in."

"And then?"

"I began to secure the scene, and as more officers showed up, I gradually handed off to them."

"And who eventually took charge of the investigation, if you know?"

"Detective Polson, ma'am."

"And after Detective Polson took over the scene, what were your duties?"

"Whatever he wanted. Mostly security. Later, we did some door-to-door stuff—asking questions, seeing if anyone saw or heard anything. Stuff like that."

"Did anyone?"

"Did they what?"

"See or hear anything?"

"No one I talked to."

"How about anyone else—if you know?"

"I think Jensen—that's Corporal Jensen—said the landlord saw Tommy around."

"Objection, Your Honor," Sam said. "Hearsay."

"Sustained," Daniels growled.

"But no one you spoke with saw or heard anything?"

"No."

"No more questions," Ann said. "Counsel, your witness."

"Mr. Johnstone, any cross-examination?"

"Briefly, Your Honor."

"That would be appreciated by all, I am sure," Daniels said. Sam glanced at the jurors, who were looking at Daniels. After a few seconds, each pair of eyes turned toward Sam, and he didn't like what he was seeing.

"Officer Baker, how many dead bodies have you seen?"

"Not very many."

"Dozens?"

"No, not that many."

"Ten or more?"

"No."

"Five?"

"No."

"Officer Baker, was this the first dead body you encountered as a police officer?"

"Yes."

"And you're sure about the time?"

"Positive."

"How long were you on the scene before you found her?"

"Maybe five minutes?"

"Could it have been longer? Could it have been less?"

"Well, maybe, but not by much. I got there, looked around, broke the window on the front door, went in, and found her. Then I noted the time."

"I thought you sent the co-worker off?"

"Oh, yeah. I did that, too."

"And you were to interview neighbors—is that right?"

"Yes."

"And how many did you interview?"

"Well, maybe half a dozen or so."

"And none of them saw or heard anything that night?"

"Well, nothing that seemed relevant." The hair on Sam's neck was standing straight up. The old adage was "never ask a question to which you don't know the answer," but here, Sam had no real choice.

"Officer Baker, are you saying that some people saw or heard things that night, but that you didn't deem it relevant?"

"Well, yeah."

Sam grabbed some papers from a manila folder on the defense table. "Let's look at your report, shall we?"

"Your Honor, may we approach?" Ann wanted a bench conference. In Judge Daniels's courtroom, as in many others, when an attorney had an especially complex or contentious objection, it would be heard at the judge's bench with the microphones off, so only counsel and the judge could hear. When all parties were arranged at the bench, Ann said earnestly, "Judge, this is outside the scope of direct. Counsel is fishing."

"Your Honor," Sam began. "This is perfectly legitimate cross-examination. Counsel put on the record the investigative steps taken by Officer Baker. All I am doing is crossing Officer Baker with his own words and the report filed by the police following the incident."

Daniels stared hard at Sam for a moment. He had to allow it, under the law. "I'll allow the questioning to continue—up to a point, counsel. But keep it short."

After Ann and Sam had returned to their places, the judge announced, "Objection overruled."

"Officer Baker," Sam continued. "Please take a look at what I am handing you and let me know when you are prepared to answer a few questions about it."

"I'm ready."

"What are those papers you are looking at?"

"This is a copy of the report I filed after the incident."

"And you prepared that report—true?"

"Yes."

"When?"

"Well, I worked on it for a couple of days, but it looks like I completed and filed it November 6."

"And when you filed it, everything was still fresh in your mind?"

"Yes."

"And when you file these reports, they are supposed to contain truthful information—isn't that right?"

"Of course."

"So, of course, everything in there is true—is that correct?"

"Correct."

"So, what is supposed to go into the report?"

"Objection," Ann said. "This client is not an expert."

"Your Honor—" Sam began.

"Overruled. Answer to the best of your ability," Daniels said, adding, "Mr. Johnstone, I am running low on patience." Again, Sam was shocked. This was entirely improper on Daniels's part. Again, he looked at the jurors, who were now staring at him curiously.

"The report is supposed to contain everything that we did in connection with the investigation."

"Everything?"

"Well, yeah. I guess. I mean, everything that's relevant."

"Who decides what's relevant?"

"Well, the guy writing the report."

"So, if something happens in connection with the investigation, you put it in the report unless you find it not relevant—is that right?"

"Uh, yeah. I think so."

"Okay, so looking at this report, there is no mention of your door-to-door investigation, is there?"

"Yes, there is," Baker said, pointing to a page. "Right here, I noted the individuals I spoke with, and what time, and where they lived."

"But you didn't say in your report what any of them said, did you?"

"Well, no. Because I didn't think it was relevant."

"Officer Baker, what did Mrs. Snodgrass tell you?"

"Who?"

"Mrs. Snodgrass. 806 Custer Avenue. What did she tell you?"

"I can't recall."

"You don't know?"

"Well, I can't remember, sitting here now."

"And what about Mr. Jorgensen. He lives at—"

"Counsel, please approach," Daniels interrupted. When the parties were in place, he looked hard at Sam. "What are you doing?"

"I'm cross-examining a witness, Your Honor."

"This is going to take forever at this rate," Daniels hissed. "I won't have it."

"Your Honor, I have every right—"

"Mr. Johnstone, I'm going to order you to move along. Ask your questions, but in such a manner that we can get this witness done before the evening break."

Sam again met Daniels's glare. This was clearly improper. He snuck a glance at the jurors, who were clearly intrigued, and clearly of the opinion that Sam must be doing something wrong. "Your Honor, I object to your continually interrupting my cross-examination of this witness."

"I'll not have this kind of impertinence, counsel. Return to your places."

"Judge—"

"Return to your places!" Daniels hissed.

"Officer Baker, let me ask it this way," Sam said, after everyone was back in place. "You said earlier that some residents gave you information during your door-to-door, right?"

"Right."

"And not all of that information made it into your report, right?"

"Right."

"So, what information were you given, and by whom, that didn't make it into your report?"

"Objection, Your Honor," Ann said. "Hearsay."

"Sustained."

"Your Honor! I have no other way to elicit this information," Sam said. "It was withheld! I had no knowledge of it because it wasn't disclosed."

"The witnesses' names were in the report, Judge. He could have deposed them prior to trial," Ann said.

"But I didn't know they'd said anything not included in the report," Sam argued.

"The objection is sustained, Mr. Johnstone. Move along."

Sam looked at the jurors, all of whom were looking impatiently back at him. Daniels had turned them against him. "No more questions, Your Honor," he said, smiling at the jurors as he sat down, and getting a smirk from Juror 465 in return.

40

"Ms. Fulks, call your next witness," Daniels said, when trial resumed the next day.

"Dr. Ronald B. Laws." Ann turned and faced the rear of the courtroom, awaiting the doctor's arrival. As was customary, Dr. Laws had been sequestered prior to testifying. The doctor approached the stand, was sworn to an oath by the judge, and took his seat on the witness stand.

"Would you state your name, please, and spell your last name for the record," Ann requested.

"Ronald B. Laws, M.D. That's L-A-W-S."

"And where do you live, Dr. Laws?"

"You want an address?"

"City and state will be fine."

"I live right here in Custer, Wyoming."

"Are you employed?"

"I am."

"What is your occupation?"

"I am a physician."

"Do you have a specialty?"

"I am a pathologist, and within that specialty I am further certified as a forensic pathologist."

"So, could you tell the jurors what you do as a forensic pathologist?"

"Certainly. Pathology is a large field of medicine and is divided into two major subfields: forensic pathology and clinical pathology. So I am often involved in clarifying medical or scientific questions that come up in the courtroom, to include the investigation of sudden or unexpected death."

"Can you give the jury an idea of your medical education?"

"Certainly. I grew up in Cody, Wyoming, and attended public schools there. I did my undergraduate work at the University of Wyoming, graduating with a degree in microbiology. After graduation, I attended the University of Washington School of Medicine, graduating with a doctor of medicine degree. Then I did a five-year residency in pathology at the Hennepin County Medical Center and surrounding hospitals and labs in the Minneapolis area."

"Are you board certified?"

"I am board certified in the sub-specialties of clinical, anatomic, and forensic pathology."

"Do you work at present as a physician?"

"I do. I am a pathologist with Custer County Health and I am the appointed Custer County Medical Examiner."

"What is the medical examiner?"

"The medical examiner is the physician assigned to the coroner's office. The coroner is an elected position and does not have to be a licensed physician. The medical examiner heads the office that is in charge of investigating the two major types of death investigations: non-natural deaths—the accidents, suicides, and homicides that take place in a community every day—and sudden unexpected deaths—deaths where no doctor was in attendance to sign a death certificate. We investigate those cases."

"We?"

"Well, generally, me. I can ask for assistance from the State Department of Health if I need it."

"Do you perform autopsies?"

"Routinely, yes."

I want to go back to last November—the early part of the month," Ann said. "Were you asked to perform an autopsy on one C. Emily Smith?"

"No."

"You weren't?"

"Of course not," Laws said. "As I just explained, the decision to perform an autopsy is well within the purview of my responsibilities. No one *asked* me."

Sam smiled to himself. Typical doctor.

"In any event, you performed an autopsy on Ms. Smith during the first week in November?"

"I did."

"How is an autopsy conducted?"

The doctor embarked on a lengthy explanation of the procedure he generally followed. From time to time Ann would interrupt the monologue long enough to ask a clarifying question, whereupon the doctor would explain in excruciating detail. As a result, the direct examination took the better part of the morning. Sam was losing patience when Ann finally zeroed in on what was important. "What of significance did you find upon your initial examination of Ms. Smith?"

"The body was well-preserved, deterioration was minimal. In examination the most immediate observation was an enormous laceration of the throat and neck."

"What portion of the neck?"

"Well, really, almost ear to ear," the doctor replied, gesturing as he did so.

"Did you have X-rays done?"

"I did."

"What, if anything, did they reveal?"

"The X-rays revealed a metal object in the neck area. I later removed the object, which I believe to be a shard of metal from a knife of some sort."

"Your Honor, may I approach the witness?"

"You may."

"I'm handing the witness what I've marked as Exhibit 14," Ann said.

"Your Honor, the defendant will stipulate to foundation, relevance, and to admission of Exhibit 14," Sam said. Juror 465 was looking at him approvingly.

"Exhibit 14 is received," Daniels said.

Ann continued. "Doctor, looking at Exhibit 14. What is it?"

"This is the X-ray I ordered of the decedent's upper torso, showing the bones of the neck and skull. On the right side of the X-ray is a white, kind of triangular-shaped area. That's where I later extracted what I believe to be a piece of a knife."

"And why do you believe it to be part of a knife?"

"Well, I've seen knives, it looks like part of a knife, and the cops told me later—"

"Objection. Hearsay," Sam said.

"Sustained," Judge Daniels said. Sam noted the doctor's irritation.

"This portion of a knife," Ann began, looking at the jury. "It would have been located where on Emily's body?"

"Right about here." The doctor touched his own throat. "On what she would have deemed her left side."

"Did you remove the shard?"

"Yes, I did."

"What did you do with it?"

"I gave it to Punch Polson."

"Is that Detective Kenneth Polson of the Custer Police Department?"

"Yes. He's sitting right next to you."

Ann ignored the insult and jury's laughter. "And after removing the shard and giving it to Detective Polson, what did you do?"

"I completed the autopsy; took samples, weighed the organs, and the like."

"And following the autopsy, did you reach a conclusion as to the cause of death?"

"I did."

"What, in your opinion, was the cause of Ms. Smith's death?"

"Exsanguination as the result of the laceration to her neck," the doctor responded. Then, seeing Ann's reaction, he looked to the jury and explained, "She bled to death after having her throat slashed."

"No further questions, Your Honor," Ann said.

"Mr. Johnstone," the judge began as Sam rose for cross-examination. "How long do you suppose your cross-examination will take? I'd like to see that these good people are able to enjoy lunch."

The judge's question was entirely inappropriate but had the intended effect. The jurors were looking at Sam expectantly. He had a stark, unsatisfactory choice: he could either rush through his cross-examination to meet the jurors' judicially-induced expectation, he could risk alienating them by properly doing his job, or he could ask the judge to take a recess before commencing his cross-examination, thereby allowing the doctor's testimony to ferment unchallenged in the jurors' minds.

"Counsel, we're awaiting a response?" Daniels said, clearly expecting Sam to request to commence cross-examination after lunch.

"Your Honor, I think my cross-examination will take no more than five to ten minutes," Sam ventured.

"Well, then, make it five," Daniels snapped. "Please begin."

"Good morning, Doctor," Sam said.

"Good morning."

"You're not an expert on knives, are you?"

"I am not," the doctor admitted.

"So, you cannot say for certain that the piece of metal you extracted from the decedent's body came from a knife, can you?"

"I cannot."

"Did you estimate the time of death?"

"I would say she died about forty-eight hours before I saw her, so any time between 11:00 p.m. on the 31st and 4:00 a.m. on the 1st."

"And did she die in her home?"

"Are you asking if she had been moved?"

"Yes."

"Well, not my area of expertise, but given the blood in the immediate vicinity, I think she sustained the injury and died within several feet of where she was found."

"Was there any alcohol in her system?"

"Yes."

"How much?"

"Objection, Your Honor," Ann said. "Relevance."

"What is the relevance, Mr. Johnstone?" Daniels asked.

"Your Honor, the decedent's actions immediately prior to her death are relevant to how she died. My client has the right to inquire—"

"Overruled. You may answer," Daniels said to the doctor.

"Yes. She had a blood alcohol content of approximately .10."

"She was legally drunk?"

"Well, she was presumptively too intoxicated to safely drive, if I understand the law."

"Thank you, Doctor." Sam turned from the podium and appeared to be heading to the defendant's table when he stopped, swung around, and returned to the podium. "Did your investigation reveal the presence of any drugs?"

"Objection, Your Honor!" Ann said. "Again, what is the relevance?"

"Mr. Johnstone?"

"Same response, Judge," Sam said. "My client—"

"You may answer," the judge said, surprising Sam.

"Yes. Her blood showed the presence of tetrahydrocannabinol. That's THC, the intoxicating element in marijuana."

"Can you surmise as to how recently she had consumed it?"

"The state lab estimated within twelve hours of her death."

"Did you examine Ms. Smith's vagina?"

"During the autopsy, yes," the doctor replied, to courtroom titters.

"Was there any evidence that she had been sexually assaulted?"

"No."

"Had she had sex before she died?"

"Yes."

"How do you know?"

"There was seminal fluid in and on her."

"Do you know whom she had sex with?"

"No. Not my area of concern."

"Can you say whether it was one or more men?"

"Objection! Your Honor, the defendant is attempting to—"

"Sustained," Judge Daniels said. "Move along, counsel."

"Your Honor, may we approach?" Sam asked.

When Sam and Ann had positioned themselves in front of the judge, Sam began, "Judge, I'd like to make an offer of proof." In order for an objection to be taken seriously by an appellate court, an attorney generally had to offer proof that the evidence, if admitted, was material and could affect the outcome. Otherwise, even if the judge did commit an error in making his ruling, it would be examined under a "plain error" standard, meaning it was unlikely to be overturned on appeal.

"No. Denied," Judge Daniels replied. "Move along, counsel." Sam stared hard at Daniels, who had no authority to deny his making an offer of proof. On the other hand, there was a record of the denial, and if the jury was paying attention, they now knew that Emily Smith was drunk, stoned, and having sex with someone before she died—and that's what Sam was trying to get in front of them to begin with. Looking at Juror 465, Sam withdrew.

"One final question, Doctor," Sam began when he got to the podium.

"Yes?" Laws looked at Sam expectantly.

"From your standpoint as a medical doctor, it's true, isn't it, that Ms. Smith was killed at the hands of an unknown killer using an unknown weapon."

The doctor sat perfectly still, clearly thinking. "Yes, that's true," he finally answered.

"Nothing further," Sam said, and sat down.

Daniels scowled at Ann. "Redirect?"

"No further questions," Ann said, content with the fact that she had gotten the date, approximate time, and manner of death into evidence.

"Thank you for your consideration, counsel. Doctor, you may step down," Daniels said. "We'll break for lunch."

41

The next couple of days were painful for Sam. He kept an eye on the jurors, hoping to see them driven to boredom by Ann, who appeared determined to call and inquire of anyone who had even tertiary involvement in the investigation. Sam had objected twice, arguing that witnesses were cumulative. Each time he had been rebuffed by Daniels; each time Juror 465 beamed at Daniels approvingly, then shot Sam the fisheye. As he watched helplessly, a string of increasingly well-trained and good-looking men and women took the stand and earnestly recounted their part in the investigation that culminated in Tommy's arrest. They spoke at great length and in precise detail about measurements taken, distances from here to there, the condition of the body and the activity of neighbors, presenting a picture of a comprehensive and flawlessly executed investigation, all while Sam drank water and tried to feign indifference.

Ann was thorough, prepared, and clearly intending to get every bit of inculpatory evidence in the record. Sam understood, but wanted it in quickly and with as little discussion as possible, so where he believed it to be to Tommy's advantage, he attempted to cooperate by stipulating to the admission of exhibits and by asking few but pointed questions on cross-examination. While that tactic no doubt pleased Judge Daniels and Juror

465, it was concerning to Tommy. "Shouldn't you be doing something?" he asked.

"Not a lot to do," Sam whispered. "This is all routine stuff. We need to save our energy for the important fights."

"But they're burying me," Tommy insisted.

"I know it seems that way." Sam nodded. "But not a lot I can do right now."

"Sam, you have to eat," Veronica had said over the phone. They hadn't seen each other in days. Between Sam's preparations and her own schedule, they'd each been overcome by events of late. She'd finally talked him into a late dinner. She was having a glass of chardonnay. He was drinking sparkling water.

"I guess I've never seen you drink water," she observed. "Is this how you react under stress?"

"For most of my life, stress resulted in a lot of booze."

"But now?"

"Now, a guy's life is in my hands. I'm trying not to do anything I'll regret."

"Not true."

"How so?"

"Tommy's life will be in the jury's hands. It's not your job to win or lose. It's only your job to tell his story, and to challenge the State's witnesses and evidence," she said.

"Not bad," Sam observed. "Civics class?"

"Professor Sam Johnstone," she giggled. He liked the way she laughed when she'd had a glass of wine. That seemed healthy. "Besides, who do you think types up the judge's advisories to the jury?"

Sam smiled and pushed a roasted potato around his plate. He'd been skipping meals for the better part of two weeks, too busy to cook or sit down for a proper meal. But he could hardly bring himself to eat anything even now. He looked at the remaining half of the ribeye he'd ordered with little enthusiasm, then at Veronica.

"Sam, what is it?" she asked.

"It's just the trial," he said, taking a sip of the water and making a wry face as he swallowed. He had to stay sober. "I don't like the way it's started. I just need one juror to go Tommy's way—just one juror who will question the State's investigation and vote accordingly. But I don't see that guy or gal. I—"

"Sam, you can't take all this on. You can't make the jurors see what they cannot or will not see."

"That's my job."

"That's the ideal. Your job is less straightforward than that. You can't take this on. You didn't do it."

"Neither did Tommy."

"You don't know that, Sam."

"I know it."

"You can't know it. The only people who know what happened are Emily and whoever killed her. The rest of us are just guessing—looking for the truth."

"Right," he said.

"How is the counseling going?"

"All right. I like the guy," Sam said. "I can't see him during the trial, of course, but he gave me his phone number for emergencies and a book that's helping me understand why I think the way I do."

"Good to hear."

"Yeah. He's been some places, seen some things. Not what I expected."

"I'll bet he'd say the same about you."

"Probably." Sam smiled. "He's got me doing some mindfulness exercises."

"Are they working?"

"No."

"How do you know?"

"Because I don't feel any different."

"Sam." Veronica placed her hand on his. "These things take time."

"I don't have time. I can't have another freak-out in court."

She looked at the circles under his eyes and shook her head. "Well, you haven't had any problems yet, have you?"

"Not yet."

"What are you doing tonight?"

"I've got to get ready to cross one of their experts. Then I'm just going to try and relax."

"Why don't I come over and see if I can help you?"

"What do you know about cross-examination?" he asked, smiling.

42

"Your Honor, the State calls Cale Pleasance," Ann announced in a strong, steady voice. She was gaining confidence with every witness, Sam noted.

The deputies retrieved Pleasance and brought him before the judge while the jurors watched. He was sworn and took the stand. After obtaining identifying information from him, Ann asked about his occupation.

"I'm a fingerprint examiner for Custer County."

"And how long have you been so employed?"

"Oh, five, maybe six years."

"And have you received any specialized training in connection with your employment?"

"Your Honor, the defense will stipulate to Mr. Pleasance's expert qualifications," Sam offered. He wasn't being magnanimous; this was another effort to blunt the effectiveness of the coming testimony, and Daniels knew it.

"Thank you, counsel," Daniels replied. "Mr. Pleasance, you may answer."

"Yes. I was originally hired back east as a lab tech, then after a couple of years I was trained in Virginia at the FBI Academy, spent three years with the FBI at one of their labs, and then applied for and was hired by the State of Wyoming's Division of Criminal Investigation. A few years after that I transferred here to Custer. My wife's from here."

"And what exactly does a fingerprint examiner do?"

"I examine fingerprints at crime scenes as well as those that are recorded at the jail or are in our database for comparison with each other."

"And how is that accomplished?"

"Well, fingerprint identification has been around since the 1920s," Pleasance began. "It's a biometric process using the impressions made by the ridge formations or patterns found on the fingertips." Warming to his subject, Pleasance continued. "As you may know, no two persons have the same arrangement of ridge patterns, but what you may not know is that the patterns remain unchanged throughout life. For these reasons, fingerprints offer an infallible means of personal identification. Other personal characteristics may change, but fingerprints do not."

"So, how do you actually go about making the comparison?"

"Well, one way is that fingerprints can be recorded on a standard fingerprint card or can be recorded digitally and transmitted electronically to the FBI for storage in their database and later comparison. The FBI keeps a database of fingerprints," he added. "By comparing fingerprints at the scene of a crime with the fingerprints of a crime suspect, we can show absolute proof of the suspect's identity. Another way, of course, is to compare the fingerprint found at a crime scene with the fingerprint of a suspect. I can do that right here in Custer."

"And in November of last year, were you asked to identify fingerprints having to do with the homicide of a woman named Emily Smith?"

"Yes."

"By whom?"

"I think Detective Polson was the one doing the asking, but it might have been one of his assistants who made the actual request."

"And what were you asked to do?"

"I was asked to do two primary things. First, identify, if possible, the persons who made all the identifiable fingerprints at the scene."

"Let me stop you there. Did you collect any fingerprints at the scene?"

"Many of them, yes. Crime technicians got the others."

"Okay. So, you obtain or receive prints and then you attempt to identify them using a database of stored prints?"

"Usually."

"And what else were you asked to do?"

"I was asked to look at the prints found on certain items of evidence and tell the law enforcement officers whose prints they were, if possible."

"How would you be able to figure that out?"

"We can compare what we have with AFIS, er, the Integrated Automated Fingerprint Identification System. It's a national database of everyone who has had their fingerprints registered."

"And who is that?"

"Well, all suspected criminals get fingerprinted. Military personnel, law enforcement types, some government employees and contractors, and others working sensitive positions."

"So the match is done with a computer?"

"Initially, and then in a case like this I would personally verify. Or, like I said, I could compare fingerprints at the scene with known prints, like the decedent's."

"And did you perform both tasks?"

"For the most part, er, well, yes. I mean, there were some prints I could not identify."

"Why not?"

"Well, some prints weren't identifiable. Just smeared or otherwise unrecoverable. For others, we couldn't match because you must have a known source. If the person who left the print has never had their information put in the database, then there's nothing to compare it with, so unless you have a second set of prints left by a suspect to compare your specimen to, you're out of luck."

Ann then had the witness give an extended lecture on the difference between patent prints, latent prints, and the collection techniques for each. By the time that was done, it was time for a recess. Punch walked quickly into the parking lot and dialed Pleasance's number.

"Members of the jury, you'll recall that at the time we took the lunch recess, Ms. Fulks was inquiring of Mr. Pleasance," Daniels said, settling onto the bench. "Ms. Fulks, please continue. Mr. Pleasance, I remind you that you are still under oath."

Ann rose and stepped to the podium. "Mr. Pleasance, you were able to identify a number of fingerprints found in the decedent's home—is that right?"

"Yes, it is."

"How many sets were you able to identify?"

"Well, we know there were at least six sets of prints in the home."

"So, you identified six sets of prints?"

"No, we identified five. One set remains unidentified."

"So, one set of prints has never been identified?"

"Yes."

"Is that all?"

"Well, there were any number of prints that for whatever reason we couldn't recover. Like I said, in some cases they were smudged, in others the source material was not conducive to our lifting a print."

"So you can't be sure how many people had actually been in the house?" Ann asked, trying to take the sting out of any points Sam might make.

"That's right."

"Did you examine the prints on what's been deemed the murder weapon?"

"Yes."

"How many sets of prints were on that weapon?"

"Two."

"Were you able to identify those prints?"

"One set, yes."

"Whose prints did you identify on the weapon?"

"The defendant's." All eyes were on Tommy, who sat rigid, just as Sam had coached. Sam was thinking about a question Ann had not asked.

"And the other set remains unidentified?"

"Yes."

Ann then inquired into each location where Tommy's fingerprints had been located. It was damning stuff, on its face. At last, she concluded, "Your witness, counsel," and turned to Sam, who remained seated, obviously thinking.

"Mr. Johnstone, are you with us?" Daniels asked.

"Yes, Judge," Sam allowed while scribbling on a yellow pad.

"Well, do you have any questions for this witness or not?"

"Just a few, Your Honor," Sam said, still seated and apparently lost in thought.

"Well, get on with it!" Daniels said, drawing an approving nod from Juror 465.

"Thank you, sir." Sam rose and moved quickly to the podium to begin his questioning. "You can't be sure how many sets of prints you and your people actually located in the home?"

"No."

"So, it could be that dozens of people have visited the decedent's home?"

"Could be."

"And it's not your job to eliminate them as suspects, is it?"

"I just look at fingerprints."

"You said that fingerprint identification is 'infallible'—was that your testimony?"

"Well, yes."

"Strong word. But there can be mistakes—isn't that true?"

"Well, of course. People make mistakes."

"Can you tell the jury what a 'false positive' is as it relates to fingerprints?"

"A false positive occurs when two prints that are not alike are mistakenly deemed to be a match."

"What's a 'false negative?'"

"A false negative occurs when two matching fingerprints are mistakenly identified as not matching," Pleasance said. He wasn't enjoying having to admit the possibility of mistakes. Sam decided to change the subject. "So, six separate and identifiable sets of prints in the home?"

"Yes."

"The decedent?"

"Of course."

"The defendant."

"Yes. Lots of them," Pleasance added gratuitously.

"The decedent's mother?"

"Yes."

"Her housekeeper?"

"Yes."

"And an unidentified set?"

"Yes."

"That leaves one more set, does it not?"

"Yes."

"A set you've identified?" Sam asked, looking at Ann. Detective Polson had testified to four sets having been identified during the preliminary hearing. He'd gotten nothing from the prosecution since.

"Yes," Pleasance admitted.

"The identity of the donor of that set has not been disclosed to the defense, has it?"

"Your Honor, the State objects," Ann said. "This witness is not responsible for discovery by the State."

"Mr. Johnstone?"

"I'm just trying to figure out what Mr. Pleasance knows, Judge."

"I'll allow it," Daniels said.

"Not my job," Pleasance said, taking his clue from Ann. "I don't know what you've been told, sir."

"Do *you* know who left the fifth set of prints?"

"Yes."

Sam was conflicted. The Golden Rule for trial lawyers is never to ask a question to which you do not already know the answer. Under the rules, the prosecution should have disclosed the donor's identity as part of the discovery process. The fact they hadn't done so was confusing; the only options that occurred to Sam were that Ann was either violating the rules or hadn't been told whose prints they were yet. Tommy's prints had already been placed at the scene. It couldn't get any worse. He had to ask.

"Whose were they?"

Pleasance looked at Ann, who gazed down at her yellow legal pad. Then he glanced at Punch before returning his attention to Sam. "It was a single print, on a vase of flowers," he said. "It belonged to one Jonathon Howard."

Punch watched silently as the courtroom predictably went into an uproar. He heard Sam asking for a mistrial, saw Daniels pounding the gavel to restore order, and stood with everyone else as the jury was sent to the jury room. He listened as Daniels ordered a brief recess, after which he would hear Sam's motion for a mistrial. Punch sat back down heavily after the judge departed. Spectators, courtroom personnel, and attorneys alike chattered nervously, filling the ensuing silence.

Sam and Tommy had their heads together, Sam obviously filling Tommy in on the meaning of Judge Howard's prints. Ann was huddled with Rebecca, the two of them trying to get ready for the coming argument. Punch felt Ann should have the upper hand, because she'd obviously known the information would come out at some point.

He got up and excused himself. "I'm going to stretch."

"Don't go far, Detective," Ann said through clenched teeth. "We might need your testimony."

Daniels was pouring himself two fingers of scotch when Mary entered his chambers to check on him. The break had come much earlier than she anticipated, and she didn't have his afternoon tea prepared. Seeing the glass in front of Daniels, she scolded him. "Goodness, Judge. You cannot be drinking during a trial."

"Not now, Mary."

"What is going on?"

"The shit has hit the fan," Daniels said. "I'm going to have to grant Sam Johnstone's motion for a mistrial. Damn it! We don't have the time or money for another trial! That's what's going on. Get me my book of court rules. It's on my bench."

"I'll do that, sir," Mary said. "But first, you finish that drink and brush your teeth."

"We're back on the record," Daniels said, moments later. "Mr. Johnstone, do you have a motion to make?"

"Yes." Sam rose from his chair. "The defendant moves for a mistrial. As you know, sir, under both *Brady v. United States* and Wyoming law, the prosecution has a duty to disclose exculpatory information in its possession. Here, the State had knowledge for some time that a fingerprint belonging to the very judge who signed the arrest warrant and presided over the preliminary hearing was discovered in the home of the deceased. That's a failure to provide discovery and a staggering conflict of interest, and we ask the court to grant a mistrial."

"Ms. Fulks?" Daniels looked to Ann for the State's response.

Ann stood, looking drawn. "Your Honor, the information was not disclosed. The State admits that. But the information wasn't exculpatory to begin with, and we didn't have access to it ourselves until after the preliminary hearing, so we couldn't have disclosed it prior. There is no evidence as to how that fingerprint got on the vase, and the defendant hasn't shown—or even asserted—that he was prejudiced by not having the information. Therefore, we'd ask the court to deny the defendant's motion."

"Mr. Johnstone?" Daniels was looking steadily at Sam. "What is the defendant's response? More specifically, what prejudice do you believe has been sustained by the defendant?"

"Your Honor," Sam began. "I can't begin to answer that question, because I don't know what I don't know. I know nothing about the print—when and where it was found, by whom, etc."

"You could inquire, couldn't you? I'd certainly allow you to re-call any witnesses with relevant information."

"But I couldn't begin to know whose information might be relevant! I don't know who found what, where, or the like."

"But you could ask, could you not?"

"If you would afford me some leeway, I could make a stab at it, Judge. But clearly my client is at a tactical disadvantage here."

Punch, who was next to testify, was fully prepared for the judge to declare a mistrial. He couldn't help but think of the colossal waste of resources the trial had been—and all because Ann had disregarded her duty.

Daniels looked at Johnstone for a long time, clearly on the verge of granting the motion. "Let's take a recess; I want to think this over and do some quick legal research. We'll reconvene after lunch," he said, then stood and left the courtroom.

"Sam—" Tommy began.

"Not here," Sam said. "I'll talk to you in the holding cell. Be right there."

The courthouse holding cell was small, cramped, and bare, and Sam could smell the stale sweat on Tommy as soon as he entered.

"Sam, I still don't understand," Tommy said.

"The State failed to alert us to some information they had. Apparently, Judge Howard's fingerprint was found on a vase in Emily's house."

"When?"

"What do you mean?"

"When was the print found?"

"I'm not sure. That's part of the problem."

"Was it before or after we saw him?"

"Well, from what Ann said, it sounds like the State didn't know until after the preliminary hearing—if she's telling the truth."

"So, what's that mean?"

"Well, I think the presence of the print is exculpatory—it means Judge Howard might have been in the house at some point. They were supposed to tell us that. And Judge Howard shouldn't have signed the warrant for your arrest or heard the preliminary hearing because he had a conflict. I've asked for a mistrial—"

"Why?"

"Because the prosecution didn't turn over what they had!"

"And if we get a new trial, what then?"

"Well, we'd basically start all over. Only this time I'd have all of the information—"

"When?"

"Well, I don't know. I suppose it would probably be a few months—"

"Months? No way, Sam. I've been locked in a cage for months already."

"But it's your right!"

"I don't give a damn. Even before the preliminary hearing, you said that I needed to be prepared to get bound over—that everyone gets bound over, right?"

"Well, yeah."

"And so I got bound over, right?" Tommy was up and pacing the room now.

"Yes."

"So, what difference did it make who the judge was?"

"That's not the point."

"Sam, that *is* the point—to everyone except lawyers!"

Sam sat back in his chair. "Tommy, the prosecution has to follow the rules!"

"Screw the rules, Sam! I don't want another trial. I want to get this over with one way or another."

"Tommy, maybe with a new jury—"

"Let me ask you something," Tommy began, pacing more furiously. "The jury knows now that Judge Howard was in her house before she died, right?"

"Well, presumably. They know his print was there."

"So, this jury already knows what you'd tell them in any new trial, right?"

"Well, yeah," Sam allowed. "But Tommy, I think with this new evidence up front we could do a deal—"

"I've told you, Sam: no deals. I didn't kill her." Tommy sat down and looked at him. "This jury knows that print was there. They have to know the prosecution was trying to screw me, right?"

Sam sat quietly, looking at the yellow pad on the table.

"I want to go on with the trial," Tommy said. "Tell the judge you take back your motion, or whatever you call it. I don't care whether that judge was banging her like a drum."

"I'm advising against it."

"Got it, Sam. Now, what do you need from me? Need me to sign something to cover your ass?"

43

In the courtroom, waiting for Daniels to be seated, Ann felt sick to her stomach. All of her preparation, all of her work, going down the drain because Howard had apparently been pumping Emily and Punch didn't figure it out until it was too late. No doubt she would take the fall for this. Rebecca would assign another attorney to the re-trial. She took a long pull from the water cup on the table and set it down carefully, her hands shaking.

"Please be seated, ladies and gentlemen," Daniels began. "We are back on the record in State v. Olsen. The court has heard the argument of counsel and . . . Mr. Johnstone, do you wish to be recognized?"

"Yes, Your Honor," Sam said, already on his feet.

"Well, what is it? I'm trying to make a record before I announce the court's decision, sir."

"Your Honor, the defendant moves to withdraw the motion for mistrial."

Daniels looked around the courtroom, quieting the whispers of shock as soon as they had started. Two reporters jumped up and headed for the doors. Daniels stared at Sam for a long moment. "Very well, Mr. Johnstone," Daniels said, and then, without looking at Ann, asked, "Ms. Fulks, I'm assuming the State does not object to Mr. Johnstone and his client withdrawing the motion?"

"We do not."

"The motion having been withdrawn, are there other matters we need to discuss before the court recalls the jury?"

"No," Ann said.

"There is one thing," Sam said.

"Yes?" Daniels asked.

"I'd ask the court to remind the State of its continuing obligation to supplement discovery if and when additional information is uncovered as part of its continuing investigation."

"Your Honor, I object!" Ann was on her feet. "Counsel seems to be implying—"

"Ms. Fulks, sit down," Daniels said.

"Judge—" Ann interrupted.

"Ms. Fulks, I'm talking!" Daniels barked. Ann sat quickly, chagrined. "We have already seen the State's failure to properly disclose come uncomfortably close to derailing this trial. I'm going to remind you once, and once only, of the State's affirmative responsibility to disclose information of an exculpatory nature, and I'll tell you right now that if additional information is found to have been improperly withheld, this court will likely declare a mistrial and assess costs against the State—this time over the objection of both of you, if necessary. Am I clear?"

On direct, Punch Polson testified for an entire day. From Sam's perspective, the testimony was devastatingly effective. The detective had been thorough, careful, and complete in his investigation. He had obviously been well-prepared by Ann. The testimony provided a comprehensive overview of the investigation, connecting the dots and filling in information omitted by earlier witnesses. He calmly and professionally admitted shortcomings in the State's case: the late identification of Howard's fingerprint, the yet-to-be-identified fingerprints on the murder weapon and at the scene, the unidentified DNA, the lack of witnesses, the circumstantial nature of the case, as well as other evidentiary unknowns. He was, in short, an excellent witness for the prosecution. Ann finished her direct and sat down, clearly pleased. Punch sat in the witness's chair, drinking from a paper cup, calmly awaiting Sam's cross.

Sam faced a stark choice. He could cross-examine Polson and attempt to show the jury where mistakes or omissions had been made. But Ann had wisely already gotten the evidentiary shortcomings on the record, and by venturing down that road, Sam risked reinforcing in the jury's mind what appeared to be a competent, professional investigation. The other option was equally unappealing: by foregoing cross-examination of Polson, Sam risked leaving the jury with the impression that he had no factual basis upon which to contest Polson's decision to arrest Tommy.

"Mr. Johnstone?" Daniels was impatient.

The jury already knew about the prints and semen. "No questions, Your Honor."

44

"You're late," Veronica said. "You're never late."

"Sorry." Sam took off his jacket and dropped it on a chair. She liked the way he felt at home. "I've been on the phone with a private fingerprint examiner out of Denver. I hired my own now that I see I can't trust the State."

"Well, I'm just glad to see you," she said. "Let's eat, and then I want to watch a show on television. Sunday night's my favorite."

It was, of all things, a courtroom drama. Sam watched with more interest than he might have anticipated as a pair of improbably attractive lawyers defended their obviously innocent clients against trumped-up charges brought by overeager, politically-motivated prosecutors. An hour later, with the verdicts of acquittal having been rendered by a television jury, Veronica stirred. "So," she asked. "Are you going to put Tommy on the stand?"

"I don't know yet," Sam said. He was trying to sip bourbon from a tumbler she had given him, despite his overpowering urge to quaff the entire thing in one gulp and pour another three fingers. For whatever reason—Fear? Anxiety? Stress? All three?—he had a burning desire to get stinking drunk. It was dangerous. Before he left home, he'd read a chapter of the book Martinez had given him and tried the breathing exercises. The trial was reaching its most critical point, and the last thing he needed was to lose preparation time or show for trial feeling in less than tip-top shape.

"Well, if he's innocent, why wouldn't he testify?"

"There are a lot of reasons. First, he doesn't have to. He's got absolute right to silence."

"I know, but—"

"Second, because it's fraught with danger," Sam said. "The State's witnesses are almost all experts at being in court. Cops, criminologists, scientists—they have all testified before. They know what to say and what not to say. Hell, some of them have taken classes in how to present evidence. But your average guy doesn't know what to say or when to shut up. He's easily manipulated by a good prosecutor, and Ann is a good prosecutor."

"But even if he gets tripped, if he's innocent—"

"He's got a pretty lengthy rap sheet, and unless he testifies that won't come in. But if he testifies, his record is fair game." Sam finished his drink and reached for the bottle.

"You'd best be careful," Veronica said.

"I've got it."

She nodded. "When will you decide?"

"Probably no sooner than I have to, but certainly not before she finishes her case," Sam said. "It really comes down to weighing how well he'll stand up under cross-examination against how good Ann's case is. If I think he's in real danger of being convicted at the end of her case, I'll put him on. But if there's any chance of acquittal, then I'll try and convince him to trust me and sit it out."

"How do you think he'd do?"

"Frankly, I think he'd suck. He's immature, emotional, and naïve. He's proud, somewhat narcissistic, and angry. Any one of those traits will work against him on the stand, and I'm afraid that if he testifies Ann will pick him apart in front of the jury."

"What does he want to do?"

"Oh, he's raring to go. He thinks that if he just testifies this will all be behind him. What he doesn't understand is that if I agree to his testifying, it means, excuse my language, that he is in deep shit at that point."

"So if he testifies—"

"That means I am so certain he's gonna be convicted there's nothing to lose, or that he insists and has disregarded my advice. He's the client. It's his case. It's always his option."

They stared across the table at each other. "Your dinner is getting cold," she said.

"I guess I don't have much of an appetite," he countered.

"Well, force something down or you're going to be feeling that bourbon tomorrow. Why did you hire your own examiner, by the way?"

"Because I have an idea," he said. "It's a long-shot, but it's possible."

45

"The State calls Gus Hadley," Ann said. Sam took a deep breath and let it go, then swallowed about five ounces of water in a single gulp. He was somewhat dehydrated, but other than that not much the worse for wear from the weekend. Fortunately, the next witness wouldn't do his client much harm.

"State your name," Ann said.

"Name's Gus Hadley, just like you said."

"Thank you, Mr. Hadley. Now, do you know—excuse me, *did* you know a woman named Emily Smith?"

"I did. I manage the apartment she lived in."

"What can you tell me about Ms. Smith?" The question was vague and overbroad, but because he had a pretty good idea what the witness would say, and because the testimony was probably harmless, Sam let it go.

"Well, as I told you afore, I ain't a snoop, so I don't spend my time watching what goes on, know what I mean? But I get paid to upkeep the place, so I keep my eyes open as necessary."

"Go on," Ann encouraged the witness.

"That Emily, she was a good-looker. She had lotsa guys lookin' in on her. Some a them were young men, and some was older. The night afore she died I seen that guy go into her house." He pointed at Tommy.

"Let's take a step back," Ann said, adding, "I want to make sure I understand." What she really wanted, of course, was to have the witness repeat what he'd just said, just in case a juror or two was dozing after lunch. "Now, you were where?"

"In my living room, which looks out on the parking lot."

"And Emily's apartment is, er, was, where?"

"Right next to mine."

"So, you were at the window in your apartment and you saw the defendant do what?"

"I seen him pull up in his truck, get out, and go into Emily's house."

"And you're sure it was him?"

"'Course I'm sure."

"Is the man you saw enter Emily's apartment in this courtroom?"

"Yup. I just told you that."

Ann ignored the slight. "For the record, could you point him out, describe where he is sitting and what he is wearing?"

"Well," Gus said. "He's wearing a brown sport coat and sitting right next to Mr. Johnson, the lawyer. Right in front of me."

"Do you mean Mr. Johnstone, the defense attorney?"

"Well, I guess. I mean that fella there with the bad leg." Sam smiled in spite of himself.

"You saw him go into the apartment?"

"Yep."

"Did you see him leave?"

"Yep."

Sam sat up in his chair. This was not what Gus had told him. Gus said he'd not seen Tommy leave and that he'd had no real good idea when and if he did.

"What time was that?"

"Oh, I'd say about four," Gus offered.

"So, when was the next time you saw Emily?"

"Never did."

"But you saw the defendant leave?"

"Yup."

"How can you be sure of the time?"

"Well, I'm a light sleeper," Gus said. "I was up 'cause my stomach was bothering me a bit. I know it was about four 'cause I looked at the clock."

"Your witness, counsel."

Sam had gotten increasingly angry during the man's testimony and was now in full froth. He spent some time looking at the papers on the desk in front of him. It was almost impossible to successfully impeach a witness based on statements he'd made out of court while not under oath, but he was going to try.

"Mr. Johnstone, does the defense wish to cross-examine this witness?"

"Yes, Your Honor," Sam said. "But I wonder if we might take a brief recess?"

"Denied, Mr. Johnstone. It's been less than an hour since lunch," Daniels said impatiently. "We'll break at three o'clock."

"Thank you, Your Honor," Sam said, rising. Juror 465 made no attempt to suppress her satisfaction with the judge's ruling. His mind racing, Sam stalled for a bit more time. "Just a moment, Mr. Hadley, while I review my notes."

Sam would have to tread lightly. The admissions Hadley had made during his earlier interview with Sam had been off the record and unsworn. Today, he was both sworn and on the record. Today's testimony counted, and Sam had not expected it to change.

"Mr. Hadley, your testimony today is much different than it was when you and I spoke last month, is it not?"

"Objection. No foundation, assumes facts not in evidence—"

"Sustained."

It was a good objection, Sam knew. "Withdrawn. Let me rephrase, Mr. Hadley. Last month, you and I spoke, did we not?"

"Yeah, I think you came over to my place."

"And when we spoke last month, you indicated that, while you thought you'd seen my client go into the decedent's apartment, you had no idea when he'd left, if he left at all—isn't that right?"

"No, I don't think so. I think I'm sayin' the same thing today I always have said."

"Did you tell me last month that you'd gone to bed and watched *Bonanza* after a man arrived and went into Emily's home?"

"Well, yeah."

"And didn't you tell me that you'd gone to sleep watching that show, and that when you'd awakened the truck the man had driven was gone?"

"Well, yeah," Gus said. "But I remember now that I seen him leave around four."

"How is it you remember that here and now, but you didn't remember when I was speaking with you?"

"'Cause I remember now."

"Just like that?"

"Well, just seems like things have been coming to me, the more I think about it."

"Okay, Mr. Hadley, let's go at it this way. You saw a man you claim was my client get out of a truck and enter Emily Smith's apartment—true?"

"True."

"But that cannot be true, can it?"

"Whaddaya mean?"

"Well, because Emily Smith's apartment is beside yours, you can't actually see her front door, can you?"

"Well, no, but I can see her front porch if I put my face against the window."

The jury tittered. Sam sensed an opening. "But you're not a nosy person, are you?"

"Well, no."

"And so on the night in question, you didn't push your face against the window to watch, did you?"

"Well, no."

"So, you really don't know if the man you think was my client ever went into that apartment, now do you?"

It was a minor point, but Sam had made it and the jurors would have to take into account the lack of proof that Tommy had ever crossed the threshold into Emily's home.

"But I seen him come out!" Gus insisted.

"What did you see?"

"I seen the guy—that guy," Gus insisted, pointing at Tommy, "leaving her apartment."

"Mr. Hadley, what you're saying *today* is that you saw someone who looked like my client walking from the area of her front porch to his vehicle —true?"

"Well, yeah."

"And you don't know if he'd ever been in the house, do you?"

"Well, I suppose he coulda stood on her porch for a couple a hours, yeah," Hadley said, pleased with himself as the jurors and audience cautiously laughed.

"So, you don't know anything about what happened at Emily's place during *Bonanza* for sure, and really after the guy you think was my client arrived—'cause you're not nosy, right?"

"Well, yeah. But I know what I seen."

"Now, Mr. Hadley, you were watching Ms. Smith's apartment, weren't you?"

"Well, it's kinda part of my job."

"Did you ever go out with her?"

"Well, no."

"Did you ever ask her out?"

"Well, yeah, but we didn't go out, if that's what you're askin'."

"Because she turned you down?"

"Well. . . yeah."

"So, you were watching her house, weren't you?"

"I already told you—"

"—Because you wanted to know what she was doing, true?"

"No. It was my job."

"No more questions, Your Honor."

Javier Vargas was a small Hispanic man hailing from Brownsville, Texas. He'd been in Custer County for a couple of years now, having arrived originally to work construction. But times had gotten hard, he'd gotten in some trouble with the law, and had spent the better part of the last year in and out of jail.

"Are you familiar with a man named Tommy Olsen?" Ann asked.

"Yeah."

"How so?"

"We were locked up together," Vargas said. "*Are* in jail together, I guess."

"And what are you in for?"

"I'm doing a one-year split for possession with intent."

"And when are you scheduled to get out?"

"Next month."

"So, on or about the 10th of January, did anything happen between you and the defendant?"

"Yeah," Vargas said. "I was minding my own business and he came into my cell and started beating the hell out of me."

"Did he give a reason?"

"No."

"Did he say anything?"

"Objection. Hearsay," Sam said, standing.

"Your Honor, the statement will be one against interest."

"Overruled. You may answer."

"Well, he called me a 'punk' and a 'dirtbag.' Then he told me if I did it again, I was gonna get mine, 'just like that bitch.'"

"That's a goddamned lie!" Tommy hissed.

"Quiet down!" Sam whispered, putting a hand on Tommy's arm, which felt like a steel cable. "Let me handle this."

"But I didn't say that!"

"Be quiet and let me handle this," Sam repeated. Juror 465 was eyeballing Tommy, shaking her head slightly.

"And what did you were 'gonna get yours, just like that bitch' mean to you?"

"Objection!" Sam was on his feet.

"That he was going to cut my throat just like he—"

"Move to strike, Your Honor," Sam said.

"Sustained. The jury will disregard the answer," Daniels instructed. Sam sat down.

"No further questions. Your witness," Ann said.

Sam sat for a moment. The best way to attack this kind of witness was to show bias—that in return for his testimony, he was going to receive some sort of benefit. But since Vargas had been sentenced earlier, there was likely nothing along those lines to go after. Attacks on character and reputation for truthfulness were allowed, but Ann had wisely gotten Vargas to admit he was a felon. Sam had reviewed his file, and while Vargas's record was a long one, it was primarily penny-ante drug and alcohol stuff. Tommy had essentially agreed that things went down like Vargas said, except for the last statement. By attacking the statement, Sam would reinforce its importance in the trial. Moreover, if Sam attacked Vargas, he would almost certainly have to put Tommy on the stand, and he hadn't made up his mind on that yet.

"Mr. Johnstone," Daniels began. "Is it the defendant's desire to cross-examine or not?"

"May I have a moment, Your Honor?" Sam asked, looking through the affidavit of probable cause that was filed in connection with Tommy's battery charge.

"No."

Sam was not surprised, but in any event, he'd made his decision. "Just a couple of questions, Mr. Vargas," he began. "You were doing laundry in your room for most of the night on the evening prior to the incident, weren't you?"

"Well, yeah. I always do. The jail would have us live like pigs, and I ain't no pig," he said, smiling.

"And in fact, Mr. Olsen had asked you to stop doing laundry, hadn't he?"

"Oh, yeah. But he ain't my boss."

"And sometime during the evening, when Mr. Olsen had asked you to stop, you told him to kiss your ass, didn't you?"

Some of the jurors were smiling. Seeing that, Vargas beamed with pride. "Oh, yeah. I told him he could kiss my brown ass, but I wasn't gonna stop."

"So, when Tommy came into your cell, you knew why he was there, didn't you?"

"Yeah, 'cause he's a dickhead," Vargas replied, pleased with himself.

"Move to strike," Sam said.

"Granted. Defendant's response will be stricken, and the jury will disregard that last answer," Daniels ruled.

"And you spoke with the jailers about what happened, didn't you?"

"Yeah. Told 'em he came in for no reason and started beatin' on me."

"But there was a reason, wasn't there?"

"Ain't no reason to be beatin' on someone."

"But you knew why Tommy had come into your cell; you knew what he was mad about, didn't you?"

"Yeah."

"But you didn't tell the cops that, did you?"

"I can't remember."

"You told them you didn't know why he came into your cell, didn't you?" Sam asked, moving from the podium and shuffling through papers on the defendant's table, appearing to look for something.

"Well, maybe."

"Maybe?" Sam said, then, appearing to be reading from the paper he had earlier retrieved, he continued, "You told them you had 'no idea' why he came into your cell, didn't you?"

"Yeah."

"And that was not true, was it? Because you knew *exactly* why Tommy had come into your cell, didn't you?"

"Hey, I was hurt!"

"But you didn't tell the cops the truth, did you?"

"No. I was scared and—"

"And yet you now want us to believe that Tommy said you were 'gonna get yours just like that bitch' when you've already shown that you have lied in connection with the events surrounding the battery?"

"Objection, Your Honor," Ann said. "Counsel is badgering the witness; the question is argumentative."

"Sustained," Daniels said.

"I wasn't under oath then." Vargas folded his arms and sat back in the witness chair.

"Mr. Vargas! Please do not speak except in response to a question!" Daniels was clearly perturbed. The jurors were observing Vargas closely.

The point having been made, Sam determined to let it rest. "No more questions, Your Honor."

"Good." Daniels looked to Ann. "Does the State have any redirect?"

"No, Your Honor," Ann replied.

"Call your next witness, Ms. Fulks."

"Your Honor, the State would rest."

"Thank you," Daniels said. "Ladies and gentlemen of the jury, this looks like a good time to break for the day. Let me remind you not to talk about the case with anyone. We'll reconvene tomorrow morning at eight-thirty."

All in the courtroom stood while the jury filed out under Daniels's steady gaze. "Please be seated," he ordered. "The jury having been excused, let's take a look at where we are. Mr. Johnstone, I'm assuming the defendant will want to be heard on a motion?"

"Yes, Your Honor. Mr. Olsen—"

"I'm not going to hear it now. We'll hear the motion tomorrow."

"Your Honor!" Sam protested.

"Counsel, I've made my decision. Please be seated. The court will hear your motion tomorrow morning." Daniels thumbed through documents on his desk. "Mr. Johnstone, has your client decided whether he will testify?"

"Not yet, Your Honor."

"Well, he needs to make a decision. One way or another, I need to do the requisite advisal. I'd like to go ahead and get that on the record immediately following my decision on your motion."

Sam was hot. The fact that the judge was anticipating having to advise Tommy regarding his right to testify meant that he was anticipating denying Sam's motion for a directed verdict of acquittal. And while that was not unexpected—a judge granting that motion was exceedingly rare—his openly saying so was not only very unusual, it was prejudicial to the defense even if the jury wasn't present. Sam was half-tempted to tell the judge to forego the motion, but to do so could constitute malpractice. He now faced the prospect of spending valuable time preparing for argument on a motion that Daniels had already decided.

"Is there anything further to come before the court?" Daniels asked. Without waiting for an answer, he shot a glare Sam's way and continued, "If not, we'll be in recess."

46

"Yo, Frac," Fricke said. He was sitting in a chair in Daniels's chambers, watching Frac dust. "You remember last week I said I'd give you four-to-one on conviction?"

"Yeah, I remember."

"I'm thinking six-to-one now. You in?"

"Nope."

"Nope? Why not?"

"You said you are betting Tommy will be guilty, right?"

"Of course!"

"I don't think he did it."

"You numbskull. What you think don't matter. It's what the jury thinks that matters."

"I think the jury will . . . what do you call it when they let him go?"

"You mean acquit?"

"Yup. I think the jury will acquit him." Frac shook dust into the trash.

"What the hell do you know? Tell you what: I'll go ten-to-one. If you're right, you'll make ten bucks for every dollar you bet."

"So, if I give you five dollars?"

"Then if your boy walks, I'll pay you fifty."

"Deal."

"Gimme your money."

"I don't got no money right now."

"Hey! No backing out! We gotta deal."

"Mom has my money."

"Okay, well, you get me five bucks and I'll hold it," Fricke assured him. "If Tommy walks—and he won't—I'll give you fifty."

"Okay."

"Man, you are gonna be one sore loser!"

"So, what do you think?" Ann said. She was in Shepherd's office with Punch.

"I'm thinking we did the best we could with what we've got," Punch replied. "I'm worried about the loose ends. Juries focus on loose ends."

"I agree," Mike said.

"Well, we got it all in," Ann said.

"What do you think Sam's got?" Punch asked.

"He doesn't have anything," Ann said. "What could he have? We've got his client's prints, his client's blood, his client's DNA, the weapon with his prints on it at his house, Hadley's testimony, Vargas's testimony. Hell, he admitted to you that he was there; he's clearly the last to have seen her alive."

"What about the other prints?" Punch asked. "And Howard? And the other DNA?" He looked at Mike Shepherd, who was focused on a piece of convenience store cake he was trying to unwrap.

"That just means she was a skank," Ann said, watching both men recoil at her use of the term. "Sam's going to try. He made a big deal out of those prints and the unidentified DNA while crossing our guys. At closing, he'll throw Howard, those prints, and the DNA out for the jury to see, but without something else—an ID, a motive, or something—the jury will see it for what it is: a smokescreen."

"Do you think Tommy will testify?" Punch asked.

"No," Shepherd said as Ann answered, "Yes." They looked at each other. "Always a bad idea for the defendant to testify," Shepherd said.

"It is," Ann agreed, "but Tommy Olsen is an arrogant man, a Marine, and a career criminal. He's spent his life thinking he's tougher and smarter than everyone else."

"Sam won't allow it." Shepherd dropped the wrapper in the trash. "I wouldn't."

"Not sure he has that kind of client control," Ann said. "That's two sick puppies right there, probably sharing war stories and feeding off each other's illness. And Sam knows that testifying might be his client's only shot. We nailed this one, boys. Now, if you would, please give me a little space here. I need to get my cross-examination of Tommy outlined."

After the two men left her office, Ann swung her chair around and hit a few keys. The Department of Justice's website had a listing of Assistant United States Attorney jobs she wanted to review. A death penalty conviction would look good on her resume and would be her ticket out.

"We need to talk about whether you will testify," Sam said to Tommy. They were in the jail on Saturday morning. Tommy looked tired and edgy.

"Ain't nothing to talk about," Tommy said. "I'm testifying."

"I need to give you the pros and cons, just to make sure you understand."

"You say whatever you want, Sam. But I'm going to get on the stand and tell the jury the truth: I did not kill that woman."

"Tommy, the evidence the State put on—"

"Is all circumstantial."

"Certainly, but most convictions are obtained through circumstantial evidence. The prosecution rarely has an eyewitness, especially in murder cases."

"Sam, I'm gonna ask you a question, and before I do, I want you to know I expect you to answer the question as a human being, not a goddamned lawyer—got it?"

"Yes." Sam stood and walked to the door, knowing full well what the next question would be.

"If you were a juror, wouldn't you want to hear me say I didn't do it?"

"I would, Tommy," Sam said. "But that's not the test. The test is whether the State has proven your guilt beyond a reasonable doubt. You have an absolute right to remain silent, to make the State prove your guilt without you saying a word."

"I know that. You've explained that. But Sam, you know as well as I do that if I don't testify, them jurors will think I have something to hide."

"The judge will instruct them not to think that way."

"You're thinking like a lawyer, Sam."

Sam smiled at Tommy. True enough. "Tommy, testifying is dangerous. Ann is a good prosecutor. By testifying, you could say something—"

"Like what? I didn't do it, Sam."

"I know that. I believe you. But Ann could get you to say something that might trip you up, something that might hurt us."

"Us?"

"You."

"Goddamned right, *me*," Tommy said. "It's my ass on the line."

"I know that."

"Sam, let me ask you something. That Juror 465—do you think for a minute that if I don't testify, she's gonna vote to acquit?"

"Well, I'm not sure. But she's an alternate, so we don't have to worry about her, thank God."

"But if she was?"

Sam thought about his response for a moment, then decided to forego saying anything. "Okay, Tommy, if you're going to testify, let's get you ready."

Punch was sitting in a small diner on Custer Avenue, waiting for Ed, the proprietor—known locally as "sweaty Eddie"—to serve up his bacon and eggs, when his cell phone rang.

"Always on the clock, eh, Detective?" Ed laughed.

"No kidding," Punch said, quickly shoveling in a mouthful of hash browns before answering. "Polthen."

"Is this Detective Polson? Sounds like you're in a hole or something."

"Jutht a minute." Punch took a swallow of tepid water. "Who is this?"

"This is Simmons, DNA technician from the crime lab."

"You got something?" Punch asked, struggling to keep from hyperventilating.

"You sittin' down?"

"Yes."

"That fingerprint? DNA matches that from the semen."

"Jesus Christ! You sure?" Punch signaled for Ed. "Put it in a box," he mouthed, indicating his breakfast.

"Well, as sure as I can be. You're the only one who knows where the print came from. The DNA from the print has the same DNA as the semen. So, assuming you didn't mix something up, they're both from the same guy. I don't know whose it is, but I can say with scientific certainty—"

"I understand. Holy shit!" Punch took a swig of his coffee.

"You sound surprised. You must have had an idea."

"I did," Punch said, peeling bills off his money clip. "I just didn't want to believe it. Hey, Simmons?"

"I know, I know. Keep this between us, right?"

"Right."

Five minutes later, Punch was in Ann's office. He'd given her the news. "This is more of the same—no more or less exculpatory than the prints," Ann said.

"You can't be serious! If I'd have had this information—" Punch began.

"Well, maybe you should have, Detective!" Ann slapped her hand on her desk. "This was your investigation, after all. Maybe you should have gotten this information sooner."

"I got it as soon as I could."

"We don't even have confirmation, do we?"

"What do you mean?"

"I mean right now, all we have is a print *you* say was gathered from Howard." Ann sat back in her chair.

"I got it myself!"

"But we've got no chain of custody—nothing we could take to court if we were inclined to do so." She stood and moved to look out her window at the sunshine. The trees still hadn't leafed out. Probably warm and sunny in Denver by now.

"No, but I took it and had DNA drawn from it—"

"Without clearing it with me, I might add."

"I am the investigating officer! I had the DNA taken from the print and matched to the DNA taken from the semen sample."

"So, we have a DNA match between the print of an unknown donor—"

"Ann—"

"Let me finish, Punch. We have a DNA match between the print of an unknown donor and a stain on her sheets, right?"

"We know the fingerprint on the vase was Howard's. Pleasance said it right on the stand. And now we know Howard was not only in her house, but literally in her bed—sometime around the time of her death."

"Sometime," she said. "Assuming she even did laundry."

"Ann, we know Howard left a print on the vase and his, uh, semen on her sheets. I just can't say when either event happened."

"That's right. You can't." Ann returned to her desk and sat down. "And the jury already knows about Howard's print, and they know of the presence of an unknown man's semen."

"But they don't know the connection between the two, Ann!"

"And neither do we, to a scientific certainty, do we? Because you collected the sample, and you ordered it examined, and you did all this without following protocol!"

Punch sat back. "Do we have enough for a warrant?" he asked. "Because he's not in CODIS. Apparently, he's never given a DNA sample. But if we get a warrant, I could verify it."

"For what?" Ann said, typing into her computer. "All I know is that I just found out about a possible match and advised the investigating officer to move quickly to verify information he *might* have that *might* be exculpatory."

Punch watched her typing. After a few minutes, he got up and left, slamming her door behind him.

47

Daniels was in his chambers smoking a cigar when he got word that Detective Polson wanted to speak with him.

"Regarding what?" he asked Mary.

"I don't know, Judge. He wouldn't say."

"Well, show him in. But don't go far. He won't be here long."

Mary escorted the detective to the judge's chamber. "Thank you, Ms. Perry," Daniels said. "Sit down, Detective. How can I help you?"

"I have some information for you, sir," Punch replied.

"Information about what, exactly?" Daniels asked, lighting his cigar.

"The Olsen matter," Punch replied, watching the judge closely. Daniels slowly stopped the effort to light the cigar, placing both the lighter and cigar in an ashtray on the end table next to his recliner. He folded his hands across his midriff, sighed deeply, and looked steadily at Punch.

"Go on," Daniels said. "But be careful. Surely you know that a conversation between us at this juncture is potentially improper."

"I understand that, sir."

"And yet, you're here."

"I am."

"Does the chief know that you're here?"

"No."

"Does he know the subject matter you're here to discuss?"

"No."

"Does Rebecca Nice know?"

"That I'm here? No. The subject matter? I'm not sure. I doubt it."

"Does anyone else know?"

"That I'm here? Just your secretary," Punch said. "The subject matter, well, that's part of the problem."

"Do you want something?"

"No."

"Do you want me to do something?"

"Yes."

Daniels took another sip of scotch. Asking another question would mean no turning back. On the other hand, Punch wouldn't be here if the matter wasn't critical. Punch was a good cop. Daniels made his decision.

"What is it you think I can do, Detective?"

"I have reason to believe that certain information possessed by the State —information that is potentially exculpatory—has not been turned over to Olsen and his attorney," Punch said. There. It was done. The judge had the information now.

"Again? We've already dealt with the nondisclosure of a fingerprint," Daniels mused.

"Right, Judge."

"More of the same or new information?"

"New."

"And you're not a licensed member of the bar." Daniels knocked the ashes off his cigar, sat back, and took a deep puff.

"No."

"What makes you think it hasn't been passed on?"

"Because if Sam Johnstone had seen the information, he would be standing on your desk right now."

"How do you know he is not waiting until Olsen's case-in-chief to bring it up—maybe for tactical reasons?"

"I guess I don't," Punch allowed. "Not sure he could. No *foundation*, I think you'd call it."

Daniels smiled. "You've seen hundreds of trials, haven't you?"

"I have."

"And in your experience, has the prosecution generally turned this kind of information over?"

"Without exception."

"And this information, Detective—you believe it to be exculpatory?"

"Absolutely."

"What is the nature of the evidence?" Daniels asked, and then, clarifying, followed up. "Would you term it documentary? Video? Testimonial?"

"Not sure what category, sir. It's, uh, more in the nature of . . . forensic evidence."

Daniels was very still. Punch met his stare. "So, like . . .?"

"DNA."

Daniels had it now. No turning back. "Well, lots of DNA at a young woman's house seems natural. I would think—"

"The DNA from some of the semen on the decedent's sheets matches a set of fingerprints found in the decedent's home."

Daniels sat quietly. He reached forward and retrieved his tumbler, finishing the drink. "How do you know?"

Punch explained the process he'd used. "Good attorney could explain that away," Daniels mused. "Likely not admissible. No chain of custody. You're no expert."

"Judge—"

"Ann might be able to explain away the decision to keep the evidence out of the trial."

"Maybe," Punch allowed. "Look, I'm no lawyer, but if the donor of DNA found on the dead girl's sheets being someone other than the defendant isn't exculpatory, I don't know what could meet the definition."

"You've got an evidentiary issue, Detective," Daniels said. "Who knows about this?"

"The match?"

"Yeah. The match."

"You, me, Ann—plus anyone she's told."

"And no one knows you're here now?"

"No, sir," Punch answered. "Are you looking for plausible deniability?"

"Don't insult me, Detective," Daniels snapped.

"Fair enough. You want to know the really shitty part?"

Daniels stood and began pacing his chambers. He went into his private restroom, retrieved a tissue, and loudly blew his nose. Tossing the tissue near the wastebasket next to his desk, he resumed pacing. After a moment, he turned to Punch. "I doubt it, but go ahead. What is it?"

"You sure?"

"Of course I'm sure, Detective! What is it?"

"It's Howard's print that matches the semen."

Daniels sat back down and spoke quietly. "Are you absolutely certain?" Then, recognizing the inanity of the question, he finished his thought. "Of course you are . . . So you told Ann all of this—"

"I did."

"And you think she's refusing to turn it over?"

"She told me she wouldn't disclose, so I'm assuming she hasn't. Either that, or Johnstone is the worst attorney ever," Punch concluded.

"Or playing a tactical hand we cannot discern," Daniels said.

"I don't think she passed the information, sir," Punch said.

"But you don't know for sure, Detective—do you?"

"No."

"And you don't know that she won't turn it over, do you?"

"No." Punch stared at Daniels, who was standing again. "What are you going to do?"

"Right now, I'm going to finish that bottle."

"You know what I mean, Your Honor."

"I do."

"Do you have a plan?"

"I think so."

"What are you going to do, sir?"

"Detective, you've accomplished what you set out to do," Daniels said, filling the tumbler once again. "Your conscience should be clear. Allow me to handle this from here on out."

"You've got to let Sam know!"

"I suppose I do," Daniels answered. "But not right now."

"Will you do it tomorrow?"

"No."

"But the trial's almost over!"

"Mercifully."

"And Judge Howard did the preliminary examination!"

"He did."

"And that was a conflict!"

"We've already dealt with that." Daniels took a long pull from the glass.

"And now we know he'd been sleeping with the deceased!"

"Regrettably." Daniels wiped his mouth with the back of his hand.

"You have to do something."

"I will."

"What?"

"Detective Polson, I told you I'd handle it, and I will." Daniels stood and looked out the window of his chambers. The sun was setting. "Now, please leave me to it."

"Sir?"

"Yes, Detective?"

"You have to know my next step will be the Wyoming Supreme Court and the newspaper."

"Close the door behind you, and please don't threaten me," Daniels said. "I'll handle this; you have my word. Just give me some time."

48

"Have you decided?" Veronica pushed a pea around her plate.

"I think so," Sam said, trying to sip the single malt. "I think I've got a plan. It's not necessarily a good plan, but it's a plan."

"You are going to put him on, aren't you?"

"I think so."

"Dangerous, you said."

"Absolutely, but I've been watching the jury, and I'm thinking the only way he walks is if he personally can convince the jury that he didn't do it."

"Ann will be hard on him."

"She should be. That's her job. And I've told him to expect that."

"But they're never ready, are they?"

"Nope."

"Can you limit the scope of your direct, and try to limit Ann's cross-examination that way?"

"I can try, but Tommy's got so much bottled up inside I'm not sure it's going to matter much what I ask. I think he'll say what he wants to say in any event."

"Yeesh."

"Yeah. It's gonna be ugly."

"Have you talked with your counselor?" she asked, looking at his tumbler.

Sam looked at her and then sipped his scotch. "I have."

"And?"

"And I'm doing a lot of meditating. Look at me." He spread his arms wide. "It's the new me. I'm a smiling cloud."

They were laughing when his phone rang. The number was unfamiliar, but Sam picked it up anyway. "This is Russ Johnson. That's kinda funny, Johnson calling Johnstone—huh?"

"It's a riot." Sam shrugged at Veronica, who was looking at him curiously.

"Yeah, so I'm a technician with Stillman Forensics in Denver. You wanted us to look at some prints for you?"

Sam sat up in his chair. "Right! What do you have?"

"Well, what we have is a match between a couple of those prints you sent us."

"Which ones?"

"Well, let me see here," Johnson said. Sam could hear Johnson clicking his mouse and breathing into the microphone as he searched. "There was a print on a knife or something."

"Right?"

"Yeah, we found a match."

"To what?"

"To a print in the house, I guess," Johnson said.

"I know that!" Sam blurted out, instantly regretting it. "Sorry, under a bit of stress here. Where in the house did you find the match? Was it from the print found on a vase full of flowers?"

"No, it was from a shot glass."

"Thank you," Sam said. "I'm gonna need someone here to testify for me."

"We bill at—"

"I don't care. I need whoever ran that match to get here as soon as possible. My client will cover all fees, costs, and expenses."

"There'll be a premium because of the short notice. Our usual rate—"

"Don't care," Sam said. "Just get here. And Mr. Johnson?"

"Yes?"

"Were you able to match that print to anyone in the system?"

"I can't do that, Mr. Johnstone. You gotta have a law enforcement type do that. Your donor have a record?"

"I think she got busted years ago in New Orleans."

"Well, there you go. Should be easy."

"Thanks, see you soon," Sam said, hanging up.

"What is it?" Veronica asked.

"I might have gotten a break," he said. "I've got to get to my office, make some calls, and start getting some direct testimony drafted."

"At this time of night?"

"Yeah. Right now," he said, gathering his coat. "Look. I'll call you, okay?"

"Okay. Be careful, Sam," she said to the closed door.

Ann Fulks's secretary patched his phone call through promptly at eight a.m. "Ann, this is Sam Johnstone. We need to talk."

"I'm not going to do any deals, counselor," Ann said, sipping her coffee. "That ship sailed before opening statements."

"My expert says the unidentified print on the murder weapon matches one found in the house," Sam said. Hearing nothing at the other end, he continued. "You guys had a false negative. You got the wrong guy."

"You got your expert; we've got ours," Ann countered. "The difference is, ours was disclosed. I don't know jack-shit about any expert of yours."

"I'm telling you now. Ann, you got the wrong guy. I just need you to do one thing for me."

"Fat chance. But just out of curiosity, what do you need?"

"Run the prints against someone for me."

"Why would I run prints for you?"

"Because it is the right thing to do. You're an officer of the court."

"I don't think so."

"Ann, I'm telling you, I think you've got the wrong guy."

"And I think you are grasping at straws."

"Please, Ann, you—"

"Thanks for calling, Mr. Johnstone. I've got a case to prepare. You might be interested: I'm working on my argument to convince the jury to impose the death penalty."

"I'm not sure that we should be talking, Mr. Johnstone," Punch said. "After all, we're on different sides. Did you talk to Ann?"

"I did, but she's not interested," Sam said. "I'm thinking maybe you are different."

"Why?"

"I think you want to see justice done."

"I'm looking forward to it, counselor," Punch said. "To that end, I might attend your client's execution. If it comes to that, I mean." He was in his office looking out the window at a particularly attractive redhead walking to her car. "Besides," Punch continued, "if the match was with Howard, you wouldn't be calling now. Jury already knows about him, and we've got his print. So, the match has to be with that print on the shot glass."

"That's good detective work."

"And so, my smartass lawyer friend, there must not be a match in the system. Because if there was, we'da already found it."

"Unless there was a mistake. There was one already, when your folks failed to match the prints on the glass and the weapon. Could be someone failed to match a print to someone in the system. It's called a false negative—remember?"

"Two mistakes on one set of prints?" Punch said. "Come on, counselor, what're the odds?"

"Astronomical, I admit. But do you want to take that chance? Easier to run the prints and be done with it. Ease your conscience."

Punch was quiet, thinking. "You got someone you want me to run against?"

"Yeah."

"Who?"

"Becky Olsen. She should be in the system. Tommy says she got busted in New Orleans years ago."

Punch again was quiet—this time for even longer. "I keep wondering why I should help you build a defense."

"I think you have a conscience."

"You mentioned that. If she's got a record, why didn't she pop up before?"

"My guy will testify to the possibility of another mistake."

"Let me think about it," Punch said. "If Ann finds out about this, she'll cut my balls off. Will you send me what you got?"

"I have to; State has asked for discovery. It's in the judge's pre-trial order."

"Under the order, you have to send it to *Ann*. Send it to me, too. That way, I'll be sure to get it—but keep it between us, okay? And you know, of course, that if she isn't in the system, then you're gonna need a warrant, and to get that I'd have to go through Ann and then through Howard or Daniels, right?"

"You have my word."

"I'm not agreeing to anything, but I'll think about it."

"Ann, you've had your face in that computer all night," her mother said disapprovingly. "Keep that up and you're gonna go blind."

"I know, Mom." It was true enough. She'd been looking at apartments in the Denver area. A place in Cherry Creek looked about right, in part because there was an assisted living facility nearby. Once this trial was over, she'd start looking with a purpose, but for now it was a daydream.

"I worry about you, dear."

"Why's that, Mom?"

"Girl your age should have a boyfriend."

"Mom, I've told you before, I'm just not...I'm just not that into men."

"Goodness gracious. I never heard such a thing. Pretty girl like you, spending time alone."

"I'm not alone, Mom. I'm here with you."

"You know what I mean, Annie."

"I do, Mom," she replied, then changed the subject. "How about we go get some ice cream?"

"Okay, dear. If you want to haul an old lady around, I guess that's okay. Maybe we'll see a nice man you can meet while we're out."

"Maybe. Get your coat. It's still a little chilly this time of year."

49

Sam was immensely hung over. His head was aching, he was dehydrated, and the three hydrocodone had done nothing to alleviate how he felt. As the courtroom began to fill with spectators, he stared at the nearly empty pages before him. He'd gotten drunker than he wanted or needed to be last night, and his preparation for today was lacking. Maybe it was the pressure of the trial—lots of lawyers overdid it during trial. Maybe it was the futility of it all—just knowing that whatever he said, it wouldn't be enough, because the judge had already made up his mind.

Or maybe he was just a crazy, drunk vet.

The spectators were buzzing among themselves. While they didn't know exactly what would happen today, most understood that today's events would be significant. Most were hoping to hear Tommy testify. Others, assuming he'd maintain his right to silence, awaited the closing arguments.

When everyone was ready, Mary Perry came out and informed them that the judge would arrive shortly, and slowly the din died down. Finally, when the judge appeared, the crowd respectfully stood, silent, waiting.

"Good morning, ladies and gentlemen. Be seated. We are back on the record in the matter of State v. Olsen. When last we were here, the State had rested its case-in-chief. Are there matters preliminary before we recall the jury?"

Sam stood. "Your Honor, before the jury is returned, I'd like to make the motion the court anticipated yesterday."

"Go ahead, Mr. Johnstone, and make it quick."

"Your Honor, may it please the court," Sam began, then nodded toward Ann. "Counsel."

"Counsel," she replied.

Sam took one last swig of water. "My client moves pursuant to Rule 29 of the Wyoming Rules of Criminal Procedure for judgment of acquittal. Under Wyoming law, Your Honor, judgment of acquittal is proper where the evidence is such that a reasonable juror must have a reasonable doubt as to the existence of any of the elements of the crime.

"In order to prove my client guilty of the crime of murder in the first degree, the State was required to show that on or about October 31, in Custer County, Wyoming, the defendant, purposely and with premeditated malice, killed the decedent, C. Emily Smith—"

"Mr. Johnstone, let's cut to the chase," Judge Daniels interposed. "For which elements, in your opinion, has the State failed to meet its burden of proof?"

Sam considered putting an objection on the record but decided against it. Daniels's one-sided handling of the case would come through on a reading alone. "Your Honor, the defendant asserts the State has failed to demonstrate that my client killed the decedent, or that my client acted both purposefully and with premeditated malice. In fact, we would argue that the best evidence indicates that there must be reasonable doubt: there is one set of unidentified fingerprints on the scene, one set on the murder weapon, and the semen of an unknown male on her sheets. We know there was at least one other man present at or about the time of death."

Sam went on to attack the remainder of the State's case, pointing out shortcomings and deficiencies. Daniels eyed him steadily throughout the argument. "Your Honor," Sam concluded, "for these reasons my client asserts the State failed to meet its burden. We ask that you dismiss this matter and set my client free."

Daniels studied Sam intently, then turned to Ann. "Does the State care to respond?"

"Of course, Your Honor. May it please the court," she began. "The State has met its burden of proof to this point. As the court and counsel are well aware, to prevail at this time, the State does not have to have proven each element of the charge beyond a reasonable doubt, but rather, the State needs only to have made a prima facie case with respect to each element.

"The defendant does not appear to contest that the crime occurred on or about October 31, or that it occurred in Custer County, or that the decedent was C. Emily Smith. Those elements, then, are conclusively established. The sole issues relevant to this motion, then, are whether the State has made a *prima facie* case that Tommy Olsen killed the decedent, and whether he did so purposely and with premeditated malice.

"Your Honor, the State's witnesses have testified that the defendant's blood was found at the scene, that his fingerprints were found on the murder weapon, that his semen was found in and on the victim, that he was observed in and around her home in the days immediately preceding her death, that his name was on her planner, and that he visited with her the evening prior to her death.

"Further," she continued, "the evidence indicates that Defendant Olsen killed the decedent with a knife he brought to her house, then hid the knife in his garage, thereby indicating purpose, premeditation, and malice. Surely, Your Honor, the evidence presented is sufficient to withstand this motion, and we'd ask the court to find that as a matter of law the State has met its burden, and therefore deny the motion."

"Mr. Johnstone? Your motion; you get the last bite at the apple," Daniels said.

"Your Honor, what the State again fails to address is that there are other, unidentified fingerprints on the scene and on the weapon, and there is another man's semen on the scene. There were other appointments in her appointment book, and she had many, er, acquaintances."

"Objection, Your Honor!" Ann said, on her feet. "The decedent is not on trial."

Daniels looked at Ann dolefully. "Overruled."

"Moreover, Judge," Sam continued, "the fact that the couple was in a dating relationship and the fact that there was obviously drinking going on would all militate against premeditation," Sam argued. "Judge, we'd ask you to grant the motion and enter a judgment of acquittal."

"Thank you, Mr. Johnstone," Daniels said. "I've made my decision." Sam's heart sank. This was a bad sign for Tommy, and while it was inconceivable the judge would grant the motion at this point due to the low level of proof required, denying it with so little reflection would be seen by some as indicative of the strength of the State's case. At the State's table, Ann sat quietly and confidently, staring at the old judge, expecting the quick denial she had witnessed at each of her prior jury trials.

"I've decided I'm going to reserve decision on the motion," Daniels said.

Ann was stunned. She stole a glance at Sam, who showed no emotion. Tommy leaned over to Sam and whispered, "What does that mean?"

"It means we have a chance," Sam whispered back, as Daniels shot him a reproving stare. "But nothing more," he added cautiously, trying desperately not to raise his client's hopes.

"Ms. Fulks, is the State prepared to proceed?" Daniels asked.

"We are, Judge," Ann said, angrily shuffling papers in front of her.

"Mr. Johnstone?" Daniels took a drink of water. "Has the defendant decided whether he will testify?"

"He will testify, Your Honor," Sam said.

"All right," Judge Daniels said. He then advised Tommy regarding his right to remain silent, and the potential repercussions of testifying. Tommy indicated he understood, and explained that while Sam had cautioned him, it was his decision to testify.

"Good enough," Daniels said. "Bailiff, let's get the jury back in here."

Daniels stood and all followed his example. After the jury had been seated, the judge ordered everyone to be seated. "Is the State satisfied the jury is present?"

"We are, Your Honor," Ann replied.

"Mr. Johnstone?"

"The defendant is satisfied the jurors are present, Your Honor."

"All right, ladies and gentlemen of the jury, when we were together last, the State had rested its case-in-chief. It is now the turn of the defendant, if he so chooses, to put on a defense. You are reminded that the sole burden is that of the State; the defendant is not required to defend himself." Daniels turned to Sam. "Mr. Johnstone, call your first witness."

50

Sam stood. "Thomas Olsen," he said.

As a murmur ran through the gallery, Tommy took the witness stand, looking anything but an imposing figure. By the time he had been sworn and seated, the courtroom was silent. Adjusting the microphone, he looked like a schoolboy called to the principal's office, rather than a former Marine charged with murder. Sam took a deep breath and began.

"Will you please state your name?"

"Tommy, er, Thomas John Olsen."

"How old are you?"

"Thirty-five."

"Where do you live?"

"Here in Custer."

"And how long have you lived here?"

"My whole life, except for the fifteen hundred days I did in the Corps."

"Did you see action?"

"I did."

"Are you a disabled vet?"

"I am."

"Did you know a woman named Emily Smith?"

"I did."

"How so?"

"She was my divorce attorney."

"Are you now divorced?"

"I am not. She filed for me, oh, I guess maybe six or eight months ago?"

"So, you are a married man?"

"I am," Tommy replied, looking at Becky in the back of the crowd. Some in the audience snuck a look at her as well.

Sam then led Tommy through a rather lengthy background of how he and Becky had met, married, and loved, then how things had changed, ultimately resulting in his filing for divorce. Juror 465 sat staring at Tommy, arms folded.

"And did you ever see Miss Smith socially?"

"Yes."

"When?"

"Well, I seen her in the office, of course."

"Let me ask it this way: have you ever been in Miss Smith's home?"

"Yes."

"And when was the last time you were there?"

"Halloween night. We ran into each other at a party, then went back to her place."

Juror 465 clearly disapproved. "So you didn't go to the party with her?" Sam asked.

"No, I met her there."

"What kind of party was it?"

"A Halloween party."

"Was it a costume party?"

"Yes."

"Did you dress up?"

"Yes."

"As?"

"I was an assassin."

The audience groaned, but Sam had to ask. Better to get it in on direct. "And did Emily dress for the party?"

"Yeah. She was, well, I guess, a hooker. Lady of the evening." Tommy smiled slightly as the audience tittered nervously.

Sam allowed the low murmur to dissipate under Daniels's harsh glare before he continued. "And so you met at the party?"

"Yes, we ran into each other at the party, hung around a little bit, and then decided to go back to her place for a nightcap."

"Whose idea was that? To go back to her place?"

"Hers."

Sam snuck a look at Juror 465, whose eyes were fixed on Tommy. She looked angry.

"So, you went back to her place, then?"

"Yes. Took separate cars. She was there when I got there."

"How did you get in?"

"She gave me a key."

"So, you got back to her place. Then what happened?"

"Had a few drinks."

"Then what?"

"Then. . ." Tommy drifted off, as though he was thinking back.

"Did you have sex?"

"Yes."

"Was it consensual?"

"You mean did she want to?"

"That's what I mean."

"Yeah. Woman like that, she knows what she wants," Tommy said. Seeing the look on Juror 465's face, Sam knew he needed to follow up. The problem was, he didn't know what his client might say.

"What do you mean when you say 'a woman like that?'" Sam asked.

"I mean she was a strong, independent woman. Ran her own business —you know? She wasn't your shy, retiring, uptight type that might need a little encouragement. She knew exactly what she wanted and wasn't no one gonna tell her otherwise."

Juror 465 was almost nodding as Tommy finished. "So, you had consensual sex?"

"Yeah."

"Where?"

"What do you mean? You asking if—"

Sam intervened quickly, before Tommy said something that made Juror

465 faint. "I mean where in the house? In the bedroom, kitchen, or somewhere else?"

"Well, I guess we started fooling around in her kitchen. Then I cut myself." Tommy raised his hand as if to show the jurors the scar on his finger. "And it bled like hell, er, a lot, so we used a bandage and some tape she had to staunch the flow of blood."

"How did you cut yourself?"

"We were doing tequila shots. I was slicing a lime."

"Did you bleed a lot?"

"Objection. Witness not qualified to answer," Ann said.

"Your Honor, I'm not asking for a medical opinion," Sam replied. "I am merely attempting to elicit his opinion as a layperson as to how much he bled."

Judge Daniels stared at Sam for a moment while he thought about it. "You can answer," he decided.

"Like a stuck pig," Tommy said. "I didn't think I was ever going to stop bleeding. I guess maybe it was all the alcohol making my blood thin, but—"

"Your Honor, I object," Ann said, again on her feet. "Move to strike. The witness has not been designated as an expert."

"Sustained, as it pertains to everything after the words 'stuck pig,'" Daniels said, before Sam could reply. "Just answer the question, Mr. Olsen."

"Mr. Olsen," Sam began. "Did you bleed in her kitchen?"

"Yeah. That's where we were doing the shots."

"And so you tried to stop the bleeding?"

"Yeah, I applied pressure, then tried putting a cold compress on it using a dish towel. Then we went upstairs."

"Why?"

"That's what she wanted."

"And did you bleed in her bedroom?"

"Maybe," Tommy allowed. "First we went to the sink in her master bath. I looked for a bandage while she kept pressure on my finger. Then, when the bleeding finally slowed, I put some hydrogen peroxide I found on the wound and put on the bandage."

"Then what happened?"

"Then we, uh, went to the bed."

"And you had sex?"

"Yeah."

"Then what?"

"Well, she was sleeping."

"She was asleep?"

"Well, after, yeah. She fell asleep, and so I left."

"Why?"

"Why?"

"Why not just spend the night?"

"'Cause I had to work in a couple hours, pack my lunch, take a shower, stuff like that."

"You expect the jury to believe that you got cut slicing limes?"

"It's true. I was drunk."

Juror 465 was staring at Tommy, disbelieving. "And so you left."

"Yeah."

"Did you take anything with you?"

"From her house, you mean?"

"Yes."

"No. What would I take?"

"Mr. Olsen," Daniels interrupted. "Just answer the questions. Don't ask any of your own." Sam saw that Juror 465 was almost beaming at Daniels.

"Mr. Olsen," Sam began. "When you left, was Ms. Smith alive?"

"Oh yeah," Tommy answered earnestly. "She was alive."

"How do you know?"

"Because I heard her snoring when I left."

Sam allowed the murmurs and titters to die down before continuing. "And how did you leave?"

"I went right out the front door."

"And what time was that?"

"Oh, I'd say maybe a quarter after five."

"How do you know that?"

"Well, it was almost 5:30 a.m. when I got to the emergency room. It's only a few minutes from her place to the hospital."

"You went to the ER?"

"Yeah. I couldn't get the bleeding to stop, so I went to the ER and the doc gave me some stitches and I was good to go."

"After the ER, did you stop anywhere?"

"No."

"See anyone you recognized?"

Tommy was silent for a minute. Finally, he answered, "No."

"So, no one can attest to your story?"

"What?"

"You don't have anyone who can corroborate—agree with—what you've testified to here today?"

"No. Well, the ER docs. But other than that, it was just me and her."

"Thomas," Sam said, using Tommy's given name for the first time. "Did you kill Emily Olsen on Halloween night?"

"No, Sam. I didn't." Tommy looked to the jurors. "I would never hurt anyone. I'm a good man and a good dad."

Sam sighed. That was a mistake he'd warned Tommy not to make. By attesting to his own character, he'd opened himself up to a character attack by Ann. Sam posed additional questions on a variety of subjects, but only one thing really mattered: Tommy had denied killing Emily. That was all the jury would remember him saying on direct. He turned to Ann. "Your witness," he said, and returned to his table, dreading what was to follow.

51

"So, Mr. Olsen," Ann began, "your story is that you met Ms. Smith at a party, and then the two of you went to her home and had some tequila, whereupon you conveniently cut yourself—"

"Objection, Your Honor," Sam stated.

"Sustained," Daniels said. "You know better, Ms. Fulks."

Ann nodded briefly. "Apologies, Your Honor," she said, and returned her glare to Tommy. "And then she helped dress your wound, the two of you had sex, and then you left her blissfully fulfilled—is that right?"

Sam let it go.

Tommy was confused. "Huh?"

Ann watched Tommy carefully. He seemed truly confused. "You're telling this jury that when you left Emily's apartment, she was alive and sleeping in her bed—is that right?"

"Yes."

"Can you account for her throat being cut?"

"No."

"Can you account for her throat being cut with a bayonet that was later found among your possessions?"

"No."

"Can you account for your fingerprints being found on that bayonet?"

"Of course. It was mine."

Good answer, Sam thought.

"Now, Mr. Olsen, you've had some difficulty with the law, have you not?"

"I've had some stuff, yeah."

"And fair to say that most of your difficulties with the law have involved drugs and/or alcohol?"

"Well, yeah."

"And you've got an explosive temper—you'll admit that, won't you?"

"Objection," Sam said. It was futile. Tommy had opened the door when he testified he wasn't a bad guy.

"Overruled. Fair game now, counsel. Answer the question, Mr. Olsen," Daniels said.

"Well, I guess I can get pissed, like every other guy."

"You suffer from PTSD, right?"

"Yeah."

"Are you seeing a counselor?"

"Sometimes."

"How often?"

"I'm not sure."

"Weekly?"

"Not that much."

"Monthly?"

"Well—"

"You haven't seen him at all this year, have you?"

"No, but I've been in jail for a while now, thanks to you."

Sam cringed, but Ann ignored it. "Ever been in a fight?" she asked.

"Lots of times."

"Isn't it true that you've been convicted twice in the past year for mutual combat?"

"Objection," Sam said. Again, it was futile, but he needed to try and break Ann's rhythm.

"Overruled." Judge Daniels shot Sam a scathing look, one matched by Juror 465, who was clearly enjoying seeing Tommy grilled. "Counsel, you know very well your client put character in question. Answer the question, Mr. Olsen."

"What was it?" Tommy asked.

"Isn't it true that twice in the last year alone you've been cited for mutual combat—fighting in public?" Ann said.

"Yes."

"And it's true, isn't it, that officers from the Custer Police Department and/or Custer County Sheriff's Office were called to your home on three occasions?"

"No."

"Mr. Olsen," Ann began, "I could call—"

This was objectionable, and Sam was on his feet. "Your Honor! May we approach?"

"Please," Judge Daniels replied. When Sam and Ann had approached the bench, the judge nodded, and Sam put his objection on the record. "Your Honor, if counsel inquires about collateral matters on cross she is stuck with his answer. She may not introduce uncharged conduct if she doesn't get the response she is seeking."

"Your Honor, I'm only trying to show the defendant's propensity for violence."

"That's improper on its face, Judge," Sam said.

Judge Daniels thought about it for a moment. "I'm going to sustain the objection."

"Your Honor," Sam said, "because counsel clearly understood this sort of thing is improper, I'd appreciate the court explaining to the jury the basis for your sustaining the objection."

"Judge—" Ann began.

"No, Mr. Johnstone, I am not going to do that," Judge Daniels told Sam.

"But Judge, if you don't, the jury won't know that kind of evidence is improper, and they'll think my client is trying to hide something," Sam said, eyeballing Juror 465, who was looking at him with disdain.

"Well, maybe you should have thought of that before you objected, counsel."

"Your Honor, I'm only asking for the court to clarify—"

"I've made my decision. Return to your places."

Ann began questioning Tommy before Sam even returned to his place. "So, Mr. Olsen, you are married?"

"Objection, Your Honor," Sam said. "Lacks relevance."

"Overruled. Answer the question," Daniels instructed.

"Uh, yeah," Tommy said. "Me and Becky been married nine years."

"Happily?"

"Renew the objection, Your Honor," Sam said.

"Sustained. Move along, Ms. Fulks," Daniels instructed.

"So, you admit having sex with the deceased?"

"She was alive!"

Ann let it pass. "And your testimony was that it was consensual?"

"Yes."

"And she was sleeping when you left?"

"Yes."

"But you don't know, and can't explain, how it came to be that your bayonet had her blood on it."

"No."

"And you can't explain how a piece of that bayonet happened to be found in her neck?"

"No."

"Or why the bayonet was found at your home?"

"I live there!"

"But despite all that, according to you, she wasn't killed while you were there."

"No."

"You weren't using that bayonet to cut limes."

"No."

"You weren't showing it to Emily or waving it around?"

"No."

"It wasn't in her house at all, to your knowledge?"

"No."

"So, it can't be that you 'accidentally' cut her with it?"

"No. I never had it with me in her house!"

"And you're not sure exactly when you left?"

"No. Well, wait! I heard a George Strait song on the radio when I was leaving. On satellite."

"But you didn't see anyone or talk to anyone or stop anywhere and have contact with anyone who could verify your story or even the time you left?"

Tommy sat for a long time. He shifted in his chair and looked at his hands. "The ER doc," he said at last.

"Mr. Olsen," Ann began. "Have you ever struck a woman?"

"No!"

"Answer carefully, Mr. Olsen."

"Objection!" Sam said.

"Overruled—if it was charged," Daniels said.

"Thank you, Judge," Ann said. "Mr. Olsen, isn't it true that you lost a rank during your time in the Marine Corps for hitting a woman?" Ann watched the jury's reaction to her question and deemed it better than she could have hoped. They were angry.

"She was an officer!" Tommy began, stopping when some in the audience began to react. "She was being disrespectful of those of us who were redeploying—"

"So you hit her?"

"She slapped me!"

"So you hit her?"

"Yes!" Tommy said.

"No more questions," Ann said, seeing Juror 465 sit back in her seat and fold her arms.

Daniels allowed Ann to take her seat before proceeding. "Redirect, Mr. Johnstone?"

"No, Your Honor," Sam said. The damage was done, just as he had feared.

"Mr. Olsen, you may step down, sir," Daniels instructed Tommy, and then turned to Sam. "Call your next witness, Mr. Johnstone."

"Your Honor, may we approach?" Ann asked.

"Of course." Daniels waved both attorneys forward. When the attorneys and the court reporter were positioned, the judge turned on the "white noise" generator to preclude jurors from hearing and asked, "What is it, Ms. Fulks?"

"Judge, the State of Wyoming strenuously objects to Mr. Johnstone calling this witness! We were given no notice—"

"Your Honor," Sam interrupted, as calmly as he could. "I filed an amended pretrial memorandum with the court and Ms. Fulks several hours ago."

"That's not enough time—" Ann began.

"It's several hours more than I got on the Howard evidence, sir," Sam said levelly.

Daniels sat back in thought for a time, and then waved the attorneys away. When they were back at the tables, he stood. "We'll take a ten-minute recess, ladies and gentlemen, before the defendant's next witness takes the stand."

Juror 465 gave Sam a long look as she left the courtroom.

An hour later, after Russ Johnson, who had testified to the presence of the now-linked-but-still-unidentified prints, had been cross-examined and Sam completed redirect, Daniels informed the witness, "You may step down, sir." Then, looking at Sam and knowing it wouldn't happen, Daniels instructed for the record, "Call your next witness, Mr. Johnstone."

"The defense rests," Sam said, hearing the audience stir behind him. He couldn't blame them; Sam himself could feel the tension building. After days of focusing on the *now*, he couldn't help but begin to look to the moment when the jury delivered its verdict.

"Does the State intend to present any rebuttal evidence?" Daniels asked.

"No, Your Honor," Ann said.

"Thank you, Ms. Fulks," Daniels said. "Ladies and gentlemen of the jury, the evidence has now been closed in this matter. We will take a brief recess. When we return, the court will provide you with your instructions. Thereafter, the attorneys for the State and for Mr. Olsen will provide their closing arguments. At that point, you will begin your deliberations. Again, I beseech you: discuss this case with no one until you have been told to commence deliberations, and if anyone attempts to discuss the matter with you, report them immediately to your bailiff.

Bailiff, please escort the jurors to the jury room. We will reconvene on my order."

Daniels and all others rose as the jury departed. When the doors closed behind them, he looked to Sam and Ann and said, "We will meet in my chambers in ten minutes for final, on-the-record discussion of instructions. Barring any unforeseen circumstances, counsel, we'll hear your closing, Ms. Fulks, in about an hour from now. We're in recess."

52

Ann's closing, in Sam's opinion, was perfunctory. She began with a review of the elements the State was required to prove, then ticked off each element and the evidence she felt provided sufficient proof for the jury. Ann's closing, by Sam's watch, was fourteen minutes long—remarkably short for a murder trial. No boasting, no overstatement of what had been shown, no soaring rhetoric. It was clean, concise, and—judging by the smirk on Juror 465's face when Sam's eyes met hers halfway through—very effective for the prosecution.

Sam stood and faced the jury. "May it please the court . . . counsel," he began. "I, too, wish to thank you for your patience and participation in this case. I know it has not been an easy task for you. I recognize that your participation on this jury has been a burden for you and your family members.

"There is nothing pleasant or pretty about this case. The evidence—pictures and bayonets and blood samples and semen—are extremely distasteful. And I agree with Ms. Fulks that what happened to Ms. Smith was horrific. There is no excuse for it. When we began this trial, I asked you to keep an open mind until all the evidence was in, until the judge had given you your instructions, and until arguments of counsel had been heard. I asked you to wait until the case was over to make your judgment. That time is near.

"Now, you should know that there were things Ms. Fulks might have shown you that were probably worse than what you did see, and for that I thank her," Sam continued, cringing as Juror 465 looked with approval toward Ann. "But remember this very simple, very fundamental fact: the burden of proof in this case was upon the State. Their job was to prove to you beyond a reasonable doubt that Tommy Olsen"—here Sam pointed to his client—"is guilty of murder in the first degree.

"And they tried. They tried like hell. In so doing, they made a lot of fanciful arguments. In fact, some of them are extremely persuasive until you start scratching the surface of them. But remember, the burden of proof is never on the defense. My client didn't have to prove anything. The State had that burden. And after all the testimony and all the witnesses and all the exhibits and all the arguments, the State failed to meet that burden. Because, ladies and gentlemen, when it's all said and done, the State piled up a lot of circumstantial evidence against Tommy Olsen, but nothing conclusive.

"The State says, 'Tommy's fingerprints were all over the house.' Well, of course they were—Tommy had been there. He didn't deny that. The State says, 'Tommy's semen was in and on the victim.' Well, again, of course it was—Tommy was having an affair with her. But you know what? So was someone else. We know Judge Howard had been there, but we don't know when or why, and we don't know how hard the State tried to find out. Because once they had Tommy in their sights—Tommy, the disabled veteran who's had some trouble since he got back from overseas—they quit looking. So, we don't know who the owner of the other set of unidentified fingerprints might be or when they were left, and we don't know who else left his semen behind, because the State apparently didn't bother to look.

"Ladies and gentlemen, I submit that the fingerprints and semen that remain unidentified come from the real killer or killers, and I submit that's reasonable doubt." Sam looked at each juror in turn. He only needed one to agree with him. Juror 465 met his stare; it wouldn't be her—and he silently thanked his lucky stars she was only an alternate.

"I'm not going to re-hash everything that was said during this trial—you were here, that's up to you to recall. But I want you to remember one witness, and that's Tommy Olsen. Tommy Olsen didn't have to testify, but he did. He didn't have to answer questions, but he did. Did he have satisfactory answers to every question? Of course not. Who among us could possibly account for some of the things he was asked to explain? But he took the State's best shots and replied as best he could. He had an explanation for everything, as much as anyone could. And he was unimpeachable on one particular point: that he did not kill Emily Smith."

Sam looked again at each juror in turn. "We don't dispute that he was there shortly before she was killed, or that he had sex with her, or that he bled in her kitchen, or that his fingerprints or semen were there. Mr. Olsen has admitted all of that from day one—almost from minute one. But what he has maintained since his very first conversation with Detective Polson was simply this: he did not kill Emily Smith.

"The State's burden of proof is beyond reasonable doubt. And that goes for every element. And the State has not bothered to even offer a scintilla of evidence that Tommy Olsen killed Emily Smith purposely and with premeditated malice, or that he killed her while perpetrating a sexual assault. They've provided no evidence of motive," Sam said, his voice trailing off. "And do you know why, ladies and gentlemen? Because there was no motive. Tommy Olsen simply didn't have one. No motive, unexplained prints, unexplained DNA. That's reasonable doubt, ladies and gentlemen.

"All we ask you to do is three things. First, go into the jury room and review the evidence—all the evidence. Second, look at each element and ask yourself, with regard to the evidence supporting each and every element, 'Is there reasonable doubt?' Because if you do that, we are confident that you will do the third thing I ask, which is to return a verdict of not guilty. Again, thank you, ladies and gentlemen."

With that, Sam sat down, exhausted. Under the table, Tommy made a fist and indicated a fist-bump was in order. Sam ignored him and, one last time, glanced at each juror in turn. All avoided his eyes, except Juror 465, who smirked at him. Sam picked up his pen and tried to take notes while Ann delivered her rebuttal. Again, it was brief, and before Sam could fully process what she had said, Daniels had charged the jury and they were off to deliberate.

The trial was over.

53

Sam remained behind, listlessly shuffling papers on his table, long after Ann and the prosecution team had rolled away the file boxes. At some point, he heard a voice inquiring of him, and he looked up.

"Mr. Johnstone, you okay?"

It was Fricke, the janitor. They were alone in the courtroom.

"I'm fine," Sam replied.

"You need anything?"

"No, I'm good. Maybe a little sleep."

"I hear that," Fricke said. "Mind if I get the trash?"

"Please do," Sam said, and handed Fricke the trash can from beneath the defendant's table.

"I seen a lot of trials, Mr. Johnstone," Fricke said.

"Yeah?"

"Yeah. And that was a damned good closing."

"Thank you."

"For all the good it'll do you."

"Huh?"

"That dude's going down, sir. Jury ain't buyin' it." Fricke shook his head as he emptied the trash. "Just how it is."

Daniels had his robe and dress shoes off, donned a pair of slippers, and was pouring himself two fingers to sip while waiting for the jury to deliberate when the phone in his chambers rang. It was Joe Nelson, one of the bailiffs.

"Yes?" Daniels said.

"Judge, we've got an issue," Nelson said.

"What is it?"

"One of the jurors is sick, sir."

"How sick?"

"Chest pains."

"Christ. Which one?"

"Juror 342."

"That the big heavy guy?"

"Yeah. Front row, all the way to the left."

"Okay. Get him to the hospital. We'll have to call an alternate. Who's the first alternate?"

"Juror 465."

"Which one is that?"

"That fat woman in seat nine. Not good for Olsen. If looks from her could kill, he'd be one dead dude."

"Thanks, Joe," Daniels concluded. He then dialed Mary. "Get ahold of both attorneys. Tell them to meet me in the courtroom. We're going to go on the record, and I'm going to activate the alternate to replace number 342. He's got chest pains."

"What does that mean?" Tommy asked after the brief hearing. He and Sam were huddled at the conference table.

"That means Juror 465 is replacing 342," Sam said. That was enough. Tommy didn't need to know that the seating of Juror 465 had eliminated the remote chance of an acquittal. The best Tommy could do now would be a hung jury.

"Which one is that?" Tommy asked. Sam described her.

"But that gal hates me!" Tommy protested. "I could tell! What do we do?"

"Nothing we can do, Tommy. That's the system."

"So they can put someone on the jury who hates me?"

"Yeah."

"The system is crap!" Tommy said. Court security was moving closer.

"Well, it's the only one we've got." Sam put a hand on Tommy's shackled wrists. "Look, try not to catastrophize this. Just go back to your cell and hang tight. I'll let you know if anything significant occurs."

"Okay, Sam—but this is bullshit."

"I hear you, Tommy."

"Sam?"

"Yeah?"

"I think you did a good job. You're a good lawyer."

Sam's eyes welled up. He turned away but blindly extended his hand toward Tommy's cuffed ones. "I appreciate it," he managed to choke out. "Now, get out of here and get some dinner." He watched as Tommy was led away, certain his client's opinion of him would soon change.

After fourteen hours of deliberation, the foreman notified Daniels the jury had reached a verdict. It had been a long night for everyone. Thirty minutes later, all parties and a full audience were assembled in the courtroom. "Ladies and gentlemen," Daniels began. "I understand this has been a long and arduous couple of weeks. And I understand that for many of you, the result announced here today is as important as anything that may occur in your lives. But this is a courtroom, and I expect you to conduct yourselves accordingly. There will be no sound—not a peep—after the verdict is read. If we have any sort of noise, I will clear this courtroom."

He wouldn't, of course. But it had to be said.

"In just a few moments, I will call for the jury. When the jury is seated, we will go through a few administrative things, and then we will ask for the verdict. When the verdict is announced, the trial will be over if the verdict is not guilty. If the verdict is guilty to the charge of capital murder, we will reconvene here on Monday to conduct the sentencing portion of this proceeding.

"Does the State have anything we need to discuss out of the presence of the jury?"

"No, Judge," Ann said.

"Mr. Johnstone—for the defense?"

"Your Honor, I renew my motion for a directed verdict. Very simply, the State failed—"

"Mr. Johnstone, I've already explained that I am reserving my decision. Is there anything else?"

"But, Your Honor—" Sam began.

"Bailiff, please bring in the jury." After the jury had assembled, Daniels adopted a suitably grim countenance and asked, "Did the jury elect a foreperson?"

"We did, Your Honor," replied Sean O'Hanlon. "I am the foreman."

"And has the jury reached a verdict?"

"We have, Your Honor."

"Please deliver the verdict form to the bailiff," Daniels directed. "The defendant will stand."

The bailiff took the form from O'Hanlon and walked it to Daniels, who perused it briefly and handed it to the clerk of court. With shaking hands and a quiver in her voice, the clerk read aloud: "We the Jury, duly empaneled in the above-entitled matter, having well and truly tried this matter, find the defendant, Tommy Olsen, with respect to the charge of murder in the first degree, guilty."

Tommy went down a bit, but Sam steadied him. Muffled exclamations of relief came from Emily's family and supporters on the prosecution's side of the courtroom. Tommy's few supporters and his soon-to-be ex-wife cried quietly.

"Does the State wish to have the jury polled?"

"No, Your Honor," Ann replied, quickly sitting down. Her legs were wobbly, and her stomach was doing flip-flops. She'd done it! Her first murder conviction.

"Your Honor, the defense would like the jury polled," Sam said.

Turning to the jury, the judge asked them collectively, "Is this the verdict reached by each of you?" All jurors nodded yes, whereupon the judge addressed each juror by number. Sam watched each closely for signs of deception. The last juror polled was Juror 465. "Juror Number 465. Was this your verdict?"

"It was," she said, then looked straight at Sam and added, "And it wasn't even close."

"Thank you. Please be seated. Let the record show that all jurors have been polled and that all jurors have indicated that this was their verdict.

"Ladies and gentlemen of the jury, your duties are now complete. We thank you for having performed this sacred duty. You will get your expense checks here shortly and then be released. Please remember to take personal property with you. You may now discuss this case with anyone you wish, although you are not obligated to. One final caution: please respect the jury process and the anonymity of your fellow jurors. Bailiff, please remove the jurors."

After the jurors had been removed from the courtroom, Daniels announced a five-minute recess. As he left, he heard the eruption behind him.

"Sonuvabitch!" Daniels exclaimed angrily, throwing his robe onto a chair in the corner of his chambers. "I can't believe it!"

"What is it?" Mary had heard the commotion and come running. "What is it, Judge?"

"Guilty, damn it!"

"Your Honor, I will not have such language around here! You've heard plenty of verdicts over the course of the last twenty-five years, and I do not understand what would make you take the Lord's name in vain."

"It was wrong, Mary," he growled.

"Well, goodness, Judge. Juries are not infrequently wrong. Now, let me get you a glass of whiskey, and you calm down before you end up having another one of those atrial fibrillations like you did two years ago. I'll be right back."

"Mary, get Judge Howard on the line. Tell him I need to see him. Now."

"Well, okay," she said, turning for her office. "And it wouldn't hurt to hear the word 'please' around here every once in a while."

Daniels poured himself a stiff drink, then opened his desk drawer with one hand while feeling in his pocket with the other for his cutter. Finding it, he rose, walked across his chambers, and looked through his humidor until he found what he was looking for. Returning to his desk, he pulled out an engraved lighter his daughter had given him when he was named to the bench. He shook the antique lightly and, after suitably trimming the end of his cigar, set about lighting it. Smoke billowed satisfactorily, and he returned to the overstuffed chair with his cigar and drink.

"Another round," Ann slurred. Her secretary, the investigators, and even Rebecca Nice cheered. The whole office had made its way to the bar following the verdict. After several celebratory toasts, they'd settled in to do some serious drinking.

As Ann looked around the barroom, it occurred to her that she felt as good—as alive—as perhaps she ever had. She'd done it. Her first capital case and she'd gotten a conviction. Now, all that remained was to persuade the jury to impose the death penalty. And while she was comfortable that a Custer County jury would do just that, she knew that it didn't really matter. The fact that she had obtained the conviction was enough to give her career the boost she needed. Very soon, she'd be in a position to leave these redneck losers in her dust.

Over the top of her glass she saw Punch approaching. "Have a drink, Punch," she said, shaking the ice in her glass. She spoke carefully, trying to fully enunciate her words. "We done good."

"I'll pass," he replied. "Is there somewhere we can talk for a minute?"

"Now?"

"Yes, now."

She pointed at an unoccupied corner table and carefully followed Punch to it. He observed she was thoroughly intoxicated already. "Punch, what can I do for you?"

"I think that conviction is wrong, and I think you know it, too."

Ann raised an eyebrow. "Excuse me," she slurred. "But aren't you the one who arrested the man? Aren't you the one who put together the case against this man?"

"Well, of course, but that was before we knew about the other prints and the DNA."

"Right. And the jury convicted the man. They knew there were prints that didn't match Tommy's. They knew there was DNA that didn't match. Now, don't be such a limp-dick, and have a drink." She indicated the bar.

"But they weren't given the whole story," Punch said, recoiling. "And neither was Sam. And the judge's DNA . . . you withheld that from everyone."

"Because it didn't matter. I told you that. The information wasn't ex... excul...it didn't matter. It wasn't even admissible. In my opinion the jury would have reached the same verdict. Even when Sam hit us with that last-minute witness claiming one print matched another, it simply didn't matter."

"But you can't know that for a fact!"

"Wouldn't have mattered," Ann said dismissively.

"But you can't know that!"

"Of course not," she said, and took a long drink. "But I can and did assess the evidence, and I made the call based on my best professional opinion."

Twenty feet away a loud roar went up as the members of the prosecutor's office toasted success. Punch watched as Rebecca Nice drank a shot glass full of amber liquid.

"Did you discuss it with Rebecca?"

"That's none of your concern."

"I think it is," Punch insisted. "I need to know how far up the chain this goes."

"You don't need to know shit," Ann seethed, leaning toward Punch so her face was just inches away. He could smell the whiskey on her breath. "You need to get back to the station and type a report or eat a donut or do whatever it is you small-town cops do when you aren't rousting drunks or addicts."

The other people at the table had turned their attention from celebrating Tommy's conviction and getting drunk to watching Ann and Punch closely.

"Ann—"

"Detective, we're done here."

"I'm not letting this go, Ann." Punch met her stare. "Enjoy your drink, counselor," he said over his shoulder as he left.

"What was that all about?" Nice asked Ann when she had returned to the festivities.

"Oh, nothing," Ann said. "Just a difference of opinion."

"You shoulda listened to me," Fricke said as he unwound the cord to the commercial vacuum. "If you'da listened to me, you'da saved five bucks."

"Yeah," Frac said. "Maybe. I liked him." He was on his hands and knees, scrubbing a particularly stubborn heel mark from the courthouse floor. The hundreds of spectators blackened the ancient marble floor daily, and Frac was once again reduced to cleaning it by hand. "He's nice," he said.

"Who?"

"Tommy."

"You kiddin' me? The guy's a killer, Frac."

"No, he's nice. He smiled at me when I saw him."

"Well, what the hell does that mean? Lotta people smile when they look at you. You're a pitiful-lookin' fella; people gonna smile. Damn, you are one dumb sonuvabitch," Fricke said as he powered up the machine.

Frac returned to his scrubbing.

"I told you!" Fricke said. "The guy was guilty. I knew it from the minute I looked at him."

"I liked him," Frac repeated, taking his mop and bucket from the closet. "I don't think he did it."

"What the hell are you talking about?" Fricke asked. "A jury of twelve people said he did it. Well, he did it. That's how the system works."

"Well, maybe they was wrong."

"And maybe someday you'll be president. But right now, he's guilty and

I got your money, bitch." Fricke waved a five-dollar bill at Frac. "And I'm gonna spend it on something for myself."

It was happy hour, and by the time O'Hanlon made it across the street from the courthouse to the Longbranch, condensation was forming on the outsides of two glasses containing an acceptable IPA.

"So," Howard began, "how did it go?"

"Guilty!"

"Well, I know that. How was your experience as a juror?"

"Well," O'Hanlon began, then stopped to take a long pull from one of the drinks. "It was a helluva deal. That's all I got to say. We got in that jury room and the fur started to fly. I mean, two or three of them folks had serious doubts."

"So, what did you do?"

"Well, like you told me, I said, 'Let's look at the required elements of the crime, and then line up what evidence we got. So, once we did that, I was able to talk a couple of them folks over to our side, and that last guy, well, he's self-employed, so I don't think his business woulda survived another day, to hear him talk. But he had a heart issue and left, so they brought in Elva Miller as the alternate, and she was all set to convict even before we started deliberating."

"So, no doubts in your mind?" Howard ventured carefully.

"Well, I ain't gonna say I don't have any doubts. I mean, I know that, like you told me, this ain't *Law and Order* like on TV, but it seems to me the cops coulda done a little better job." He finished the first drink. "I mean, they had a set of unidentified fingerprints in the house and on the weapon that matched, and even some unidentified semen on that gal's sheets, and we never did get any kind of motive for why he killed her. I'd feel better if I knew all that."

Howard took a long pull of the IPA. "Seems to me you folks did a good job and reached the right verdict. Glad you got yourself elected foreman, too."

"Well again, your advice was key. I just volunteered right when we got back there. None of the others wanted the job, and being foreman allowed me to set the schedule, just like you said it would."

Well, let's keep that between us, shall we?" Howard suggested, signaling to the bartender.

"Judge, I got a question for you," O'Hanlon began. "Your prints. What was that all about?"

"It was nothing. A family member of hers died. I sent some flowers, is all. Pete, another for my friend here."

Sam was walking to the jail to see Tommy when his phone rang. "Mr. Johnstone? Russ Johnson here. I'm waiting for my plane back to Denver."

"How can I help you?" Sam said. "I'm in a hurry."

"Well, I got to thinking about those prints and your client. I wish I could have been of more help."

"It's a little late now."

"I know, but I got to thinking . . . you said your client's old lady—the gal that left the prints—you said she got arrested in New Orleans?"

"I did," Sam said, crossing the street. "So what?"

"Do you know when?"

"No, does it matter?"

"Well, maybe."

"What do you mean?" Sam asked, moving aside to avoid foot traffic. "What are you saying?"

"Well, it's a long shot, but a lot of stuff—evidence, I mean—got lost after Hurricane Katrina."

"So, you think—"

"Well, now, I ain't sayin' anything, other than just to tell you what might have happened."

"Okay, Russ. Thanks, I've got to see my client."

"Okay, counselor."

The absolute worst part of a trial lawyer's job was meeting with a client who had lost at trial. Inevitably and invariably, when clients prevailed, they celebrated the righteousness of their cause. When they lost, they blamed their lawyer. Sam sat heavily opposite Tommy in the small cell reserved for defendants and counsel.

"Tommy, I don't know what to say."

"Nothin' to say. We lost."

"I know. And we'll appeal. But right now we have to start getting ready for the next phase. The sentencing phase."

"Sam, they're gonna stick a needle in my arm and put me to sleep, ain't they?"

"Not if I can help it, Tommy."

"Yeah, well. To be truthful, your record ain't so good so far, is it now?"

"I know."

"I mean, you did your best, but like we used to say in the Corps: 'results count.'"

"They do."

"And to date, your results have sucked," Tommy said, slowly warming to his subject. "I mean, you lost every argument, every motion, every objection, and the goddamned trial! So, either that judge and jury was against me from the start, or you don't know what the fuck you are doing!"

It was unfair. Sam felt his ire and knew his face was reddening, but he held his poise. "There is another possibility, Tommy."

"What's that, Sam?"

"That the jury reached the right verdict."

"You sonuvabitch!" Tommy exclaimed, standing. "You never did believe me, did you?"

"Well, I did," Sam said, standing as well. "But you have to admit the evidence was overwhelming, and you made the decision not to do a deal or plead not guilty by reason of mental illness or deficiency. Either one of those things would have been a better solution. But you said no."

"Sam, I said no 'cause I didn't do it! I did not kill that woman! I keep tellin' you and anyone who will listen that!"

"I hear you. Look, we've got to get through this, Tommy," Sam pleaded. "I need to start preparing for the penalty phase. I'm going to need your help."

"Lotta good being cooperative's done me so far."

"Tommy, I need you to trust me."

"I keep telling you, that ain't worked out so well for me so far."

"This is not over, Tommy! I need you to trust me and work with me. Please."

"Lemme think about it."

"Tommy, we really need to—"

"I said lemme think about it! I'll let you know Sunday."

"Tommy, whatever you decide. But I'm telling you right now, I won't quit. I'm going to work my ass off for the sentencing phase and I'm going to try and get you out on bond when we appeal. You can help me, or not. But it would be a helluva lot easier with your cooperation."

Tommy sat still, staring at the floor. "Whattaya think?" he asked at last.

Sam looked at Tommy for a long time. "No."

"No?"

"No. Tommy, I do not believe any jury will sentence you to death."

"I wanna believe you, Sam," Tommy said. "But to date your record of predicting what the jury might do ain't been so good."

"That's fair." Sam nodded, then changed the subject. "Tommy, when was Becky arrested?"

"Oh, hell. Long time back."

"Before the hurricane?"

"Right before. She had to take a bus back," Tommy said.

"No shit," Sam said, thinking. "What are the chances?"

"What do you mean? That dumb bitch—"

"Look, there's something I've got to do," Sam said, standing to leave.

"What's that?"

"I need to talk with Becky."

54

"Well?" Punch demanded. He had stormed past Mary and was standing in Daniels's chambers, angry to the point of being out of control.

"Well, what?" Daniels asked. "Do I need to call security, Detective?"

"You admitted you had to tell Sam! You said you would!"

"I thought I would probably have to," Daniels admitted, pointing to a chair in his office. "Sit down, Detective."

"But you didn't say shit!" Punch made no move for the chair.

"No, I didn't. Not yet."

"So, a guy who might be innocent just got convicted!"

"Indeed, but Detective, as I recall it was you—not me—who charged him."

"Your Honor! How could you let it happen? You knew there was exculpatory information out there, yet you allowed Ann to keep it from Sam. You said you had a plan."

"I did."

"So, you've left me no choice but to go to the Supremes and the newspaper."

"That would be a mistake."

"Why?"

"I told you I would handle this," Daniels began. "And I will."

"How?"

"Be in court tomorrow at eight a.m."

"But there's nothing scheduled for tomorrow. It's a Saturday. The trial's over!"

"There will be a hearing tomorrow," Daniels said. "See you at eight a.m., Detective. Now, get out of my goddamned chambers and close the door behind you."

The small apartment was on the end of a row of dilapidated units. Rent was low and subsidized. Toys littered the small, weed-infested yard in front of each. Hip-hop was blaring from one of the windows. Sam found the unit he was looking for. "Mrs. Olsen," he said through the screen door after knocking loudly. Inside, he could hear children playing. "I'd like to talk with you."

"About what?" she said, coming to the door.

"About the murder of Emily Smith."

"What does that have to do with me? Tommy was convicted. I was there."

"Well, I wanted to thank you for supporting your husband."

"A lot of good that did, huh?"

"And I wanted you to know there's been a development," he continued, eyeing the cigarette on the broken end table. "Could I come inside for a second?"

Becky stood behind the door, seemingly using it as a shield. "Do I have to?"

"Why wouldn't you?"

"Well, I've got the kids, and it's just about time for their lunch."

"I guess I'm a little surprised you don't want to talk."

"About what?"

"About your husband's case."

"You lost. What is there to talk about?" She waved him in, then sat and lit a cigarette.

"Want a beer?" Sam removed a six-pack of bottles from a paper bag.

"Why not?" she replied, opening the beer Sam handed her and drinking greedily.

"So, there's been a development."

"Yeah?" she said, wiping her mouth.

"Yeah. I hired a fingerprint expert and he matched up some of those unidentified prints in Emily's house."

"I know that. I heard him testify. Didn't mean shit," she said. "They couldn't identify who they belonged to."

"True, but I think it means something."

"What?"

"I think it means Tommy didn't do it."

"So, what—you think that old judge did it?"

"No." Sam put his beer down. "I think you did it."

"Are you kidding me?" Becky laughed, which generated a prolonged coughing fit. "Seriously, why would I kill that little bitch?"

"Because she was bonking your husband."

"Oh, hell, he was screwing anything he could get his hands on," she said, taking a deep drag and letting the smoke out through her nose. "If I tried to kill everyone he was sleeping with, I'd be the only woman left in town."

"I think those prints will match yours."

"Yeah? So what if they do?" Becky said, putting the bottle down and leaning toward Sam. "What you think isn't worth shit, because the trial is over! You lost the case and got my husband convicted, and now you come in here with some wild-ass scheme tryin' to save what's left of your reputation. Well, it ain't gonna work on me. Now get your sorry ass out of my house!"

"Becky, it's only a matter of time—"

She had moved around the table, getting close enough to him so that he could smell the smoke and booze on her breath. "If I did kill her—and I ain't sayin' I did—there ain't shit you can do about it! That bitch was screwing my husband and she deserved whatever she got! Now, maybe you need to go see what you can do about keeping him from gettin' the death penalty."

"I'll just take the ones we drank and leave the rest," Sam said.

"Goddamned right you will," she said. "Least you can do after getting my husband convicted and all."

"So what now?" Rhonda asked Punch, who was attacking a plate of spaghetti. The kids were at practice and he was trying to choke down something before they went to pick them up.

"Up to Judge Daniels," Punch said between mouthfuls.

"I know, but what do you think he'll do?"

"I'm not sure, but I think it'll be the right thing. He knows if he doesn't, I'm going to the paper and to the Supreme Court."

"Are you sure you want to do that?"

"I am. What else can I do?"

"I'm not sure. When will you know?"

"Tomorrow at eight a.m. He assured me he has a plan."

"I wish he would get on with it," Rhonda offered.

"Me, too. I don't want to wish my life away, but . . ." Punch shrugged. "Hey, get your jacket—it's still a little cool. We'll grab the kids and maybe get some ice cream."

As they left their house, Punch's phone rang. "Don't answer it!" Rhonda pleaded. "You promised the kids."

"I know," Punch said, hitting the button to answer. "But I gotta do this."

"Who is so important as to make you break another promise to your children?"

"Sam Johnstone."

"The lawyer."

"Yeah." Punch put a finger to his lips. "Just a second. Let me take this." He stepped into the den and closed the door behind him.

"Detective Polson?" Sam asked.

"Yeah, Polson here," Punch said, ignoring Rhonda's look. "What is it?"

"This is Sam Johnstone."

"I know. What's up?"

"I spoke with my expert earlier."

"Yeah?"

"Yeah. I got an explanation for Becky's prints not being in the system. She got arrested in New Orleans—"

"You told me that."

"I did. But what I didn't know was that it was 2005, right before the hurricane. According to my guy, a lot of evidence was lost in the flooding—"

"And that's why nothing was in the system," Punch concluded.

"Yes! It makes sense! Can you help me?"

"I . . . I don't know," Punch said. "I really ought to get some guidance on this."

"From who? Ann? I'm telling you that Becky killed her!" Hearing nothing on the other end of the line, Sam waited for a moment. "At the very least this will provide reasonable doubt. All I need is for you to match her prints with a known print." Punch was quiet. "Detective?" Sam said. "Do the right thing, please. Look, I—I can't live with another man's life on my conscience. Five men died already because of me. I need your help. Tommy needs your help."

"I've got a wife and family," Punch said simply. "If Ann finds out . . . Let me think about it."

"There's no time!"

Sam listened to Punch breathing into the phone until at last Punch said, "I'll need a print."

"I got some—on a beer bottle."

"How?"

"Does it matter?"

"No, I guess not," Punch said, having made his decision. "Look, Sam, I've got something else you need to know." He closed the door behind him. Moments later, he opened the door and emerged. Rhonda took one look at him and knew.

"The trial's over!" she said. "'Judge Daniels is going to do the right thing,' you said."

"I know," Punch said. "But never too late to right a wrong—and I might have been way, way wrong." He dialed the lab as he closed the door behind him.

55

"Sit down, Jon." Daniels pointed to a large, overstuffed chair on the other side of a small end table. The table and chairs formed a kind of sitting area in Judge Daniels's chambers. Howard was momentarily taken aback, for even in private, judges rarely referred to each other by their first name. Whether through custom, habit, or as a matter of mutual respect, most judges addressed each other formally even in otherwise informal settings.

"Thank you," Howard said, taking a seat.

"Cigar?" Judge Daniels offered the humidor. When Howard shook his head, Daniels asked, "Drink?"

"Uh, no thanks. My afternoon opened up so I had a couple at the Longbranch. I was just on my way home. I'm good."

"I wanted to talk with you," Daniels began. "And I want you to know up front this isn't a social call."

"Okay. What's up?"

"You know that Olsen kid got convicted."

"I heard."

"You know that's the wrong verdict, Jon."

"Well, juries make mistakes." Howard shrugged.

"Not this one. This one decided the way it should have, given the evidence."

"Well, what do you mean, then?"

"I mean they didn't have all the evidence," Daniels said, tapping ash into a silver tray before puffing on the cigar and blowing a huge cloud of smoke toward the ceiling.

"I guess I don't know what you're talking about," Howard began. "More importantly—"

"You know your fingerprints were in her house."

"I know that. Everyone knows that. It came out at trial."

"What'd you tell Margaret, by the way?"

"I told her Emily—Ms. Smith—had a death in the family."

"She buy it?"

"Of course!"

"Red roses for a death in the family?"

Howard reddened. "Look, I've been there. I'm not denying that. But even if my fingerprints were there—"

"They got your DNA from her sheets."

Howard was silent now, considering. The silence lengthened.

"What are you thinking now, Jon?" Daniels finally asked. "You got some lame explanation for how you left pecker-tracks on her sheets, too?"

"Judge, just because my fingerprints and DNA were there doesn't mean anything. We had a relationship."

"One you didn't disclose."

"Of course not. My wife—"

"You did the initial appearance!" Daniels exclaimed. "You signed the arrest warrant and heard the goddamned preliminary hearing!" His face was red and the infamous vein in the middle of his forehead was pulsing.

Howard was silent. His judicial career was over—of that he'd been certain since O'Hanlon told him the fingerprint was disclosed. He might have explained that away, but DNA was different. Daniels was bound by his oath of office to disclose what he knew, and no canon of judicial behavior was more revered than a jurist being uninvolved in the outcome of the proceedings. He'd be suspended pending an investigation within hours of Daniels making a call.

"Good God, man, I don't know what the hell you were thinking!" Daniels said. "I don't know what you were thinking when you were screwing her, and I certainly don't know what you were thinking when you didn't disclose it as soon as you were assigned the matter. You could have given the case to someone—anyone—else."

"Judge, you know how she was," Howard began. "I was . . . scared. Embarrassed. Afraid. Afraid for Margaret."

"Maybe you should have thought of Margaret before you started banging Emily! Jesus, Jon. That's the same sad-sack, criminal-thinking bullshit you and I hear from defendants every day! You were afraid you were going to get caught. That's what you're afraid of."

The two men sat quietly, Howard looking at the floor and Daniels puffing furiously on his cigar and occasionally taking a swig from his glass.

"That DNA thing—that come out in trial?"

"No."

"How did that happen?"

"Ann had the information but didn't disclose it."

"Holy shit! She's gonna have her tit in a wringer," Howard surmised. Then, apparently cognizant of the irony of pointing out Ann's ethical lapse, he added, "I didn't kill her, Press."

"Jon, the best thing you can do right now is to shut the hell up."

"What are you going to do?"

"Well, I'm considering the options. I suspect Johnstone's going to find out right about now that the DNA wasn't disclosed. He's going to flip out. Probably renew his motion for a judgment of acquittal."

"Well, maybe, but I'm not sure you could grant that. Under the rules, you can only enter that judgment if the evidence was such that no reasonable jury could find against Olsen," Howard offered.

"No shit. And because of you, that wasn't the case, now was it?" Daniels snapped. "I sat on that motion twice, and Sam's client didn't do himself any favors when he testified. There was plenty of evidence for the jurors." He was looking out the window of his chambers. "Goddammit, Jon. I was hoping they'd acquit so you could quietly resign, and we could put this behind us."

Howard got up and poured himself a drink from Daniels's bottle, then sat back down and took a long pull from the glass.

"What I'll do," Daniels continued, "is order a new trial."

"Sam would have to make a motion."

"He will."

"Why would he do that? He doesn't have any idea—"

"He will momentarily."

"How?"

"Punch Polson is going to tell him, that's how. Polson's convinced I'm covering for you."

"I appreciate the fact you tried."

"I didn't do it for you. I did it for the system," Daniels said. "People have got to believe in the system."

Howard sat very still. "Who knows?" he finally said.

"Punch, you, me, Ann. Not sure how many in the prosecutor's office or the PD."

"Why didn't Ann disclose to Sam?"

"She wanted to win this thing." Daniels shook his head. "I think winning was so important to her, and she was so convinced of Tommy's guilt, that she rationalized it away."

"Bad decision," Howard observed.

"Please tell me you're not going to throw any yellow flags here," Daniels said. "Anyway, this thing is coming apart."

"She got the right guy, Press. I didn't kill her. You gotta believe me."

"I told you, shut up."

"It doesn't matter, does it?"

"Well, career-wise, no. You're screwed. And you should be," Daniels said. He turned from the window, moved to his chair, and sat down. "But that might be the least of your problems."

"What do you mean?"

"I mean Punch is probably crafting a search warrant right now. I sure as hell would be." Daniels leaned forward in his chair. "And Jon, let me be honest with you: when I see the damned thing, I'll sign it. I expect you're gonna be interrogated tomorrow. You better get a lawyer."

"Jesus! Press, can you give me a day? I got some things to wrap up. Margaret and I—"

"No."

"Please, Press. We've been friends."

"Jon, I'm meeting with counsel at eight o'clock on the dot tomorrow morning. After that, I'm gonna call the Wyoming Supreme Court and tell them what I know. I figure by noon, as the senior judge in the district, I'll have an order from the Supreme Court telling me to have you escorted out while an investigation is undertaken." Daniels finished his drink. "You'll get paid, probably."

"You've been considering this for a while, haven't you?"

"Ever since I got the word that was your print," Daniels said, offering the bottle to Howard. "I made up my mind when I found out that was your DNA."

"Please, just let me—"

"I'll give you tonight to clean out your desk, of course, but the whole thing might be easier if you just packed your shit right now."

"I'm . . . I'm sorry, Judge."

Daniels sat quietly. "I know you are, Jon," he allowed at last. "Things happened. But we've got to deal with it now."

Howard stood. "This was the best job I ever had. Every day you've got the ability to make a positive change in someone's life. Every day might be the day where you can see something click or give someone what they've never had—hope. I did the best I could every day, Judge. I just . . . I just couldn't leave her alone. We had a one-nighter a while back and when we got back to town, well, I—Oh, hell." He turned to leave, his huge shoulders hunched as if against a stiff breeze.

As Howard breached the door to his chambers, Daniels said, "Jon, you were a damned fine jurist for a lot of years. You made mistakes—hell, we all have. But it's time to do what's right."

Without turning, Howard said, "Thanks, Judge, that means a lot," then stepped through the door and closed it behind him.

Daniels poured himself the last of the bottle.

"Answer the phone!" Marci said.

Daniels got his bedside phone out of its cradle on the third ring. "Judge

Daniels," he croaked. He'd been dreaming about basketball, of all things. In his dreams he could dunk like LeBron.

"Judge, Punch Polson here."

Daniels wasn't surprised. "What is it?" he asked, knowing the answer.

"We got a body in the park. I'm gonna need a warrant."

"Howard?"

"Yeah. How'd you know?"

"I had a hunch. He leave a note?"

"Yeah, but how'd you know it was him?"

"Call it judicial intuition. He admit?"

"To what?"

"Whattaya mean, 'to what?' To killing Emily."

"No, but he sort of admitted being at her house and having sex with her that night."

"That's all?"

"Yup."

"So, if he didn't admit to killing her, why did he off himself?" Daniels asked.

"I didn't say he did."

"What? Are you telling me someone killed him, too?" Daniels was sitting up in bed now, reaching for his glasses on the nightstand.

"I'm not saying anything until I reach a conclusion. Right now, all I'm saying is we've got his body in the park, and it looks like a suicide."

"But there's a note, right?"

"There's a note."

"What's it say?"

"Judge, I'm gonna hold onto that information. No offense—"

"Damn it, Detective! You call me in the middle of the night—"

"It's my job," Punch said.

Daniels took a deep breath. "I know. If he didn't do it, you got any ideas?"

"I do."

"A hunch?"

"Better."

"I'd love to know."

"I think by noon I'll have confirmation."

"How is Margaret?"

"On my way right now. Jensen says she's distraught."

"They were married thirty-nine years," Daniels said, recalling that he and Marci were coming up on forty-two years of marriage. "Will you give her our best? Marci and I used to play pinochle with Jon and Margaret years ago."

"Yes, Judge."

"Thank you," Daniels said, and hung up.

"What is it?" Marci asked, rolling over to look at her husband.

"Jon Howard killed himself."

"Oh my God! What happened? Why?"

"Long story," Daniels said. "Long, sad, shitty story. Might as well put on a pot of coffee."

"At this hour?"

"Yes. I'm not gonna be getting any more sleep tonight, honey."

56

"Judge, we need to talk—before we go on the record!" Sam slammed his briefcase on Daniels's conference table.

A red-eyed Daniels, Sam, Tommy, court security, Ann, and the court reporter were in Daniels's chambers. Just as he'd told both Punch and Howard, Daniels had convened a Saturday morning hearing, and he knew now that Punch had contacted Sam. An injustice had been done to his client, and Sam would brook no interference in getting it fixed. So, Daniels knew that while he had docketed the hearing, Sam was going to have his say.

"Detective Polson has told you about the additional evidence?" Daniels asked.

"Yes. He told me about the evidence, and about the conduct of the investigation! About the State's refusal to turn over exculpatory evidence— stuff I'm told you were aware of!"

"Who said that?" Daniels looked at Ann.

"That isn't important," Sam said.

"The hell it isn't!"

"What's important is that the State suppressed evidence that it was bound by law to turn over. What's important is that you knew about it and have disgraced your office—"

"Now you just hold on there!" Daniels said, pounding on the conference table with his fist. "You can't come in here and accuse me of violating my oath of office—"

"Oh, Judge, I'm accusing you of much more than that."

Daniels sat back in his chair. "What in the hell are you talking about?"

"I'm accusing you of covering for Judge Howard," Sam said.

"The judge didn't know, Sam," Ann interjected quietly. "At least, no one in my office spoke to him."

Sam looked at Ann and then the judge. "I'm told differently, and I've got witnesses who will testify the two of you had a number of *ex parte* communications before and during the trial."

"You've got people telling you Ann came to my chambers on a number of occasions—that's what you've got," Daniels said. "I will not stand for these unfounded accusations! Now, I can understand how you feel—"

"The hell you can!" Sam stood and loomed over both Ann and Daniels, nearly out of control.

"Sit down!" Daniels barked, and Sam reluctantly complied. "I just found out some of what's been going on recently. Now, I called you and Ann in for a reason."

"Judge—"

"Mr. Johnstone, be quiet!" Daniels said. "In five minutes, we're going to go into that courtroom, whereupon you are going to move for a new trial based on newly discovered information. You will outline that information—fingerprints, semen, and whatever else you know—in general terms. I'm asking you not to use Judge Howard's name for the sake of Margaret. Don't know if you heard, but it sounds like he killed himself last night."

"Oh my God!" Ann exclaimed.

"Indeed." Daniels trained his reddened eyes on Ann. "Ann is not going to object to a new trial—are you, Ann?"

Ann stared at her swollen feet—the trial had taken its toll. "No, Judge," she said.

"Then I'm going to grant the motion, Mr. Johnstone, whereupon you are going to ask me to reconsider bond and ask that your client be released on his own recognizance with terms sufficient to ensure he appears for all further proceedings, whereupon Ann will tell me she has no objection—won't you, Ann?"

"Yes, Judge."

Five minutes later the parties were assembled in court, and five minutes after that, Daniels set aside the jury verdict, granted Sam's motion for a new trial, and ordered Tommy released on his own recognizance. Tommy seemed not to realize what was happening until court security came over and unshackled his hands.

"Give me a minute, will you?" Sam asked, and the two large men stepped back. When Tommy was ready, they'd transport him to the jail for out-processing and he'd be a free man. The few spectators who had assembled for the short-notice, undocketed Saturday morning hearing were abuzz as Sam turned to shake Tommy's hand. "Tommy, you'll have to go on over to the jail for out-processing and to claim your stuff."

"We got some guys standing by, so you ought to be released in an hour or so," a guard said. "Counsel, do you need another minute?"

Sam took one look at Tommy's stunned face and smiled. "No, get him out of here. Tommy, come see me Monday."

"Uh, where?"

"My office."

"Where's that?" Tommy asked, and Sam realized he and Tommy had only seen each other in jail and the courthouse. He'd never even seen Tommy in civilian clothes, except for the cheap suit he'd purchased for the trial. Sam gave him directions and patted him on the back. "Get going—and Tommy?"

"Yeah?"

"No booze."

"Ahh, Sam!"

"Seriously. Now is not the time."

Several hours later, Sam was listening to the buzz in his head. He knew he shouldn't—things were happening way too quickly—but he ordered another scotch. He was celebrating Punch's phone call: the prints matched.

"That's three," Veronica said gently. "Be careful."

"You counting?"

"I'm sorry. It's just, well, I worry. And you've got to get ready for another trial, right?"

During dinner, he'd tried to explain what was going to happen, but Veronica clearly hadn't understood.

"I don't think so. Can't see them bringing charges against Tommy again, barring some new evidence. Howard's print and his DNA might have been enough for the jurors to find reasonable doubt—that's why Ann didn't disclose in the first place. And any jury in the state will know she hid evidence. You can try and screen the jury, but they'll know he already got a raw deal."

"So, Judge Howard killed Emily Smith," Veronica said, shaking her head. "I still can't believe it. He was such a nice man. A gentle giant, we all thought."

"I'm finding it a little hard to believe myself." Sam nodded in agreement. "And now, with Becky's prints at the scene and on the weapon, I'm finding it even more unlikely."

"I guess the important thing is that Tommy is out of jail."

"Yeah," Sam said, finishing the last of the double and clinking the ice. "I guess it doesn't really matter who did it."

"I want my money!" Frac said. He and Fricke were in the maintenance office. Frac had closed the door and was looking at Fricke with his hand extended.

"Now, wait a minute," Fricke countered. "Tommy got convicted. That's what the bet was. No one said anything about the verdict getting overturned."

"I want my money," Frac insisted. He took a couple of steps closer. "Fifty bucks. You said."

"Damn it, what don't you understand? I told you we were betting on what the jury said. You were just too stupid to understand that."

"Money. Now." Frac inched closer.

"Screw you. Get outta here," Fricke said, waving Frac off.

Frac's brow furrowed momentarily, then he struck Fricke with a heavy blow. Fricke was stunned, and when his head cleared, Frac was holding him by the collar, prepared to shake him.

"Money! Money!"

"Okay, okay!" Fricke said. "Jesus, I'll get you your money!"

"What's going on here?" It was Daniels, in the courthouse late for some reason.

"Nothing, Judge," Fricke said. "Just horsing around."

"Well, you boys better knock it off," Daniels said. "Someone could get hurt. You okay?"

"Fine, Judge. Fine."

"Okay, well, good night, men."

57

Sam walked up to Becky Olsen's door, again dodging the toys and garbage strewn along the sidewalk. "Mrs. Olsen?" he said through the open screen.

"What the hell do you want?" she asked, looking through the screen door. "I told you to get your ass out of here."

"Do you take the newspaper? Listen to the radio? Social media?"

"Why? What's this about?" she asked, wiping hair from her eyes.

"The trial verdict was set aside."

"What? Why, for God's sake?"

"New evidence came up. Evidence the prosecutor had but didn't turn over to the defense. Seems Judge Howard had been having an affair with Emily. His fingerprints and semen were in her house. That's evidence that should have been turned over to the defense."

"So what?"

"Well, Tommy was released."

"Tommy's out of jail?"

"Yup. Judge Daniels set a personal recognizance bond."

"But I thought—"

"It's complicated, I know. But I still think most wives would be interested in finding out how they might help their husband."

"Most wives weren't married to Tommy Olsen!" Becky said. "Besides, he's out of jail and we're getting a divorce. I left with the kids, remember? He might come after me!"

"Why would he do that? You were at the trial supporting him every day."

"Only because you thought it would look right. 'Good optics,' I think you said—whatever that is."

"So, can we talk?"

"Come in," she said, and stepped to the side. "Sit yourself." She cleared a chair of papers by sweeping them to the floor.

Sam stepped gingerly over the papers and took a seat. He watched as Becky began to pace about the room. "What's this really all about?" she asked.

"I don't think Tommy killed Emily."

"No shit. If you'll recall, you already told me you think I did it!" Becky said. "But now, you've got that judge's prints. Maybe he did it."

"Well, maybe," Sam said. "But Howard is dead."

"How?"

"Looks like suicide."

"Well, there you go."

"Maybe. But I've got some new evidence."

"What evidence?"

"Forensic stuff."

Becky was picking up toys and papers and tossing them all into a toy box. "What kind of forensic stuff?"

"Those fingerprints we talked about last time?"

"What about 'em?"

"They're from a smoker."

"So? Lots of people smoke."

"They're yours."

Becky stopped picking up toys, turned around, and looked at Sam. She inhaled smoke and blew it toward the ceiling. "Mine?"

"Yup. I got them off the beer bottle from the other day."

"You are an asshole."

"Yeah, well, what can I say? Polson had your prints run. They match the ones on the weapon and on the shot glass."

"So what? Someone planted 'em."

"You expect me to believe that?"

"Not really. You don't know what the hell to believe. If you'll recall, you're the dumbass who got my husband convicted."

"It's over, Becky," Sam said. "Tommy's out of jail and the police are going to be looking at all the evidence with a fresh set of eyes."

"And what's that mean to me?"

"It means you probably ought to find a sitter for your kids. Long-term, I'm thinking."

58

"Sam, come in and sit down." Paul gestured to the chair Sam had sat in hundreds of times when they'd worked together. "How are things?"

"Better than they were a couple of days ago," Sam said. "What's up? Case I failed to close?"

"Look, Sam, I just wanted to say that I'm sorry for the way things worked out."

"What do you mean?"

"Well, giving you the heave-ho when you took on Tommy's case. I think that was a mistake. I was worried. I mean, I built this," he said, gesturing at the walls and ceiling. "It's not much, but whatever it is, it's sort of what I've done with my life. I was trying to protect—"

"I understand, Paul. No hard feelings. I can't blame you for that. You've got ties to the community and a family to feed. No reason to risk that for a guy you hadn't seen much of for twenty years."

"Really?"

"Really."

Paul looked tired. "Sam, what are you going to do now?"

"I'm going to go fishing."

"Of course you are." Paul laughed. "I was thinking more long term."

"I'm not entirely sure. Haven't given it much thought."

"Would you consider coming back to this office?"

Sam sat quietly for a moment. "Not sure."

"I mean as a partner, this time," Paul said. "Anyone who can try a murder case deserves partnership."

"I lost."

"Well, the State hid crucial information about Judge Howard from you. Maybe things would have turned out differently had you had all the information. That's why Daniels granted your motion, right?"

"Right. But Tommy's still technically a suspect. Eyes are still on him."

"I know. So, will you think about it?"

"I will. What's the buy-in?"

"I'm not sure. I'll get with my accountant—our accountant, maybe?— and see what he thinks. While you think about it, I mean. I'll just ask sort of parenthetically."

"Okay."

"Where you going?"

"Not sure, except that it'll be somewhere I've never been. I'll get the maps out, look for blue lines, pick one, and see if there's any fish in the creek. Just wander around, really. Clear my head."

"You deserve it."

"Thanks, Paul."

"I'll have something for you this week?"

"That'll work." Sam stood to leave.

"Thanks, Sam," Paul said, extending his hand. "And again, I'm sorry. I didn't mean . . . I panicked. I mean, I know this place don't look like much, but . . . Will you think about it?"

Sam took Paul's hand. "I will. At least until I get near the water. After that, I can't make any promises."

"Judge, I have a question." Mary placed a cup of coffee on the desk in front of him. She didn't have to do that, of course, and she knew it. But she'd been his judicial assistant for more than twenty years, and made certain allowances—primarily because he appreciated it.

"Yes?"

"Were you surprised at all?"

"About?"

"About Judge Howard and Emily?"

"Not really. I've heard all the same rumors you have."

"I mean about the fingerprints. And his, uh, his DNA at the house."

"Well, I didn't think he'd gone that far, of course."

"I can't believe he did it."

"Well, we don't know he did yet."

"He killed himself. That's enough for me," Mary said. "I heard he left a note admitting to everything."

"You did?"

"Yup. Word on the street is that he admitted it and felt so ashamed for everything he did to Margaret that he just decided to kill himself. Good riddance, I say. Man that age running around with young women. And a judge!"

Judge Daniels smiled and sipped his coffee.

"Can I ask another question?" she asked.

"Of course."

"Why didn't you stop the trial when Punch came in here and told you?"

"Listening through the keyhole, were you?"

"Of course not!" Mary answered. "But these walls are thin."

"I thought about it," Daniels said. "But a couple of things. First, evidence has to be turned over to the defense if it is exculpatory—if it tends to show the defendant didn't do the crime. There's at least some argument to be made—and Ann would have made it—that given the amount of evidence against Olsen, the presence of Judge Howard's print and even his DNA wouldn't have mattered. And there is no evidence that she knew about the first print until after the preliminary hearing."

"It was unfair."

"Right. Just as important, though," Daniels continued, "I thought Johnstone was doing a good job—holding his own or better. Easy decision at that point. The match with the semen sample was more of an issue. My thinking was that if Johnstone had walked Olsen without the Howard information, then everyone goes home happy and no lives would have been ruined. Remember, when they got the case, the jury knew the judge's fingerprint was there, that there was a matching set on both the weapon and the shot glass, and—as far as they knew—there was unidentified DNA there. They knew *someone* else had been there, and if they were paying attention, they knew *two* people besides Olsen had been there around the time of her death. I thought Johnstone might get them to bite on reasonable doubt or get one juror—that's all it takes—to bite on that and hang the jury. I would have made Jon step down, of course, but at least his pension would have been good. Margaret deserves that."

"Judge, can you do that?"

"Well, I did it," Daniels said. "But two things happened. First, Olsen testified. I think there was at least some doubt in some of the jurors' minds before he took the stand. But like most defendants, he didn't fare well under cross-examination. Second, Juror 465 got put on the jury, which killed any chance of an acquittal."

"But if your plan had worked and if Olsen was acquitted, Judge Howard would have gotten away with it!"

"Well, Judge Howard would have resigned immediately after the trial— I'd have seen to that. Punch would have continued his investigation—he never really stopped. And honestly, we don't know that Judge Howard killed Emily. Someone left those other prints."

"So when the jury said guilty—"

"I had no choice, and when Johnstone found out about the DNA evidence, I granted his motion to set aside the verdict and start a new trial."

"You took a chance," she said. "Will you get in trouble?"

"Perhaps," Daniels allowed. "What I did was unconventional, to be sure. I made what I thought was the right decision. Of course, I'm not in the 'right' and 'wrong' business, so it may be that I'll get my ears boxed. I can live with that."

"Will there be another trial?"

"I don't know. Depends on what Polson finds out. Olsen . . . well, there's some degree of doubt there, although there's still a bunch of evidence against him. The State will have to find a new prosecutor; Ann's tainted at this point. She's probably already been shown the door."

"But who killed Emily? It had to be either Tommy Olsen or Judge Howard, didn't it?"

"I don't know, and we won't know until another jury looks at it. Hell, I was convinced it was Olsen. That's the beauty of the jury system. You give one man or woman power to judge and punish, there's a good chance human emotion, bias, prejudice, or just plain clouded thinking will get in the way. Juries make mistakes, of course, but in my opinion we're a helluva lot better off having twelve people look at the facts and make the call."

"Well, all I know is what's being said. And right now, everyone thinks it was Judge Howard."

"Well, a week ago, everyone—me included—was convinced it was Tommy Olsen," Daniels said. "Maybe everyone misjudged him. Maybe everyone is misjudging Howard, as well. Let's wait and see what Detective Polson digs up."

59

Punch and Becky Olsen were in an interrogation room at the justice center. He'd explained to her that she wasn't under arrest and was free to go at any time, but that he wanted to ask her some questions.

"So, Mrs. Olsen—" Punch began.

"Call me Becky."

"Becky, what happened?"

"What do you mean?"

"I think you know what I mean."

"It's a long story."

"I've got all night. Coffee?"

"Can I smoke?"

"Sure."

"Then I'd like coffee. With sweetener, if you have it."

Punch nodded toward the one-way mirror. Jensen was back there observing; he'd get her a cup. Becky rooted through an expensive purse and eventually extracted a pack of cigarettes and a lighter. She lit one, took a long drag, and exhaled smoke. "It's a long story," she repeated.

Punch simply stared at her.

"I guess I don't know where to begin," she said.

"Well, why don't I ask you a few questions?"

"Okay."

"How is it that your fingerprints came to be on that bayonet?"

"What bayonet?"

"Oh, Becky, please don't insult me. The bayonet used to kill Emily. The same one found in your husband's garage."

"How would I know?"

"Well, who else *would* know?"

"I'm sure I don't know. Tommy probably showed it to me at some point."

"That could explain it."

"Of course it does."

"Ever been to Emily's house?"

"I guess I don't know what you're getting at."

"I'm simply asking whether you've ever been in Emily's home."

"Why do you ask?"

"I think you know that."

"I can't remember."

"You cannot expect me to believe that you can't recall whether you've ever been to Emily's house," Punch said. "I simply don't believe it."

"You can believe whatever you want, Detective."

"I believe you've been there—you wanna know why?"

"Why?"

"Because, as I already told you, your fingerprints are there," Punch said. He let that sink in, but she showed no emotion, just inhaled smoke and blew it to the ceiling. "You're denying that you've ever been there, but your prints say otherwise. You're lying to me."

Becky said nothing. "Your fingerprints are on the murder weapon," Punch reminded her.

"I told you, he showed it to me one time."

"You had access to Tommy's place."

"Of course I did! It was my house until I packed the kids and left his ass."

"You could easily have put that bayonet in the garage."

"You think I killed Emily?"

"Tell me you didn't."

"I don't have to talk to you, do I?"

"No, but you should," Punch said. "More importantly, I know you want to do the right thing."

Becky sat quietly. "You killed her," Punch said. "Why, I don't know. But I know you did it. And I can prove it."

"Yeah, well, you *proved it* with Tommy as well—didn't you?" Becky lit another cigarette.

"Becky, tell me what happened," he urged her.

"Nothing happened. I'm telling you, you're wrong. I had nothing to do with killing that little bitch."

"Where were you on Halloween night between eleven p.m. and six a.m.?"

"How the hell do I know? Do you know where you were?"

"No, but I'm not under suspicion of murder," Punch said. "Becky, now that I've got your prints. . . we'll find some DNA."

"I'm sure I was home with my kids."

"Can anyone corroborate that?"

"Of course not! Unlike my husband, I wasn't sleeping with anyone else!"

"How did you know he was sleeping with Emily?"

"What?"

"How did you know he'd been sleeping with Emily?"

"It was obvious!"

"Tommy said he'd only slept with her that night. In fact, he'd only been with her that one time."

"Tommy's full of shit."

"So, unless you were following him, how did you know he was sleeping with Emily?"

"I just knew. Women know these things."

"Come on. You can do better than that."

Becky looked at Punch for a long time. "It was good when we started, you know?" Punch nodded, and she continued. "But he was never the same when he got back. Angry, yelling all the time. No patience with the kids, couldn't hold a job. I could live with all that. But then he started fooling around with other women. That . . . hurt."

"I'm sorry," Punch offered.

"You know what else?"

"What?"

"He's never asked to see the kids. Not once since I moved out."

"I'm sorry." Punch motioned for Jensen to get her more coffee. "Becky, what happened?"

"When I left with the kids, I thought maybe that would get him to change. Maybe he'd think things through and say he was sorry and maybe we could do counseling or something." She lit another cigarette. "But instead he just hit the bars and picked up whores."

"How did you know what he was doing?"

"Because I'd put the kids to bed and follow him! Wasn't hard. Wasn't like he cared. He was just out looking to drink and get laid. Meanwhile, I'm stuck at home with the kids, tryin' to make ends meet. No money for rent, food—or for me to have a life!"

"So, you followed him to Emily's house?"

"It was actually kind of an accident. I was on the way to the store to get some cough syrup for the little one. And I seen Tommy going the other way in his truck. Looked like he was following some fancy little car. I turned around and followed Tommy, and bigger than shit I seen that little car pull up to some house, then Tommy went inside and he and that bitch started making out. Can you believe that?"

Punch said nothing. She stubbed out her cigarette. "They were all dressed up in costumes. I watched for a while and then I drove home and took care of my kid for a couple of hours. His kid too, you know? And then, when everyone was asleep, I went and got that knife from Tommy's house and was driving to that bitch's house when Tommy went on by—going home, I suppose. So I parked down the street, walked to her place, and rang the doorbell."

"She answered?" Punch asked.

"Oh, yeah. I think she thought maybe Tommy was coming back for seconds. She was surprised to see me. Shoulda seen the look in her eyes. She knew she was in the deep shit."

"So what happened?"

"You know what happened."

"You killed her."

She sat quietly, smoking. He let her think about it. At last, she exhaled toward the ceiling, looked at him, and nodded. "I did," she said. "Followed her upstairs. Was gonna do her in her room, but I got mad. Didn't take much—she was weak. Then I went home, cleaned up, and gave the kids breakfast and got 'em off to school. Because that's what I do. I'm a good mom, goddammit!"

"I know you are." Punch positioned himself between Becky and the door. "Then what?"

"Then I took the knife back to Tommy's house," Becky said. She looked at the floor and then lifted her eyes to meet Punch's stare. "How'd you know?"

"Well, I didn't, for a long time. I thought it was Tommy," Punch admitted. "The evidence seemed overwhelming. Then with Howard's DNA and print I started thinking maybe he did it. But just one print? And how would he get the weapon in Tommy's house? And I kept thinking about those two unidentified sets of prints. I mean, you being his wife, it wouldn't have surprised me if your print was on the bayonet. But my lab guys said the extra print on the bayonet didn't match a print in the house, so I didn't worry about it and eliminated you as a suspect early on. Sam and his experts saw it differently. Failure to match prints that should match is called a 'false negative,' I've since found out. Later, when I tried to match your prints with those on the scene and the weapon, you didn't have any in the system. I couldn't figure it out until Sam told me that your arrest in New Orleans was before the hurricane. That explained the lack of prints in the system. Then he gave me a beer bottle with your prints. Once I had them, I had your prints run and—"

"And they matched, like that lawyer said."

"They did."

"So I might have gotten away with it if not for Sam Johnstone?"

"Well, I like to think I'd have figured it out at some point," Punch said.

"I misjudged him. I thought he was just another crazy, screwed-up vet. Like Tommy."

Punch smiled despite himself. "Finish that smoke, and I'll have you stand up and turn around."

"What? Why?"

"I'm placing you under arrest—suspicion of murder, in that you did, on or about October 31, in Custer County, Wyoming, murder one C. Emily Smith."

"What about my kids?"

"They'll have to stay with grandma for a while," Punch said. Jensen entered the room with a fresh cup of coffee and Punch motioned for him to set it on the table. "She'll take that to go. Let her finish this butt, then read her rights and get her a room, will you?"

60

Ann awaited Rebecca's arrival. In the five years that she had worked as a deputy county attorney, she had been called into Rebecca's office exactly three times. Rebecca arrived and took her seat without even looking at Ann. "This is a disaster," she said without preliminaries.

"I got a conviction," said Ann. "I did what I had to do. How was I to know the defendant had been framed? What is this, *Perry Mason*?"

"I'm not saying that you could have known," said Rebecca. "I am saying that everyone in the world expects that you would have figured it out, if you were paying attention to what was going on. Worse, you had exculpatory information. You were supposed to turn that over to the other side. You convicted the wrong man!"

"I understand that, but there's nothing I could have done. I did my job and convicted the person who best fit the evidence. I was given bad information by these stupid redneck cops. What else do you expect me to do?"

"I expect—no, I demand—that my staff convict the right person, the *right person* being loosely defined here as the one who actually did it!"

"The evidence indicated that Tommy Olsen was responsible for Emily's death," Ann said. "That's where the evidence took us, and that's what we told the jury. There was no way for me to know anything different. That hick detective couldn't figure it out!"

"That is not good enough."

"It has to be good enough! That is how the system is designed and that is how it must work. No one says the system is perfect. No one says the system never makes mistakes. Everyone has to understand that we are all human and we make mistakes."

"My office *is* perfect, at least as far as the public knows. We don't make mistakes in death penalty cases. We don't ask the public to understand when we convict the wrong person for murder."

"So where do we go from here?"

"That depends on you."

"What do you mean?"

"Is it your intent to resign, or do I need to terminate you?"

"You have to be kidding me!" Ann said. "You saw the exact same evidence I did. You believed the same thing I did. You know what I did was what any reasonable prosecutor would have done—proceed based upon the evidence in the prosecution of Tommy Olsen. You would have done the same thing!"

"But I didn't know what you knew."

"Sure you did," Ann said. "Mike had to tell you. He's too weak to keep something like that from you."

Rebecca wrote something on a legal pad in front of her. "Think he'll remember that?"

"My God, you are hanging me out to dry!"

"I am willing to give you the opportunity to do the right thing and resign. Failing that, I will terminate you for cause—an 'ethical lapse,' I think I'll call it. I need your decision by noon."

Sam and Veronica stood silently, respectfully, as the horse-drawn caisson passed by. Arlington National Cemetery was eerily quiet on this Friday morning, due in part, Sam supposed, to the rainy weather.

"What's the significance of that?" Veronica nodded toward the caparisoned horse.

"Symbolizes the last ride of the rider," Sam whispered. "For the same reason the saddle is empty and the boots face to the rear. In twenty minutes or so, you'll hear a three-volley salute. Then the bugler will play 'Taps.'"

"My goodness. It's so formal," she said, looking around her. "How many people are buried here?"

"I'm not sure. I think something like four hundred thousand."

"Oh my God! Do they go through all of this for four hundred thousand men and women?"

"No, most people don't get buried with full military honors. All gave some, but some gave all."

"So—?"

"Yes. My men all got the full deal. It's the least this country can do."

They'd been to the grave sites earlier that morning—all five of them. Sam had spent some time alone at each, head down and eyes closed in prayer and thought, while Veronica stood by, nodding at passersby and thinking about just how quiet the cemetery was. At each grave he had straightened, rendered a salute, and left a gold coin on the headstone. She'd asked him about it moments ago, but he just shook his head and said, "I'm not ready to talk about it."

"I understand," she said. "This place. It's so . . . so reverent."

"It is."

"Will you be buried here?"

"I'm not sure."

"But you could be."

"I could be," he said, nodding to a man pushing a wheelchair occupied by another man, who was wearing a hat emblazoned "Army." "But right now, I want to think about living. I want to focus on the future."

She kissed him deeply and put her arm through his. "Come on, Captain. Let's go watch the changing of the guard. Then maybe you can show me around D.C."

ONE AND DONE

When an all-star college athlete is charged with murdering a fellow student, attorney Sam Johnstone must solve a crime that isn't as clear-cut as it appears.

After an impressive performance in front of a full house, local college basketball stand-out Davonte Blair celebrates the victory with a few friends. But when a fierce argument over drugs ensues, the evening takes a violent turn—and one member of the group goes missing.

When police discover the body of the basketball team manager, the town turns into a tinderbox of emotions. The media is calling it a hate crime. The college president is desperate to avoid a scandal. And the police department is under intense pressure to solve the horrific case.

As defense attorney Sam Johnstone looks into the murder, the case grows even more complicated. Ronnie Norquist, the son of Sam's longtime friend and law partner was the dead student's roommate—and Ronnie was there the night his roommate disappeared.

His personal and professional worlds colliding, Sam can tell Ronnie knows more than he's letting on. But what is it that Ronnie witnessed? And whose guilt does it prove?

Get your copy today at severnriverbooks.com/series/sam-johnstone-legal-thrillers

JOIN THE READER LIST

Never miss a new release! Sign up to receive exclusive updates from author
James Chandler.

Join today at
severnriverbooks.com/authors/james-chandler

ABOUT THE AUTHOR

James Chandler spent his formative years in the western United States. When he wasn't catching fish or footballs, he was roaming centerfield and trying to hit the breaking pitch. After a mediocre college baseball career, he exchanged jersey No. 7 for camouflage issued by the United States Army, which he wore around the globe and with great pride for twenty years. Since law school, he has favored dark suits and a steerhide briefcase. When he isn't working or writing, he'll likely have a fly rod, shotgun or rifle in hand. He and his wife are blessed with two wonderful adult daughters. Misjudged is his first novel.

Sign up for James Chandler's newsletter at
severnriverbooks.com/authors/james-chandler
jameschandler@severnriverbooks.com